FATAL
DESTINY

Robert K. Swisher, Jr.

SUNSTONE
PRESS

SANTA FE

Printed in the United States of America

Library of Congress Cataloging in Publication Data:

Swisher, Robert K., Jr. 1947-

  Fatal destiny / Robert K. Swisher, Jr. -- 1st. ed.
      p.   cm.
  ISBN: 0-86534-110-9 : $ 26.95
  I. Title.
PS3569.W574F38   1991
813'.54--dc20   89-39445
                                                CIP

Published in 1991 by SUNSTONE PRESS
          Post Office Box 2321
          Santa Fe, NM 87504-2321 / USA

TO
THE
COWBOYS

PROLOGUE

There was peace here, a moment to forget the world and the time and all the planned and chance happenings in one's life that had created the man. His destiny, some called it. This ridge had always given him peace. When he was a child he would walk up from the house and sit looking out from the edge of the cliff for hundreds of miles. Out to what seemed to be the end of the universe, then down the straight 200-foot drop to the river that twisted and turned through the ranch, continually cutting the gorge deeper and deeper. Here he would come and forget all the childhood miseries that at the time seemed so earth-shattering. Lost to the world as the lizards with their brown and black spots scurried from rock to rock. He would stand there and let the wind whip up through the gorge and feel his hair dance to its wild tune. Here he could reach out and touch the black crows as they squawked across the sky, and at times even the hawk would sail over his head as he remained still, wanting to catch the soaring creature. He had stood here when his sister died, and had let the wind dry his tears. He had stood here after the news came that they must sell the ranch. His mother had found him, asleep in a tight knot in the morning, nestled in the rocks. So alone, yet a part of the gorge and the rocks, the lizards and the crows. He did not return to the ridge after they had packed the wagon to move. His father was deathly silent, as if his sun-dried face had forever lost the sun. He moved, not knowing anything else to do, and loaded the wagon. His father had sold what few horses were left to the neighbor. Leaving the ranch, he looked once more with his childhood eyes at the cliff and it was as though he was once again standing there, watching the family move. Something so grand, it was beyond sadness or pain, as he pictured himself standing on the edge of the flat-topped granite rock that perched on the rim. There he saw himself soaring up into the sky and sailing into the wind. Out he flew, over the fence his father had strung for the cows, the ditches he had dug to water the garden, and over the small mesas with their stands of gamma grass that the horses would eat to the ground. With a great surge the wind tore at his face and carried him over the small white cross where his sister lay and where, suddenly, he lost the sensation, only feeling the jolts of the wagon wheels as they bounced over the white rock that made up the road. His mother's head bobbed as she urged the horses on and his father sat straight and stiff in the saddle, as though he was afraid to look back at the ranch.

There and then he had sworn to himself that he would never be poor. His sweat and toil would not end as his father's had. He was just a boy, but he would never forget this parting from his home.

(I)

Cam Stearns slid easily but wearily out of the saddle and let the reins drop to the ground. The bay gelding flicked its tail at the buzzing flies on his rump and snorted, gnawing a clump of grass that grew through the cracks in the rocks on the edge of the cliff. "Easy boy," Stearns muttered through his thin, cracked lips, "that will be enough for today." He removed the saddle and his bedroll and slipped the bridle smoothly from the horse's head. Patting the horse on the neck he felt the wind touch his brow and a fleeting moment of calmness came over him. "Stay close now, we're far enough ahead to take a break." The horse moved off slowly, shaking as if to rid himself of the memory of the rider over the last hard days. He sat down on the saddle and looked out over the cliff. It was the same, time had not been here. It had not been here with the wind and the rocks.

The last rays of the sun sent red slivers cutting into the valley below, causing it to be light enough to make out the old road from the house to the river. It had been a long time since he had been here, too long. But, for the moment, he was safe. He took his rifle and set it beside his bedroll. He placed the 44/40 pistol under where his head would be and lay back, too tired to eat his jerky or to bother with a drink of water. For now he would rest and sleep and before dawn move out once again, eating and drinking as he traveled.

The dark came quickly. The stars danced as they only do in the mountains. Far off down the river he could hear a pack of coyotes. This made him remember the nights in bed when he heard his mother stir the embers in the fire, and heard the familiar lonely cry of the coyotes filling the night. There were some nights when he would lie for hours listening to them and feel strange sensations coming over him, causing him to imagine that the coyotes knew where he was and knew where he was going. His father called the coyotes, children of the night. He felt that they were men with lost souls who came to find what they had lost in another life. And he would lie there, his eyes staring into the dark unafraid, as if he was with them and the moon, these souls seemed to love.

He awoke to a dull, grey horizon, the crickets still chirping. He found the horse contentedly eating a short distance away. "Sorry fella," he muttered, "but there's nothing I can do." He wanted to stay and look out once more as the sun rose, and feel the wind touch his brow. But that was dead now and even the memories had lost their feeling. They were just ghosts. It was too late to turn back. He pulled his limp, dirty hat tight on his head and headed out away from the cliff and deeper into the mountains. He thought, "I'll go where they will never find me. They willnever put me away again," he vowed. His deep green eyes set themselves on the peaks of the distant mountains as he put his horse into an easy lope.

_____

Sheriff Sutter slammed his large round fist on top of the desk. "I leave for two days and you two lousy bastards can't even keep one prisoner in jail," he roarted.

The two deputies wanted to be anywhere but here this morning. They had talked in low whispers for the past day knowing what would happen when the sheriff returned. Sutter had been Cam Stearns' father's friend for years. He had even been a pallbearer for his funeral and had gone out of his way to help his poor widow. But he was the law, and no matter what his feelings were they did not interfere with his duty. Sutter was a big man, not all toned muscle, but round, which gave strangers the impression that he was soft, until his large iron fist sent them flying and his brown eyes locked into theirs. He wasn't quick to shoot, but when he did, he didn't shoot to wound, only to kill. "I aim to get old," he would say, "ain't no wounded son-of-a-bitch going to put me in the grave." On this day, Sheriff Sutter stormed around the small outer office of the jail. "Just how in the hell could he get out of here?"

"Hell, you know Sheriff, he was half-snake, half-Indian. Me and Jim locked the door to get a bite to eat and when we came back, he was gone. No hole in the wall, cell still locked. Beats the hell out of me."

Sheriff Sutter sat down heavily in his chair and rubbed his hands through his thinning hair. "I don't suppose you took the keys with you?"

The two deputies looked at each other and wanted to swallow their tobacco.

"Fine buncha lawmen I got," Sutter snarled. "Get outa here and leave me the hell alone!"

The two deputies scurried for the door. For a few days at least, it would be better to stay out of sight. The Sheriff leaned back in his chair and rested his boots on top of the desk. There was no rush. The law was the law, no need to hurry into things. He could wire Santa Fe in a few hours and put the word out. Cam Stearns, he thought to himself, good luck. He closed his eyes and tried to blank out his mind. Fuckin' life, how could it get so mixed up. At times he thought, this damn job is too much for me. He knew Cam, knew him since he was a boy when he and Cam's father used to hunt deer on the old ranch. Cam always had that wild look about him. Stand-offish to the rest of the people, but not shy, just different. It was as though he had a pain in him that no one could ever touch. He seemed a cousin to the dry, dusty mountain wind or to the cactus that cling tenaciously to the ridges. He was a person who should be left alone, but with not enough space to be alone. Then aloud, "Cam, Goddamnit, I hope you make it."

Bill Lakey watched the two deputies run from the office and laughed to himself. He watched them, like the day they went to lunch and he walked in and let Cam out. Just that easy, he had opened the door, opened the lock with the keys left on the hook and Cam had walked out. Bill had given him his horse, what money he had, some jerky and he was gone. "Good luck boy," the old man had told him, "I was a friend of your paw's." They called him Old Man Lakey, but what did the people of this town know? Where were they when people like Cam's father and he had come out and settled this wild land? Where were they when he had worked ed all day and half the night? Where were they when there was no law, only yourself and a few friends? In this time, a man had slapped Cam's mother, and Cam had shot him. Now this was considered murder, but years ago they might have skinned the man. But he was a respectable, restaurant owner and all. He was a leader of the community. It was just dumb if you ask me, Lakey thought, everybody in town knew Cam Sterns could be mean. He was real quiet, slow to anger but once mad, he was downright mean. Some people said he was dynamite, just waiting to blow up.

Las Vegas, New Mexico was a haven for all breeds of the west. The railroad had just been completed through the edge of town bringing with it hotels, gambling and girls. Money was fast and people were fast. The white gamblers and men on the run hated the Mexicans as much as the Mexicans hated them, and the Indians were somewhere in-between this animosity. It was a thriving town, celebrating the fact that it had beaten Santa Fe out of its railroad line. Santa Fe was never to have a railroad. Instead, the track would run through the small town of Lamy, fifteen miles to the east. Men of all distinctions, from Teddy Roosevelt and his Rough Riders to Bat Masterson and Billy the Kid, walked the streets. It was a boom town that never slept. During the day the wives of ranchers shopped for cloth and food; and, during the night, men without names told tales of the badlands and mountains, and eyed the girls going to and from the upstairs rooms. Rooms were a buck in the cheaper places, and forty dollars in the Montezuma hotel that lay on the edge of town. Fancy dans that promenaded in their new suits from the east rubbed shoulders with cowhands at the bar. It was into this setting that Cam Stearns rode. He had heard about Las Vegas, but the stories did not match what he saw. Wagon upon wagon filled with all imaginable goods filled the streets. Men cursed and hollered at stubborn animals and the crack of whips filled the air. Children ran among the throng of horse riders and wagons, lost in some game that the adults had long forgotten. The ladies of the night smiled down at the riders. Cam smiled back, and tipped his hat at the girls above the Dead Horse Saloon. A small circle of men surrounded two men fighting in an alley but Cam paid it no more than a passing glance. He wanted a bath, a room and a train ticket out of here. Where, he did not know, but he knew it was somewhere. The man at the livery stable didn't look up as he came through the door.

"My horse is for sale," Stearns said, eyeing the short stocky Mexican. The Mexican looked up from the forge and spit sideways from his large toothless mouth. He walked around the horse not speaking, and went back to the forge.

"Twenty-five dollars, with the saddle, fifty-five." The Mexican said. Stearns took the gun out of the scabbard, and put the bedroll over his back. "I'll pick the fifty-five up tomorrow morning," he said, and walked out into the fading light. It was April 12, 1898.

The town changed with the approaching darkness. Women and children could no longer be seen on the streets. Instead, men with hats pulled low on their heads began to appear in groups. Cam Stearns walked into the lobby of the nearest hotel. "Room and bath," he told the man behind the counter. The smallish, thin man, with an accent Stearns did not recognize, gave him a key.

"Bath at the end of the hall." he said in a bored tone.

As Stearns started to walk away the desk clerk noticed the well worn holster

7

and the rifle. He said, "there's good women at the Dead Horse, and good food at Molly's down the street and to the right."

Stearns nodded his head and trudged up the stairs. It was a small room with no windows, a bed and washbasin. He unrolled his bedroll, took out his clean pants and blue shirt and headed down the hall. Sitting in the bath he closed his eyes and let the hot water soothe his tired muscles. It was a weariness that neither a woman, nor a steak, could help. After his bath, he lay on the bed and listened to the sound of the night echo through the small room. Occasionally a shot rang out, or he could hear the yelling of a group of men. It was midnight before he decided to go out for a drink. Strapping on his pistol he took the knife out of his bedroll and stuck it down his boot. The rifle he tucked under the mattress. There was a different man at the desk as he came down the stairs, and he passed him without a word.

The Dead Horse consisted of hard men, smoke, hollering and the smell of cheap whiskey. He noticed a short man with large thick glasses sitting at a table with many men around him. They seemed like a rich looking lot lost in some important talk, cattle or ranch land he imagined. He walked to the bar and ordered a beer from the large, burly bartender who looked like an ex-fighter.

"Girl?" he asked, sliding the beer down the bar.

"Na," Stearns answered, "can't afford one."

After three beers he felt better and began to look more closely around the room. The little man with the glasses seemed to be getting into a heated conversation with the other men around the table. The house's best whiskey sat in the middle of the table.

"We'll wipe them out in three months," Stearns heard him say above the roar of the bar. "Go over, get it over with and be back home with the boys before the first winter snow."

Stearns knew from looking at him that here was a man of power. Although he was small, he had the glow about him that conviction brings, that certain feeling that sets some men apart from others and makes them leaders.

Stearns continued to observe the man, without knowning why. He was not unusually strong, tall or good looking. He didn't look like a killer, but one sensed he was completely unafraid, almost suicidal. A reckless abandon lay behind the bottle-bottom thick glasses. Stearns felt he knew this man, and it was a strange and unusual feeling for him. He had never felt as if he knew anybody, not his father or his mother or the few people his life had touched, but, this man he knew. These two could communicate without words.

The bar seemed to be growing quieter as man after man stopped and began listening to the mustached man in his glasses. "My God, man," his voice carried over the subdued din of the bar, "those bastard Spanish have sunk our boat in the harbor, killed men and boys of our country and we just sit. Sit like helpless women. If we had any balls we would declare war on those half-brown bastards, blow them into the ocean and make Cuba ours."

Stearns noticed the fire in the man's eyes but couldn't tell whether it was an act for the crowd, or truly his own feelings.

"I'll take any wager that within a week we declare war on Spain and me and my

Rough Riders will carry the war to the damned Spaniards.''

Most men in the bar could care less about Cuba or Spain. What did it have to do with New Mexico or Las Vegas? Most could not look past a few card games and running out of town or the next batch of whores coming in. But Stearns watched the man and felt the power, the liberation of a people, the cheering crowds and the smiling children. He turned from the men at the table back to the bar. "One more beer, bartender.''

By now it was two in the morning and the bar had recovered from the temporary spell cast by the leader of the Rough Riders. Men half-drunk were now fully drunk, counting change for one last whack at the girls or pushing each other around in their stupor. Cam Stearns looked around and felt the urge to go. It was trouble time, and his own problems outweighed any that might arise in this bar. He drained the last swallow of his beer and turned to walk toward the door. As he turned, he bumped into a large black-skinned Mexican. It was the man from the livery stable. He apologized and kept walking. Stearns heard the man behind him, say through clenched lips, "Fucking gringo.'' Then he felt the man's hand on his shoulder, and he turned like a cat, drawing the 44/40 and dropping to one knee. He moved the gun upright with such speed the Mexican could not make a move before the pistol was within one inch of his throat. Stearns looked into the Mexican's face, the gun unmoving, and without raising his voice he said, "Friend, you owe me fifty-five dollars in a few hours and I want you around to collect it. Now just smile if you want to pay me and keep hollering if you don't.''

The bar had grown completely silent. Stearns, with his gun still in the man's throat, reached into his pocket and removed a fifty-cent piece, and pitched it on the bar. "Buy this man a drink when I leave.'' He slowly remove the pistol from the man's throat and slid it causally into his holster. "In the morning,'' he said, as he walked out the door. The Mexican snarled and turned to the bartender.

Teddy Roosevelt watched the man walking out the door. He thought, now there is a man of action, 'there is a man who would kill you in a minute but also give you a chance.' He replayed the night in his mind and sealed the thin face into his memory. "Five-feet ten, sandy blond hair, no mustache, clean shaven. I'll bet when he sleeps, he sleeps coiled. I'm glad the Spaniards aren't like that.''

Stearns crawled into the bed. 'Cuba, I wonder where Cuba is', he thought as he fell into a restless sleep.

In the morning as Cam Stearns walked down the stairs from his room, the thin man with the strange accent was back at the desk. "Mr. Stearns,'' he said as Cam went by the desk, "a message for you.''

Stearns stopped and looked at the man. "Read it to me. I can't read.''

"I would like to talk to you. Room 21 at the Montezuma Hotel. T. Roosevelt''

Stearns didn't pay much attention to the message, he only thought of collecting his fifty-five dollars.

The toothless Mexican eyed Stearns apprehensively as he came through the stable doors. Stearns noticed the double-barreled shotgun propped in the corner and quickly judged the distance between it and the livery man. It was too far away from the Mexican to be a threat. "Came for my fifty-five dollars,'' Stearns said, looking into the dark eyes of the Mexican. The Mexican reached into his dirty shirt pocket, walked slowly over to Stearns and handed him the money. Without a word, Stearns turned and walked out the door. The Mexican spit scornfully and went back to work.

The Montezuma Hotel was nothing like Stearns had ever seen. It was three stories high with beveled glass in all the windows. The lobby was carpeted from wall to wall, had large polished wood tables and stuffed leather chairs arranged for maximum quiet. The doorman greeted Stearns, eyeing his rough clothes and pistol, but not saying a word to the negative.

"Room 21 please," Stearns said.

Ladies and men stood in the lobby. The ladies in the latest fashions from the east stood and clustered behind men in top hats and suits. Stearns caught the aroma of their perfume as he walked by and could not help but feel aroused as he looked at the clean, fine women. 'This isn't like the bars', he thought to himself. The ladies, seeing his garb, did not eye him across the room and the men seemed slightly ill at ease as he passed. The pistol and the worn holster were a menace to their world.

The doorman knocked on the door. "Mr. Roosevelt, a gentleman to see you."

"Come in, come in," came from behind the door.

Stearns smiled to himself. 'Gentleman, now that was a first.' If he thought that the lobby was grand, he had never seen anything like this room in his life. Two red velvet chairs sat with a mahogany table between them, radiating in the morning light. The bed was large enough for four people and the pillows were covered in a shiny material he had never seen. The walls were a light, brown wood and the table that sat in the middle of the room matched them. Four chairs were pulled around the table, but only the man he had seen in the bar sat eating his breakfast. He did not rise but motioned for Stearns to sit down.

"That will be all, doorman," he said, setting his coffee cup down.

Stearns removed his hat and sat at the table opposite the man.

"Colonel Roosevelt," Roosevelt said, extending his hand. "Coffee?"

Stearns nodded. "Cam Stearns," Cam said, returning the handshake. Roosevelt poured the coffee and Stearns took the cup.

"Do you have any idea why I wanted to see you, Mr. Stearns?"

Stearns shook his head no and savored the coffee.

"Do you know that our country is about to be plunged into war? We need strong able-bodied men like you to help us."

Stearns smiled and looked at the man. "The Cubans never did anything against me. I don't even know where Cuba is."

Roosevelt eyed Stearns approvingly. 'Here was a real man, not someone looking for excitement or glory. Just a man, a true man of the west.' "Been out here your complete life, Mr. Stearns?"

"Yes, sir," Stearns answered, "born on a ranch, lived there until the railroad grabbed it from my father. Then lived in a little town south of Santa Fe until I got the bug – to move. Not much in town after living on the ranch. Pa died, my mother works for a man in a restaurant."

"And what do you do, Mr. Stearns?" Roosevelt asked.

Stearns looked into the eyes magnified by the thick glasses. "Mind my own business, Mr. Roosevelt."

Roosevelt put down his coffee cup and laughed. A deep, unafraid laugh. "I forgot sir, excuse me. But traveling from the east coast to the west and coming from an area where all people want to know is what you do, I forgot the unspoken law of the west."

Stearns relaxed. "Guess you could say I pushed cows and horses and hunted. If that be a trade, then that is what I do."

"Use a gun, too?" Roosevelt cut in.

"And use a gun," Stearns agreed.

"Quick action with that man last night in the bar. You could have blown his head off."

"Yes," Stearns agreed, "But no need, he was just taking it out on me 'cause I was the closest man to him. Besides, he owed me fifty-five dollars."

"I need men like you, Stearns. Join me, help me win this war, I'll make you a sergeant and put you in charge of a group of men. Men need people they can follow, people who will fight. What do you think?"

Stearns set the coffee cup down. "How can you make me a sergeant?"

Roosevelt laughed his deep laugh again. "Because I am the man in charge, and I can do what I want."

"How much money?" Stearns asked.

"Sign up for two years and you'll get sixty-five dollars a month, starting as soon as you put your name on the paper."

Stearns stood up from the table. "I don't know, I never thought much about the army. But I'll let you know."

Roosevelt watched the man leave the room. 'I wonder what he's running from,' he thought 'I've seen too many men to not know when they're running.' He made a mental note to check into Stearns' past and poured himself another cup of coffee. The camera man was coming today to take photographs of him and a few Indians they had rounded up. Something for the papers back on the coast. 'Newspapers,' Roosevelt snorted, 'what could one do without them?' 'I need this war,' he thought, 'I need this war.' Roosevelt felt his destiny. He was a leader, a man born to overcome all opposition. He was a man born to get what he wanted. And for some reason, he wanted Cam Stearns, and he would get him.

Roosevelt walked down to the lobby of the hotel and up to the doorman. "Find the sheriff for me please, and tell him I would like to eat lunch with him in a few hours. Tell him to meet me here at 12:30."

Sheriff Ed Moore watched the cameraman with amusement. The four Indians stood in full-dress regalia around Roosevelt, who stood like Napoleon, dwarfed by their height, his eyes fixed straight into the camera. 'I wonder what bullshit he'll think up to tell the people back home about this one,' Moore thought. Moore didn't like strange men in his town. He believed that they brought more trouble than they were worth. He would be glad when this Rough Rider business was over and things could get back to normal. It seemed as if the government had moved in ever since Rooevelt had come to town. 'Let the damn government get out and let me get back to doing my job,' Moore thought. His job consisted of looking the other way and waiting to get old. Railroad men owned this town and

Moore worked for them. It was that simple. A few drunks were rounded up and spent the night in jail, but everything else ran wide open. Keep it quiet and it was fine.

Roosevelt spied the sheriff and strode over to him after the cameraman told them that was all. "Make sure the Indians get paid." he told the bored-looking aide as he passed. "Sheriff Moore, my good man," Roosevelt put his arm around the sheriff's shoulder. "Join me for a bite of lunch. The quail here is extraordinary."

"Thank you, I'd like that," Moore replied.

They sat by the large windows that looked out across a large expanse of green rolling hills without a tree. On the horizon, like faint mirages, the outline of the southern Rockies could be seen.

"Beautiful country, isn't it sheriff?"

The sheriff wondered if he had to cut the quail with a knife and fork or if he could pick it up. Roosevelt, seeing the look of bewilderment on his face laughed. "Pick it up my good man, this is not Washington."

Moore smiled. At least Roosevelt had a touch of home in him. "Yes beautiful country sir, the best in the west."

Roosevelt eyed the sheriff. 'Here was a man that was not looking for trouble. Here was a railroad man. In many ways smarter than being a staunch law man. There was no law here, but there would be some day, at some point much later. Too much law results in too little freedom. Every country needs land like this. Land that is wide open and free.' Roosevelt looked Moore straight in the eye. "Mr. Moore, I would like a little information about a man, but I don't want any action taken if the information is bad."

Moore looked at Roosevelt. 'He was honest at least, no beating around the bush.' Moore had prepared himself for a lunch of sitting and trying to figure out what it was the man wanted. He hadn't called for his company at lunch to talk about the beautiful free country. Moore wiped his mouth with the napkin and looked away from Roosevelt and toward the window. "It's a new country out here, Mr. Roosevelt. Some men come for different reasons. Some bad men turned good, some good men turned bad. I find it best to mind my own business and let what is be. If a man treats this town right then I can see no reason for looking into his background."

"This is different, Mr. Moore," Roosevelt cut in. "This man is just passing through. All I want is a little information." And with a pause, he added, "You will be paid for your service." Then, reaching into his back pocket he placed two fifty-dollar bills on the table.

Mr. Moore smiled. "I see you understand the west very well, sir. What is the man's name?"

"Cam Stearns, He's from south of Santa Fe."

Moore smiled, the fresh greenbacks in his pocket. He looked at Roosevelt. "I just got a wire on him today. He killed a man in Bernalillo, and Sheriff Sutter wants him back. But if Sheriff Sutter wants him, then I guess Sheriff Sutter'd better come and get him."

Roosevelt poured more wine into Moore's glass. Their eyes met. It was good enough. "To the west, Mr. Moore," Roosevelt toasted, "to the west and the law of the west."

_____

Cam Stearns sat at Molly's chewing his beefsteak slowly. The desk man had been right, this was the best steak he had ever eaten and Molly was a fine looking woman. She smiled and fussed around his table. It was three-thirty in the afternoon and he was the only customer. Molly, a big breasted Swedish woman with a small, delicate waist, waited on his table herself while the Mexican waiter talked to the cook in the back. Stearns had felt relaxed from the moment he walked in and saw her light complexioned face break out into a big grin. "Come on in," she greeted him, taking him by the arm and leading him to a clean table with a starched white tablecloth. It was not a large place. It had only eight tables, but it was spotless, "My steak's the best in the west, and you look as though you need one." she laughed. And before he could say a word she had hollered to the back, "Steak, biggest in the house, fried potatoes and corn and lots of hot bread."

Stearns sat down. You could argue with any man, but with this woman you might as well forget it, and he bowed to her greater power. After that, she had left him and did not return until she brought his food out piping hot. She stood watching while he took the first bite and chewed it.

"Well," she said, "is it or isn't it the best steak in the west?"

Stearns smiled at her. "You're right, lady, this is the best steak in the west."

"Good, mind if I join you? My feet are killing me. Poncho," she hollered, "bring two cups and some coffee. Coffee's on me, the rest is on you."

Stearns laughed. "I take it you're Molly."

Molly looked at him though hazel blue eyes. "That's right, and you?"

"Cam," he answered, "Cam Stearns."

"Glad to meet you, Cam."

He could not help noticing the cream color of her skin, or the way the lace neckline of her gown touched the top of her breast. She noticed his shy gazes but said nothing. At least he wasn't like most of the men in this town, who only pinched and hollered. Molly watched the man eat. Quiet, slow eating. She had noticed the well-worn holster but he did not look like a gambler or a gun for hire. He looked kind of like a cowboy but not wild like cowboys. 'Maybe he is a federal law man or a ranch foreman,' she thought. Whoever he was she liked him, and it was nice being admired.

Stearns finished his steak and took a deep breath. Molly poured him a cup of coffee. "Black, no cream please," he said.

"Please, please, it is," she mimicked. She saw his green eyes sparkle for a moment, then immediately close up again. 'A hard one,' she thought to herself, 'close-in'. 'If someone could break that shell, they'd find a lot.' Stearns finished the coffee and set the cup down. "Well, I guess I should be going. That was a fine meal." He felt more rested and relaxed than the last hectic weeks could allow.

"My pleasure," Molly answered.

He reached into his pocket and put a ten-dollar gold piece on the table. "The rest is yours for the conversation."

"No, I couldn't," she was about to say when he stopped her.

"No, the rest is yours," and she could tell by his voice he was not used to being told what to do.

13

"Well then, thank you." she smiled. "You come back," and with a pause she added, "please." She stood by the window, hidden by the red paint of the M in Molly's, and watched him walk down the street. There was something about him, something fearful and wonderful. She did not know which one infatuated her, but she wanted to find out. Poncho came out of the kitchen, trying to hide his smile. "Nice gringo, huh, Molly?" he said through his heavy Mexican accent. "You need a man."

Molly's cheeks turned red with anger. "When I want your opinion on my love life I'll ask for it."

Poncho faked a fit of fear, and started in a fluid run of Spanish. Molly laughed and followed him into the kitchen. Dinner rush would be soon and there was a pile of potatoes to be peeled.

As Cam Stearns walked down the street he could not seem to get the creamy white skin and the curve of Molly's breasts off his mind. 'I don't need that,' he tried to convince himself. 'Not now.' 'All I need to do is get out of this town and start my life somewhere else.' As he entered the hotel, he thought of his mother. But it was too late for that. He had acted in a fit of anger and nothing could bring that man back to life. He would write her when he got settled and send her money, by hook or by crook, he knew not which one, but one way or the other he was going to make money.

Col. Roosevelt sat in his room and watched the sun touch the horizon. It was beautiful here. Tonight not a cloud dotted the sky and the land stretched as if it was some great, grey ocean that was waiting to be sailed. He walked from the window and sat down at the mahogany desk. 'What was it about this man Stearns.' Roosevelt thought. 'Hell, he was just another cowboy on the run.' I should let the sheriff have him and be done with it.' But there was something, something behind those green eyes and small thin features. Something Roosevelt could not put his finger on, and he was a man who was used to figuring out other men and using them for his purposes. This bothered him, it disturbed him. He reached for the decanter of Scotch and poured himself a double. Raising the glass to the setting sun he toasted, "Here's to you, Cam Stearns, whatever your destiny is, here's to you."

The sun dipped behind the horizon and the dark came suddenly.

Cam Stearns did not have time to grab the pistol under his pillow. The double barrel 12-guage in his face was enough to stop him from that foolishness. Sheriff Moore clicked the hammers back one at a time. "If you're a brave man try it, Mr. Stearns."

Stearns shook his head. Moore stepped back slowly, the two barrels aimed straight at Stearns' face. "Okay now, up nice and easy and put your clothes on."

Moore struck a match and lit the kerosene lamp on the chest. The light illuminated the room so that Stearns saw the badge on Moore's shirt. "Didn't make it too far did I, sheriff?" Stearns was pulling on his pants. Moore looked at Stearns. "I'm not paid to talk. Get moving."

When Stearns was fully dressed Moore motioned for the door. "All right now, don't try anything. Let's just get this over with."

Stearns opened the door and headed toward the stairs that led to the lobby.

"No, we'll go out the back way and try not to arouse much attention."

Moore dropped the shotgun from Stearns back and pushed him lightly toward the back fire escape. Once out in the alley, Moore directed him through the maze of buildings. Stearns noticed that they were not headed toward the jail. Soon they were in front of the Montezuma Hotel, and Stearns gave Moore a quizzical look over his shoulder. Moore said slowly. "Okay now, just mind your manners and when we walk through the lobby, it's just like you and I are good old friends."

Stearns nodded his head, and as they entered the hotel he stayed even with the sheriff.

"Mr. Roosevelt's room, please," the sheriff said to the doorman. Stearns' head spun toward the sheriff and the sheriff gave him a gentle tug on his elbow. "Follow the doorman."

The doorman knocked on Room 21.

"Two gentlemen to see you, Mr. Roosevelt."

"Come in, come in."

Neither the doorman nor the sheriff seemed at all disturbed about the fact that it was around three in the morning. Stearns entered first and took in the complete room. Roosevelt sat behind the desk, dressed in his army uniform. The flat brimmed hat sat on the edge of the desk. The sheriff stopped at the door and motioned Stearns to move forward.

"Mr. Stearns," Roosevelt said as he rose, "good to see you again. Sit down."

Stearns sat down and looked at Roosevelt. "What is this?" he said in a cool, even voice. "I told you I would give you an answer."

Roosevelt poured a shot of Scotch. "Scotch, Mr. Stearns?"

"No thank you."

"Well, you don't mind if I do then." And without waiting for an answer he poured the shot and tipped the shot to his lips. He rose and walked to the window, and with his back toward Sterans he began to speak. "I don't know what it is about you Stearns. Your eyes, the way you carry yourself, the way you handled that man in the bar, I don't really know. But we are one and the same. Not in breeding or the way we were raised but we're still one and the same. I need men like you, men I can trust, men I know who will not tell me what I want to hear because of my rank, but true men, and that's why I had the sheriff look into your background a little."

With that he turned from the window. "It's very simple, Mr. Stearns. I'm giving you a choice. Either join me with the offer I gave you, or go with Mr. Moore here to jail."

Stearns looked at the sheriff and looked at Mr. Roosevelt. He looked down into his hands, and the last years of his life seemed to move like a parade through the front of his mind. He was riding his first horse as fast as she would gallop, the wind was making his eyes water and he had never felt so free, so alone, as if he could ride forever. For those few minutes there were no worries or cares, no yesterday nor any future, just the sound of the horse's hooves as they struck the ground, and her great lungs gulping the air. He moved his gaze to the window and the dark outside. For a brief instant he felt like running and jumping, letting the sheriff's slugs tear through his body. At least then it would be all over, no more pain, no more wondering, no more lost direction. But he looked at Roosevelt and felt that he knew this man, this little giant among men, and a small smile crossed his lips. "I guess you have yourself a sergeant, Mr. Roosevelt."

Roosevelt crossed the room and extended his hand. "Let's hope neither one of us has made a mistake, Mr. Stearns. You can go, Mr. Moore."

Moore tipped the rim of his hat and walked out of the door. Stearns looked at Roosevelt. "What about him? He knows."

"Don't worry about that," Roosevelt said, and Stearns could tell by the sound of his voice that there were no worries. "Now, how about that drink?"

Stearns nodded his head. "I think I need one after this."

Roosevelt filled two shot glasses and raised his high in the air. "To the war. Yes, to the war and to destiny."

Stearns touched his glass to Roosevelt's and noticed the sun was turning the horizon a faint grey.

"You will come with me at seven in the morning with all your belongings. The men are camped west of town. From this time on you are a sergeant. I will bring you your uniform to the room and fill you in on the rest then."

Stearns looked at Roosevelt. "You mean I can go now."

Roosevelt nodded his head. "I'll see you in your room in a few hours."

"Thank you, Mr. Roosevelt."

"Colonel Roosevelt to you, soldier."

And with that, Roosevelt turned in his chair and looked out the window. 'Now to win the war, war must be declared soon,' he thought. 'Those fools in Washington will have to get off their asses and move before it is too late.'

Cam Stearns walked down the main street of town. It would be easy to run now, go to the livery and buy his horse back and head down the trail. North, south, what did it matter, this country was too large for any law to catch up with him. But he pushed it from his mind, and walked to his room.

Inside the room he poured water from the pitcher into the basin and splashed it on his face. He lay down on the bed and fell asleep, relaxed.

He awoke shortly afterwards, shaved, and waited impatiently for Roosevelt to knock. He did not have to wait long before the strong knocks came on the door. He opened the door, Roosevelt walked in briskly and tossed a paper-wrapped package on the bed. "Here are your new clothes, Mr. Stearns," and he sat in the chair by the washbasin. Stearns unwrapped the package and put on the brown wool army pants and the beige shirt with the two upside-down V sergeant stripes on the sleeve. He put the oval brimmed hat on his head and placed the strap under his chin. He put on the brown buckle boots, and tucked the pants into the accompanying leggings.

Roosevelt watched the man dress. Here was a soldier, he thought to himself. When Stearns had finished dressing, he looked into the mirror. The straight creases of the uniform seemed to match the hard lines of his thin narrow face and dirty blond hair. His eyes sparkled with a hard intensity that would make his stripes hold up to even the biggest man.

"A true soldier, Mr. Stearns," Roosevelt commented, "a true soldier." And

Cam Stearns could not help but feel proud, a part of something exciting and somewhat mysterious.

"All right, Sergeant Stearns, the men are going to ask you questions. So here is your story. You have been with Colonel Billings in Colorado for the past three years. You heard I was forming a group of fighters and asked to be with me. The rest is up to you. Half of being in the army is how well you can bullshit and the other half is how well you can lie, so you shouldn't have any trouble."

Stearns put the army holster around his middle and adjusted the belt. He took the 44/40 pistol from under the pillow and slid it into the holster.

"You won't need the rifle, it isn't army issue, but the pistol you can keep because you have a right as a sergeant to choose any pistol you would like. You will also be issued a 35/40 KREG. Bullets for your pistol you have to pay for yourself, but imagine I can scrape you up a few boxes or so."

"Thank you, sir," Stearns replied. He took the rifle and propped it in the corner. The extra set of uniforms he placed in his bed roll, along with his shaving gear. He slipped the knife into his boot. "Ready and willing, sir."

Roosevelt rose and opened the door. "What day is it, Sergeant?"

"I don't know sir."

"Today is April 25, 1898, and the United States has officially declared war on the Spanish over Cuba."

Stearns looked at the Colonel "That's what you wanted, sir."

Roosevelt looked at him without answering.

(2)

On the ride out to the bivouac area, Roosevelt briefed Stearns on military manner and how to distinguish rank. "I'm sure you'll have no trouble, Sergeant," he said as they entered camp. Stearns felt the excitement of the camp as they rode in. Men moved around the straight line of tents with the stacked arms in front of each one. He was amazed at the number of men, it had to be close to a thousand. Lieutenants seeing Roosevelt began barking commands and he noticed how the men began to fall into line with the sergeants first in each line. The lieutenants in front. Roosevelt stopped his horse and a sergeant grabbed the reins.

"Morning, sir."

"Morning, Sergeant," Roosevelt answered briskly.

"I heard the news, sir, the men are ready and willing, sir."

"Good Sergeant, good. Send for Lieutenant Williams please, I have a sergeant for his platoon."

The sergeant gave a snappy salute and lead the horse off.

"Tie your horse over there, Sergeant, you won't be needing him anymore. Only officers ride," Roosevelt said to Stearns.

Stearns smiled to himself and did what he was told.

"Follow me." Roosevelt ordered.

They strode briskly along the line of tents until they entered one in the middle of the line. Officers jumped when Roosevelt entered, but he dismissed them with a hearty, "Good morning, gentlemen. I suppose you have all heard the news."

The men paid no attention to Stearns and he was amazed at the differences among the group of officers. Some were in their forties, showing signs of many battles behind them, and others were no older than himself. Roosevelt, although shorter than the majority of the rank, was immediately the focus of everybody's attention. He strode across the tent and sat down behind a portable military table. Removing his hat, he seemed to survey the room with his gaze. Finally with a wide grin he said, "Jolly good, gentlemen. Now let's see what the famed Rough Riders and Teddy Roosevelt can do."

The men laughed and from somewhere a bottle emerged.

"To the end of the Spanish," a lieutenant toasted. The straight shots of whiskey were chugged down to the end of the Spanish. A lieutenant brushed by Stearns standing at the flap of the tent and stopped in front of Colonel Roosevelt. The man came to a snappy attention and saluted. "Lieutenant Williams reporting as ordered, sir."

Roosevelt returned the salute. "A shot of whiskey for the war, soldier?"

"Yes, sir," Williams answered.

Stearns noticed that he did not seem to be taken in by the war fever as did the other men, and that the other officers did not pay him very much attention.

"To the war, sir," Williams toasted, draining the shot. Roosevelt motioned for Stearns. "Sergeant, this is your platoon commander, Lieutenant Williams. Lieutenant, Sergeant Stearns. A good man, I knew him a few years ago. I am putting him with you. You can trust him."

Stearns saluted the lieutenant, and the lieutenant looked at Stearns. "Come with me, Sergeant, I'll show you your new accomodations."

Stearns saluted Roosevelt and they turned and left the tent. "Strange, isn't it, Sergeant," the lieutenant said as they walked by the other tents, "how some men look forward to war."

Stearns looked into the dark eyes of the lieutenant. He noticed the dark curly hair and the well kept pencil-thin mustache. "Aren't you excited, sir?"

The lieutenant gave a light look of exasperation. "I'm only excited about getting back home, Sergeant, I have more important things to do than kill a bunch of little brown bastards that are killing other brown bastards."

Stearns looked around him and watched the soldiers move in and out of the tents. What a grand feeling it was, for the first time to feel as though he fit in somewhere. A part of a moving group of men, each dependent on the other to live or to die. He only hoped that he had learned quickly enough not to draw attention to his masquerade. They stopped in front of the last tent in line. "Well, this is it, the first bunk on your left is yours. I'll get you your rifle. Stroke of luck you getting here. Our other sergeant went back to Virginia, his wife died and Teddy let him go. If nothing else we have the most outspoken Commander in the army and the most daring. Known him long, Sergeant?"

"No sir, not that long."

"Well he must think a hell of a lot of you. This entire outfit is hand picked by him almost. Crack shots from the west and men he knew in school who were outstanding athletes. You must shoot like hell or you wouldn't be here."

Stearns smiled at the lieutenant. "I can shoot a little, sir."

"Well, let's hope so. Fall the men out in an hour, we have a speech by the Colonel."

"Yes sir," Stearns saluted and the lieuteant walked off. Stearns entered the tent and twenty faces turned and looked at him from his feet to the top of his head. A man about Stearns' age with short blond hair and sparkling blue eyes stood and hollered, "Look here men, it's our new sergeant."

The men all stood. "Three cheers, hip, hip, hurray, hip, hip, hurray, hip, hip, hurray."

Stearns smiled and dropped his bed roll on the first bunk on the left. "I can see this is going to be a memorable experience," he laughed. He reached into his bedroll and pulled out a bottle of dry gut whiskey. "Well gentlemen, not like the officers, no glasses, but pass the bottle around and let's hope we all get home to pat the girl or the wife on the ass once again."

Stearns took off his hat and sat down on the bed. It had been an extraordinary few weeks. In a few weeks, he had gone from being as close to the bottom of the barrel as one could get to being a sergeant in the army in charge of twenty men. He looked around at the laughing, cussing men passing the bottle and lay back on the bunk. Before he shut his eyes, he looked at the blond haired man with the sparkling eyes. "Wake me in thirty minutes, friend, we have to fall out in an hour."

"You bet, Sergeant," he drawled.

Must be from Texas, Stearns thought as he dozed off. The dream came quickly. *The hawk glided in slow even circles higher and higher above his head. Looking away from the hawk and down the cliff he could see his mother hanging the wash on the line and the thin curl of smoke rising from the fire under the wash tub by the house. Down from the house the sound of his father chopping wood behind the barn echoed dully off the face of the cliffs. He returned his gaze to the hawk, which was now a mere dot among the white, darting clouds. He saw the dot and remembered his sister's empty bed in the corner of the house and the small flower-like cross that marked her grave, and, for the first time since she died he began to cry. He had stood by his mother while the preacher talked, but it was as though the preacher was saying nothing. He had seen his father's tears and his large rough hands around his mother's shoulders but still he hand not cried. The first night there had been little conversation in the house and he had spent the night looking at his sister's empty bed as though any minute it would all be a dream and she would roll over in her sleep. As he cried and the hawk reach-ed the pinnacle of his climb and dove toward the valley floor, he could see, through his tears, the talons of the hawk dig deep in a rabbit running below the cliff. But he did not understand.*

"Sergeant, Sergeant, wake up."

Stearns sat up and looked into the blue eyes. "Fall out," he mumbled, rubbing his forehead, erasing the dream from his mind.

"Ya fell out okay, Sergeant, like a log, ya was out. Where ya from, anyway, Sergeant?"

"Right here," Stearns answered, "Yourself?"

"Texas, Texas-born and raised,"

Stearns smiled. "And what's your name, soldier?"

"Folks call me Smiley. Best dang squirrel hunter in west Texas."

Stearns stood up and stretched. "Well, let's hope you can shoot Spaniards as well as you can shoot squirrels."

The Texan smiled from ear to ear. "Right where I wanna hit 'em, Sergeant," he drawled. "right where I wanna hit 'em."

Stearns looked down the tent. All the men were dressed and ready to fall out. These are good looking soldiers, he thought to himself. 'Who knows what stories could be told right in this tent and how many different paths led these men to this place in time.'

The bugle sounded outside and the men scurried for the flap. Stearns did not have to holler fall out or even push a slow man to start. 'Thank God,' he thought, at least since they were the last tent he would have time to fall back slowly and observe how the other sergeants stood. The men stood in two neat rows of ten and he stood slightly to the left and the front. The lieutenant came in front of him and stood at attention. Stearns, noticing what the others had done, saluted and spoke, "All present and accounted for, sir."

The lieutenant spun on his heels and stepped directly in front of the men, his back to them. Presently, from down the center line of the tents, Colonel Roosevelt walked by with two majors behind him inspecting the ranks. He was saluted by all men as they passed by a presentation of rifles. He did not change his stern look, but all could see the color in his cheeks and the way his eyes seemed to soak in the glory at the thought of leading.

The men carried his courage, his spunk, one could see it in their faces, feel it in the way their back bones stretched for the last bit of straightness as he passed. They were his men, his Rough Riders, ready to obey his beck and call. Roosevelt turned and walked to where he was directly in the middle of the troops. "At ease, Major," and the major barked "at ease," a chorus of sergeants followed suit and the mens' left legs and rifles moved to the "at ease" position.

'Like a machine,' Stearns thought, 'like a machine.' 'One mind, one body, one soul.'

Roosevelt took off his hat and wiped his brow. He seemed to take in the entire force and one could feel the pride boil up inside of him. "You think it's hot here?" We ship to Florida in ten days men, and take our ship to Cuba with our banner of freedom."

A large yell began in the middle of the formation and spread like a grass fire through the ranks. Roosevelt raised his hand and all was quiet. "I want you all to know you are the best men in the army. The best shots, the best disciplined, and I feel proud and honored to have you with me in this time of our glory. "Freedom," he yelled, "freedom for all men!"

The soldiers, caught up in his mood, took their hats off and the sky was filled with a thousand flying hats. "The rest of the day off, men," Roosevelt ordered.

"Fall out," the major hollered, and the sergeants did not have to say a word. The men retrieved their hats and stacked their rifles in front of the tent. Some stood in groups and others walked back into the tents.

"Chow in thirty minutes," Smiley told Stearns. "Best chow in the army. Roosevelt is a real stickler on food. If it ain't done right he gets all over the cooks. Of course he don't eat here, he stays in town in the ritzy hotel."

Stearns laughed, "pays to be a big rock."

Smiley spit a large gob of tobacco. "Takes all kinds, cain't be no big rocks without all us little ones."

Stearns looked at Smiley and knew he had found a friend. Thinking about it later sitting on his bunk, he realized he had never had a friend before. It had been a good day, the best day he could remember in a long time.

The mess tent was a milling line of men gorging on ham and beans and corn bread. Talk circled the tent as to when Colonel Wood would show up. For the first time Stearns found out that Roosevelt was second in command. A burly sergeant next to him with a large upturned mustache and dark tattoos of dragons on his forearms told him between spoonfuls of beans, how Wood would show up when all the work was done which was now. Also as far as he was concerned, Roosevelt was the only one to follow anyway. Wood was some paper pusher from Washington who was not good enough to shine Roosevelt's boots. Stearns sat quietly and listened to the buzz of conversation.

"Ya know," one soldier said, "Roosevelt had a ranch up in the Dakotas and pushed cows just like me and my daddy for several years until the snow wiped him out."

Stearns looked at the man. "Where did you hear that?"

"Read it in the paper, read it right along with the story they did on us being here training and all to fight the Spaniards."

Stearns felt better and better all the time. At least Roosevelt knew his men, but he could still not figure out why he had given him the break he did.

Walking back to his tent he thought of Molly. 'I just might get a day pass and go into town,' he thought, and see Molly.

The tent was quiet when taps sounded, the low, sad tones of the bugle surrounding the men. Stearns lay looking into the darkness as the horn grew quiet. From down at the end of the bunks a voice came through the darkness. "Me and the men just want to tell you we're glad to have you along, Sergeant Stearns."

Stearns could not speak but lay looking into the darkness. The crickets came out and the stars dotted the sky, a slight breeze rustled the grass and they slept. A thousand faces in a row, a thousand dreams.

Sergeant Stearns stood in front of the store window and looked at his reflection. It was different walking in town wearing his uniform. People noticed him now, and the ladies smiled shyly from behind their bonnets. It was not like when he had ridden in before, a faceless drifter to be ignored. He felt pride swell up inside him and the sergeant's stripes seemed to shine when the sun hit him. He walked into the store and a short, stocky lady behind the counter said merrily. "Sergeant, come in. May I help you?"

"Yes ma'am," Stearns answered, "I'd like a present for a lady. Not too expensive, though," he added.

21

The woman swished from behind the counter, her long skirts dragging on the kerosene soaked floor. "Follow me, I'm sure we can find something. I want you to know, Sergeant, that we are all proud of you men and what you are doing. Those poor Cubans over there, the papers are full of the deprivation and death they have been put through."

Stearns smiled to himself. If nothing else in the army, he would have to learn how to read. His mother had been careful to teach him to write his name but to this day he had never read a newspaper or a book. His father had always felt it was more important to work on the ranch. He knew horses and cattle and the signs of the weather, but when it came to reading he was unable. His speech was not bad, but it had taken much practice and coaching from his mother. She had told him often, "there's more to life than horses and cattle and guns, Cam."

Now he wished he had gone to school, and then and there he put it in his mind that he must learn to read.

The lady stopped in front of a glass case filled with fancy engraved brushes and combs, rows of ribbon and bolts of cloth. Behind the counter were sun bonnets and dresses. Stearns felt ill at ease. The lady smiled and looked at him. "What color are her eyes, soldier?"

"Blue, blue," Stearns blurted out.

With much wisdom, knowing a soldier's pay, she reached under the counter and pulled out three dainty, lace edged handkerchiefs and a roll of blue ribbon. "She would like these, they come all the way from England. Blue ribbons for her hair."

Stearns looked at the hankies and the ribbon as though they would bite. He had never thought of anything like this, his mother had never had any of the nice things in life.

"You can have them all for two dollars, Sergeant."

"Could you wrap them, Ma'am?"

The lady hurried from behind the counter smiling. "She will be so happy, Sergeant, you mark my words."

She watched the sergeant leave the store. 'Such a handsome man,' she thought, but a tinge of sadness came over her. 'War, there always seemed to be a war.' 'Why should it be so sad, to be honorable?' She said a small prayer that he would return home safely.

Molly saw him walking down the street and she hurried from the restaurant window to look at herself in the mirror in the back, tucking in place the blond hair that was hanging in front of her ear. She brushed her dress and came out into the dining room as he entered. Her blue eyes scanned his figure and a warmth spread around her throat. "Why Cam, you devil," she laughed, "you didn't tell me you were a sergeant in the army."

"You didn't ask," he countered.

"Sit down, sit down, it's good to see you."

Stearns sat down and set the package on the table.

Molly looked at the package and asked, "Someone having a birthday?"

Stearns looked into her deep blue eyes. "No, it's for you, Molly. I've been thinking about you lately out in the camp, and I thought I'd buy you a little something.''

She sat down and picked up the small package. Trying to hide her excitement, she opened the paper so as not to tear it and giggled as she took out the three handkerchiefs and the blue ribbon.

Stearns blushed slightly, engrossed in her graceful fingers as she toyed with the ribbon. ''For your hair,'' he said.

She looked up from the ribbon and leaned over and kissed him on the cheek. He felt her breast push into his arm. ''Thank you, thank you, this is the nicest surprise that has ever happened to me in this town.''

She rose from the table and hurried into the kitchen. In a few minutes she was back and she had taken the ribbon and pulled it around her forehead and down underneath the back of her neck. Her long blond hair cascaded down her shoulders. In front was the smallest of bows.

Stearns smiled. The lady at the store had been right. ''You're beautiful,'' he said quite unintentionally.

Molly grew quiet. A moment later she answered, ''Thank you, Sergeant, thank you very much. Now enough of this, what would you like to eat?''

Stearns was hungry, but what with the room in town and the present for Molly, he was just about broke. ''Just coffee, please.''

Molly, sensing his plight, said, ''Now, that will never do. How about a ham sandwich and some cole slaw?'' And she added, ''A gift from me to you. Fair is fair.''

''Sure, okay,'' he answered.

She sat down at his table. ''Poncho, ham and cole slaw and coffee, two cups.''

From behind the door Stearns could hear the Mexican cook's guffaw, and the sound of ham hitting the frying pan.

Molly watched him eat. It was a warm feeling she had for this man. A feeling she had not had in three years and tried so hard not to have. It had taken two years to become human again after the accident. But she had done it. Working night and day in the restaurant, running it, keeping it, and starving with it for the first year. But she did not want to go back to the east. Not after all the dreams they had shared about moving out west, the land of freedom and how their children would grow up and never see the hardships and suffering they had known, the long hours of working and sewing. Hector, her husband, working for twelve hours a day. Barely with enough money to stay alive, nevertheless, continually saving for the day they could leave. The long wagon trip out west ending in his sudden death. One day alive and the next dead, run over by a runaway supply wagon. For six months she had thought she would never survive, crying herself to sleep at night. Waking in the morning to feeling of nothingness and of abandonment. But, with her Swedish strength she put every penny they had saved into this restaurant and through guts and work she had pushed these memories away until once again life shone in her face and her eyes danced with renewed color. And for the first time in three years she had that feeling again, that warm feeling toward a man. This Stearns was no ordinary cow bum. She could tell he had once been hard, but there was something inside of him, something that set him apart from most men, a soft part, a lonely part. Here was a man used to being alone, not fighting his aloneness but making it a brother, a friend.

23

Molly smiled as Stearns pushed the empty plate away from him and broke the silence. "That was good," he said, reaching for the coffee cup. He looked at her face and then down at the table. It was easy to think the words but hard to say them. "How about you and I going for a walk this evening after you close up? We're shipping out in a few days and it would be nice to walk with you."

Molly looked at his thin face and the way his green eyes seemed to dissect everything they watched. He was like a cat, quiet and subdued but ready at any moment to reach out with lightning speed. "I'd like that, we can even go to my house and have coffee or tea afterwards. Come and get me at eight tonight, Sergeant. Poncho can close the restaurant up."

Stearns stood and put on his hat. "Thank you, Molly. I'll see you at eight."

He left the restaurant and whistled to himself. Half way down the street to the bar he stopped. He didn't even know her last name. He had enough money for one beer and four hours to drink it until eight. He made a mental note to ask her for her last name.

The bar was pulsating with activity. It seemed as if all the soldiers who had a pass were in the bar. He adjusted his eyes to the dim light and saw Smiley across the room. Smiley noticed him and motioned over the bobbing heads to come and join him. He noticed when he got there Smiley was looking at a newspaper. "Look at this, Sergeant," Smiley drawled, "here we are again."

Stearns looked at the blond Texan and said, "Smiley, I can't read."

"Well, hell then, I'll read it for you."

Stearns watched and Smiley sensed his urge to read and placed his fingers on the headlines:

"'Roosevelt's Rough Riders to sail. It has been this newspaper's contention that we, the United States of America, should have been at war many months ago, but through the inept handling of foreign policy by the present administration it has taken months for this country to see the conditions facing our brothers in Cuba before we have had the courage to do something about it. One man, Lieutenant Colonel Roosevelt, has tried for months to spur on our war effort and he, with his Commander, Colonel Wood, have trained and readied the best fighting force this nation has ever drawn together in freedom's name. In just fourteen short days these brave men will be headed from Florida to liberate our friends the Cubans from their cruel oppressors.'"

Smiley looked up from the paper. "And then it goes on about General Shafter bein' in charge of the army and something about some navy admiral named Sampson but that don't mean nothin' to us. Hell, we're the Rough Riders."

Stearns laugh. "Well Smiley, let's drink one to the Rough Riders."

He reached into his pocket and pulled out his last coin. "This is it for me, guess I don't need money where we're going."

Smiley threw back his head and grinned his boyish grin. "Never ya mind, Sergeant, never ya mind, I got enough coins for you and me to drink enough beer to piss us a river from here to Florida and back."

And they started to drink. After four hours of drinking Stearns looked at Smiley and asked, "How in the hell did you ever end up here in New Mexico with Rough Riders?"

"Well my Dad and I run a small spread down by Amarillo and one day in town there was a poster sayin' there'd be a sergeant come though town lookin' for men who could qualify for a crack outfit in the army. Ya had to be a crack shot and ride like the wind," Smiley laughed, "this was before I knew only the officers rode. Well the day he was in town, see, I go in and shoot the socks off ever one around and the sergeant tells me, sign up boy, see the world and all and here I am. But to tell ya the truth, I love it Sergeant, I love the shootin' and the trainin' and the marchin' and the drinkin', and the wild girls when I can get up enough nerve to go ask one if she wants to go to the top of the stairs. It beats punchin' them cows in that Texas sun."

Stearns looked at Smiley. "Might make it a career, huh?"

Smiley tipped up his beer and a few drops spilled on his shirt. "Just might, Sergeant, how about you?"

"Nope, not enough money. There's a place I want. I don't know how I'm ever going to get it, but I can't do it in the army."

"Two more beers, bartender," Smiley hollered. "Well, here's two more for dreams, Sergeant. Let's hope we all see at least one dream come true."

It was 8:15 before Stearns remembered his date. "God, I'm late." And he turned, leaving Smiley by himself. Smiley, not being one to be concerned about other people's actions, just watched him run out of the door.

Molly sat at the table as he dashed in the door of the restaurant. "First date I've been on in years and he shows up late," she teased. She rose and walked over to him and put her arm around his. Smelling the beer, she said, "Last night in town and all you could do is belly up to the bar."

Stearns looked at her and the blue ribbon and smelled her perfume and could not speak for a moment. "I'm sorry, Molly," he finally stammered. "I'm truly sorry."

"Forget it," she replied, "if this was the worst thing that ever happened to me I'd be lucky."

They walked down the board sidewalk as far as it stretched and stepped down to the dirt. The stars shone bright and merry and a slight breeze cooled the evening. "Beautiful here at night," she mumured. "No place like it on this earth. It seems as if the whole sky is a blanket and you can lie down and count the stars forever. What do you think, Cam?"

Stearns felt her warmth on his arm and looked at the stars. "I never really thought of it like that, Molly, it has always been peaceful to me. Just quiet, a time to rest, nothing to think of, just let my mind go blank."

They stopped by a large cottonwood tree that grew in the middle of town. "Tell me about yourself, Cam," Molly said.

Stearns leaned up against the tree and looked at the stars between the branches. "I was born about 150 miles from here, raised on a ranch. Didn't and don't know much of anything except cows, horses and guns. Guess that's why they like me in the army. I don't know a trade, can't even read, but I know I want to."

Maybe it was the beer, maybe the night, but Stearns felt secure with Molly and he went on. "Seems most of my life I've been looking, looking and seeing but never finding. I never looked much past day to day, except now, I know where

I'll be in a few days, but I know I'm not going to stay in the army."

Then suddenly he turned and looked at Molly. "You know what I want?"

"What?" she asked.

"I want to learn how to read."

She reached up and touched his face. "You know what I want?" she asked.

"I want you to kiss me," and she pulled his face down to her and kissed him.

Their lips melted into each other's and the breeze seemed to sway them in rhythm with the leaves. He drew away from her and put his arms around her and held her close. "I like you, Molly."

She felt his heart beating and stared off into the darkness. "I like you too, Sergeant Stearns."

They were silent during the walk to her house and when she asked him if he wanted to come in for coffee he said no. He had to catch the wagon back to camp. "Thank you for the walk, Molly," he said as she stood inside the door. She watched him leave and fade into the darkness. She was slow to get into bed this night and slow to fall asleep.

Stearns squeezed himself among the men on the wagon. Most were drunk enough that the bumpy, jolting ride to their camp did not wake them from their stupor. Stearns saw Smiley's bobbing form near the front of the wagon and could tell he would need help reaching the tent. It was a slow ride, and among the groans and songs from some of the men he could not get his mind off Molly. It was not until they reached camp that he remembered he had forgotten to ask her her last name.

In the morning one could tell which of the men had passed to town. They were the ones drinking the steaming hot coffee and not talking while the others seemed to be engrossed in stories of how the war would go.

Stearns was issued his 34/40 rifle and drew comments of admiration at his expertise with the weapon. "Too bad it shoots out so much smoke," was his only comment after firing. "Better fire it and move," he told the men. "Won't take too much to see where these blunderbusses go off from."

He liked his pistol much better, but knew it was of limited use for long distance firing. This method of shooting one shot and then reloading was for the birds. During rifle practice he wondered why there was not more attention paid to knife fighting, as it would seem that there would be more hand to hand fighting than anything else going on. From what he had heard, Cuba was a hot, sticky place with lots of bugs and rain. He wondered how bearable it would be with the wool pants and shirts on. They might be prepared for the fighting but these clothes were not the best.

They had five days to ship-out date and all passes were suspended. He spent the days thinking of Molly and each day sent a sinking feeling in his chest. There would be no way to get in touch with her. It seemed such a loss to him, he knew he did not love her, but she was the closest he had ever felt toward any woman. So instead of feeling the excitement grow with each day closer to leaving, he felt duller. There was no way he could get into town, it would not be worth the possibility of getting caught and destroying in one moment all he had gained in the last weeks. When he was on the train he would have Smiley write a letter and address it to her restaurant. She might get it. At least it gave him a glimmer of hope.

He had not thought of his mother in the last days. It was almost as though a part of his life had died that night in the hotel room with Roosevelt. His life on the ranch, the cliff, and all passed into some dark corner of his mind.

The next to the last day in camp he asked Lieutenant Williams if he could get him an appointment to see Roosevelt, and Williams said he would see what he could do. That evening after chow a sergeant came to the tent and told him Roosevelt would see him in his private tent. The last few days Roosevelt had spent in camp, having checked out of the hotel.

Stearns knocked on the wood frame around the door and heard the familiar "come in" from Roosevelt. He entered and saluted the sitting form on the cot. "At ease, Sergeant," Roosevelt said, rising. "Sit down."

Stearns sat down in a folding chair across from the cot. Roosevelt picked up a bottle of Scotch from the table. "Scotch?"

"Don't mind if I do," Stearns answered.

Handing Stearns a glass, Roosevelt sat down once again on the cot. "Well, how's army life treating you?"

"Just fine, sir, better than I imagined."

Roosevelt noticed Stearns shining face and how good he looked in uniform. A true soldier, Roosevelt thought, still intrigued by the man. "What brings you here, Sergeant?"

Stearns sipped the Scotch. "I was wondering sir, if there was a way part of my pay could be sent to my mother, while I receive the other part."

Roosevelt looked at the man. "Of course, Sergeant."

He reached and got a piece of paper from the table and a pen. "Just write down her address and I'll make sure the paymaster gets it. How much do you want to send her?"

Stearns looked at Roosevelt. "I can't write, sir, just my name."

Roosevelt displayed no surprise and took the pad and pen. "What is her name?"

"Rachel Stearns. Bernalillo, New Mexico."

Roosevelt set the pad down. "I've heard you are popular with your men, as I knew you would be, and that you can shoot the eyes out of a gnat."

Stearns smiled. "That's one thing I can do, sir."

Roosevelt's expression grew serious. "Are you ready, Cam?" It was the first time he had ever used Stearns' first name.

Stearns looked at Roosevelt and saw the seriousness and he also saw the concern he felt for him and the other men, as though the dead would forever lay on his conscience. "I've been in trouble one way or another my whole life, sir, but I've never been in a war. Everyone I've met is my friend and I suppose I'm as ready as the next man. But I suppose I'm less informed than most about the cause and all."

Roosevelt rose and refilled his glass, not offering more to Stearns. "Men go to war for a lot of reasons, Cam. Some to fight because that is all they know and will ever know. Some to prove themselves and see if they are cowards or not. Countries go to war for multitudes of reasons, most to mask the truth I suppose.

Freedom or slavery, power and gain. A day is just another page of history. Some countries fight some wars for peace. But real war is what we are, Cam. Not newspaper articles, not causes or reasons, but our compulsions are molded and framed in wars and causes. It is as though men like us are drawn to it, not because we want it, but because it is there, and somebody has to do it."

He looked at Stearns and shrugged. "I suppose my mind has been traveling these last days. At night I don't sleep, but lay and hear the guns. And looking at the faces of the men in the morning I realize some of these men won't return to this country. They will have honor and medals and glory but they won't have life, and I wonder at times why it is me who's in charge, why this drive to be there, to be first, to have such conviction that I am right.

Stearns looked at Roosevelt and for the first time he realized he was just a man like the rest of them. No matter that his power or his bearing made him a leader, he still was a man and he was as afraid as the rest of them.

It was one of those fleeting moments when the truth sinks in, when the reality of war, a real war and as opposed to the preaching of war becomes easily differentiated and very clear. Not just a day in the field practicing war. "I don't know, sir, I'm not as educated as you are. I suppose I've never really thought of things like that."

"Yes you have, Sergeant. All those days of your life fighting something or somebody, all those nights of laying awake with nothing in your mind but a feeling you couldn't put your finger on, it's all the same. It's just a feeling, a knowledge that education or manner or bearing doesn't bring out. We are the true men, men bred for war."

"I don't want to fight my whole life, sir," Stearns said.

"Nor I, Sergeant, but at times I see the future and it seems as if it is on fire."

"Tell me a little about yourself, Sergeant."

Stearns rolled the glass between his fingers. "I was born on a ranch in New Mexico. The early part of my life was riding, chopping wood, shooting. I never felt like a little boy, never had toys. I had the stars and the animals and my rifle and pistol. My dad was a hard man but a good man. Quiet, he was. I know now he loved all of us, but it seemed it was always work. My mother worked her whole life and is still working.

"Funny, there was a cliff on that ranch. I used to go there all the time. It was about a quarter of a mile from the house and you could see out for hundreds of miles. I would sit there for hours when I was caught up with my work and watch the hawks and the animals below.

"I had a sister who died when she was five and it seemed my mother was never really the same after that. It seemed like my whole world began to crumble from then on. My dad lost the ranch and I swore I would have it back one day. I swore I would never be poor again.

"Well, we moved to town and it was as though the move broke my dad. He did odd jobs and worked but mostly he just drank a lot, and one day he just died. My mother started working for a man in a restaurant and I did cow work mostly. Broke horses, but there was never enough money. I saw my mother slowly working herself to death, always needing but never complaining.

"Then one day the restaurant owner hit my mother, and when she came home and I saw her face I just blew up. I ran to the man's house and kicked in his door. I threw a gun at him and told him to pick it up, but he just stood there crying and blubbering. He wasn't a mean man like me, but I shot him in the face."

"I didn't even fight the deputies. They knew me, there was nothing to do. Sitting in the cell I felt like hanging myself until this old man around town just walked in and let me out one morning, gave me a horse and some money and let me go!"

"And the rest you know. Except one part. Riding here I rode by the old ranch. I slept on the cliff and felt the familiar wind, like when I was a boy and I left it with a vow. I vowed I would never be poor, no matter what, I would never be poor."

Stearns stood up and set the glass on the table. "Well, I've taken enough of your time, sir."

He saluted. "The best to you, sir, and thank you for everything you have done for me."

The officers rode around the men in ranks. Gone were the tents and any sign of life except for the bare trodden ground which showed that a thousand men had lived here for over six months. The lieutenants stood to the left of the troops with their shouldered arms. Col. Wood and Lt. Col. Roosevelt rode in front of the columns. They would give Las Vegas a show as they left. Roosevelt had made sure that the town knew when they were leaving and that the newspapermen from the east were there. There would be a band and the colors at the train station would tell the whole country that Teddy Roosevelt and the Rough Riders were on their way to win the war.

Forward, march! reverberated down the lines of faces, and they began to move, snaking down out of the rolling grass hills toward the town. As they entered the town the band broke out in the Star Spangled Banner and all the men felt the chills run up and down their spines. Stearns marched, feeling the power grow within him, and his face showed the expressionless, stoney glare of an old time army sergeant. He did not see Molly run out into the street until she was right beside him, but he felt her touch on his arm and he smiled down at her, fighting the urge to pick her up and whirl her around in the air. She skipped to keep up with the marching men and jumped and kissed him on the cheek. "You take care of yourself now, Sergeant Stearns," she shouted above the blaring of the band, "and get yourself back here in one piece. Here's something for you to remember me by," and she took out an envelope and pushed it into his hand. He turned his gaze to her and smiled, but could not find any words to say. She stopped walking as the men neared the train station, and the last she saw of him was his back disappearing into the train.

Stearns sat by the window of the train and watched the dark landscape fly by. Occasionally sparks flew by the window, illuminating for a moment a tree or a bush. Smiley sat beside him, engaged in a heated conversation about catfishing with another man from Texas who was assigned to another platoon. He reached into his pocket and pulled out the envelope and opened it slowly. Although he could not read, he knew what he saw was her address. Enclosed also was a strip of blue ribbon with a small braid of her hair attached. He took the ribbon and tied it around his neck and returned his gaze to the window and the dark. It would be a long ride to Florida. A long time to sit and contemplate the dark and the days ahead. His adventure had begun. He felt the excitement, and somehow he knew he would return.

(3)

The train ride was long and tiresome. At each town the men were ordered to fall out in ranks in order to be greeted by the milling crowds and the bands. It seemed that the whole country knew they were leaving. In every town the men were greeted by shouts and speeches from local politicians. Col. Wood and Lt. Col. Roosevelt made speeches from the flag-draped podiums that were hastily constructed for their arrival. Small boys ran in and out of the ranks of soldiers, dreaming of battles and heroic exploits. The men enjoyed the break in the monotony, and the attention the young girls showered on them. With each stop Stearns felt more and more a part of the unit. At some stops they were given packages by the ladies, that once back in the train were hastily opened to bring out cakes and cookies and fruit which were greedily gobbled up — a welcome change from the bland army food. Roosevelt was seen little, sharing a Pullman with Col. Wood. The lieutenants were with the men in the cramped cars, which if nothing else helped to break down the weight of rank and bring a closer tie between the lower brass and the men, an important quality in a good fighting team. Card games went on for days and some men lost many months pay. Stearns avoided the card games, intent on watching the winners and the losers alike. He was never one to gamble, not prone to believe in luck and not willing to lose what little money he was making.

It was dark when they pulled into Orlando, and unlike the other towns there were no bands or speeches. There was just an empty, hushed railroad station suddenly filled with the noise of men falling into ranks and the following marching orders. They marched for a little over an hour until they were dismissed in front of wooden barracks with orders that no one was to leave. A cot was a welcome relief from sleeping in train seats, and tired, cramped muscles were allowed to stretch. Sitting on the cots the men were strangely silent as they knew their days were numbered now, as soon the fighting would begin.

Smiley walked over to Stearns' cot and sat down. "Well, looks as though we made it," he drawled.

Stearns rubbed his tired neck. "I was wondering if that train ride was ever going to end."

"But wasn't it something?" Smiley said.

"It was something," Stearns agreed.

"Could you imagine livin' in one of those big cities, havin' one of those fancy carriages with the fringe and all? Sittin' there like mom's plum pie tippin' your hat to the ladies."

Stearns stood up and pulled off his shirt. For the first time Smiley saw the blue ribbon. "Lookey here," he hollered. "Sarg's got himself a fancy one," and he whistled.

Stearns could feel the blond hair rub against his chest, and he threw Smiley a look that told him he'd better quit laughing.

"Hope it brings you luck, Sergeant, I think a lot of us are gonna need it."

The weather was nothing like the cool nights and dry days of New Mexico. The men sat around during the day, the hot muggy air seemed to put them into a trance. Several old soldiers having been there years before, spread stories of Cuba. "You think it's hot here, there it's hotter than this at night and the bugs are big enough to carry you off. Never a break from the heat, even the shade's like a sweat bath."

The heat made the men irritable. After all the months of training they were ready to go. All had it in their minds that it would be over soon. What son-of-a-bitch could stand up to them? They would get there, bury the bastards and be home.

That afternoon there was mail call. Most of the soldiers had no wives or families but the ones who did stood anxiously around waiting for their name to be called. Stearns was surprised when he heard his name, and walking back to his bunk he looked at the envelope and felt his heart beat hard in his chest.

He found Smiley engrossed in conversation with a man, and he stood there for several minutes before he could ask him to come to his bunk.

He looked at Smiley, sitting on the bunk with a serious expression, and it took him several more minutes before he could muster the courage to ask him to read the letter for him. Smiley opened the letter carefully, making a neat cut with his knife across the top. "Smells like springtime," he muttered, unfolding the paper and reading:

THE LINKS OF FRIENDSHIP'S GOLDEN CHAIN
BIND MANY HEARTS TOGETHER
WITH A TIE SO STRONG THAT JOY NOR PAIN
NOR OUGHT THAT TIME MAY DO OR SEVER
BUT WE ARE BOUND BY HOLIER TIES
THAT THOSE WITH FRIENDSHIP MAKES
A FRIEND'S LOVE WILL FOREVER LAST
THOUGH EVERY FRIEND FORSAKES.

and it was signed simply, Molly.

Smiley looked at Stearns and handed him the letter. He was silent for a moment, looking out the window of the barracks. "Wish I had me a girl who'd write like that," he said. "You sure are a lucky fella."

Stearns folded the letter back up and put it on his pillow. "I've never had anyone say anything like that to me," he murmured.

"Sergeant, she loves you, that's all there is to it, she loves you."

Stearns rubbed his head. "How can she love me when we have only met twice?"

"I don't know, my daddy sent for my mother from letters they wrote back and forth. She mailed him a picture and he mailed her one and one day she came and

31

they were in love. Men smarter'n us have tried to figger it out and can't, but I'm tellin' ya, she loves you, Sergeant.''

Stearns stood on the steps of the barracks. The sun had just set and the air was filled with the buzz of insects. A slight muggy breeze blew, rustling the tops of the palm trees. He felt the soft touch of the ribbon around his neck. He sat down on the steps.

Once when he was a little boy he had hiked up to the cliff. It was a day in the fall and all the scrub oak were in their prime red and yellow colors. The mountains looked like a painter had taken all the shades of red and yellow and dropped them on the top of the mountain. He was sitting there thinking of the deer and how they would leave the mountains soon, when he saw his mother and father walking below the cliff. They were walking slowly and holding hands and it was the first time that he had ever seen them holding hands. All he could remember was them working and his father falling asleep exhausted every night. A strange feeling had swept over him, a feeling he had never known, and for the first time he realized his parents had been alive and had done things before he was born. It was the first time he realized he did not share in their feeling for each other and he had been angry and happy. Angry because it had made him feel alone, but happy because he knew that they loved each other. He had sat on the cliff until the sun perched on the edge of the mountain and a chilly fall wind had swept across his face. Once back at the house he did not tell his parents that he had seen them from the cliff.

Later that evening Lieutenant Williams came to his bunk. "The Colonel sent this over to you, Stearns," he said, handing him a book and a pad of paper with several pencils. "Said to tell you to study and practice and it wouldn't take long."

Stearns looked at the book. "What is it, Sir?"

"Teaches you to read and write, Sergeant."

Stearns turned the book over in his hands several times. This small book was the key. The key to a world he had never visited but knew was there, and this was the key, the opening of a door to whatever awaited him.

From that time on, during every minute of spare time, Smiley and he went over the book. Smiley, in his slow, Texas style, pointed out the letters and the words. As they walked around camp he showed him words until after a few days he knew some words by sight. He played them over in his mind and wrote them slowly and deliberately each night from memory. He copied the a's and the b's hundreds of times and continued on through the alphabet, until after a week he could, with much thought and difficulty, write a few sentences and thoughts. A warm, satisfied feeling came over him, when he looked at the words he had written. Not the physical satisfaction he felt after having roped a cow or broken a horse, but a true feeling that he had accomplished something very important. Smiley cheered him on laughing and joking, and even the Lieutenant began to help him. The Lieutenant seemed to have finally resolved himself to the fact that he was going to war. Occasionally he would carry on about the uselessness of it all, but more so he seemed to put his attention into teaching Stearns how to read and write. The three would sit for hours on the steps of the barracks, going over and over words. The Lieutenant would write words and have Stearns sound them out. His dark eyes would beam when Stearns got one right. "Very good, Sergeant," he would say.

The Lieutenant had graduated from Harvard, Stearns found out, with a degree in law. After a year of practice he had grown tired of law for reasons that were too complicated for Stearns to comprehend. Somewhat of a dreamer, the Lieutenant seemed to be one of those men who are destined never to find happiness. He was too intelligent to accept the world and he could never see past the hypocrisy or cruelty of life. He didn't enjoy being in charge of men. He hated the responsibility of their lives on his conscience, but it was something that he could not get out of now, and more and more he put his trust in Stearns, who radiated an animal power from within him.

The men were attracted to Stearns. Although he was not boisterous like the other men were, he was a man that men followed. They knew he would not falter in a pinch. The Lieutenant liked this man, who was raised so much differently than he. It was as though he gained his strength from Stearns and in return he patiently taught him how to read and write.

Stearns devoured words like food. Everything around him was pushed into the background. Nothing mattered during his waking hours except words, letters and practicing writing. A whole new world had opened up to him and he was bound and determined to capture it. It was as if the words would disappear unless he grabbed all of them before they were gone.

One hot afternoon the Lieutenant and Smiley walked into the barracks and saw Stearns practicing writing words in his diligent manner. The words were written with firm, bold strokes. Except for the army uniforms the two men looked like small boys, who had just successfully pulled off some outrageous prank. Walking up to Stearns, they stood by the bunk. "And how's the star pupil," Smiley drawled.

Stearns looked up. "Seems the more I know the stupider I find out I am," he laughed.

The Lieutenant nooded his head, "There's more truth in that statement than you know."

Stearns noticed the Lieutenant was standing with one hand behind his back. He looked suspiciously at both men, but didn't know what to say. The Lieutenant began, "Smiley here was playing cards in the other barracks this morr.'ng and he just happened to be winning for once." Smiley had a reputation for not knowing how to play poker. "And this private from over there ran out of money and couldn't pay his losses so, while Smiley was going through his belongings he came across something he thought you might like to have."

From behind his back the Lieutenant handed Stearns a black book. Stearns looked at the cover. In gold, embossed letters it read, DICTIONARY. Stearns looked at Smiley and the Lieutenant and they were both laughing. He stood up, and said "Thanks, Smiley."

Smiley started to walk away. "Now you can write some letters and I won't have to teach you so much. This time is getting into my poker time."

The Lieutenant stood by the bunk. "Payday tomorrow, Sergeant. And I understand they are going to give the NCO's and the junior grade officers a day in town. So why don't you have the men write down what they want and you and I can pick up a few thing for them when we go in?"

"Yes sir," Stearns answered.

The Lieutenant walked off and Stearns sat with his new book. He thought of his mother and the nights when he watched her sit by the fire. He remembered all the arguments she would use with his father about sending the boy to school. He wished she could see him now, and for the first time in many weeks he missed her. A pang went through his chest. He saw her tired form, the rough and chapped hands from the toil they had known. He knew she had already received some of the money from his last month's pay. What little it was would be a god send to her, he knew. In a few days he would be ready and he could write to her. He felt like a small child with this thought. He was sure she would be very proud of him.

Lieutenant Williams and Sergeant Stearns walked down the paved street. He had never seen a town like this. Every imaginable item could be seen through the store windows. Candies of every shape and color. Men's suits and ladies dresses. In one part of town there had been fish and pineapples piled as high as a man, and creatures they called crabs and lobsters. There had been a smell there, a different smell than the mountains and plains, but a smell of the earth, and he had enjoyed the tough talk of the vendors and the sound of large fish being thrown on scales and wrapped in heavy brown paper. He marveled at the people and the number of black people there were. And he was amazed at the fancy and rich dress of the whites compared with the rags and tattered clothes of the blacks. They had walked along the docks and he had been awe struck. The many ships with tall masts and sails wrapped neatly, but the ones that fascinated him the most were the great steel ships with the shiny metal glistening in the sun. "That one, that one there," The Lieutenant told him, "that will take us to Cuba."

Stearns stood and looked at the ship and large cannon barrels that protruded from every conceivable part of the ship. "How does it float?" he had asked the Lieutenant, and the Lieutenant had laughed. "It floats because it has air inside of it. It's powered by engines that gobble up coal like it was hay and turn large propellers underneath the water."

Stearns found the ship so exciting, he couldn't wait to see the inside and feel the pull of those engines that the Lieutenant had talked about.

They ate lunch at a small outdoor cafe, drinking cold beer and eating greasy fish served on paper.

It was late in the afternoon when they staggered back to the camp carrying the men's cigars and writing paper and various other sundries that were ordered. Stearns sat on the bed and the men crowded around asking questions about the town, about how many women, about what it was like. They could smell the beer on his breath, and kidded him about how nice it would be to be a sergeant and drink a few beers in town. They did not believe that he didn't look for a girl, but each walked away from the bunk like little children with their assorted treasures.

It was dark when Stearns stood up on the bed holding two bottles of whiskey in his hands. "All right men," he ordered, "break out the glasses."

The men scrambled in various forms of undress and the rest of the night was spent listening to old war stories and whorehouse exploits. They laughed and joked and for a few hours the agony of waiting was forgotten.

joked and for a few hours the agony of waiting was forgotten.

It was quiet when Stearns lay down. Looking down the neat row of cots he was struck for a moment with the reality of the situation. Here they were, men of all walks of life. Some educated, some east coast men, some cowboys. There had to be more than one like himself, hiding from the law and being given a break. But here they were, about to travel across a small portion of the ocean to fight and kill a race of people they had never seen. It struck him as something terrible but also as something beautiful in its own way, something grand and powerful. The engine of the war machine had been started and there was no turning back. Bred for war stuck in his mind as he dozed off. Roosevelt had said there are some men bred for war, men like you and I, Mr. Stearns.

What the soldiers waiting to be sent to Cuba did not know was that the army was waiting for word from Rear Admiral William T. Sampson as to the whereabouts of the Spanish fleet. Intelligence reports had confirmed that Spain had sent a fleet to Cuba under the command of Admiral Pascual Cervera y Topete. On May 28 Sampson's fleet located the Spanish fleet, which was anchored in the harbor of Santiago. Upon receiving this news the army hastily prepared to assualt Santiago by land.

Major General William Shafter walked into the smoke-filled room. The majors and colonels jumped to attention as he entered.

He was a serious man, this Shafter. Now in his early 60's, he looked very much the part of the old warrior. A medal of honor recipient during the Civil War, he carried his power with a steady and unequalled grace. "Sit down, men," he said through his white-flecked mustache.

Several aides hastily followed him. He stood in front of the brass and looked over the men. "Many of you I know," he said slowly, "many I don't. Let us hope this fight is over soon and I don't have to meet you." He laughed in a dry, infantry laugh and sat down, too old to have the vigor for battle. "We leave in two days, gentlemen."

A low hum spread through the room, with the knowledge that the weeks of waiting were finally at an end. "My aides are passing out all the information necessary for you to have, so that this meeting will not take long. The navy has the Cuban fleet blockaded and we are going to land a two-pronged attack. One group will land at Daiquiri and the other at Sibarney. Luckily we don't have to walk, we'll let the navy handle that!"

A controlled laugh spread among the officers, many visualized themselves in the General's place in a few years. "I suggest you inform your lieutenants tonight in order that they can inform the men and let them have time to write letters and get their affairs in order."

He rose with the slow grace of an old bull. Leaving, he stopped by the door, and said "To a quick and decisive victory," and he was gone.

The Colonels and Lieutenant Colonels shook themselves from his trance and sat back down. "Jolly good," Roosevelt said above the din of the room. "It's about time we get this bloody mess over with."

It was midnight when the Lieutenant woke the men. "We leave in two days, boys," he said. "Ammunition will be issued tomorrow evening. Sleep well, good luck.''

After he had left a few men spoke in subdued tones. ''It's about time,'' one said, ''let's get this thing on with, by God.''

Others were quiet, staring into the dark.

Stearns lay on his bunk and looked into nothing. He thought of the cliff and remembered the feeling he had at times that he could jump from the cliff and the wind would carry him far off and up into the sky.

But there was no cliff here, no wind and no blue, cool New Mexico sky. Just the wool army blanket and the endless drone of the insects outside.

Dear Molly,

He began with slow, deliberate strokes of the pen. His writing was not excellent, but it did not look like a small child's, either.

I am sorry it has taken me so long to answer your letter, but I have been learning to read and write. I am happy to say that this is the first letter I have ever written in my life. The men and I have been sitting here for the past several weeks waiting for our order to ship out, which finally came last night. We leave in one day. At least now the waiting is over. It is both a blessing and a curse. It is strange to look around me and know that some of us will not return to this country. The train ride here was a great experience. I had never dreamed in my life that there were so many things in the world. For a country boy like me it seems as though my mind has been opened and filled with more sights and sounds than I can remember. I want to thank you for your poem and I have it in my bedroll. There are times sitting here at night that I think of you and the tree downtown and how the stars were so bright that night. I am sorry I did not have much to say to you that last day in town when you ran up to me. I have the ribbon with your hair around my neck. It makes me feel very good. The smell of your letter comes to me in the night when I sleep. I hope your restaurant is busy and you are in good health. The newspapers are making quite the thing out of this war. Tell Poncho, your cook, hello for me and take care of yourself. I am always your friend.

And it was signed, *Cam Stearns.*

Next he wrote his mother.

Dear Mother,

There are so many things to tell you. First of all I am writing this letter by myself. I have learned to read and write and keep studying every chance I get. I know by now that you must know I am in the army by the money you receive. I hope it helps you. I want you to buy some nice things for yourself, some new dresses and some lotion for your hands. I know how you always wanted some nice lotion. I am a Sergeant in the Rough Riders. How this all came about I will tell you when I see you the next time. For now it is enough for you to know I am well and in good spirits. We are in Orlando waiting to be shipped to Cuba tomorrow. It is a good feeling to know we are fighting for freedoms sake. You will be receiving money every month from the army from me. I wish I could send more but there are some things I need. Be careful, mother.

Love, your son.

Sergeant Stearns sealed the envelopes and dropped them in the mail pouch. Letters were such amazing things. Traveling so many miles with thoughts from one person to another. Lord, what a feeling. He felt warm and relaxed lying in bed that night. He could feel Molly's breast mold into his arm and smell her perfume, and he could see her blue eyes with the ribbon around her blond hair coming closer and closer to his face. She loves you, he heard faintly in the background and he was asleep.

(4)

There is no feeling in the world like the feeling of men going off to war. The sound of heavy boot-laden feet hitting the pavement. The shouting sergeants and movement of the officers around the marching troops. It is an immortal feeling, which is passed from father to son with only the weapons changing with each generation. They marched, chests bursting outward, boots shined so one could see a dull reflection of one's face. The rifles shone with their coating of oil and the men's eyes showed the fear and the bravery all mixed into the day. It was their day, a soldier's day. The bands had played, the women had cried and waved and they had marched into the great steel heart of the ships. They had stood by the railing as the faces slowly turned into mere dots on the horizon and all one could see was the endless ocean all around them. The ship was steel and paint and navy men were running to and fro. A few soldiers and navy men threw jibes at one another with animosity. The men lined the decks and sat in three-tiered hammocks below deck, sweating with the hot summer humidity of the Caribbean. A few men were seasick but most adjusted quickly and laughed at the ones running for the rails or the latrines. Most, though, were anxious to reach land and get back on the good old Mother Earth.

Stearns stood by the rail and let the breeze blow around his face. It was peaceful here, like the cliff when he was growing up. Although there was nothing to grace the eye, the endless ocean brought rest to the mind. There were no mountains to clutter up the brain. It was as if God gave man the ocean to cleanse his mind, not just to rest it. Here it was, the ocean, and everyone including the navy men knew the ocean was supreme. You sailed on her only at her will. She was a grand woman, who men dreamed of making love to. No matter the boasting or the charms or the gifts presented, it was still the woman who allowed the love making to start. He did not think of the cliff for long, standing by the rail, nor did he think of Molly or his mother. It was as if there was nothing else in the world except him and the ocean. The talking, milling men around him were somewhere in front of or behind him in time. He stood there and his world enveloped him, he could smell the gun powder and hear the curses of men. Somewhere off to his left a man fell and another fell behind him. Two more rushed passed them, curses and yells emitting from their fierce faces. He heard the whine of bullets flying over his head but he felt no fear. He fired his rifle and ran, firing and running. The butt of his rifle tore into the face of a man in front of him, exposing jaw bone stark white to the sky, he saw the fear in his eyes as his boot crashed into his temple and the body shook and convulsed as he moved farther up the hill.

"Sergeant, Sergeant," broke him from his spell. He turned his gaze from the ocean and Smiley stood beside him. "Well, here we are, Sergeant. Sure don't look like Texas or New Mexico, does it?"

Stearns smiled. "Nope, sure doesn't look like New Mexico."

"You afraid, Sergeant?"

"Yea, I'm afraid, Smiley. Afraid I might never get the chance to do the things I have to do. Afraid I might die over here and never find out what my life is about."

"I'm afraid too, Sergeant," Smiley said, looking over the rail of the ship, "but I s'pose that's what it's all about. Do ya think they're afraid?"

"Who?"

"The Spanish. Do ya think they're afraid?"

Stearns looked at Smiley. "Sure they're afraid. They're just like us only they believe different. They're people, they don't want to die either."

"No, I s'pose they don't. Well, see ya in the ship tonight. There's a card game on the other side. I'm gonna see if I can change my luck."

Stearns stepped back from the rail and began to walk toward the door that led down to the troop quarters. He noticed Lieutenant Williams standing separated from the men by the rail. He walked up next to him and looked out without speaking. The Lieutenant turned his gaze toward him. "Hello, Sergeant," he sounded far away. "It's about time, isn't it?"

"Yes, Sir."

"I've been dreading this day it seems for years now, Sergeant. All the training and shooting, a million times it has gone through my mind. I can see it, it's like a fire, the death and the killing, all this to kill and burn."

Stearns stood silent beside the man.

"Isn't it amazing, the newspapers, the flags, the banners, all the activity and excitement over the last months to lead to this. Murder, that's all it is, Sergeant, murder. Here we go off to another country to kill people for someone else and do you know why?" He continued without letting Stearns answer. "Because a group of powerful men back in the states see an opportunity for this country to gain land and therefore gain more money for their companies and themselves. It's not freedom or lack of freedom, it's power and simple greed that sends us off to this war, Sergeant. Just greed."

Stearns looked once more out upon the ocean. "I don't know, Sir," he said, "I only know it doesn't matter anymore. We're about there, and there's nothing we can do about it. Hell, I don't even know why we're going."

Lieutenant Williams stood up straight and chuckled. "For that, my friend, you are most fortunate. You can still believe in freedom and causes."

He walked away, not with the swagger of a young army lieutenant, but more like an old man who had seen too much of life to smile and carry on.

Stearns went below deck, an empty feeling in his stomach which did not feel better until he had reread the poem he had received from Molly. I wonder how she is, he thought smelling her perfume. He had never thought of it before but

now he wondered if she had met another man and the thought bothered him.
_____

Molly found herself doing more and more work around the restaurant. She had been nervous the past weeks. Every day she hurriedly bought a newspaper and read of the developments leading to the war. The trip across the nation by the Rough Riders had been covered daily. The bands and shouting crowds had been explained and explained, the proud words of Roosevelt and Wood and the sad words of McKinley, urging the country to war. She could sense that McKinley did not want this war and thought what a terrible burden it must be to be a President and to have so many men on one's conscience. She would find herself at times rewiping tables she had already cleaned, and sitting at night in her chair by the window lost for moments without a thought, just a feeling of the terrible things that brave men would see and do in war's name. It was grand and it was terrible. She would work all day trying to make herself tired so sleep would come easily once she was home. Poncho had told her many times to slow down and take it easy, and that she was working herself into a frenzy. Although she never mentioned the soldier, he knew that he was the source of her anxiety, and he went out of his way to make her smile and laugh. She felt his concern and tried her best to look rested and at ease during the day.

She was sitting, drinking coffee and reading the paper the day it was announced that the navy had the Spanish fleet surrounded in Santiago Harbor and that the soldiers would be there soon. She felt the blood rush to her face and her heart beat madly in her chest. It was close now, and in her mind, she could see Stearns marching beside the men the day they marched through town. It seemed like so many months ago they had left, but it had really only been a few short weeks. That evening she walked slowly back to her house, picking up the mail with little attention. It was not until she was in the house and the lamps were lit that she noticed the strange envelope with the dark, deliberate writing. She opened the letter hurriedly and read the words from Sergeant Stearns.

Sitting by the window that night, the letter in her lap, she felt rested and at peace. Molly, my girl, she thought to herself, it must be love. If you ever see him again you won't let him get away. He might be a no-good cowboy in the army, but it's love and you're not going to lose him. Then, a sudden feeling of dread came over her and she felt he would be killed. He would be killed and she would never hold him in her arms, and a wave of passion swept over her body, like none she had ever felt before. She wanted him there with her, naked in her bed with his lips kissing her, down her neck to her breasts, and she felt the fire rise in her nipples and spread to her thighs and she wanted him inside her, inside her, warm and safe. She went to bed early that evening, dreaming of his touch and her sleep was little and troubled.

(5)

On June 22, 1898, with the navy ships under Rear Admiral Sampson blockading

39

the Spanish fleet inside the harbor of Santiago de Cuba, General Shafter began landing 15,000 troops on a two-pronged attack. The forces, split almost evenly, landed at Daiquiri and Siboney south and east of the harbor. The men had sat quietly the night of June 21, the ships bobbing peacefully in the ocean. Occasionally a light could be seen coming from the land hidden by the darkness. There was no loud bragging or card games. Everyone seemed to have found their own personal corner and crawled into it. In the morning would start the real thing and the bullets would be the enemy's.

Stearns sat and thumbed through his dictionary. He could at any moment lose himself in the search for new words and spelling. Each new word seemed to let a light shine into his mind that had never been there. He knew he was not educated, but by not being so, the small insights he gained through the words were that much more important and wonderful in his memory. Lieutenant Williams had stopped by to see him earlier in the evening and Stearns could tell that he was half drunk. "You should watch the booze Sir," he had told him. The Lieutenant had smiled, "One must become insane to do insane deeds," he had said. "Tomorrow our glory is our stupidity."

Stearns watched him stagger off and hoped the Lieutenant would pull himself together. It was his job to watch after him and he put it in his mind to keep the Lieutenant in sight at all times.

It was dark when the ships moved into position and with the first rays of light the great guns began their bombardment of the Cuban shore. Tremendous flashes of light spit out from the barrels sending the charges hurtling at the unseen enemy. The men, quiet and nervous, walked in full gear up to the decks and began to holler and shout, their faces shining with sweat in anticipation of the upcoming battle. Stearns would never forget the feeling as the boats neared the shore. The sound of the men yelling as they scrambled up the beach. But they were not met with a wave of enemy fire as had been expected, but only a few occasional rounds that buzzed harmlessly over their heads. It was over before it had really begun, and they were deployed in lines above the edge of the white sandy beach.

Sergeant Stearns stood and looked at the line of men lying on the lush grass above the sand. His fears about the Lieutenant had been unwarranted, for as the boat had neared the shore the Lieutenant had seemed to finally take note of the situation and the reality and resigned himself to the fact that no matter what his inner convictions were he was here, and if he wanted to survive he had better get with the business of fighting. Running through the few feet of water to the beach he had spurred the men on. "All right, may God bless us all," he called, "Let's go get those fuckers."

Stearns had been exhilarated as he ran from the craft. The few moments of uncertainty soon turned into disbelief as the enemy was not there. Now the men lay on the grass and smoked and talked, nervous laughter came from a few but most still had the dazed look of disbelief upon their faces. The Lieutenant looked at Stearns "I guess it was not supposed to be this day, Sergeant," he said, sounding relieved, "but I fear there will be a day."

Sergeant Stearns looked past the reclining men and his eyes fell upon the most beautiful land he had ever seen. Here were lush areas, the grass as green as any he had ever seen anywhere. To the west he could see the vague outline of a large mountain range and upon its crest a thin layer of clouds. Farther inland he saw the edge of a stand of trees that looked like a different type of pine tree than those found in New Mexico. Cattle, he thought, looking at the grass, and he could visualize cattle scattered over the low land.

"What do you see, Sergeant?" the Lieutenant asked.

Stearns looked at the Lieutenant. "Nothing, Sir, just looking."

It was not as hot as the stories had told. In fact, it was not as bad as Florida. A cool breeze blew in from the ocean and the slowly building clouds promised rain before the day was over. The men did not know it, but this was the biginning of the rainy season, which would extend well into October. About the only thing Stearns found annoying about the place was the constant low buzz of the every present mosquito. He could hear the men cursing and slapping at the pesky insects. "These little fuckers are worse than the bullets," the Lieutenant had said, swatting one on his face.

Soon the order came to move inland and the men moved out cautiously in a thin line. Even after the many weeks with the Rough Riders, he had no idea the size of the force deployed against the Spaniards. It was a compelling sight, seing the line of men slowly move up and away from the beach. He took one last look at the ocean as they moved into the trees. It had been a warm and friendly companion, but he soon forgot it as the night neared and they stopped to make camp, the whine of the insects increased in intensity.

The Lieutenant was gone for several hours during the night. Returning, he sat down by Stearns. "We are to move inland for a few more miles and then swing east and join the other forces at Siboney. According to reports there were only two casualties during the landing. Tomorrow we'll march through a small town and make as much progress as possible. It's only about five miles to join the other forces."

The men sat in small groups, guard duty was assigned for the evening. It was different being on land once again and also different knowing they were in a war, having not really tasted this fact. After Stearns ate his rations, he rose and walked among the men. They all nodded and said hello and although he did not talk to any of them except Smiley and the Lieutenant, he felt as if he knew them all. Smiley was busy carving off a piece of chewing tobacco when Stearns walked up to him. Smiley put the chew in his mouth and began the process of chewing to soften up the mess.

"One of these days you're going to be running and swallow that garbage," Stearns laughed. Smiley spit and Stearns could see the merriment in his eyes. "Nope, Sergeant, not me, This here stuff is to me just like the ribbon around your neck is to you. You can have anything I got, ceptin' my tobacco."

"You okay, Smiley?"

Smiley patted the rifle beside him. "Just fine, Sergeant."

As Stearns started to walk away, Smiley called to him. "Keep your head down, Sergeant!"

In the morning they formed ranks and marched down a road that lead through the small town of Daiquiri. Stearns had never seen proverty like this, small, thatched homes cramped close to one another. The children ran around in shorts and tattered shirts, barefoot, alongside the marching men. Women in dresses that long ago should have been discarded looked at the men from the doorways. Old toothless men and young men stood silent as if this was just another force they must contend with in their fight to stay alive. There were no bands nor banners, no great joy at having been saved. Just the look of the poor and underprivileged. The Lieutenant did not avert his gaze from the road in order to prevent the image of these people from sinking into his mind.

By three in the afternoon they were on the outskirts of Siboney, and a man on a horse rode up to them. He conferred with Roosevelt briefly and rode off. Roosevelt talked with one of his majors, and the men swung in a different direction. It was evident that they would camp soon. To the left and to the right of them they could see American forces setting up camp. This was to be the staging area. Already tents were standing and cooks could be heard cussing and yelling at the unlucky ones pulling KP. Some coffee would be good, Stearns thought, and a tent before the rain started.

Every afternoon the clouds boiled up and dropped a torrent of rain. It was not a cold rain like in the mountains, but it was cooling. Although the heat was not intense it was sticky, and the rain gave a slight relief from the stickiness.

They marched until they came to an open area that had been left for them. Tents ready to be pitched were in a row. Men from the ships must have unloaded them and other men, taking up the rear, brought them in during the night. The men stacked arms and jovially fell into the work of setting up the camp. "Friggin' rain be here soon, gents," Stearns heard one man say, "so let's get these tents up. If I want a shower I want it out of my clothes."

Stearns could see the other platoons down the line begin working. It was a good sight. Within thirty minutes it looked as though they were back in New Mexico. The instant tent city. Some of the men sat on cots and unrolled their gear. Others stood outside and watched the sky darken. When the rain started it seemed to lift everyone's spirits. Soap came out and soon the tent was surrounded by laughing, naked men showering in the rain.

Stearns soaped his narrow, taut muscles and looked at the country. The thought of cattle still clung in his mind. What a place. No freezing winters to kill off one's work, plenty of deep grass, a mild semi-damp climate. There was a fortune to be made here if one knew the right people. He didn't know how, but he did know that there was a fortune to be made here.

Sitting on his bunk, clean and listening to the rain, he thought of Molly for the first time in days. It was as though the last days had melted together, with no break between one moment or the next. The body stood up to the challenge and then slowly unwound to rest and regain the needed strength for what the future held. It was always strange to think of Molly. At times it was as though he had known her his whole life, as if she has been with him through everything he had ever done. He felt as though he could talk to her and she would listen. But, at other times, he would feel stupid in his thoughts of her, afraid and confused that he could feel at all for a person he had only met a few times. But, this feeling would soon vanish and he could feel the warmth of her as she brought herself close to him. He would remember the fire of her kiss as it touched his ckeek and a hunger would come over him unlike he had ever felt before.

Molly nervously scanned the front page of the newspaper. It had been a glorious landing by the American forces. There was no word that there had been little resistance, but carefully drawn diagrams showed the landing and the advancement of the forces to Siboney. Two long paragraphs described the landing and deployment of the Rough Riders and told of the courageous manner in which they conducted their operation. Recorded were the words of the cheering crowds that greeted them marching through the liberated villages. But there were no words of the distrustful gazes from the peasants or the fears of the women that they would be raped as they had been by the Spaniards. There was no account of the casualties, only that they had been light, and the Spaniards had suffered horribly. But there was the promise that it would be over soon. Molly set the paper down on the table and Poncho came and sat down with two cups of coffee. "He'll be fine, Molly," he said in his clipped English. Molly looked at Poncho and smiled. He could see the strain around her thin red lips.

Oh, this love, he thought to himself, it is such sorrow and such grief at times.

The landing and the march to join the two advancing armies had been uneventful. The forces united, they rested for two days and moved out early on the morning of the 24th. The men were in good spirits with many feelings each day would be as the past two. It was around 10 o'clock when stiff resistance was met and the smiles were instantly turned into the full fledged horror of battle. One moment the men were walking and talking and the next shells fired from the Spanish implacements at La Guasimas sent bodies ripped and torn flying into the air.

Sergeant Stearns, walking beside the Lieutenant, saw two men several yards from Smiley suddenly twist and jerk and knew that they were dead before they hit the ground. "Run for cover," he commanded. The Lieutenant for a brief moment did not move, but Stearns' pulling on his arm sent him scurrying for what cover he could find. The advancing line of Americans dug in and waited for the shelling to stop. Officers on sweating and foaming horses ran up and down the line returning to the brass with reports.

In what seemed like an eternity, but in reality was only a few short moments, the outer left and right flanks were ordered to advance and circle the Spaniards. The middle, composing the Rough Riders, was ordered to hold and wait for orders to charge. The men readied their weapons. Stearns checked the knife in his boot and scanned the faces of the men. He could see it on their faces now; this was it, the first test.

As rounds flew into their ranks a lieutenant on horseback galloped up and talked to Roosevelt. Stearns could see the look on Roosevelt's face, it was not a look of fear, but an expression which told that he had been there before. It was his destiny, and he faced it head on. He pranced his splended bay horse in front of the men, and pulling his sword out of the scabbard he raised himself in the stirrups. "Colors to the front," he ordered. The colors were waved and the cade of the Rough Riders rose, and charged into the fire. Bullets nipped the ground and whined through the ranks. Soon the placements could be seen and the Rough Riders, with deadly accuracy, began picking off the heads and shoulders of the Spanish

43

that peered above the placements. Stearns heard men scream as they were hit, but the advance was so quick that there was no time to see who or where. The Rough Riders rushed into the middle of the Spaniards and could see the skirmish going on around the outside of the perimeter as the American forces to the left and the right converged. Stearns saw the Lieutenant stumble and fall, and a man raise his rifle in order to club him. Stearns dropped to his knee and shot his 44/40 from the hip, and the Spaniard fell to the ground clutching his face. The Lieutenant regained his feet and placed a shot into the man's neck.

Just as suddenly as it began it was over. Brown men, their hands held high and talking in Spanish, began walking toward the American forces. Small groups of Americans poked them with rifles and slammed them to the ground roughly. A bugle sounded and, among the powder and the stench of battle, the brass could be seen riding up and down the ragged lines of men. Soon the Spanish brass were brought forward and Lt. Col. Roosevelt and Col. Wood saluted them as the Spaniards lay down their arms.

"Call your men to order, Sergeant," the Lieutenant ordered. Of the men standing in ranks Stearns counted four missing. To his relief Smiley was there, but with a bad gash over his right eye. He walked up to Stearns. "He was tryin', Sergeant," he drawled, "must be my Texas hard head."

Stearns patted Smiley on the back did not speak.

"Four men missing," Stearns reported to the Lieutenant.

"Pick two men and go look, Sergeant."

Stearns could see that the Lieutenant was shaken.

Stearns picked two men and the three of them began to walk back over the battle ground. Men could be seen to the left and the right with other details from other platoons heading toward them. Occasionally a cry would be heard and the men would turn sharply to see a soldier doubled over in pain. They found two of the Rough Riders together, their bloody remains torn and twisted into a black ooze. One of the men looked at Stearns. "That one is Rogers, Sergeant, I can tell by his red hair. I think O'Reilly was beside him when we started."

"Did you see O'Reilly in ranks?"

"No, no I didn't."

Stearns reached down and took the dog tags from around the necks of the dead soldiers. A Private Graves was found farther back, the left side of his face gone. One eye staring into the nothingness left to his gaze. Private Summers was found walking around with his hands in front of him whimpering, "I can't see, someone, please help me, I can't see."

The men coming up to him propped him up between them, and soothingly talked him back to the front. "It'll be okay, soldier," Stearns said. "Just take it easy, we'll get you to the medics."

The hastily set up medic area was filled with men on stretchers. A low moan engulfed the area and cries came from the tents where the doctors sewed and cut the wounded flesh.

The three men walking back to the platoon seemed to have aged in a few moments. They were quiet as Stearns dismissed them. Details had already been chosen to set up the camp. Farther down the line, men could be seen starting to chow. Stearns scanned the faces of his men and noticed the hard lines. It was war now, no matter how long or how short, it was war, and this one day had been like a year.

Stearns sat drinking coffee by himself. Overhead the clouds had parted to reveal the stars. It was quieter. Some of the men talked in low tones while others walked guard around the perimeter. The smell of gunpowder still hung in the air and mingled occasionally with the smell of burnt flesh. Lieutenant Williams walked over and sat down across from Stearns. "Thank you, Sergeant," he said, his eyes veiled by the darkness. Stearns did not speak. "I guess I owe you my life."

Stearns drained the coffee. "Part of the job, Lieutenant." He noticed the Lieutenant looked drawn.

"I killed him, Sergeant. I shot him while he was lying there."

"Don't think about it, Lieutenant," Stearns interrupted. "You can't think about it."

"I suppose you're right," the Lieutenant continued, "there's nothing I can do. It just seems so incredibly that here on this lush, beautiful island I have killed a man."

"He was trying to kill you, Sir."

The Lieutenant rose, "does it matter, Sergeant?" And he walked off.

Stearns rolled out his bedroll and lay down on top of it. It was quiet now, as if the day had never been. The flying shells seemed to have been just a dream and the dead soldiers from both sides seemed to have never been alive.

For five days the forces rested and regrouped after the battle at La Guasimas. Scouting parties were sent out and after several days it was discovered that the Spanish forces were at three strongholds around Santiago. El Caney was nor-theast of the port city, while San Juan Hill and Kettle Hill were almost directly in line from Las Guasimas. The scouting reports were clear that the three locations were heavily armed and ready for a sustained battle with the American forces.

From his Command Tent, General Shafter read and reread the scouting reports and carefully and with deliberation mapped out his plan. It was obvious to him that the Spanish forces were far inferior to the American forces, and a quick and decisive victory would put an end to the struggle. He had learned through the Civil War that hesitation only gave the enemy time to regroup, leading him to believe that once a march was on, it was better to continue than stop for rest. Satisfied that all the information he had received was correct, and that the Spanish ships were still blockaded by the combined ships of Admirals Sampson and Scheley, he called in his unit commanders.

Over the past days Sergeant Stearns had seen Roosevelt off and on each day. Not close enough to talk to him, but close enough to observe his behavior. Roosevelt was ill at ease and irritable. He wanted to move and engage the enemy, and each passing day with nothing but scouting reports made him more and more on edge. He did not call on his junior officers nor spend time with Colonel Wood. He would rush by the men as if each moment was a passing moment of glory he would not attain again in his lifetime.

Stearns, on the other hand, in between carrying out the duty rosters and posting the guards, spent his time going over his dictionary. It was a quiet time. As if the war had gone away and the time in camp was restful. The afternoon showers found him in the tent copying words and reciting letters. The majority of the squad spent their time playing cards or sleeping.

Smiley, walking around with a bandage on his head, seemed to smile more now that he had a mark of war on him. Stearns wondered how many different tales would come out of that wound before he died. It seemed that a smile was always on his face, whether assigned to guard duty or K.P. Life was life to Smiley. There was nothing to read between the lines, no power or glory with which he grappled. If all went well, he would live to a ripe old age and accept death just as he had accepted life.

The next morning Stearns was standing outside the mess tent when he saw a captain come up to Roosevelt, salute, say a few words and depart promptly. Roosevelt seemed to relax and a smile came across his face. Stearns knew they would move out soon. He knew that smile. The way the eyes would draw up, seeing for years in the future, but also catching every color and movement around them.

He walked to the tent, not feeling afraid. There had been the battle, now there was no more fear. Fear was not the word anyway. He knew he didn't want to die, but he also knew he had no choice in the matter.

The Lieutenant saw Roosevelt ride off and at the same time he saw Stearns watching Roosevelt. He had never figured out the connection between these two men, although he knew there had to be one. Why else would a Lieutenant Colonel in the army make sure a lowly sergeant had books to learn how to read. The Lieutenant did not know Roosevelt very well but he knew that he was a man willing to make adjustments to create his destiny. He had watched him during the fighting and had seen the almost mad look in his eyes as he galloped through the shells. It was eerie how he had flaunted his life. It was as though he dared death to play with him, as if he challenged his fate. The Lietuenant knew Stearns. He knew he was quiet, accepting in many ways, and dedicated. To what exactly, he did not know. He only knew Stearns was a man who wanted something. Love, power, money, he did not know, as Stearns was too closed within himself to let others read him. Like Roosevelt he had that look that tempted death. It was as if they both laughed at life. They had been born with an insight that other men would never know or feel. He liked and respected Sergeant Stearns but he also feared him. Seeing Roosevelt ride off he walked over and caught Stearns walking into the tent. "What do you think of that?" he asked.

"Looks like we're about to move out, Sir."

"I think so too, Sergeant."

"The men are rested and ready, Sir."

The Lieutenant looked at Stearns and saw the stark cut lines of his face and the way his chin squared off. His face set so that when he smiled, which was rarely, it was as though he was forced to smile. "How's the reading?" he asked, to take his thoughts from the upcoming battle.

"Coming along, Sir." Stearns continued, "do you think we'll ever get a mail call?"

The Lieutenant looked at the ground. "I heard the mail would catch up in a few days, Sergeant."

"Is that all, Sir?"

"Yes, that's all."

Stearns went into the tent. It would be dark soon. In the morning they would get the news. The Lieutenant would be called in and they would stand around while they were told that this life of sleeping, guard duty and KP was about to end once again. _____

General Shafter sat casually behind a fold out desk. The various unit commanders stood around the desk and eyed the map hanging behind him. "We will divide our forces after a march of four miles. Colonel Hays, you will take your men and assault El Caney on the morning of July 1st. Colonel Roosevelt, you will proceed with the remainder of the forces. You and your Rough Riders will assault Kettle Hill, while the remaining units will attack San Juan Hill. After we have captured these locations we will regroup, leaving enough men to hold the areas and prisoners, and advance on toward Santiago.

Shafter eyed his commanders. They were all good men. One was outstanding. Roosevelt reminded him of himself earlier in his life. The same drive, ambition. All of this was a game to this man, a stage to play out his personal drama. Here was a man with ambition, pride, tact, but a cunning that made his every breathing moment a plan for advancement. Here was a true politician, and Shafter knew the army would not be his final dream. As he had dreamed of the star on his uniform Roosevelt dreamed of a far larger and more glorifyng position. True, it was Roosevelt who had brought fame to this war, if that is what it could be called. Leader of the expansionist as it were. They wanted the world. The American way, from one side of the world to the other. At times he could believe in their cause but at other times he felt in his heart he was an anti-imperialist. He was part of a growing voice in the country who wanted no part in helping to spread the cause of America around the world. Let the world be what it wanted, and let the U.S.A. live within its own boundaries. After all, isn't that what the revolution had been all about? He conceded that this was a strange time in history. The country had grown and prospered and now it wanted to flex its muscles. He only hoped it would not flex too much. He knew America was an emerging power, but he also knew that power had many manifestations. Some of which were not what people bargain for. He dismissed the officers and sat behind his desk unmoving, until the whine of the mosquitoes stirred him from his deep thought.

Lieutenant Colonel Roosevelt stood in front of the men and everybody including Stearns could see the heated glow that surrounded him. He had not dispatched his junior officers with the orders, but instead had called the men to formation to break the news himself. He knew this would be the battle, as he would proclaim in later years of his life, "the charge up Kettle Hill was the best day of my life."

He stood and looked over the men, so many of which he had hand picked. He felt a deep pride within him as he watched them. From the captains down to the privates they were his, trained, nurtured, developed into the fighting force that they were. The men loved him, he held a power over them, he could do no wrong. They would kill and die without question for Roosevelt, no matter what the cause or the reason.

"Men," he began, "tomorrow we move out for what will prove to be the decisive battle of this war. The day we have all waited for and trained for draws near. Our navy has the Spanish fleet blockaded. With one swift attack we will destroy the enemy's will to fight and insure our foothold in Cuba. Tonight let us all be one in thought, and tomorrow let us move with the knowledge that we fight in freedom's name."

With that, Roosevelt turned and strode toward his tent. Walking by the milling men he noticed Sergeant Stearns. He had not thought of him in the past weeks. He had been too engrossed with the details of his command. He walked up to him. Stearns snapped to attention and saluted. Roosevelt smiled and returned the salute. "At ease, Sergeant," he said, his eyes showing the kinship he felt for this man. Stearns relaxed and looked deep into Roosevelt's face. "Well, here it is, Sir, the day you have wished for."

Roosevelt reached out and put his hand on Stearns shoulder. "Come with me, Sergeant, let's have a drink to New Mexico."

They walked to the Colonel's tent and many eyes followed them. It was obvious that they were friends. Roosevelt poured the scotch into two glasses. "Did you get my books, Sergeant?"

"Yes, Sir," Stearns answered enthusiastically. "I've already written some letters."

Roosevelt looked impressed. "Good," he said, "and how is the world of letters?"

Stearns took the glass from Roosevelt. "It is as if a new world has come to me, Sir. A world that I never knew existed."

"That is what I want for these people, Sergeant," Roosevelt broke in. "So many people in the U.S. don't understand. Damn the anti-expansionists. They don't see what good we can do around the world, how many allies we can draw into us, teach the children, open schools, provide medicine, elevate them to a life-style they never would have dreamed of. Like you reading and writing, it is a new world, a pushing away of the dark."

Stearns saw the fire in his eyes, the absolute resolve that he was right.

"But what if some people don't want that, Sir?"

Roosevelt looked at the Sergeant, somewhat surprised. How many men would be brave enough to go against his will? To dare to ask questions that did not agree with his statements? "They do, Sergeant, they just might not know it."

With that he raised his glass. "To New Mexico, Sergeant, to New Mexico and cowboys and people who speak their mind."

Stearns raised his glass and drained the Scotch. "Sir, what will we do with this land when this war is over?"

Roosevelt walked over and sat down behind his desk. "Well, Sergeant, men will come in and set up businesses, land will be leased to farmers with the know-how to produce. New markets will be introduced for American goods and goods made here. There will be an economic boom. The people will be taught new skills and trades enabling them to take further care of themselves."

"What if a soldier would want to buy some land here, Sir, is that possible?"

Roosevelt eyed Stearns carefully. "Your life has found a goal, Sergeant," he said.

Stearns nodded his head. "A goal, but no knowledge to achieve the end."

"What is your idea?"

Stearns stood and for the first time Roosevelt saw a wanting in him, a desire to reach out from himself and be more than a man going through life without direction.

"When we landed Sir, and I saw the lush country, the tall grass and the rain, the rivers that run clear and pure, I saw cattle, Sir, cattle not killed by winter snow or dried and parched by summer heat so bad it burnt the flesh from their bones. I saw cattle big and fat and I saw money, Sir. Enough money to live off and have time to do more than work."

Stearns went over his words. "Oh, I mean, at first it would be work, hard work, but in time it would be easier."

Roosevelt stood. "Sergeant, when this is over you get hold of me and we'll see what we can do about getting you some land for those cattle you saw in your mind. Now I must be going, I have men to brief and dispatches to get in order."

Stearns saluted and walked out once again into the day. He felt a nervous excitement grow within himself. Roosevelt was a man of his word, he would help him. Walking back toward the tent he visualized a house with a garden, and him sitting on a horse on a small knoll looking out over his cattle. His cattle, not another man's cattle.

Back in the tent he was greeted by shouts from the men. "Roosevelt, huh, Sergeant? A sergeant with the Commander."

He could see in their eyes that they were impressed and he knew that because of his friendship with Roosevelt, the men would follow him without hesitation.

He sat down on his cot and dug out his paper and pencil. He felt better than he had in his entire life, and the first person who came to his mind was Molly.

Dear Molly,

I do not know what the newspapers back in the states have been saying, but so far there has been little action. Which pleases me as I do not really want to be killed. I have continued studying my books and the Lieutenant and a private named Smiley gave me a dictionary which I read whenever I get a chance. What has impressed me the most over here is the country and the natural state of things. There are many brightly colored birds and the sky in the afternoon is as beautiful as anywhere I have ever seen in my life. There is enough rain to keep the grass green at all times and cool down the evenings. I have never seen a place more suited for cattle and livestock. I suppose it is just a dream but I see opportunities here after this war for men who are willing to work long hours to make a good living. It is strange but I think of you often, especially the first time we met and you sat and drank coffee with me after I ate. I hope your restaurant is doing well and Poncho is not giving you any trouble. I do not know when you will receive this letter. I have been told there will be mail pouches in the morning to put letters in but the army is not always on time. I look forward to hearing from you.

Your friend Cam Stearns, Sergeant United States Army.

Putting the letter and paper and pencil back in his bedroll he rose to go to chow. The men in line were boisterous this night, laughing and shouting. The brief encounter and swift victory over the Spaniards days earlier had bolstered their courage. Army men have a way of dismissing the dead soon, a man dead could just as well have been themselves and they knew this was a chance they all took. The rifles fired during the funeral and the glory of fighting was their call. They were soldiers, and not expected to think like carpenters or doctors or other respected professionals. Theirs was a life of work and cussing, fast women and fast death. There were no intangibles, it was simple, cut and dried.

Stearns did not join in the conversations this night. He stood and watched the sun set over the rolling hills, and heard the familiar hum of the mosquitoes beginning to rise. There was only one problem, how would he raise the money? A soldier's pay would not buy land, at least not enough to run cattle on. If there was anything that stood in his way it was the money.

It was still dark when the men fell out and formed into ranks. After a quick breakfast of canned meat and coffee, they started moving. Scouts patrolled the perimeters and the men marched, knowing this day would not end as quietly as it began. Occasionally, Roosevelt rode back along the ranks, talking and shouting to the men. His face shone with the excitement of the day. It was as though he already basked in the taste of victory, with never a doubt about winning. The men called back to him, "Bully," his favorite word having become the company word. "Bully," they would shout and smile as he passed, raising their free hand.

It was a warm day, not a cloud dotted the sky. Occasionally a slight breeze blew, cooling the marching men. It was around ten in the morning when shells could be heard in the distance, the sounds of the other forces meeting their objective. The sound of the guns spurred the men on and soon a low murmur spread through the ranks, men talking to each other, building up their nerve, and shaking the last bits of apprehension. At ten thirty they were under fire. Roosevelt rode, never faltering. Looking back, he spurred his mount into a trot, making the men run to keep up with him. "To the top," he shouted, "to the top."

The men began running faster and faster, until they were running as fast as they could. The fire was horrendous, bullets cut down men in every direction but still they ran. Soon the Rough Riders' guns answered the fire and the bodies of Spanish soldiers were at their feet. Some jabbed by bayonets even though they were lifeless. Stearns followed the Lieutenant, watching the man when possible. His rifle shells were gone and he discarded it, drawing his pistol. Cannons roared in their faces and screams and cries filled the day. The fighting became hand to hand and he lost sight of the Lieutenant. He kicked, gouged, and pushed his way through the Spanish ranks. His arms ached and he felt the blood pounding in his ears, but still he fought. He lost awareness of time and place, it was just fighting, shooting, stabbing, slashing.

And then suddenly he felt as though a hot poker had been shoved with the force of a club into his arm. He staggered, fell, and a blackness covered him.

"Hello, Molly," he smiled, "it's been a long time."

He felt like running to her and lifting her in the air, but he did not. Instead he watched her face as she ran to him, throwing her arms around his neck and letting the tears come to her eyes. He put his arms around her and squeezed, and for a moment he felt the emotion build in his throat, but he caught it and held it in check. Her blond hair tickled his face. He looked into her blue eyes and saw

the ribbon in her hair. She wiped the tears from her face and smiled. "I love
you," she said, "I love you."

He touched her cheek with the back of his hand and whispered, "I love you
too, Molly."

Two men stood over the cot. "Here he is, Private. Not too long, mind you," the doctor said, "He's just now coming to. He's been pretty groggy for the last few days and doesn't know yet what has happened to him."

Smiley looked at Stearns lying on the cot. He had lost all the color in his face and the straight lines of his face looked drawn from the ordeal he had been through. His eyelids were fluttering, fighting to gain consciousness. The Lieutenant had excused Smiley from all duty so he could wait until Stearns could talk. Morphine was a strong drug and the effects could be devastating at times. Smiley looked at the body on the cot. The left arm several inches below the shoulder was gone. At least it wasn't his right arm, he thought. He only wondered how Stearns would take it. He had not seen the Sergeant go down. The fighting had grown so furious that all he could remember were bits and pieces of color. At times the men were so close to each other it seemed the enemy was part of their forces. When it was over he had found Stearns and tied off the mangled arm to stop the bleeding. The medic told him it had probably saved his life, but he would never tell the Sergeant that. The Lieutenant had been the most shook up, looking down at Stearns. "My God," he had exclaimed, "not his arm."

Each day for the past two days he had sent Smiley over for reports on Stearns. Stearns had lain tossing and moaning unintelligible phrases. Occasionally, he could discern "Molly, Molly." He only hoped the Sergeant recovered and gangrene would not set in.

Today Stearns' eyes opened. He saw Smiley through a grey haze. "Smiley," he said weakly, "why didn't you wake me?"

Smiley pushed Stearns gently down when he tried to rise. "Take it easy, Sergeant," he drawled. "You've been more than asleep."

Stearns rolled his head on the pillow and blinked his eyes as consciousness slowly came back to him. He thought he felt an itch on his left hand and reached over to scratch it. A look of horror spread across his face. "Oh God, my arm. They cut off my arm."

He began to thrash and scream. "Fucking bastards, you cut off my arm."

Smiley held the trashing man down. "Sergeant, Sergeant, he yelled, "they had to, they had to."

Stearns felt all the strength drain from his body. His brow furrowed and beaded in sweat. He rolled his head into the pillow. "Smiley, my arm," he cried, "my arm."

Smiley stood and looked at his friend. "It'll be okay, Sergeant, it'll all be okay."

The medics came and gave him another shot of morphine. Smiley watched as he slipped once more into dreams.

"It's rough, Private," the medic said. Smiley looked at the medic.

"Yeah, it's rough."

The Lieutenant sat finishing off a bottle of Bacardi. "Good rum," he slurred as Smiley entered the tent. Smiley saluted. "Forget that, Private. How was he?"

Smiley sat down and poured himself a glass of rum. "Not good, Sir, he came out of it and found out his arm was gone. I had to hold him down and the medics put him back under."

"All our brave men," the Lieutenant slurred, "look at what we do in freedom's name.

Smiley looked at the Lieutenant. He had been this way since the fighting stopped. Unshaven, dirty. Mumbling on and on about the deaths, the maimed.

"It's over, Lieutenant," Smiley said. "You have to understand, it's over. We'll all be going home soon.

With that, the Lieutenant looked up. "Home."

Home seemed to wake a sleeping part of his mind. A portion he had shut off during the fighting and after. Home, and he thought of his wife and small son in Boston. He suddenly realized that he had not thought of them lately, only of himself. "I'm sorry," he mumbled half to himself. "I've been a fool."

Smiley rose. "Clean yourself up, Sir. Tomorrow let's both go see the Sergeant and try to make him understand."

The Lieutenant watched the Private go. Home, he would be home soon, no more war. He stood and fell to his cot, exhausted.

The story of the Rough Riders' charge of Kettle Hill made headlines from coast to coast. Molly read wide-eyed and horrified at the accounts of the bloody fighting and the staggering amount of casualties. She had received Sergeant Stearns letter a week earlier and knew by the date it was mailed before the assult on Kettle Hill. If she had been nervous during the past weeks, now waves of fear racked her body. Poncho, seeing this, took her by the shoulders. "Mollee, Mollee, he eez ok, you wait and see. Poncho know he eez ok."

Molly rubbed her eyes and began to cry. "Oh Poncho," she moaned, "I'm so worried."

Regaining her composure, she read on that the Rough Riders were now in bivouac and that negotiations had begun with the Spanish over the surrender of Santiago and the end of the war. A related article in the paper raved on and on about the invasion of Puerto Rico and the plan to invade and capture the Phillipines. What had a first been an all out favoritism toward the war had now turned into a heated debate in the Senate, with many Americans vocally disapproving of the United States' intervention in foreign affairs. These Americans did not believe in holding other races by force. Their motivation, of course, rested mostly on the fact that they did not want to run the risk of having to haggle with colonies or be forced into trade deficits created by new and cheaper markets and labor forces.

Molly found herself becoming aligned with the anti-imperialists as the days passed, and she began to confide more and more in Poncho her opinion that the country should mind its own business and keep its soldiers at home.

The days became endless to her as she rushed home in the evenings, praying she would find a letter from Cam and thereby know he was all right. Each day with no word left her tired and exhausted. She was outwardly brave to the townspeople who did not know of the Sergeant. She seemed like the old Molly, cheery and smiling at the restaurant, but Poncho and the other help at the restaurant knew what she suffered through, and it become their obsession to help her and try to make her smile. "Thee poor lady," Poncho said to a small, dark eyed Mexican girl who Molly had hired to wait on tables. "Eet eez terrible for her."

Finally, on August 17th, a letter came to Molly, written in a different hand from Cam's. She sat down in her living room and opened it with trembling hands.

Dear Molly,

I wish to apologize for the deceit I have had to partake in by writing this letter. I found your address while going through the gear of Sergeant Stearns. I wish to say that Sergeant Stearns is a great soldier and a friend of mine, both in combat and as a man, but I am at a loss as to what to do, so I am writing this letter to you. During our charge up Kettle Hill, which you have undoubtedly read about, Sergeant Stearns was badly wounded in the left arm. During his confinement in the hospital, and before he had regained consciousness, his left arm was amputated.

Molly's heart sank and she began to sob, partly out of relief that he was alive, but partly out of grief for his great loss.

He is now out of the hospital, but he moves around camp in a complete daze. As you know, he was never a man of words or great commitments to other people, but now he has lost all interest in everything. He does not read or study his writing. He does not talk and he has begun to drink heavily. I cannot be one to criticize because I must confess I have done the same thing in my life, but it bothers me greatly to see this man in this state. I do not know your relationship with Cam, but I know he wears your braid around his neck. During his stay in the hospital, I heard him many times in his delirium say your name over and over. I beseech you to write to him and tell him something that will bring him back to himself. He is in great need of someone he will listen to.

The letter was signed, Lt. Williams.

Molly dropped the letter to the floor. She wanted to rush to Cam and hold him close to her bosom and stroke his hair. Life has so many twists, she thought. Now we are miles apart and I cannot be with him when he needs me.

Smiley walked into the dark and deserted tent. He saw Sergeant Stearns sitting on his bunk, the lost and dazed look on his face. On the floor sat a half empty Bacardi bottle. Smiley walked up to the Sergeant. "Mornin' Sergeant, looks like another nice day outside."

Stearns raised his bloodshot eyes and snorted, "good."

Smiley sank down on the bunk next to his. "Sergeant, you gotta get over this, it ain't no good. Men've been hurt before. You gotta get your life back together."

Stearns looked at Smiley. "Why don't you just leave me alone? I'm sick and tired of you and all the men bothering me. Just mind your own damn business and leave me the fuck alone."

Smiley looked at the man and rose. Walking away he stopped, and his voice was half pain and half anger. "Well then, you be what you wanna be, you just sit there and drink and let the world go by. It's easier anyway, to quit. But I never woulda thought you would, Sergeant, I never woulda thought you would."

Stearns did not flinch at the words or let them sink in. Alone in the tent once again he picked up the bottle and tipped it to his lips. He was a sorry sight. He had not shaved in over a week or washed, his hair was astray and the uniform dirty. He could not remember when he last ate or had even moved from the bunk except to take a piss behind the tent. At first the men had tried to help him, laughing, talking about small matters. But soon they grew impatient with him, and only the Lieutenant and Smiley continued in their efforts to bring a spark of life back to his face. He had forgotten his dream about cattle. He did not think past each day, except for how he would get a bottle. The Lieutenant had put him in for a medal, which he did not know and which Roosevelt would review in a few days. He thought of Molly a lot, sitting on his bunk. He remembered wrapping his arms around her and holding her off the ground. But he had slowly tried to push even her from his mind. For what was he now, a cripple, and what good was a cripple to anything or anybody.

Colonel Roosevelt looked over the recommendation for the Silver Star. He immediately signed the paper and dispatched it to the brigade commander. He stopped looking over the paper work and thought about Stearns. Terrible, he thought to himself, to lose an arm. But he knew Stearns' character, and he knew he would pull through. He could picture him laughing with the men. He had his badge of courage to carry proudly the rest of his life. Thank God it didn't gangrene, he thought. He called in his aide. "Lieutenant, go find Lieutenant Williams and tell him to tell Sergeant Stearns to report to my tent this evening after chow."

Watching the aide go he rose and walked around his tent. It had been a glorious battle. The men had been so brave. It had been as though the world had stopped and only the heart and soul of the men on the hill were alive. The screaming and yelling, the sound of the deadly rifle fire. It had been a day that the gods watched and sent their angels to help the victors. What could be a better cause, freedom for all men. Roosevelt strode around his tent. He had not come down from the high the battle had given him. His men had been the best in the invasion. Not one man had fled from the fire, not one man had to shoulder the responsibility of being a coward for the rest of his life. For Roosevelt there had never been such a day, and through his life and the great honors that would be his there would never be a day like this again. To his closest friends and relatives he would retell the story many times. When the parties were over, and with his drink nestled warmly in his hands, he would tell the story and his eyes would see the green landscape and the sound of the running men and the way his horse foamed and frothed at the mouth. "Bully good show," he would say, "bully good show."

Lieutenant Williams walked into the tent. Stearns was passed out and curled in the fetal position on his bunk. The Lieutenant looked at the man as though he were his son. Poor bastard, he thought, poor fuckin' bastard. He noticed two privates in the back of the tent playing cards. "Come here and help me," he ordered, and the privates jumped, noticing the tone of his voice. Stearns was too drunk to resist and the Lieutenant and the two privates dragged him to an area that had been set up for bathing. They threw him, clothes and all, into a tub of water and watched as he blubbered and spit, not knowing where he was. He tried to rise, but the Lieutenant pushed him down. Regaining some matter of consciousness, he looked at the Lieutenant.

"Roosevelt wants to see you, Stearns, and no matter what you are like inside when you go see him, you're going to look good on the outside."

Stearns started to rise to strike out at the Lieutenant, but he noticed the two young faces beside him and the way the Lieutenant was standing. It was not the time for an argument. "Make sure he bathes, shaves and gets into a new uniform. When he is done one of you come and get me. And if he gives you any trouble, you two have my permission to kick the shit out of him." And the Lieutenant walked off.

Stearns stood before the Lieutenant, and for the first time the Lieutenant treated him like a sergeant under his command, and not a friend. "You are a representative of this platoon, you will conduct yourself as such and as the position you command. You have been a disgrace to the unit and to your men. When you see Roosevelt you remember this, do you understand, Sergeant?"

Stearns looked at the Lieutenant through red-rimmed eyes. "Yes, I understand."

The Lieutenant barked, "Yes what, Sergeant?"

Stearns looked amazed. "Yes Sir, I understand, Sir."

"You are dismissed. Colonel Roosevelt wants to see you."

Stearns walked along the row of tents. He was clean and he felt better than he had in weeks. For the first time he noticed other men walking around with wounds. There was a man with an eye bandaged, another with crutches hobbling along. It was not until he saw a private with no legs sitting in the sun with his friends around him, that a slight ray of light began to enter his mind. The private laughed and talked to the men, as Stearns passed. Seeing Stearns' pinned up sleeve the private called to him. "Got you too, huh? At least it's only one."

Stearns could only manage a feeble smile as he passed. He thought of his past weeks, drinking, yelling at the only men he had truly been friends with, and he felt like a small boy, not a man, certainly not a Sergeant in the army. And here was a private with his legs gone, smiling and laughing.

You've been a fool, he thought, disgusted with himself. You've been a stupid fool. If the Lieutenant and Smiley and the others had not liked him, they wouldn't have bothered or given a damn. God, what a fool I've been. And he thought of Molly and an emptiness came to his stomach deeper than the pain of losing his arm. "Molly, Molly," his mind said.

Roosevelt smiled broadly as Sergeant Stearns entered the tent. He noticed immediately the look on Stearns face and the shallowness of the expression. It had been harder than he'd supposed on him. He walked to him as Stearns was about to salute. "Forget it, Cam," he said, tenderness in his voice. "Sit down, just sit down."

Stearns felt rested in the chair. It was like being at home, here with Roosevelt. There were no pretentions or games to play. Here was a man like himself, he felt, although his last weeks' behavior left him embarrassed and ill at ease.

"Drink?" Roosevelt asked.

"No Sir," Stearns answered, "I've been hitting it a little heavy lately."

"Well, as long as it doesn't ruin you, Cam."

There followed a strange silence as each man felt for words to say. For the first time Stearns noticed Roosevelt was a man of about fifty years old, and that he was just a lad to him, and to Roosevelt his own life was just beginning. It was not over because he had lost an arm. It was just a part of life, a unique experience that had happened to him. Sad, painful, yes, but no reason to lie down and die.

Stearns broke the silence. "Well, we whipped em', Sir, we drove their asses all the way to the ocean."

Roosevelt felt the silence broken and his eyes shone with their usual fire. "We whipped them bad, Cam. Now they beg for peace."

And the two men talked about the battle, the sounds, the bugles blowing and Stearns felt the power once more come over him, the strength one gains from surviving. They talked late into the night, and with each hour that passed they were more relaxed. Roosevelt saw the light begin to shine in Stearns' eyes once again, and he was relieved for the man. This man was as he, he had a destiny, and so, he must not fall short of his potential.

It was late when Roosevelt looked at Stearns. "You're getting a medal, you know. The Lieutenant put you in for one. In his report he says you faced the enemy with unnerving calm. Your men were spurred by your actions and you fell watching out for others. It is a very strong recommendation and I have approved it and sent it on down the line."

Stearns did not know what to say. "Many men deserve medals, Sir," he finally said, clearing his throat.

Roosevelt looked once more at the man. "How about your cattle dream, Cam?"

Stearns looked at the floor and noticed the familiar hum of the mosquitoes. "Haven't thought about it much lately. Guess I've been mostly thinking about myself and feeling sorry for myself."

Roosevelt laughed. "Well, we all do that at one time or the other, the important thing is that we learn from our mishaps and continue on in this difficult life. Well, when you have thought about it some more you let me know, now, Cam. This country is going to need brave strong men to get it on its feet. I know you could stand to the test."

Stearns knew it was time to go. "I'll let you know, Colonel."

When he reached the tent flap he looked back at Roosevelt. "I want you to know, Sir, that you are the damndest man I have ever met in my life and that serving under you has been my pleasure. I will treasure our friendship for as long as I live, no matter how far apart we become. Remember, in me you will always have a friend."

Roosevelt stood up from behind his desk. "Mr. Stearns, I take that as a compliment and plus to human nature. Good luck to you, Sergeant, in whatever you may do."

Stearns walked back along the line of tents. The cool evening breeze blew across his face and the clouds darted in and out between the stars. It was a beautiful night. It was as though he had never seen the sky before this night. But tonight the stars shone for him and the wind blew only to his ears.

Back in the tent he walked over to Smiley's bunk and looked him in the eyes. "I'm sorry Smiley, forgive me."

Smiley spit a large wad of tobacco into the can by his bunk. "Nothin' to forgive, Sergeant, nice to have you back."

Stearns walked to his bunk and saw the letter lying on his pillow. He knew it was from Molly and he sat down and spent several moments figuring out how to open the letter with one hand. He looked at a soldier watching him. This would take a little practice, but he did not ask for help.

My Dearest Cam,

I have just finished reading the accounts of your battle at Kettle Hill. You and your men are very brave and I am relieved that the fighting is over. The paper has covered the signing of the armistice and the advancement of the other troops in the Phillipines and Puerto Rico.

This was the first time Stearns knew there were other forces fighting on other islands. He had thought the battle in Cuba was all there was.

There has not been much going on around here since I last wrote you, I am happy to say that the restaurant is doing fine and Poncho is as well and jovial as ever. I would like most dearly to hear from you but suppose what with your duties and all you have not had much time to write me. How are your studies coming? I am checking to see if I can send you some books to read and will know soon. There is much debate going on in the country now as to our involvement in Cuba and many people have come forth violently opposing our takeover of another country. It seems at times that we, a free country, would follow in the footsteps of the country we fought for our own independence. But policies change with the moods of men and I suppose, who am I to judge what is good for a country. I think often of you and wish you could be here and I could cook you one of our special steaks. I know the army food cannot match mine. Please write soon as I am concerned with your safety.

Sincerely, Molly

Stearns set the letter on the bunk and the aroma of the perfume carefully dotted on the paper rose to his nostrils. She had not betrayed the fact that she had received word on his wound or that he had lapsed into dejection and despair, nor did she mention her anguish over not seeing him. Stearns picked up the letter and carried it to Smiley's bunk. "Smell this," he beemed.

Smiley breathed deeply the letter held under his nose. "Purty as a Texas rose," he said, his eyes sparkling. "Would I ever love t'have me some fancy white lady with somma that between her tits."

Stearns smiled and sat down beside Smiley. "I'm in love, Smiley, and I don't know what to do."

Smiley looked at the Sergeant. "Well, I'll tell ya what I'd do if I had me some purty lady writin' me sweet smellin letters. I'd sit down right quick and write her one, and tell her I love her afore some fancy dan beats me to the punch."

Stearns looked at his friend and a seriousness came over his face. "Get out of the army with me, Smiley. Get out and stay here and you and I will build us a cattle ranch."

Smiley looked at Stearns' face and knew he was not joking. "Cattle, here?"

Stearns went on, "cattle and horses, look at the grass, the climate, they'll thrive over here and make us rich."

Smiley looked at his hands. "Mebee, mebbee, Sergeant, you might have

57

something there."

Stearns stood up. "We'll talk about it later, but Roosevelt said he'd help me."

Smiley watched him walk away. Cattle, my own boss, my own ranch. The idea burned in his mind and there was nothing he could do to not think about it. And with Roosevelt's help, he thought. It was a big step, an even larger dream.

Stearns looked at the paper and began to write. The letter began simply.

Molly,

I am sorry it has taken me so long to write you, but I must admit I have not been myself the last few weeks. I have lost my left arm and lived in a world of self pity for many days. I scorned my friends and if not for them and their concern I might still be in my stupor. It is over now, but I thought you should know this before I continued. I am not looking for your sympathy.

He wanted to fill the pages with poems and pretty words, but try as he may he could not, and continued.

Molly, I don't know why or how, and it may seem childish, but I love you and my hours are spent thinking of you. I want so much to be near you and see your smile and your blond hair. I have never felt this way toward any woman before and really don't know what to say to tell you how deeply I feel. I can only hope and pray that you love me too, but, if you do not I will understand and will always be your true and dear friend. It seems so strange to me how I can know beyond a doubt that I love you. I really do not even know you that well. I only know that you make me feel warm inside and that I miss you very much. I would be pleased to receive books from you. Tell everyone hello for me and tell Poncho he is a very lucky man to be able to be with you every day.

I am yours, Cam Stearns

He addressed the envelope and lay down on the bunk. It had been one long day. He closed his eyes and sleep covered him immediately. That night he did not dream but slept blanketed in a mellow peace.

Stearns sat at breakfast shoveling down large forkfuls of eggs and ham. The cooks had done their job well, trading with the peasants for chickens, pigs, even, at times, large fish. The men didn't know what kind they were, but fired like American catfish they were just as good and filling. He had not eaten well in weeks, letting the Bacardi rule his system, and he bolted his food hoping he would gain back the lost pounds all in one meal. Smiley carried his tray next to Stearns and sat down. He was strangely serious this morning. Eating slowly, he watched the Sergeant out of the corner of his eye. Finally, he said. "I've been thinkin' about those cattle you were talkin' about, Sergeant. Do you really think it'd work?"

Stearns swallowed the last bite of egg and slurped the black coffee. "I've worked ranches all my life. Saw cows get fat and winter kill them, saw droughts and dry kill them. I've never seen grass like this. True, it's not large, but I bet a man can keep five cows to the acre here, maybe more. A thousand acres, five thousands cows. No large range to work, little fence. Help by the hundreds and a market just across the ocean to buy. I think it would work."

"Where'd ya git the cattle, Sergeant?"

"In the states. Buy calves, make a deal with the seller that he can have first option on our cattle. Start with a few hundred. I'm going to get disability now, and what with the money you'll get by getting out, savings if you have any and bankers in the U.S. looking for new horizons, we might be able to swing the deal. We can even buy in Texas and ship here, there's a lot to be looked into."

Smiley saw the distance in Stearns' eyes. He knew he had seen the ranch, dreamed it. Laid out the fences and the outbuildings. All it took was filling in the pieces. "Well," Smiley said between bites of ham, "count me in. I got six more months left. You, yer out as soon's ya git back to the states, with that arm, and all."

Smiley winched when he said the word arm, but to his relief Stearns didn't flinch. That was over. The arm would not grow back and it was ended.

Stearns reached out and took Smiley's hand, shaking it vigorously. "Six months, and it's a deal. I have some business back in New Mexico I have to attend to and then let's do it."

The next weeks passed quickly and quietly. Stearns did not draw any duty and with his time he persuaded the Lieutenant to let him use a horse and rode around the country.

To the south of them and on the edge of the ocean lay a beautiful range of mountains. Here, the pine trees grew and the clouds coming in off the ocean dropped their rain, filling the rivers that ran down to the valley below. Here cattle could be run if the valleys dried. The valleys stood three feet high in grass, and sugar cane fields grew around them.

To the east lay lowland marshes, and a region that could hold cattle but was not to Stearns' liking. He saw scattered groups of cattle as he rode and explored this new land. They were good fat cattle, not like the undernourished workers who tended them. With a little cattle know-how they could be fattened up more and bred into a strong breed. The people who at first had been wary of the soldiers now waved and chattered to Stearns as he rode by, satisfied that the Yankees were not like the Spaniards. There were strict orders to the soldiers about behavior toward the native people, the swift justice to those foolish enough not to obey. The people of the rural areas of Cuba were as the people of the United States, a slow, tough people, used to long hours and toil. A smiling race, they seemed to feel a new age was upon them and that life with the Yankees would better their lot.

Each day after riding, Stearns would report his sightings to Smiley and Smiley would see through Stearns' excitement and descriptions a ranch springing out of the ground. Each day passed, and with what once had been a dream, a small seed of reality had been planted.

The Lieutenant was relieved that Stearns was himself again. In fact, he had to concede he was far better than before he lost the arm. His life seemed to move, he was not idle nor set back from the men, but talked and laughed and joked. He did not ask why Stearns wanted the horses to ride but thought of it as therapy. What better therapy for a cowboy than a horse, he thought. He had no idea of Stearns' plans or dreams as he rode the countryside.

On September 27 the majority of the men received their new orders. The Rough Riders were being disbanded. Colonel Wood, now a General, had been placed in command of the government in Cuba. It was a job he did not relish, but duty dictated it. Smiley was being sent to Colorado to join a cavalry post and Stearns would be discharged upon his arrival in Florida. The rest of the unit would stay and hold positions until the exact fate of Cuba was settled. The few newspapers the men received ranted on and on about the battle in the Senate over the fate of the newly acquired nations. By only one vote the peace treaty was ratified, and Puerto Rico and the Phillipines were put under U.S. control. Cuba would be given independence and the sum of twenty million dollars would be given to Spain for the titled lands she owned. Stearns, reading this, could only shake his head. Good men had died and now the country was giving away the spoils of war. "Dumb fuckers," he muttered to the Lieutenant one evening as they sat in the chow tent. "More and more I think you're right, Lieutenant. What is this war, anyway?"

The Lieutenant looked at Stearns. "Never thought I'd hear you say anything like that, Sergeant."

Lieutenant Williams was going home. He had gained weight and his dark, curly hair and mustache were immaculate. "Going back into law in Boston," he told Stearns. "I have the stomach for it now. If you ever need a lawyer, call on me. I'll be glad to be of help anytime."

Stearns wrote down his wife's address and promised he would. He had never mentioned his plans to the Lieutenant, there had been no need.

The day before they were to ship back to the states, Stearns received a letter from Colonel Roosevelt, delivered by his aide.

Sergeant Stearns:

I am going back to Washington to continue my career in politics. When you have the details figured out about your ranch, please cable me and we will go from there. The best in your life.

T. Roosevelt

Stearns folded the letter and put it in his bedroll. "You were made for politics, Roosevelt," he said to himself, "you know it, and I knew it, this war was just the arena for the beginning of your true destiny. The press, the pictures, the hand-picked men, it was for your purpose, your cause. I hope your desire never backfires on you."

It was quiet the night before most of the men shipped back to the states. Many of them had become close friends, but they knew they would never meet again. They had shared a war and been forced into becoming like brothers. Comments like "pat a white girl on the ass," "keep your head down," and "luck with your life," filtered through the ranks as the men going home began their march to Santiago and the waiting ships. Stearns and Smiley walked together, it was not the disciplined march of training or going into battle. The men walked in groups, Lieutenants and brass uncaring, it was the relaxed walk of the victors going home to tell their stories and get back to law books, doctors, cowboys and farming.

Santiago was a beautiful town nestled on the harbor as well as a town of poverty and vice. Here could be found cigars and booze, cloth, chickens and other welcome items. The men were given leave for the evening but most were content to sit on the ship and watch the city from the rail. Cuba was over for them, it held no fascination, no glamor. There were women back in the states who interested them and beer, good American beer. "Good riddance to those bastards," one said, spitting into the ocean.

Stearns watched the city and was both revolted and fascinated. He would get to know this city and the other cities of Cuba. One day his cattle would load here and men would shake his hand as they climbed back aboard. Here he hoped his children would be born and see a world their father had never known. They would work their own land and they would not lose it. Stearns would see to that, if he did get his land he would never lose it. No man would take what was his and live to tell about it. The ship pulled away from the docks in mid-morning and Stearns and Smiley stood until the land could be seen no more and the seagulls squawked above their heads.

The crowds that meet them back home in the states were unbelievable. Women threw colored paper and men offered cold beer and sandwiches. Booths along the streets sold cups with Roosevelt's face on them and Rough Riders in gold letters around the handle. Little boys ran up to the men. "It's the Rough Riders," they would holler, and seeing Stearns and his empty sleeve would look with pride and admiration at a true veteran of the war.

Stearns and Smiley had a drink together at a bar. The next day Stearns had been mustered out, told he would receive a hundred and eighty dollars a month until he died, and was given a suit of civilian clothes. The last words he told Smiley were, "write Molly, she'll be able to tell you where I am."

They had not seen the Lieutenant, either on the boat or when they landed. They didn't know that he had contracted yellow fever and had not made the ship. They did not know that he would lanquish in pain for several months before dying in a hot, humid hospital room in Santiago, muttering in his last hours of life unintelligible phrases about war and the army and the son he had never seen.

(6)

Cam Stearns had grown accustomed to army life, and so, the train ride back to New Mexico was at time baffling and mysterious. The civilian suit was uncomfortable, and at a stop in St. Louis he bought several pairs of trousers and loose fitting shirts. The undisciplined movement of people in and around him bothered him at first, but he soon became accustomed to the crowd and began to relax. The trip introduced him to many different people who shared the seat next to his, and so the miles passed, wrapped in conversation. The ability to read had made him feel more confident, and he found himself talking more, and even voicing opinions on many varied subjects. For three days he had ridden with a traveling salesman, a Mr. William R. Fisher. A short, round, happy fellow with small, dark, beady eyes that got lost in the flesh of his face. "William Fisher", he announced, sitting down heavily by Stearns early one morning. He paid no attention to Stearns' arm, and never once mentioned the war or any facet of the war now appearing in the papers. Stearns was relieved at this and found the good natured humor and presence of this man quite refreshing. He was a multitude of dirty jokes and knew all the whore houses in all the towns west of the Mississippi. Getting off the train in Oklahoma he laughed to Stearns, "now in Albuquerque on Fourth Street if you go, you tell Sally that Mr. Fisher will be there soon."

He picked up his large bag, the contents of which he had never divulged, and hurried through the train station.

As the train crossed into New Mexico Stearns became restless and spent the long last hours before Albuquerque looking out of the window and thinking of Molly. He had not written her to tell her he was coming. Nor had he received a letter back from her with her reaction to his confession of his love for her. At times he would be overjoyed in thoughts of Molly, feeling in his heart that she loved him and would marry him as soon as he asked. But, at other times he was lost and bewildered, not possessing the strength to think of walking up to her and taking her away with him. If, nothing else, he would get his mother and take her to Cuba. He swore to himself that his mother would not stay in New Mexico and work any longer. She would come with him to Cuba and be on the ranch. He would have a maid for her and a cook. Labor in Cuba was cheap and his pension would more than cover a few years of rest for his mother.

He stepped off the train in Albuquerque and breathed deeply the dry air. It was September 4th and the air was hot and dusty. Breezes whipped and sent the dry, light-brown dirt flying into the air. He caught a ride to Bernalillo on a wagon and slowly refamiliarized himself with the landscape. The Mexican driver did not speak or even acknowledge his presence during most of the way, content to sip from his bottle of gin and swat the flies that hovered over his wagon.

He jumped off the wagon on the outskirts of town and followed the alley to his mother's house. It was safer. The sheriff might see him, and now that Roosevelt was gone it might not do him any good to have such an important friend. He felt his temples throb as he neared the house, and when he got there he saw immediately that something was wrong. The windows were boarded up and the yard was in shambles. His mother had always kept the house immaculate and kept the yard filled with flowers. Her flowers had been her lease on sanity, and sitting in the yard in the evening she seemed to become one of them. He looked through the cracks between the boards and could see the draped furniture and the dust that covered the tables and floor. He suddenly felt in a panic. He walked to the neighbor's house and, trying not to show his concern, knocked on the door. A middle-aged woman answered, obviously working over a hot stove, her face sweating. She was not rude, but not friendly, either. Seeing Stearns she asked bluntly, "what do you want, stranger?"

Stearns tried to smile. "I was passing through town and a friend of mine wanted me to look up a Mrs. Stearns. He told me she lived in the house right there but it looks deserted."

The woman scratched her nose and said, "poor wretched lady," and Stearns could see her features soften. "She died six weeks ago. No one knows where her son is, I never met him, just know he was gone somewhere, heard he went off to war."

Spying his arm she asked, "did you know him?"

Stearns, devastated by the news, had begun to amble off. "I knew him," he stammered, "he was killed, and I wanted to tell her and arrange for his pay to come to her."

"Well, she don't need it now, Mister."

Stearns, feeling much grief, walked slowly down the dusty street.

It was beginning to cool off as the sun rested for the last moments on the horizon. He spent the night behind the livery stable, and with first light he bought a horse and a saddle. Before long, he was at the old ranch, standing on the top of the cliff. The morning light magnified the yellows and greens on the valley floor and he could see sparrows darting in and out among the branches of the oaks that grew by the river. So many times the cliff had brought him peace, but this day it only intensified his heartache. He could see his mother working and slaving each day. The years slowly building one on one until there was no more time to think of rest or that trip she had always wanted to take to San Francisco. Funny, he hadn't thought of that in years. His mother clipping all the pictures she could find in magazines about San Francisco. She guarded the little scrap book like it was a treasure, and some evenings sitting on the porch she would go over each page as if it was a magical book taking her up in a wisp of wind and sailing her to San Francisco. Now he realized it must have sustained her. A dream, a dream she knew she would never see, but still a dream. Just feasible enough to keep her going, but far enough out of reach to keep her sane and in tune with the reality of her life.

He sat for many hours by the cliff, and threw rocks that banged and created small avalanches crashing toward the valley floor. He left the cliff in mid-afternoon. "I will see you no more," he said out loud, taking in one last scan of the land that he had known for so many years. "But you will not change, you will still stand proud and free, kissing the sun and the moon when I too lie in the ground."

He did not spur his horse the rest of the day but let the horse walk, and pushed forever from his mind thoughts of his mother and his birthplace.

––––––

Molly sat stunned for several minutes. The letter had lifted her to a joy she had never known, but had also brought back memories of a love that she had tried so hard to forget over the past years. "My poor husband," she said. But, a few moments later she reread the letter. She would have to write and tell Cam, as he didn't know she had been married. A man must know that. She could not live alone forever, but she would never forget her first husband. He had been a good man, a kind man and time nor love for another man would ever change that.

The next day, Poncho had seen the lightness in her step as she came into the restaurant. He did not mention it to her or in any way change his normal actions, but he knew that she must have received a letter, and during lunch he stole out the back door and swiped a rose from a lady's climbing rose bush. He laid it on the table where Molly sat drinking coffee and smiled as she looked at him. "Why, it's beautiful, Poncho."

"Eet eez for your smile today," he grinned, his dark eyes looking mischievous.

"You are truly wonderful, Poncho."

"My wife, she say that too when I watch all the leetle ninos, but I wonder why it eet eez for."

Poncho had six children, all of whom adored Molly. They would scamper into the restaurant, shouting for their father. Poncho would make a great fuss about disturbing the customers and getting fired by Misses Molly. But, after herding them into the kitchen, he would hand them each a cookie as they marched out the back door, their mission accomplished. At times when Molly would see Poncho with his children and see the pride on his face, her heart would yearn for children of her own. Such a happy family, she would think, how beautiful.

Poncho was one of the few men born into life that did not question his fate. He had a wonderful, fat wife who cooked and sang in the kitchen.

Each new child was brought up filled with love and plenty of beans and tortillas to eat. With each child he would pat his fat wife on the fanny and say, "you see, eet eez not a miracle."

His life was pleasing to him, and working for Molly was pleasing. He loved the smell of cooking food and the satisfied looks on the faces of people who enjoyed their meals. He was never one to complain or question the day. His life was made up of God, his wife, and his family, and the rest would take care of itself. He did not read or write or carry a gun or dream of a life anywhere but in Las Vegas. Others of his race were already organizing and beginning to fight the white man. He pushed this from his mind as stupid, people were people, white, black, brown, what did it matter. Life was too short for such nonsense. Each evening, lying in bed with his wife, he would pray. "Eet's been a good day, Lord, let eet be another one tomorrow," and he would sleep, warm and content.

"You go home early tonight," Molly told Poncho. It was Saturday, and Sunday they would not open. The restaurant had been opened for so many months seven days a week, Molly finally decided it was time to take a day off. She had money in the bank, the bills were paid and it was time to rest. Giving Poncho five dollars over his pay he left, happy and whistling. "Buy something for your wife," she had told him. A deep, thoughtful look crossed his face, and he laughed, "maybe, first a beer for me."

Closing the curtains she looked over the empty restaurant. Everything was in order.

The night was cool as she locked the door. Pulling her shawl closer to her body she noticed a man down the street walking toward her. She didn't like to meet people at night and many times had been told by Poncho that she should leave before dark, but she had never listened. As she walked, the form drew closer to her and she felt a pang of fear. She hurried her steps, hoping to speed the passing. She saw the form stop and look at her, and she moved closer to the line of buildings so as to be as far as possible from the man. When they were opposite each other he turned to face her. "Molly," she heard her name. "Molly, it's me, Cam!" She was overcome with joy, and losing all her inhibitions, she threw herself into his chest. "Oh, Cam, Oh, Cam, I've worried so," she said, as she buried her face into his shoulder. She felt his arm around her and the warmth of his body. She breathed deeply the musty smell of his clothes and she was at peace.

They just stood there for a moment, holding each other, until she felt him move and release his grip. Standing back she saw the pinned sleeve and felt the shock travel through her body, but she quickly masked her feelings. Grabbing his right arm she began to walk, pulling him in beside her. "Cam, I'm so happy you're here."

As she walked towards the house the words began to flow from her in a great torrent. She told him of the restaurant, the fights, the attempt to rob the bank. All the details that had made up her life. He walked in silence as she talked, content in her words and the way the moonlight shone off her golden hair. She was more beautiful than he remembered, and all the apprehension during the train ride soon vanished. He felt her breast tight against his arm and the smell of her perfume made him dizzy with happiness. The sound and feel of this woman was a pleasure he had only dreamed of in the past months. He hesitated as they walked into her house. "Don't be silly," she laughed, "I'm a grown girl. My father doesn't have a shotgun."

He sat in the living room as she busied herself in the kitchen making coffee. He looked at the lace curtains and the dainty figurines that seemed to fill every available space of the house. It was good, it was warm and comfortable. Molly came from the kitchen with a tray and two cups. He was different looking now, more mature and settled. Behind his eyes she saw that he had seen many strange and exciting things. He looked traveled and fatigued but he looked secure.

The evening progressed and she felt his new strength, his voice and his readiness to speak. They would both talk and and then lapse into moments of silence when their eyes would lock and they would look deep into each other, looking for the moment to say what was really on their minds. Molly sat on a deeply stuffed divan, while Cam sat across from her in a straight backed wooden chair. In a period of silence he rose and walked over to her. She noticed how handsome he was, his boyish features, so hard and yet so tame. His green eyes bore into her as if she could hide no secrets from this man. He sat down beside her and she wanted to protest, but the words would not come. "Molly," he said, picking up her hand in his. "You know why I've come." There was no hesitation in his words, he had rehearsed the lines a million times over the past week. "I've come to marry you. Will you marry me?"

There had been more he planned to say, but it seemed inadequate now. Molly felt his hand around hers and she watched the words form in his mouth. She did not jump up and blubber like a school girl, nor did she blush, but she looked at Cam and her eyes showed her love. "I would love to marry you, Cam, but first there are some things you should know."

Cam looked at her and waited for her to speak. "I was married once before, Cam, my husband died, he was a dear man and he and I were very happy."

Cam looked at her. "That doesn't matter, Molly. Time has passed, life has changed, I love you. There is nothing more."

Molly buried her face in his shoulder and began to cry. "Oh, Cam, I love you so. You don't know how I missed you these months, worried about you. It's all so strange, yet so wonderful."

Stearns held her close and breathed deep the scent of her. He brushed his lips along her neck and closed his eyes. After a moment he said. "I must tell you a few things now."

She leaned away from him and dabbed her eyes with her hankie.

"I want to move to Cuba, Molly. The land is beautiful. I have a chance to start a new life, be my own man. I see cattle, Molly."

Molly looked at him and saw the intent in his eyes, the drive. She looked a little bewildered, but said, "If I marry you Cam, I go where you go."

"It will be a wonderful life, Molly, it will be a wonderful life."

He wanted to pull her close to him, run his hand down her back and slowly unfasten the buttons one by one. He wanted to pick her up and with her dress hanging from her shoulders, carry her to the bedroom and undress her standing by the bed and then, undoing her hair, lay her down and run his eyes all over her creamy-skinned body. He felt the heat grow within him as he held her. Coughing, he stepped back, and she could see the red in his cheeks and smiled to herself.

"I think I'd better go, Molly."

She stood, he could have her if he wanted. "Stay here, Cam," she saw the uncertainty on his face. "Stay here on the divan."

He sat down in the chair. "I'd like that," he answered, "I'd like that very much."

When the house was dark he lay on the divan listening to Molly's footsteps in her bedroom. He heard the bed springs creak and he thought of her breasts and her lips upon his.

He slept late until the sound of pans rattling in the kitchen woke him. She heard him rise and walked into the living room as he was pulling on his pants. Showing no embarrassment she laughed, "breakfast soon, Molly's best, pancakes, eggs over easy, biscuits and gravy and apple juice."

Cam smiled at her. "Sounds delicious, but I don't know if I have the three dollars."

"Well, for some people things can be worked out," she answered, turning and going back to the kitchen. He watched her skirt swish around the corner and looked out of the window. Down the street children were running and laughing. He heard the distant caw of a crow. It was a beautiful day, a grand day. They would have to go for a walk around town.

Molly beamed at him across the table as he ate his food greedily. "I can tell you were in the army," she laughed. He smiled, wiping his face on his sleeve. "How?" he asked. "Just a woman's way," she mused. He looked at her dancing eyes and her thin lips. "I've never been happier, Molly."

She smiled at him and patted his hand. "Let's go for a walk after I've washed up."

"My plan exactly," he answered, getting up from the table. He started to pick up his plate.

"No, you sit on the porch and I'll be out when I'm done."

He walked to the porch and sat down. It was a beautiful day. One of those days in a person's life that seemed as if nothing could dampen one's spirit.

(7)

In late September the New Mexico fall begins to touch the earth. The high aspen and birch covered peaks turn a vivid yellow, in deep contrast with the green of the fir and pine. The green mountainsides slowly fade into the brown green of the pinon covered 7,000 foot plain. It is a lively time of year in the mountain villages. The people scourged by flies and heat during the summer begin the mad rush for firewood and pinon nuts. Men who would scowl at one another for the rest of the year smile and laugh during this time of rapidly changing season. Soon the snow will cover the peaks and one morning the town will awaken to a blanket of snow and cold. Once again people will begin to trudge and work. It is a temporary respite from a harsh environment. A break in a life that is both beautiful and sad.

Cam Stearns and Molly decided not to walk this day, and went laughing to her neighbor's. Mr. Escavar was not one prone to sentimentality, but seeing the laughter on their faces moved him to loan them two of his horses with the promise that they would be back before dark. They rode east of Las Vegas to the edge of the mountains. The cool air made their cheeks rosy and the horses lively. Cam would ride beside Molly and then, filled with his joy and love, would gallop far ahead. Molly watched how he mastered the horse, his form being so in tune with the animal that he did not need two arms. She thought to herself, if nothing else, Cam Stearns, you are a man afraid of nothing, willing to try. Succeed or fail, I love you truly.

Stearns stopped the horse and watched her ride to catch up with him. She was not a ranch lady like his mother. She was a person raised differently than he, but she was a worker. A brave lady, he knew, one who had been through heartache and pain and had survived. He felt as though his complete mind and soul rode with her. If she hungered, so did he, if she laughed, so did he. It was a tremendous feeling, one that left him exhilarated, but also a little afraid. What would he do if he ever lost her? Watching her ride toward him, he looked at the blue sky, the slowly passing powder puff clouds and prayed aloud, "Dear God, if you don't grant me anything else in this life, let me die first."

Molly pulled her horse up beside his. He looked at her and laughed, "well, a horse woman, you're not."

She pinched her face into a scowl. "Well, I guess, mister smart guy, you'll just have to teach me how."

"Put your toes out more in the stirrups and bring your heels down. Now just relax and let the horse move under you."

It was early afternoon when they stopped. A small spring came to life under an outcropping of brownish black limestone. Cottonwoods and rose hips grew circling the water, already browned from the night air. Cam helped Molly out of the saddle. As her feet hit the ground he pulled her close to him and kissed her. She melted into his chest and they stood, the breeze curling around them, and felt their lives merge. "My life is your life, Molly," he whispered. "I love you dearly."

Cam unrolled his blanket from behind the saddle and they sat down. "Isn't it beautiful?" Molly said.

"You should see Cuba," Cam answered. "The ocean is as blue as the sky is here. Where the ocean touches the beaches the sand is as white as snow and the mountains are greener than anything you've ever seen in your life. Birds that I can't describe fill the trees and it's always warm."

Molly looked at Cam. "I know I'll love it Cam, if you feel so strongly about it. I know I'll love it."

As he reached out with his hand to touch her hair, his hand accidentally rubbed against her breast. A fire spread through Molly's body and she looked into his eyes. Cam pulled her close to him and kissed her neck. The smell of sweet soap filled his nose. He did not ask, he did not feel afraid as he cupped her breast with his hand. Gently kneading the flesh, he felt her skin warm and her breathing deepen. He moved her back onto the blanket and unbuttoned her dress. He looked upon her body. She was beautiful. Her hips rounded and flowed into her thighs. Her breasts, firm and proud, responded to his touch. Lying half on her and half beside her he kissed her breast and ran his hand down her stomach. He felt her shudder and relax. "Now Cam," she whispered, "now, my love."

It was as though the world had stopped. She was warm and responsive to him. He had never made love like this in his life.

As he lay upon her, slowly the world returned to him. He smiled down into her face and kissed the tip of her nose. She giggled and pushed him over onto his back. "That wasn't very lady-like," she said, sheer joy and contentment in her eyes.

He watched her rise and stand naked before him. Putting on her clothes, she picked up his pants and flipped them over to him. "It was beautiful, Cam. Whatever else we do all during our lives, let us never forget this day or this place."

He watched the breeze touching her hair, the blue sky outlining her form. He rose, and could not speak, but his heart was filled with a thousand songs and his spirit flew as high as the mountain hawk, circling and playing with the wind.

(8)

Private William Stone pulled the collar of his blue army winter coat tighter around his neck. The breath of the bay horse he rode made small circles of white around his nostrils. Three more months, Stone thought to himself, then the army could take it and stick it. "Smiley, huh?" he snorted, looking at the snow covered peaks of the mountains. "I haven't smiled in months." He settled himself deeper into the saddle and shivered. The army had not been the same since he had com-e-back to the states. The Rough Riders, the glory, the feeling that had swept over him had been replaced with a dull complacency over the past months. Screaming sergeants, inspections, spit and polish was not his idea of living. What had once filled him with pride, now left him grumbling and forlorn. He had not seen any of the men he had served with in Cuba. He supposed that they were scattered all over the country. It was during these patrols over the mountains that he thought most of Stearns and his dream of Cuba. But mostly he supposed he thought of the warm weather, and the sparkling dark eyes of the girls in Cuba. Stone reached down and wiped the gathering snow off the horse's neck. "It's okay fella, we'll git back soon. Thirty minutes tops, and you'll be eatin' oats and hay and talkin' with yer buddies about this fucked up army."

The horse plodded on, unmindful of Stone's words. Stone looked at the sky, the snow that began earlier was growing in intensity. Large, quarter-sized flakes drifted lazily down to the already covered ground. The temperature had dropped over ten degrees in the past hour and already he could feel the chill creep down his backbone. The sun, a dull glow in the grey sky earlier, was now invisible and was about to set. He was not afraid but he was apprehensive. For one thing, he was not prepared for a night in the cold. Matches he had, food none, and by his calculations he was five miles from the post, but the snow had so changed the look of the land that he couldn't be certain. Stone did know one thing, if it grew much darker he would have to stop and build a fire. No need to go deeper and deeper into the mountains in the dark. He would sit it out and stay warm and move again when it finally broke.

Fifteen minutes later he dismounted. "Well pardner, reckon me'n you are gonna spend a hungry ole cold night together."

By now the snow had become heavier and a wind kicked in gusts, sending the snow one moment into his face and the next down his neck. Stone stood rubbing his numb hands and surveying his situation. Spotting a stand of pine, he led the horse over to it. He had no ax or tools, but he tore the smaller branches that he could and leaned them between two close pines for a windbreak. He found some others and laid them in front of the break to sit on. He then unsaddled the horse, placing the horse blanket over the tree bows on the ground.

Finding dry wood was difficult under the snow, but the snow was dry and easily kicked around. By the last moments of light he had a sizable pile. He took his pocket knife and splintered small branches of dry wood and slowly and painstakingly placed them in a pile. He reached into his pocket and pulled out his matches, counting with shivering hands that he had fifteen. "Make 'em last, God," he murmured. The dry splinters caught with the first match, and in a few minutes he had a two-foot fire at the edge of his windbreak. The warmth spread through him and slowly the feeling came back to his fingers. Sitting by the fire he looked the picture of contentment. The fire lit up the area for five feet around the make-shift camp. The horse stood on the edge, its large dark eyes surveying the man with no sign of fear or dread. "Well shit, fella," he said to the horse, "let's hope this son of bitch blows over tonight. I sure am hungry."

The horse pawed at the ground and nibbled at the dry brittle grass that lay under the snow. Stone looked at the saddle and the rifle. He had twelve rounds. "First thing that moves, sparrow, squirrel, you're my dinner." he chuckled, but there was nothing that moved.

Sky that Sings stood outside the flap of his tepee. He watched the smoke rise from the dozen tents that were the camp, and he enjoyed the sight. They had stopped at his wish, wanting to move on yesterday, but he had made them stop. But he had read the clouds and knew there would be a great storm. He had made the men and women gather huge piles of wood and pitch the tepees. It would have been too hard on the children to travel through the storm. The elders had stomped off in disgust when he had looked at the sky and told them to camp. They were looking forward to the winter ground with the hot water that bubbled from the ground, and after many days on the trail, everyone had been excited about getting there. It was only a short distance more, and he had to quell their excitment. He remembered hunting deer with his father when he was a boy. The sky had been a vivid red, and small clouds that a bird could fly through had coverd the sun when it set. His father had made a large pine tree hut and had dragged trees to just outside the door when the storm had come upon them. Nine days, they had sat in the hut. The wind and snow howling outside, with the warm safety inside the hut his father had built. It had been the same sky, and although he had wanted to continue as much as the others, he had ordered them to stop to erect the tepees and gather wood. He looked at the people moving into their tepees and knew that they would talk of his wisdom as they sat around their fires in warmth and thought of the cold they could have been enduring. He turned and entered his tepee, the smokey inside smelled of warming deer meat and his wife smiled at him. "Sit, my husband, and eat," she said. He sat down on the wolf hide that covered the floor and took a large chunk of deer meat from a stick over the fire. His two boys played alongside the wall of the tepee. He smiled at his wife and she could see the satisfaction in his face. "It will be a bad storm," he said, chewing the meat, "but we are warm and our stomachs are full." He eyed his wife and thought of her warm skin. It will be a good storm, with much sleeping and playing, he thought. He let the fire warm him and smiled in his wisdom and contentment.

Smiley figured it to be mid-morning. The intense cold that follows dawn had passed and although he was still cold he knew it was not as cold as it had been. The night had been miserable. He had kept the fire going, fighting the weariness that overcame him, but some time in the early morning he had fallen asleep and awakened with a jolt, the snow covering him, and the fire nearly out. He had frantically brushed through the snow searching for wood, and with shaking hands had managed to get the fire blazing again. Enjoying for a moment the comfort of the heat, he noticed the tracks of his horse leading away from camp. Now sitting by the fire the tracks were covered. The snow fell in what seemed even larger flakes than the day before, but at least the wind had died. Although he had the fire, it was impossible to keep from getting chilled. The front of his body was warm but the cold crept down his backbone, until he would be forced to turn his back to the fire.

He rose and tromped through the snow, breaking through the fine powder and digging out the dry branches that littered the ground. He worked for what seemed hours, fighting the cold that came over him, and piled up enough wood to last through another night. He had given up hoping for a break in the weather. He knew now it would be a test. Not of bravey and bullets, but of nerve. He knew better than to strike out into the storm. He would sit and wait it out and try to ignore the hunger that gnawed in the pit of his stomach.

It was sundown when he once again walked from the fire in search of wood. His all-night supply had dwindled down to nothing. The grey-black snowing sky showed no sign of letting up. Dragging his feet through the snow he noticed for the first time how really hungry he was, and every step seemed to take more and more of his energy. By the time he had gathered enough wood he was shaking again. He sat by the fire with his knees to his chin and bent his head down into the front of his coat. Even with the fire his body was racked with cold and pain, and his mind began to jump from one thought to another.

When it was totally dark the snowflakes glistened in the firelight and the wind began again. The lean-to did nothing to curb the cold icy bite of the wind, and he told himself he would build it larger and enclose it in the morning. Sleep did not come this night, only the sound of the snow and the wind playing with the branches of the trees. ————————————

Sky that Sings opened the flap of the tepee and watched the snow. Already the snow covered the edge of the tepee by at least three feet. It would be worse than he had thought, and he closed the flap to the bitter cold. He went over and sat down by his wife who was covering the sleeping children. She smiled with her large doe eyes, and he began to untie the front of her dress. Laying bare her breast, she rose and walked to the wolf rugs. She giggled as she crawled in beside him and he felt a tingle of excitement as her thigh touched his leg. He had a great prize in this woman. She had been only two horses, and although she did not cook as well as many wives, she was very bouncy in love, and had amazed Sky that Sings many times by the different joys she could perform with relish. He placed his hand behind her head and slowly forced her head down to his stomach. The familiar warmth spread over him, and he shut his eyes. ————————————

By nightfall of the third day, Smiley sat, resigned to the fact that he would die. The snow had not stopped and the wind continued, howling through the trees. He knew his toes were frozen, but his fingers were so stiff he could not use them to pull off his boots and try to rub the circulation back into his toes. The fire he had fought so hard to keep burning was now but a small pile of embers. The snow was so deep he could no longer forage for dry wood.

Hell of a way for a Texas boy to go, he thought, dying in the snow. He was not hysterical or in anguish, he had faced death many times and already made his peace with life. He only wished it would have ended another way.

Slowly the fire gave way and his eyes closed. Wonder how mom is, he thought as a warmth spread over him and enclosed him in darkness.

Sky that Sings woke early. The children slept under their warm wolf hides and his wife slept, a small smile on her dark-skinned face. He threw his blanket over his shoulder and stepped out into the cold. The snow had stopped during the night, and the sun sent its yellow rays sparkling over the mountains. He smiled on the day, and did not notice the horse until he reached down to pick up wood for fire. The horse stood with its head down, and Sky that Sings noticed the army brand. He dropped the wood and walked over to the animal. "Easy boy," he said gently. The horse snorted and walked toward him. The icey breath from his nostrils froze on his whiskers and made his muzzle white. "Where is your rider?" the Indian asked. The horse pawed the ground in search of frozen grass.

71

Sky that Sings left the horse, and took the wood back into the tepee. Bringing the fire back to a blaze, he sat until the children stirred. The children looked at their father. He was the chief, and the pride shown in their eyes. He was a great man, and his blood flowed in their veins. He smiled at their dark eyes as they came to the fire. "The snow has ended," he said, patting the children. "Soon we will leave."

His wife moved. He watched her dress, and when she had finished, he stood up and took his rifle from the floor. "We need meat, I will be back."

Hunting was Sky that Sings' love. He had made his place in the tribe at a young age by his ability to hunt. He had shot his first bear when he was only ten. His father had sat and talked for hours to the elders about his son and how he had shot the bear.

The icy cold cut into his face as he walked. It was a feeling he was accustomed to and one he loved. The deer would be up soon, after the three days of lying under the trees. They would rise and stretch the cold cramped muscles and be not as weary as they should be.

Not more than a half a mile from camp he came across the drag marks of three deer through the snow. He could smell the hot humid scent of their steaming bodies. It would be easy today. His family would eat. He smiled and followed the tracks into the woods. He stared up into the sky and thanked God for his good fortune.

It was very hot and very dry. Smiley stood far back from the fire lest the heat bring more sweat to his brow. Down the face of the cliff he could see the deer nibbling on the short green grass that grew stubbornly between the rocks. He thought of his rifle and was tempted for a moment, but it was summer and all animals should have peace in the summer, but in the winter he would return here for his deer. The blazing sun hung straight overhead, and he dreamed of the cool mountains and a spring he knew of that was shaded by large, towering fir trees. He would love to take his dusty range clothes off and plunge into the icy cold water. He felt the sensation of the water on his skin and shivered, hoping for a cool breeze. But it was hot, so hot that in an instant his lips were cracked and large red gashes appeared on his fingers. Blood began to ooze from his lips and the sweat pouring down his face made them sting and burn as though a branding iron had been put to his face. He began to run frantically, clawing at his face, but the burning would not leave and he fell to the ground, grinding his lips into the earth. It was hot, he was on fire and then, blackness.

Sky that Sings raised the rifle and took careful aim. As the rifle fired, the deer lurched, and instead of the bullet entering the heart, he saw the slug tear into the lungs. The deer jumped and ran into the trees. Sky that Sings looked disdainfully at the fleeing deer. Now he must work, a shot in the lungs and the animal might run for miles. He sat down under a tree and took the dried fish from his coat. He would eat, the deer would hear no pursuit and bed down to grow stiff and cold, enabling him to walk close and finish the animal with no more pain. Twenty or thirty minutes later, he rose and followed the deer tracks. At first they were far apart and the red drops of blood flashed vividly in the snow. After several hundred yards the tracks showed the deer had slowed to a walk and was dragging his hind feet. He would be close. Sky that Sings brought his rifle to ready and inched through the snow. His eyes scanned the trees, his mind was lost to the world except for the animal and the sound of the forest.

Behind what looked like a wall of pine branches he saw the black legs of the deer. He knew by their position the animal was dead. He lowered his rifle and walked toward the deer. He had been lucky, it had been a bad shot but the deer had died without the necessity of another precious shell.

Rounding the edge of the branches he saw the man. He was lying with his face in the snow, deep guttural sounds emitting from the icy form. "The fire, the fire," the body said. Sky that Sings looked at the blue army clothes and felt the anger in him begin to emerge. Another soldier. Another of the men who had taken his people's land. His hand tightened on his rifle, whitening the knuckles, but then slowly relaxed. He walked to the prostrate form and kneeled down. Placing his hand on his shoulder he rolled him over. He saw the frozen eyebrows and the swollen blue cracked lips. "You are alive," he said, "and I will help you." He quickly drew his knife and gutted the deer. Taking his rope he hung the deer from a tree and picked up the man.

Carrying the soldier back to the camp, Sky that Sings wondered why he did not let him die. It was not that he did not want to, it was just that he was tired of fighting. He had killed many blue legs like this one and seen many of his braves die, but there must be no more. He knew this, the killing must end.

His wife gasped as he struggled into the tepee and dropped the soldier heavily on the floor by the fire. "He is frost-bitten. Heal him."

Sky that Sings' wife looked deep into the eyes of her husband. She had witnessed the soldiers kill his brother, she knew she hated them. But, she did not speak, and began to undress the unconscious man. Laying his naked body close to the fire, she began to rub his hands and feet, slowly bringing back the circulation to his limbs. She had the children bring snow in a pot which she heated. She dipped a cloth into the warm water and placed it on his face. He was a handsome man, and soon she did not think of his color, only that she must save him.

Sky that Sings had left without another word. When he returned he hung the deer outside the tepee. Cutting off a leg, he entered. "He will heal and become strong again, and maybe he will never hunt another Indian."

His wife looked at his face and was proud of this man. Truly, he was a man of wisdom.

The fire had ceased, but the sun did not shine. He was surrounded by blackness, and even though he opened his eyes there was no difference in the light.

Then there was the smell of smoke and cooking meat. A warm cloth on his brow that cooled and refreshed. There was no darkness nor swirling figures that sprang in front of his mind. His eyes opened and he saw the broad, dark face of a woman. Her eyes were black like the night as she smiled and pushed him back as he tried to rise. She spoke to him in a language he did not understand, but he did not resist, and lay back down on the fur blankets. It was warm. His mind was not necessary, his body knew it was warm and he was alive.

He rested four days. Smiley now knew he was in an Indian camp, but he did not ponder his fate. He had no power, no pistol or rifle. If they had wanted to kill him, he would be dead and under the snow. The woman fed him and gave him back his clothes. The man, serious and quiet, would watch him for hours at a time, speaking in low tones to his wife. The children played and laughed as though he were not there. Theirs was a child's world, not yet filled with hate or prejudice. On the fourth day, he awoke to the sound of breaking camp. He had been picked up and placed on a litter behind a horse. The sky was clear, the air cold, biting his face and hands. Some women piled furs around him and he muttered "thank you."

It was three or four in the afternoon when the procession of men and women stopped. He knew now that he had been in the chief's tepee by the way the men followed him with their eyes. The chief spoke to two braves who unhooked his litter and picked him up and propped him on his horse. One of the braves took the reins and they headed through the trees. Coming through the stand of trees he saw the fort with the smoke rising from the stoves. The brave handed him the reins and pointed. Smiley felt an enormous sense of relief. But before he could say anything the braves were gone. He leaned over the saddle and pointed the horse toward the fort. The guards saw the hunched figure on the horse coming toward the gates. As the gates were swung open to let him in, Smiley turned and looked back toward the trees. He would not fight again. To his dying day the Indian would be his own, and Smiley vowed to write Stearns and pursue his dream of Cuba.

(9)

Cam Stearns paced back and forth across Molly's restaurant. He felt uncomfortable in the black suit with the stiff white shirt collar choking his neck. Poncho sat at a table drinking coffee. "Relax," he said, "eet eez only marriage, you not go to war."

Stearns smiled nervously, "I know."

Poncho watched Stearns continue to pace. He looked at the handsome man, even more handsome with his one jacket sleeve pinned up. His brown-blond hair was slicked back and his face was slightly red from shaving too close.

"When my wife and me, marry, my wife's family, they all come. Brothers, seesters, uncles, cousins, forty-nine of them, there were. One of her brothers, he was a priest, but several they were banditos. You think you afraid? I could not sit or eat and every time when I start to feel better her father and the brothers who were banditos, they would watch me and they do not smile. Not until after the wedding did they smile, but you know they keep me all night drinking and would not let me go. The seesters, they take my wife in a wagon and drive her around all night, laughing while I drink and no can leave. "When the sun was coming up, her father and brothers they take me out of town where her father, he gives to me the few acres and the house where we now live. Her father he embrace me and they ride off. My wife, seeing her father and brothers, runs from the house with a shotgun and shoots it over their heads. "Ah, you should have seen her then. She was young and skinny, three days we spend in bed. And now each year we remember that first night and we laugh together about it. Her father he eez dead, the two bandito brothers they are in prison, and the priest, he was killed by Indians. This was the last time her family was truly together. One big step, eet eez, but we must laugh and make love and the world she goes by."

Stearns sat down by Poncho. "Come with us to Cuba, Poncho."

Poncho looked at Stearns. "I would like to, but thees, she is my home. The mountains, the plain with her cold winters and her hot summers. My children they were born here and will die here. Me, I am happy. I am not like you, Senor. I have no dream that both follows and drives me. Eet eez for people like you to go to new places."

Stearns reached out his hand and shook Poncho's hand firmly. "Wish me well, Poncho."

Poncho stood up, in his brown suit with the Mexican short-waisted jacket. "We go now, Senor Stearns, eet eez time and the padre he waits."

There were few people in the church. All of Poncho's children with the two eldest daughters acting as the flower girls. They were as pretty as a mountain sunset, with their yellow dresses and their bouquets of black-eyed susans. Their dark eyes shined as Molly and Cam walked down the aisle. Poncho's wife cried and when the wedding was over she hugged Molly to her bosom. "I am so happy for you," she sobbed.

Poncho waited outside in the driver's seat of the buggy as the two newlyweds ran through the shower of rice. The buggy clanked and rolled down the street. Cowboys seeing the cans and old boots behind the buggy shot their pistols into the air and hollered as they passed. Cam smiled at Molly as he helped her out of the buggy in front of the house. Poncho tipped his wide-brimmed hat. "Vaya con Dios. Go with God, Cam and Molly Stearns."

Cam picked Molly up and carried her toward the house. At the door he looked back at Poncho and shouted, "see you in three days, my friend."

Smiley dismounted wearily from the horse. He tied the horse to the hitching rail and walked up the wooden steps to the door of the restaurant. This had to be it, he thought, the only Molly's in town. Entering, he was greeted by the warmth of the wood stove and the smell of steak and potatoes. The ride had been cold, but he had had his experience with cold and was prepared. Never again would he be caught short in anything he did. It was March 1899, and Smiley was beginning to feel old. He hoped Stearns was here, it had taken longer then he hoped for his hands to heal and they would carry forever the marks of frost bite. The army had tried to badger him into reenlisting, but to no avail. He had taken his money, his horse and rifle and left Colorado. To catch Stearns if he could, and if not to head back to Texas, a little older and a little wiser.

Poncho watched the tall, lean man enter the restaurant. He noticed the deep blue eyes with the smile lines, but he also noticed the touch of grimness around the corners of the mouth. There were many hard men in this country. Men running from anything one could imagine. Men running from broken hearts, but this

75

man did not run, Poncho knew. But he had a look of lostness about him.

Smiley flashed a quick, explosive grin at Poncho and in Spanish spoke. "It is cold, my friend, and the food smells good."

Poncho pointed to a table by the stove. "Sit here, warm your bones and I will bring you coffee."

Smiley sat and Poncho could sense he was ill at ease. Placing the coffee before him he said, "the steak and potatoes you need, no, Senor?"

Smiley put his hands close to the wood stove. "Steak it is, medium with no ketchup."

Poncho laughed, walking off. He yelled into the kitchen, "one steak, Texas size, with too many potatoes."

Smiley sat and drank his coffee. It was nice to eat in a restaurant. He could see the touch of a lady's hand around the place. He wondered if Stearns had married the girl that wrote him, or if he was in another part of the country somewhere between here and now, mending a broken heart. He was looking into his coffee cup when he saw the long-fingered white female hands that placed the food in front of him. He looked up, smiled and Molly was captivated by his genuine smile. "Here it is," she said, "hot and ready."

Smiley knew immediately this was Molly. The blond hair, the blue velvet eyes, here was a woman Cam Stearns could love. He looked at the steak and the mountain of potatoes and then back to the woman. His eyes scanned her figure, down her breasts and to her small waist. Molly looked at him. "Like what you see?"

Smiley looked away quickly. "Sorry," he said, "I was just thinking of a friend of mine and now I know what he saw in you."

Molly looked perplexed. "What friend?"

Smiley did not want to continue. What if he was gone, denied his wedding. He did not want to anger her. But she stood there and did not move, the question still on her face. "Cam Stearns," he said barely above a whisper. "I was in the Rough Riders with him and he used to write to you."

Molly leaned over and grabbed Smiley and hugged him hard. "Smiley," she squealed with glee. "You must be Smiley!"

He felt her warmth and was immediately taken over by her charm. He didn't know it now, sitting in a small western town, that she would prove to be his dearest friend and they would forever be as close as brother and sister. Molly pulled the other chair out from under the table and sat down. "Cam will be so happy to see you, you just can't imagine how he talks about you. Him and Cuba and you, he has been a man possessed these last months, waiting for your letter."

Smiley chewed the steak and felt rested. He had found a home. There would be no Texas, maybe not even Cuba, but he had found a place. He noticed the ring on her finger. "Married ya, did he?"

She smiled, looked at the ring. "Almost three months ago."

"He's a good man, I'm real happy for ya both. Where is he?"

"He'll be back in an hour or so. He went to the telegraph office. Roosevelt is Governor of New York now. Cam just found out and he sent him a wire. He really wants to go to Cuba. Cuba, Cuba, that's all I hear."

"He's got a dream, Molly."

"I know," Molly smiled, "but I hope it doesn't destroy him."

Smiley looked at the woman and saw the touch of worry on her face and then it vanished as quickly as it came. "And what do you think of Cuba, Molly?"

Molly looked at Smiley, "I don't know," she answered truthfully, "but if it's half of what Cam raves on and on about I'm sure I will be perfectly content."

Smiley chewed the steak. One day, he thought, one day I will have a woman like this.

Molly got up from the table and took his empty plate. "More coffee for the gentleman," she called to Poncho, "and a large piece of that apple pie that's hot in the back."

Poncho hurried over with the coffee pot and refilled his cup. "One nice lady, eh, hombre?"

"She's my friend's wife," Smiley answered.

"It is good," Poncho said.

"Yes, it is good," Smiley said, "it is very good."

Cam Stearns took the telegram with a steady grip, took a deep breath and opened the envelope.

Cam Stearns . . . Received your message, good to hear from you . . . will send you all information necessary in the mail . . . keep your dream and your spirit . . . your friend . . . T. Roosevelt.

Walking back to the restaurant, Stearns could hardly hold in his excitement. The fever had grown in him over the past months. He would dream of Cuba, the cattle, and the ocean. At times he would pick up a pencil and paper and draw houses and outbuildings and the way his fences would run. And now it was close, the dream was beginning. Roosevelt had not lied, he would help. With the sale of the house and the restaurant and a few backers they would go, he and Molly, to start a new life in a new land. A land where no one knew him except from the day when he had stepped off the boat. Molly would be excited, she seemed to sense his yearning, and although at times Cam knew she was frightened at the thought of leaving, it did not dismay him. He understood. It was comfortable here for her, the business went well, they were not rich by any means but they were comfortable. But she would go with him, without a look back she would go, unafraid of the future because he had a dream. It was as it should be and he loved her the more for it.

The night was cold, but he did not feel the cold as he entered the restaurant and banged the door closed. He saw Molly sitting at a table by the stove with a man who looked vaguely familiar. It was not until he was standing by the table that he recognized Smiley. All thoughts of Cuba and Roosevelt immediately left his mind. "Smiley!"

Smiley jumped up and the two men hugged each other. "You old Texas son of a bitch, you've come, you've come."

Molly watched the two men embrace and saw the look on their faces. It was a warm feeling, a feeling only men who have shared hardship can ever possess. It is a friendship beyond friendship, one of time and moments that remain silent, but forever recorded in one's mind.

Poncho stood by the kitchen door and watched the commotion. He went back to the kitchen and came out with four glasses and a bottle of wine. Placing it on the table, he drew up two more chairs and they all sat down. He opened the wine and poured the glasses full. "To old friends," he toasted. The four raised their glasses high, and each was in his own way, happy for the other.

It was well past midnight when Molly finally got the two lost friends on their feet and headed out the door. First there had been one bottle, then another and another. Poncho was asleep on the floor. She tucked him in with table cloths and coats and left him.

Sandwiched between the two drunk and reeling men she felt the warmth of both of them at her sides. Men, she thought, wars, battles, causes, dreams, but still boys, big boys. She let them both fall on the sofa in the living room and straightened her jostled dress. They sat with their heads together, passed out. "You two may be the death of me yet," she said, "but it will not be dull. It might not always be comfortable, but it will never be boring."

She walked up the stairs, singing a lullaby she knew as a child. Standing in front of her mirror with the kerosene light behind her she slowly removed her clothes. The light shown down her shapely form, around the long thin neck, molding into her shoulders and well-formed breasts. She placed her hands on her stomach and stood very still. Cam did not know yet, but he must soon. She felt full of joy and fullfillment but she was afraid. She did not want the child to stop Cam from going to Cuba. If need be she would say nothing until they were on their way. Children must not stop his dream. Without the dream, there would be no Cam Stearns. There would cease to be the look that came over him when he gazed out past the mountains to the ocean that lay somewhere. It was a fire that must not be quenched until it burned itself out.

It was not easy for Molly to say goodbye to all she had dreamed and built. All the trying times came back to her as she looked over her belongings. Her first husband, and how they had laughed and struggled until his untimely death. The years they had been broke, until the bank was paid and the restaurant was in the black. It was not easy for her, but she hid her pain well and always met Cam with a smile and sat listening as he talked on and on about Roosevelt and Cuba. Now as the train pulled away from Lamy she felt a great sadness come over her and she wanted to run from the train, but she sat silent as Cam and Smiley toasted.

It was dark when the spell broke. Cam placed his arm around her reassuringly. "Let's go eat, Molly. They say the food on this train is the best in the west."

She smiled up into his green eyes and they rose and walked past the assortment of people who sat staring into the darkness. Smiley saw her mood of sadness and dread but did not speak. At times Cam was so deep into his vision he could not read Molly's moods, but Smiley always knew, and he would help her in any way he could.

They had sold the house and sold the restaruant to Poncho. Poncho would make his payments to the bank, from which Cam could draft from while he was in Cuba.

Three weeks after the telegram from Roosevelt, Cam had received a letter in the mail. General Wood had been promoted and was now acting governor of Cuba. Roosevelt had notified him that Cam and his wife would be landing in Cuba.

He would give every assistance to Cam and help him get started. A wealthy banker friend of Roosevelts, a Mr. Samuel Johnson, was to be contacted in Florida happy he had been when the papers to the restaurant were turned over to him. His wife had beamed and walked around the kitchen. They would add tacos and enchiladas to the menu. When Molly was taking one last look around the restaurant, Poncho had picked up her hand and kissed it. "Eet eez God's will," he had told her. "Follow what life brings to you, we cannot fight our destiny."

Molly had almost cried then, but seeing the glow on Cam's face she had turned to see Smiley watching her. A grip of compassion came over Smiley and he smiled as if to say, take heart, beautiful one, it is an adventure you will long remember.

There was something that puzzled Molly. Cam, who she loved so dearly, and would follow around the world was, at times, like a total stranger. Lost in his plans to Cuba, or living somewhere back in the past, driven to be wealthy and so, never feel the pang of hunger again. Cam, who could touch her and send her into hours of passion, and then seem as far away as the ocean. And then there was Smiley, who with one look could say, "I know how you feel. There is nothing you can do."

She found herself growing closer and closer to Smiley. He would not talk of Cuba or cattle. Content to let Cam do the dreaming, he and Molly would talk of trivial things. A few times he had mentioned the war and how brave Cam was, but mostly he talked of Texas and when he was a child. The cows and the wide open spaces. He talked, and she would listen to his slow drawl, laughing when he told of escapades with made cows and drunken cowboys. Smiley was a simple man, a good man, not one like Cam, driven to be something or somebody. Just a man who found in Cam a true friend, a man he could follow and help when necessary, a man with a strong back and the ability to work, sweat and laugh through it all. Molly felt no threat from Smiley. She knew that no matter what his feelings, he would never betray a friend, and she grew closer and closer to him each day.

(10)

Mr. Samuel Johnson stood by the doorway and looked intently at his secretary. She was a striking woman. He looked at the secretary once more and returned to his desk. There were a few letters yet to be opened and then he could leave. He was escorting the mayor's daughter to the opening of a musical tonight and wanted to be at his best. He knew they were the talk of the town. Mr. Johnson, the womanizer, having divorced just a month earlier and already out with the mayor's daughter. Let them talk, Johnson knew who he was and what he wanted. He sat down in his leather chair and sorted through his unopened mail. He picked out the most important looking letter and opened it. Being president of the largest bank in Florida had its advantages, and one of them was discarding mail that

79

was not important. But upon quickly scanning the letter he knew this was worth his most precious time. It began.

Dear Sam:

There will be a man to see you in the near future. His name is Cam Stearns.
He was a Rough Rider in my regiment and lost one arm in the fighting. Help him
in any way possible. Men like him will make Cuba a profit-making venture for
the home country. Hope all is well with you and your wife.

Sincerely, T. Roosevelt.

Johnson placed the letter on his desk and reclined in his chair. Payback time, he thought. It had been several years and at times he wondered if Roosevelt was going to let him by, but now he knew he was wrong.

He remembered the look on Roosevelt's face the day he had been summoned to his office. Under Secretary of the Navy, and proud of his job, Roosevelt had looked over the six-foot frame of Johnson, who stood looking neat and proper in his dark, hand-made business suit. Johnson, used to pushing and using people, saw at first glance Roosevelt was not a man to fool around with and soon melted under his steady and menacing gaze.

Finally, Roosevelt spoke in a voice that left no room for explanation. "We will take the loan from your bank."

Johnson shifted his weight from foot to foot. Roosevelt rose from his chair and opened the door. As Johnson walked by, Roosevelt looked at him. "One day you owe me one, Mr. Johnson," and he had bowed his head politely. Johnson had left the office and made immediate plans to leave, taking the train to Florida the next day.

Here in Florida his life had been good. He managed through marriage to tie into the largest contruction company in the state, and after two years, he had left her. He would never forget her tear-stained face after finding out about his numerous affairs. He had tried to tell her that it was nothing personal, that no one woman could satisfy him, but she had grown more and more hysterical. The only daughter of a wealthy family, her heart had never been hardened for real life.

Samuel Johnson took the Havana cigar from his inside jacket pocket. Cuba, he thought, a land of dreams and opportunity. Mr. Stearns, he thought, lighting the cigar, this may be the opportunity of our lives. He must play it carefully. Roosevelt grew in power every day. He was not a man you would want to play with, nor would you want to hurt one of his friends.

Walking past his secretary, who stood bending over a file cabinet, he patted her on the rear. "Why, Mr. Johnson," she blushed, but he could see the smile hidden behind her look of alarm.

"Good night, Mrs. Carmichael. See you in the morning. Nine o'clock sharp, now."

Cam and Molly watched the bellman leave the room. Molly turned and stepped into Cam arm. "It's lovely, Cam, such a hotel."

"Only fit for a woman who is the wife of a man about to make his fortune in Cuba." Cam said. He held her close to him and looked down into her blue eyes. "Glad the train ride is over?"

Molly walked over and stood by the window which looked out on the ocean. She untied her hair and let it cascade down her back. "It's beautiful here," she said. Look at the ocean, so large, one wonders if it ever ends. Which way is Cuba, Cam?"

Cam walked over and stood beside her. "That way, that way over the ocean."

She turned and began unbuttoning his shirt. He felt her fingernails brush lightly over his chest. He wanted to leave immediately to find this man Johnson, but he looked into her face and the halo effect of her hair. "You little, darling," he said, picking her up with his arm. "Take off your clothes and meet me in bed."

Molly laughed and began undressing. Cam talked while she undressed. There was something different about Molly lately. Her color, the way she stood, he didn't know exactly, but he knew there was something. He looked admiringly over her naked form, but thought nothing of the slight weight gain her body showed. Climbing under the sheet with her he felt her breasts push gently into his side. He rolled over and nibbled on her ear. "Welcome to Florida, lady," he said, stroking her stomach. "Welcome to the gateway of our adventure."

Smiley stood by the window of his room and looked out upon the harbor. A few large sailing ships could be seen, but mostly the smoke stacks of the iron ships filled the harbor. The sailing ships most likely belonged to smugglers, he figured. He had read all about it in the paper. He felt slightly uneasy, standing looking out upon the ocean once again. He could not place what exactly made him feel uneasy but he knew it was not right.

He knew he did not like the way he felt for Molly now. The days in Las Vegas and the day on the train. Cam running to and fro and he and Molly talking. He would think of her all the time. He would love to make love to her, but that wasn't what bothered him, as it was natural for men to want to sleep with every good looking woman they met. But it was the way he felt when he was with her. How his life seemed to lighten when she talked and smiled. She and Cam had several small arguments on the train. Nothing to speak of, pent up excitement on both parts, she at leaving what she knew, and Cam anxious to get started in Cuba. But with each argument Cam would say. "Take her to the bar, Smiley, would you? Maybe you can make her smile."

And he would take her to the bar. Watching the admiring glances of the men in the train as they passed. Careful to open the doors for her and pull out her chair and she would smile so sweetly at him and soon be laughing and happy with his conversation.

It was dangerous, he knew, but it was not out of control. She sensed nothing of his feelings, only his friendship. "Cam is so impulsive at times," she would say. And Smiley would agree.

Once when Cam had left them sitting on the train, he had noticed Molly looking pale and faint. He had gone and brought her a drink of water. "Here, Molly, drink this."

And it had suddenly come over him when her face had turned to his. She was pregnant, he could tell by the color in her cheeks and the faint dullness in her eyes. "You're pregnant," he had gasped.

Molly had smiled, "Yes, and don't you tell Cam."

81

"You mean he doesn't know, Molly? My God, if anyone on earth should know, he should."

"No," she had said, putting an end to the matter. "Not now, not until we're in Cuba. I will not stifle his dream."

He loved her more after that. Even with child, she would not stand in the way of Cam.

Smiley turned from the window, the sun set in a large orange globe on the surface of the water. Cuba, he thought, what do you have in store for me.

Cam Stearns stroked the hair of the sleeping Molly. He looked out the window at the quickly darkening sky. How strange it was. From poor ranch hand, to killer, to the army, and now married and on the way to Cuba. Each day brought a new restlessness to him, which caught him up in a frenzy that was subdued only with a supreme effort. He was young and untaught, but he knew the power was there. Money, money was the answer. Money for your children and family. No stooped backs from working, only the best schools, maids, fine homes. In his visualization of his dream he really only saw himself, dressed in fine clothes, riding a thoroughbred horse over his land. He felt growing in him the beginning of true power. Power over men. He had felt it at first in the army. His quiet ways had not bred friends, but he had men follow him. His voice, with the strange whip-like crack to words, even when he was trying to be friendly, had a way of making men see as he saw.

He rose from the bed, slowly taking Molly's arm from his stomach. What a beautiful woman you are, he thought, looking at her peaceful form. But even Molly was different to him now. The intense drive that had taken him back to New Mexico was gone. The deep burning feeling he had for her had changed over the past months. He knew he loved her, but it was as though she was at the edge of his world, and not the center. She was in his dream, but not the dream.

He stood by the open window and let the cool ocean breeze whirl around his body. The wind tossed his hair and Molly, opening her eyes and sensing him gone, saw his form by the window. Seeing the dark envelope him, she felt a pang of fear. It was as though the dark was swallowing him, taking him from her. But you can never have him, she thought. I have his baby, he is forever mine. Cam turned from the window and smiled at Molly. "Awake?" he asked gently. Molly ran from the bed and clutched him. "Cam, Cam, I love you."

Cam stood quietly for a moment, feeling her arms around him. "I love you too," he answered, but his gaze stayed with the night and the ocean.

Mr. Samuel Johnson eyed the man sitting across from him. He was not expensively dressed but he was in the latest fashion. He judged him to be in his early twenties. Aggressive, uneducated, but not unlearned. One of Roosevelt's boys, he thought, same drive, same look in the eyes, cold, unexpressive eyes. Eyes that seek and find answers, but give none in return. But Samuel Johnson knew this Cam Stearns. The look, the feel of him. Here was one not afraid of anything. A winner, for sure. "Mr. Stearns," he began, "Mr. Roosevelt told me you would be here."

He picked up the letter from Roosevelt and let it fall carelessly to the desk. "He says you are one hell of a man and that I should assist you in any way possible.

But first tell me what it is you wish."

Stearns watched the man carefully. Here was a man his senses told him not to play with. By his bearing alone Stearns knew he could make or break many men. "I was in Cuba with the Rough Riders."

Johnson did not speak or show any sign of emotion. Stearns continued cautiously, "and while I was there I saw pastureland as green as anywhere in the world, water for the asking, and cattle."

With this Stearns became braver in his statements. "Cattle that could fatten and be shipped to the states with enormous profit both for the grower and the seller. I need the money for the stake."

Johnson took a cigar from the mahogany box on his desk and offered one to Stearns, who refused. Cutting the end of the cigar with a gold clipper, he lit it and slowly blew the smoke into the air. A dreamer, Johnson thought, but a worker as well. "Ever thought of sugar, Mr. Stearns?"

"Sugar," Stearns said, puzzled, "no, never thought about sugar."

"Think about it, Mr. Stearns, think about sugar and come and see me tomorrow at three."

Mr. Johnson rose and walked to the door. Stearns stood and followed, confused. All the months, all the nights of dreaming and this was all. "At three," he said, disappointed.

Johnson watched him walk through the office. Closing the door, he began to laugh. "It's sugar for you, my country yokel, you don't know it yet, but sugar will be your fortune and mine too."

Cam Stearns walked down the street. He wanted to strike out at something but there was nothing. Just the movement of the ocean town, a few carriage with pretty women and the hum of the stores. "Sugar, sugar," he spat, "what in the hell was sugar?"

Molly saw the anger on his face as he entered the room. She helped him off with his coat and brought him a drink. Smiling, she sat down beside him on the arm of the chair. "How did it go, Cam?"

"Like Shit."

Cam rarely swore in front of Molly and it took her by surprise. Noticing this, he patted her on the leg. "Not like I imagined," he said in a more gentle tone. He set the glass down on the table and rose. "Let's clean up and get Smiley and go eat at one of those fancy restaurants, Molly."

Molly thought that she must be dreaming. The waiters wore full-length tuxedoes and all the people at the tables seemed to be the elite of Ft. Lauderdale society. Ladies with lace and gold and plunging necklines spoke and laughed. Men, dark and handsome, eyed each other's women in only the way gentlemen can.

Smiley watched Molly and felt her excitement.

Cam had been silent through the meal. Not engrossed with the red snapper cooked in pouilly fouisse or the stuffed mushrooms. Stearns felt out of place, he agonized through the meal, being careful to remember which fork to use, and to eat slowly. He felt embarrassed and ashamed, but Molly only beamed at his foolishness. Life is more than a dream, she thought, watching Cam.

Smiley picked up the conversation by making witty remarks about the stuffed shirts and the plunging necklines of the women. Molly saw the gleam in his eyes as he looked at the pale flesh above the necklines. "You need one of those women, Smiley," she joked.

Smiley flashed a smile. "I need what's in the neckline," he laughed, "but not one of these. I'm no fool."

Molly faked a blush. "You'd be perfect with this crowd."

Smiley looked at her and beamed. "No, Molly," he answered seriously. "Not me."

Molly felt the need in Smiley and reached over and patted his hand. "Someday, Smiley, someday you'll find her."

Smiley took a bite of his baked Alaska. I already have, he thought.

Stearns watched the people in the restaurant. They were like the chandeliers, all glittering and crystal. Reeking of wealth and culture. He noticed that some were no more cultured than he, but by the looks of the others in the restaurant he knew that they were wealthy men. It all boils down to how much money you have, he told himself. You could be the biggest clod in the world, and people will fuss and fawn over you. But without the money you are just a face. A small object like everything else in the world. Cam sat, and Molly and Smiley talked. Sugar, and tomorrow at three burned in his mind.

Molly slept and Cam stood by the window looking out at the ocean. It didn't really matter, he supposed. Cattle, pigs, sugar, it didn't matter. If it was sugar that was needed, then sugar it would be. Mr. Johnson was a man of the world, he knew. Who was Cam Stearns to question a man of success. He slipped into bed beside Molly, kissed her on the cheek and fell into a troubled sleep.

Smiley stood at the bar. Earlier he had noticed the stunning brunette by herself in the corner. But thinking she was waiting for someone he had forgotten her and ordered another drink. Now several bourbons later, he looked once more in her direction and she smiled. She was alone. Smiley walked over to her table. "Good evenin', Maam," he said, exaggerating his drawl, which in the future he would consciously hide unless beneficial. He did not want to be known as a hick in Cuba.

The lady looked at him with dancing black eyes and bent forward enough to show him a glimpse of her cleavage. "Mind if I join you?"

"Not at all," she answered in an accent he did not recognize. Smiley sat and looked at the woman. She was in her early twenties. Dark hair that sat bunned perfectly on her head. Her facial features were sharp, blending gracefully into a long, thin neck that seemed to melt into her breast. Her arms were bare and her hands long and thin. "Texas?" she asked, eyeing the stranger.

"Texas," he answered. "Texas born and bred, but not wed."

She laughed at his humor and Smiley felt her knee touch his thigh. She looked at him without moving, her eyes burning into his.

"Your room or mine?" he said, reaching under the table and rubbing her leg.

"Yours," she answered. They rose and walked from the bar. He smelled her perfume and noticed the grace with which she walked. She didn't look like a whore, but who was he to tell. Smiley closed the door behind them. "My name is Roslyne," she said, dropping her purse on the divan. "I'm not a prostitute, if that's what you're thinking. Let's just say I'm getting even."

Smiley watched her as she moved around the room. "I found out about my husband several months ago, but did nothing until tonight. I was sitting at home alone,
knowing he was with his lover, wrapped in her arms. I dressed and came here, to
find me a man and love him all night."

She stopped walking and turned to face Smiley. Her eyes were like coals. Her
long slender arms went behind her back and with one movement she was standing
naked before him. Smiley's breath shortened. She was beautiful. Under her dress
she wore nothing. She slipped the shoes from her feet and walked over to Smiley.
"Love me like you have know me all your life," she murmured. "Love me like I
am yours."

Smiley picked her up and carried her to the bed. He laid her down and took off
his clothes. She opened her arms to him and pulled him close to her. Her mouth
awaited his and they blended into the night, both on fire, both filling a need that
was more than the craving of the body.

Samuel Johnson talked as the smoke from his cigar trailed through the air.
"You've made a wise choice, Mr. Stearns, a wise choice indeed. It's sugar that is
king now. Sugar for cookies, sugar for cooking, sugar for candy, bread, why
everything this country eats has sugar."

Stearns sat looking at the man. He had gone on and on for the past ten minutes.
Ever since Stearns had told him, "do what you think is best." It was as simple as
that. He had walked into the office and told him. "Cattle or sugar, Mr. Johnson, I
need your help."

Mr. Johnson, feeling victorious, had gone into his dissertation on the might of
his choice. Stearns sat slightly defeated, but still better than when he had started.

Johnson continued. "I know a man in Cuba who knows where there are several
excellent sugar plantations for lease. Ever since the Platte Amendment guarantee-
ing us the right to lease land and keep the military in Cuba, large companies have
been moving in and leasing up the land. These two plantations have held out, but
now are up for grabs. If we move quickly, Mr. Stearns, they shall be ours."

Johnson watched the glow slowly rise in Stearns' eyes. Ours, the word ours had
done it. Here was a man who wanted something, something in his own name, not
working for a large company. "You do the work, organize the labor, get the
sugar to the refinery and shipped to specific companies over here and forty percent is yours, Mr. Stearns, and then when you have built up some of your own
capital we can talk about your cattle dream. Live there, see Cuba, learn her people and then build your ranch."

Mr. Johnson stood up from his desk and for a few moments he was not the fifty
year-old-maker or breaker of men, he was not the powerful
president of a bank, but he was Mister Johnson, twenty years ago. Much like Cam
Stearns. He placed the cigar in the ashtray and looked at Stearns. "You have the
drive, the ambition, I can see it written on your face, like Roosevelt must have
seen it. But be careful, Mr. Stearns, go slow, there are years left in your life.
There is a fine line between success and failure. Place your cattle ranch in the
background. Who knows, in several years you may live to hate Cuba, but with
the money you can make and save you will have your chance. I promise you, Mr.
Stearns, you will have your chance."

He returned to his desk and when he sat down he was once again Mr. Johnson, the banker. "You will be manager of the Overland Sugar Company. Who owns it, what owns it is not your business. You pay the workers, keep the books, tend the land and make all necessary arrangements for the sugar. Out of your forty percent you pay your expenses, pay the workers and live. A little work, a little cunning and in a few years you could have the start of a fortune."

Stearns looked at the man. He looked at the fat, pudgy face with the beady eyes. The look of a man too fat, too much good food, too many fine women. Left to make more money and more money until dead. "Why me, Mr. Johnson?" he asked, looking into the face of the banker.

Mr. Johnson laughed, here was a pure son of the west, short and straight to the point. "Let's just say I owe a favor, shall we, Mr. Stearns? And Roosevelt sees you in a dream of his own. Don't you see, Mr. Stearns, you and men like you are Roosevelt's dream. You are the people after the wars who do the real work. After the armies and the killing you tame the land, rebuild the soil for the country and glory."

"But it's not for country or glory, Mr. Johnson," Stearns broke in.

Mr. Johnson picked up the cigar from the asktray. "That's what we all say at first, it's for us and family, but soon, Mr. Stearns, you too will be stuck in the mud and it will be for glory and country. Already you are part of the trap."

Mr. Johnson handed Stearns a brown envelope. "Here are your tickets to Cuba, yours, your friend's and your wife's."

Stearns looked puzzled. How did he know he was married and traveling with a friend?

"Make your friend into something, pay him a good wage. Your ship leaves in two days for Havana. Once there, go see General Wood, acting governor of Cuba. He will be notified and he will take charge of all your needs. I expect a monthly report on all happenings on my desk. It is not an easy undertaking, Mr. Stearns. Tempers still boil, white faces are not greeted with kindness. Cuba is growing, trying, it is a good place to test oneself."

Cam Stearns held the envelope close to his side as he walked down the street. Sitting in the buggy riding toward the hotel he opened the envelope. He noticed the tickets, along with a white envelope. Opening the envelope, he gasped. Inside was five thousand dollars, all in fresh one hundred dollar bills, and a note that read: *"Enough to settle in. My best to your wife. S. Johnson."*

Five thousand dollars! He had never before seen that much money at one time and it was all his. He stuffed the money in his jacket pocket and sat back in the buggy. It was a fine day. The seagulls circled on the horizon and the faint smell of the ocean filled the air. Cuba, sugar and maybe cattle. There was no rush, the cattle could wait. The money settled into his pocket and made his body feel warm.

Samuel Johnson wrote quickly on the note pad. Calling Mrs. Carmichael, he folded the note and watched as her form glided into the room. Send this out by wire as soon as possible.

Cam laid the money face up on the table. Molly and Smiley stood unspeaking. When it had all been placed neatly, Cam began to laugh. "Five thousand dollars, can you imagine?"

They had sold the house for sixteen hundred dollars and the restaurant for eight hundred down, with payments of four hundred a year for three years, and had felt rich, but this, this was five thousand dollars with no strings attached. Some people worked for years for this kind of money.

Molly stood speechless.

Smiley looked over the rows and rows of smiling Ben Franklins. "Jesus, Cam," he finally said, "five thousand dollars, and we haven't even reached Cuba."

General Leonard Wood sat with the sweat pouring down his body. He hated this fucking Cuba. He hated the air, the heat, the humidity and the damn mosquitoes. At least now they had defeated yellow fever. Wood sat drinking Barcardi with lime. A small Spanish boy with a white starched jacket ran up to his side. "Telegram," he said in good English. Wood grunted and took the telegram from the tray. "Get out of here," he said gruffly.

Opening the telegram he showed no sign of emotion. *"General . . . I have found our man . . . more later . . . Mr. Stearns will be in touch within the week. S. Johnson."*

General Wood put down the telegram. Johnson, you old son of a bitch, you old son of a bitch. He stood up from the cane chair. "Miguel," he bellowed, "go fetch me Adelina. Have her make ready my bath."

He staggered down the corridor of the large sprawling hacienda. Soon his wife would join him. His wife with her Virginia bearing and her stuffy attitude toward life. What did she know? he shrugged.

Closing the door to his room he heard the barefooted patter of Adelina's feet on the red tile.

Adelina smiled as he got into the large tub with the hot water. Not until his back was turned did her face change and the lines around her mouth harden. Yankee pig, she thought, one day we will cut your throat and this country will be ours truly.

Wood let the water soak his body and relished the thought of sugar and the company he owned with Johnson. At least his stay in Cuba as puppet governor was not for nothing. He would retire soon, retire a distinguished military man with his Cuba pay filtering discreetly into his plantation in Virginia. "Johnson, you old son of a bitch," he murmured again. "You old son of a bitch."

(I I)

Molly stood on the portal and looked over the gently rolling hills that ran down to the cane fields. She loved this part of the house with the square red tile and the boganvias growing profusely over and around the portal. She would come here early in the morning before the intense heat of the day, and at the end of the day she would return to watch for Cam and Smiley riding back from the fields.

They made an impressive pair as they rode in. Cam with his knee-high riding boots, white pants and white cotton shirt open at the neck, with one sleeve pinned up to cover the stump and the other left long and flapping in the breeze. He had grown a long mustache which he curled at the corners, and wore a round brimmed straw hat that seemed to reflect the sea green of his eyes. General Wood had presented him with the coal black Arabian stallion he rode. A fine beast, prone to fits of anger and bad temper, but one suited to Cam. He was a striking figure and already had made himself a reputation to the men working in the fields. He could be both severe and gentle. He was not one to mess with. Curled from the horn of his black saddle lay his nine-foot whip, and around his waist the black hoster with his 44/40. He had never used either one, but lately with rumors of bandits in the hills and the constant turmoil of the people for independence, he had begun to carry the pistol wherever he went. He looked the part he played, and even though he did not own the plantation, he looked like the regal master of the land. He had given Smiley a share of the dividends and had never treated him as an employee. Smiley had two rooms of the twelve-room hacienda, and ate all his meals with Cam and Molly.

Molly had taken immediately to plantation living. She had two maids, one that cooked and one that cleaned. She could have had more, but told Cam that she needed to have a few things to do.

The humid heat had taken the most getting used to, but after several months and a complete change of wardrobe, it was just part of being alive now. Even the mosquitoes with their constant hum in the evening became a thing of beauty.

Smiley was not the dashing figure Cam was, preferring to dress in the traditional clothing of a Texas cowboy, except for the dagger-like spurs he had picked up in Havana. He was wherever Cam needed him, and seemed to Molly to be the only man who could keep up with Cam's constant drive to improve and make more use of the land.

The year 1900 was a year Molly knew she would never forget. She felt a pain jolt sharply through her side and sat down wearily in the cane chair on the veranda. Bertha, not her real name, but the one everyone called her, saw her sit down. She was a short, rolly polly Cuban lady in her fifties. She was content in her position around the house. She had seen too many revolutions and too many of her children die, to not enjoy the kind treatment and happiness of Molly. Molly would help her cook, and took delight in Bertha's never-ending cheerfulness.

Now, with the baby so close to being due, Bertha would keep one eye on Molly at all times. "The white women, they are frail," she had told the other maid. "At times, I think they need us more than we need them."

Molly sat and placed her hands around her round protruding stomach. "Little fellow," she murmured, "soon, and the world will be yours."

It was funny, during the ocean trip Cam had not even noticed her. Then, they had stayed with General Wood for a week. Each day Cam would be gone for hours, going over paperwork, talking with the General. Meeting growers and planters and people who owned the sugar mills. There was more to do than Cam had imagined. He had been given tours, shown how to keep books and warned about the people.

Smiley and Molly had spent the time touring Havana. What a city. Teeming with Blacks and Indians, Spaniards and Cubans. Great blocks with fruit and chickens and pigs squealing. Sections of large haciendas, and then miles of paper shacks of a poverty Molly had never seen. She had wished Cam could be with her instead of Smiley, and even though she laughed a lot, Smiley could tell she was troubled, "Does he know yet?" he finally had asked one afternoon as they sat in a small open-air restaurant.

Molly picked at her avocado salad. "No, not yet."

Smiley had grown angry. "My God, Molly, why don't you tell him?"

Molly had looked at Smiley, "In time, Smiley, in time."

And then toward the end of the week, Cam had burst into their room. "It's done, Molly, it's done."

Molly was not feeling well, and for the first time could not respond to his excitement. Noticing this, he stood perplexed. "What is it?" he asked.

She looked up at him and began to cry. "I'm pregnant, Cam, and you don't even know."

He reached down and touched her gently. "Why didn't you tell me, Molly?"

She stood and buried her head in his shoulder. "You've been so busy, so excited, it wasn't the time."

He gently stroked her hair. "Molly, I'm sorry."

He pushed her away from him and looked at her. "Stand sideways."

She stood sideways and he looked at her now beginning to protrude stomach. "Yep, you're pregnant."

He picked her up with his one arm, her arms around his neck, and swung her around. "Girl or boy?"

"Boy," she answered.

"Girl," he laughed, "girl with blond hair and blue eyes and a smile just like her mother."

He put Molly back down on her feet and kissed her forehead. "Well, it's time we had a home, Molly. Tomorrow General Wood takes us to our plantation. Everything has been arranged. It's all done, the workers are there, two servants for you. Isn't it grand?"

Molly watched Cam. He seemed so different from when they were first married. She knew he loved her, but at times his drive took him so far away she felt he would never return. She loved him so much that she had forgotten about the rest of her life. It was as though she had no life until him, as though her life had started the day they were married, since then, her love had only grown deeper and more encompassing. Molly was never to learn about men. That their love is not like a woman's.

"Dinner tonight with the General, Molly," Cam said. "Freshen up and wear one of those new dresses you bought."

Cam had given her several hundred dollars to buy clothes, and she and Smiley had gone all over Havana picking out what Cam would like. Thin, lacy dresses that moved with her form. Cam had loved them. "Striking," he had told her.

General Wood had immediately fallen in love with the blond lady from New Mexico. Every evening Cam, Molly and the General would sit and talk of Cuba and America. Lately Wood had seemed relieved, now that Cuba had drawn up a constitution and the Platte Amendment had been passed, assuring America the right to intervene in Cuban affairs. "Let the Cubans have Cuba," he would say. "We own the best plantations, let our military establish a few bases and then let's get out of here."

He would never leave Molly out of the conversation, but would turn and look at her. "What do you think, Mrs. Stearns?" and Molly would reply. The General would laugh, "that's what I like, a woman with conviction. You are very lucky, Cam," he would say, "very lucky indeed."

Cam and Molly stood in the corner talking with a navy commander who had been sent to Cuba to oversee the building of a base at Guantanamo. As the General entered the room, he smiled at the group and took his place at the head of the table. Immediately the guests took their assigned seats. The waiters and maids came from nowhere, and the feast began. First there was gaspacho, followed by a delightful baked fish, and ice cream for dessert.

After dinner, the conversation on the veranda turned to the rebels in the hills. Senor Romane, a leading grower of tobacco in Cuba, was in a heated conversation about the rebels with an American. "Rebels, rebels, every week there is some new rebel with his cause. Feed the people, build schools, but then there is a revolution and it is the same story. The workers will always be workers, they don't need schools."

Molly looked at the American. "But they do," she said, "they do."

Cam shot her a stern look. The General smiled to himself.

"These Cubans," the American continued, "what do they care of their own people? A person with money, power and influence has everything he wants, one without these things, has nothing, but a life of back-breaking work in the cane or tobacco fields. It's the same everywhere, but in Cuba it's more pronounced."

The young navy colonel, quiet during the meal looked at Ramone and broke into the conversation. "Senor Ramone, who will win the election?"

"Palma, Palma will," Ramone answered. "He is a powerful man. With the Spaniards he grew very wealthy. But with his poor background he has many of the people behind him. He will give the people a dream."

"But can he keep it?" Cam asked. Ramone lifted his brandy and took a sip. "That is to be seen," he smiled.

"And if he doesn't, then what?" the General asked.

"If he doesn't, then there will be another revolution and your troops will once again be in Cuba."

The General raised his glass toward Ramone. "Very smart indeed, my friend."

Cam stood and listened to the men talk. It was a strange place, this country. A country of bandits, crooked politicans, landowners and industrialists. Roosevelt had been right, it was a land of opportunity, but it was not a place for a weak man. The weak would soon be swallowed here.

He watched Molly and noticed the glow that covered her face. She loved the dinners and the people. The dashing officers with their uniforms and the ladies with their expensive dresses. She loved the way she was treated and fussed over. It was a good life for her, not like his mother's life. This was the life for a woman.

He was to be a father. He had never thought of it when they were married.

Never entered his mind, but now here it was. Soon he would be a father. He must make good now, now it was doubly important. The wineing and dining would be over tomorrow. The week of being shown ledgers, seeing how cane was planted, the way rows must run, would begin. He drained the gin and tonic and once again his attention focused on the conversation around him.

Senor Ramone was talking to the navy colonel. "Yes, guns are coming into the country. Spanish guns yes, but we have reason to believe that they do not come from Spain. Spain through history has had the reputation of knowing when they are beaten. Why would they send guns? Whoever and whatever sends them are important people."

The colonel looked at Ramone. "Where do the guns go?"

"To the mountains, to be hidden in caves and trees. Already leaflets spread around the country, saying 'out with the Americans.' There is a young rebel named Galindo who moves into the small villages. They feed him, hide him and he gains a few young men from one village and then the next. Already they have destroyed several bridges and robbed some trains."

"Are you worried?" the colonel asked.

"Not from this one," Ramone answered. "He is just a peon. A leader with an education and I will worry, but this one, he will hang and the vultures will eat his flesh."

Molly listened to the men talk and she felt a pang of dread. She looked at Cam and he could tell she wished to leave. He excused them from the room. The men bowed to her as they left. The General kissed her hand. "Enjoy your plantation, Mrs. Stearns," he said. "It is most beautiful."

Molly beamed at the General. "I'm sure it is as beautiful as you say, especially since you have had first-hand knowledge of its choosing."

"Mr. Johnson is a dear friend of mine, and Roosevelt was my company commander during the war."

Molly held Cam's hand firmly as they walked toward their room. "There is so much going on here, Cam," she said, "bandits, revolution."

Cam laughed, "there is much going on everywhere, my love."

She held his hand tighter and thought of the baby. What a life you will see, little one.

_____

The swift sailing ship traveled briskly out of the Florida Keys. The Captain, a large big-boned man in his early forties with a scar that crossed his forehead, let the ocean breeze cool his brow. A few more of these, and Johnson could find himself another man. He would have enough money to go to San Francisco and live by the sea, not on it.

The next day they sailed the coastline of Cuba until just before dark, when they made a heading into one of the secluded coves below Trinidad. He didn't know why they couldn't meet these rebel bastards on one of the many deserted islands that circled Cuba, but he only followed orders. From the dense jungle that bordered the bay a light blinked three times and then was dark. Several moments later, it blinked twice and was dark again. The Captain ordered the fifteen crates brought up on deck, and they waited. Soon the sound of oars dipping into the water could be heard and the ladder was thrown over the side. Six men crawled up the ladder looking dirty and hungry. They were bearded and wore various odds and ends of military clothing. "Where are they?" a hoarse voice said in Spanish. The Captain lit a light and opened the boxes one by one. Laying in neat rows were new Spanish rifles, greased and unfired. "The bullets," the Cuban said. The Captain shook his head. "No, tonight the guns, tomorrow the bullets. The money," the Captain said gruffly. The Cuban searched his face in the light of the lantern. The Captain did not flinch. The Cuban looked at his companion who scampered back down the rope ladder and returned with a box. "Count," the Cuban said. The Captain shook his head no. He knew the money would be there, they needed the guns. Without the money there would be no bullets. What were guns with no bullets. The Cubans grunted, lowering the crates to their waiting boats. "You'd better be here tomorrow," a Cuban muttered, disappearing over the side. The Captain bent over the side and looked down into the boat. "Don't worry, pig," he snarled. Mr. Johnson had picked him for this job because he knew he hated Cubans. He hated Mexicans, and Cubans were worse.

———————

General Wood stood on the veranda and looked out over the ocean. The harbor lights of Havana glimmered in the warm October air. Senor Ramone stood beside him. "Beautiful, no, General?"

The General did not take his gaze from the harbor. "Careless tonight, Ramone," he said, "letting that colonel get you into talking about guns."

Ramone looked nervously at the profile of the General. "There was nothing I could do, General, nothing."

"Don't let it happen again. Even a little slip could spread suspicion."

Ramone sipped his drink nervously. He had gained too much to start trouble now. These Americans with their might and new power, what did they know about Cuba? But they had the money and the guns, and the General was one man who would work for the dollar. Life was nothing to him, all his work for the people had been a mere facade to get Palma into power. Under Palma the U.S. would continue to have her bases and land, there would be no trouble. The trouble was the people, the volatile people of Cuba. Poverty stricken for generations, they would flock to Galindo.

The General moved from the veranda, Ramone following discreetly behind. Turning, he looked at Ramone. "Nothing to Stearns mind you, he knowns nothing. In time, yes, but not now. The planters are just planters now, but soon the rebels will burn and destroy their work and they too will be pulled into our cause.

Ramone looked at the General. What cause, he thought. You are no better than us. In your might, you are no better than us.

———————

Bertha helped Molly up from her chair. "It is soon," she spoke, her dark eyes serious. "Soon the little one will be alive and clinging to your breast. It is a wonderful time."

As Cam and Smiley galloped into the courtyard, he looked toward the veranda but could not see Molly in her usual place. Two Cubans ran and grabbed the reins to the horses, Cam patted the horse and headed for the house. Mary, the other maid, met Cam at the door. "Where is my wife?" he demanded. "She is in the room with Bertha," Mary answered. Cam hurried toward the room, with Smiley taking large steps to keep up with him. "Maybe it's time, Cam," Smiley said.

Bertha came through the door and closed it behind her. Cam started to go in but Bertha barred his way. "It is my turn, now, Senor," she said. "Senor Smiley, you will please take Senor Stearns to the bar." She said as if she was in charge in this matter, and Cam did not fight her authority. As he and Smiley walked toward the bar he said. "God Smiley, it's time."

Both men sat looking out the window. The sun set over the green hills and in the faint glow of dusk Indians and Cubans could be seen walking into their shacks. He had improved the shacks, but they were still very inferior housing. They sat in a clump past the hacienda beside a large grove of pineapple trees.

Molly lay in bed, Bertha had undressed her and placed her large, dark fingers on her belly. "Soon, my lady," she said, "soon I will be back."

Cam and Smiley could hear the commotion as several women came into the house and went to the kitchen. There was much talk and laughter, and then the kitchen was quiet at they heard the women move down the hall to the bedroom. Mary came into the bar, smiling. "Bertha says dinner when you want it."

Cam shook his head. "No, not for me. I'm too nervous to eat."

Smiley, on the other hand, always ate when he was nervous. "Yes," he said.

Mary brought him a boiled chicken, which he devoured while Cam paced and drank.

It had been good the past months between Cam and Molly. When Cam had found out Molly was pregnant, he had paid more attention to her, and Smiley had more time to himself. He oversaw all facets of the work, and squelched trouble before it could begin. He would say, "Cam, why don't you go see Molly?" and Cam would ride off.

Molly had blossomed in the last weeks into a fat, duck-footed balloon, plodding around the house, ill one moment, bubbling the next, and Cam had catered to her every whim. "You spoil me," she would say, "you spoil me."

Cam would smile and place his head on her great protruding stomach. Feeling the tiny feet kicking, he would say, "mean little bastard, whatever it is."

By the time Bertha entered the bar, Cam was drunk and had passed out. Smiley stood by the window looking out into the night. Bertha looked at Cam and then at Smiley. "Just like a man. It is a little girl, Senor Smiley."

They tried to wake Cam, but he would not move.

Smiley entered the room quietly. Molly lay peaceful, half asleep. The sheets had been changed and a tiny headed bundle lay beside her. Hearing the door, Molly turned with glazed eyes. "Cam?"

Smiley stood over her. "No, Molly, he drank one to many while he was waiting, and he passed out."

She smiled up at him. "It's a girl, Smiley, a little girl."

Smiley took the light blanket that covered the baby, and with his calloused hands pulled the cover from her head. It was Molly in miniature, he thought, as he looked at the sleeping baby, her tiny hands knotted into fists. A lump came to Smiley's throat and he looked at Molly. "She's beautiful, Molly. You and Cam should be very proud."

Molly smiled, and her head dropped to one side as she kissed the child's head.

Smiley leaned over and kissed Molly lightly on the forehead. "That's my girl," he said, and left the room.

Cam awoke and it was dark. Smiley was nowhere to be seen. He ran to Molly's room and crashed through the door. A candle burned on the dresser by the bed, and he stopped and walked slowly toward the bed. Molly slept with the small doll-like object beside her, nestled deeply into her bosom. He stood for a few minutes, looking in wonderment at the two of them. A girl, he thought, a little girl. He left the room and walked out into the night. Across the way a few lights could be seen in the worker's shacks, and out over the cane fields a slight breeze rustled the tall cane. It is good, he thought, it is very good.

_____

Estrada Palma took office in 1902 as the first president of Cuba. It was met with joyous partying in the streets. The people drank and cheered for three days. The planters, puppets of the American-based corporations, were too busy with the cane and tobacco to really be involved. The shipping out of the troops bothered them, but small garrisons of American troops were stationed around the area to secure their safety. A permanent naval base at Guantanamo was under construction and it looked as though peace would reign. General Wood shook hands with Palma with satisfaction and relief.

When General Wood boarded the ship for the United States several weeks later, he took his last look at Cuba. Already his accounts were bulging with money from the guns and sugar. It would be a good life in Virginia. Now, after so many years, he could write and fish and spend time with his grandchildren. He was a tired, old man. Tired but content. He had succeeded in the American dream.

(12)

Antonio Alfonso Madrid sat comfortably in the cane chair on the veranda. Elizabeth Ray Stearns played happily in the boganvias, keeping ever mindful of the stares of Smiley. She was nine months old and already a rolling ball of energy, forever keeping her mother and the two maids scurrying about the house. Molly had grown even more beautiful with motherhood. Fussing over the baby, it seemed she became more lovely each day with her love of the child and her love of Cam.

Cam poured himself another brandy and sat down across from Madrid. "Well, I suppose the people are happy now," he sounded weary.

Madrid looked at his American friend and shook his head. "You Americans," he said, "to you life is so simple, so cut and dried. There will be no change. Don't you see?"

He could not understand these Americans. A people who would send men to fight and conquer a country, and then leave with nothing more than a few bases and some plantations. Pouring the spoils of war into the country they left. Captialism, he would snort to himself, you hide behind many disguises.

Stearns finished his drink. "There is change already. Already the workers receive more pay."

Madrid shrugged his shoulders. "Yes, but soon what was once five cents will be a dime, and what is more pay?" Peons will always work the fields, don't you see if you pay everyone the same, then who will work the fields?"

Stearns did not understand all this, politics was not his game. He knew about cane now, already having sent back to the states over nine hundred thousand dollars in pure profit, and putting into his own account two hundred twenty thousand.

Molly took careful account of all the records and had been amazed at the profit they showed. This season had been a loss, but with everything else, Cam would still have over a hundred and fifty thousand in the bank. At times, Molly thought that it was almost too good to be true. Her child grew happy and healthy and Cam was prosperous. There had been several raids on neighboring plantations by rebels over the last months, but nothing serious. She was too involved with her husband and child to become involved with rebels and wars. They were mens' games and of no importance to her. But at times she could see the strain on Cam. He would come in at night, too tired to play with the baby or say much to Molly, eat in silence and then fall asleep.

But when Cam was too tired to pay attention to the baby, it seemed that Smiley never was. No matter how dirty or sweaty he was, he would pick up the child and toss her into the air. She called him "oncle," as she pronounced it. "Oncle," she would say, pointing a tiny finger when she saw him, her blue eyes wide with life. At times Smiley would be playing with Elizabeth and he would look up to see Molly staring at him, a puzzled looked on her face, and at these times she would look away quickly as if to say, I was not looking at you.

In the past months Cam had very seldom made love to Molly, and she would find herself during the day wishing for his touch. She would dream of running naked with him through some secluded area. His reaching her and grabbing her, and their falling to the ground together. But her advances at night were meet with a grunt as sleep overcame him. She knew he worked hard and there were many things on his mind, but she only wished he could forget them for just a few nights. She was still a woman, young and with desires.

Smiley sensed a distance between Cam and Molly, but he never mentioned it. He took on more and more of the load around the plantation, trying to give Cam a break, but Cam would just go to another project, working himself into the ground each day, and continuing to be exhausted each night.

Madrid rose from the chair. "Now you, Molly and Smiley don't forget. In one week, next Sunday at my ranch, there'll be a big party, and you must come. El Presidente is coming. Also the Smiths from Havana and many of my friends. There will be dancing, food, it will be a grand time."

Molly looked excitedly at Cam. "Cam, please, let's go."

Cam smiled faintly at his wife. "Okay," he answered, rising, "we'll be there."

Molly rose and stepped to his side. "Thank you for inviting us, Mr. Madrid," she said.

"My pleasure," he answered, taking her hand and kissing it. "See you Sunday,"

"I'll walk with you to your horse." Smiley said.

Molly moved closer to Cam's side. "Don't go back to the fields," she said, "let's you and I have an afternoon together."

Cam put his arm around her. "Sure," he answered to her surprise, "let me take a bath and then let's go for a walk."

Cam sat in the sprawling living room of the ranch house and for the first time in months, he felt relaxed. As his mind settled he noticed the room around him, and he was struck by the beauty of the house. He sat in an overstuffed red chair, and his eyes scanned over the red brick floor and the white stucco adobe walls. It was a large room, twenty by twenty, situated in the center of the house. Off of this room were doors to the hall which led to four bedrooms and into the dining room with its entrance into the kitchen. Off of the kitchen was a doorway to a small hall that led to two helpers' rooms. He noticed for the first time the woven rugs and little vases of flowers Molly had placed around the room. In the middle of the room on the woven cane rug he saw a small yellow wooden duck, and a pang of regret bolted through his body. It suddenly came upon him that over the past months all he had done was work. From Havana to here, he had spent his days and nights only for the ranch, the cane. The cane grew, the workers worked with no problems and already he had more money than he had ever dreamed of, but what of Molly and Elizabeth? He stared at the yellow duck and heard Molly walk into the room. He stood up and looked at her as she came toward him, and he felt filled with remorse and the love he had known for her in New Mexico flooded into him. "Molly," he said, "I love you so much."

Molly, radiant in a light white cotton dress, looked puzzled.

He pulled her to his side and kissed her lightly on the cheek. "The work, the work," he muttered, "I've been a cad toward you and the baby."

Molly started to speak, but Cam kissed her on the lips. "We need more time together," he said softly.

Molly pushed gently away from his grasp. "Let's go for a walk, Cam," she said, pulling his hand.

They walked out onto the veranda with the boganvias growing over the sides and walked out into the lush yard with the green grass and carefully bordered flower beds. "It's beautiful, isn't it, Molly?" And for a moment Cam was back in New Mexico, and his mother was sweating over the wood stove while his father struggled to stay awake in front of the fire, his dirty and swollen fingers too tired to pull the boots from his feet, and Cam remembered the feeling he would get looking at his father. A yearning, sad feeling. "Always work, always work," he muttered.

"What?" Molly asked.

Cam looked at her. "Oh, nothing, old thought, dear," and he took her hand and they continued to walk.

Molly had always been touched by the beauty of the ranch. Just ninety miles from Havana it lay, sprawling in rolling green hills. There were so many birds that she couldn't identify, and exotic flowers that grew year round. During the day, sitting on the veranda, she would look out and ponder the twist of life that had brought her here with two maids and a lovely child.

"Funny, isn't it, Molly," Cam interrupted her thoughts, "months and months of laying out my cattle ranch and now miles of growing cane. Planted, cut, hauled to the mill. Burn the fields and start all over. Sugar. Johnson was right, sugar it is."

They walked out from the house, past the corrals with the horses and down the lane that ran to the main road to Havana. The cane grew ten feet tall here, and Molly could see the half-naked men working the fields. She had never really seen the hands before. But today, seeing the half-dressed men and women, she noticed the rags they wore for clothes and the utter exhaustion that covered their faces.

Cam noticed her distressed expression. "Just Cubans and Blacks. They're used to it."

Molly looked at Cam. "No Cam, they're people, just like you and me. We could be the ones working those fields."

Cam didn't answer her. What did she know? If Cuba had not outlawed slavery, these Blacks and half-blacks would be working for nothing. As it was, he paid twenty-five cents more than the government proclaimed and didn't beat his help.

Once in a fit of rage when a drunk driver had overturned a wagon of cane, he had lashed out with his whip, but Smiley had caught his arm. "No, Cam," and Cam had looked at him and coiled his whip and rode away. The helper was gone the next day. These people were necessary to Cam, but he didn't regard them like the maids. The maids were part of the house, living, speaking people, but these workers were just that, workers. If they didn't work for him, then they worked for someone else. Other planters he knew treated them like animals, beating them and underfeeding them. Cam fed them well, as hungry workers didn't work to full potential, and he didn't work them on Sundays. Of course, the stable boys did not work as hard, but they were trusted men who had proven themselves better than the others.

Lately he had been pondering getting a driver for Molly and the baby. She shouldn't have to drive her own buggy, and he had even thought about having Johnson ship over one of those new automobiles that were the craze of America.

Although Cam didn't keep contact with many planters, he knew his stature was growing. To the other planters he was strong, hard working and efficient. If he said it, he did it, and through the months Cam had begun to acquire the manner of his position. His walk was brisk, his manner more curt, and what he said he expected to be done. Each morning he shaved and dressed, making sure every button was in line, the shirt sleeve pinned just right. It was as if to say, look at me, I have become somebody.

Smiley had noticed the change in him more than Molly, but Smiley always believed in the old Texas saying, you can't argue with success, and he said nothing. Although he knew Cam was still his best friend, it was as though there was a wall between them now. Cam was the planter, the overseer of the ranch, while Smiley was just a man. A man with a high position, but a man without the entire say, because of Cam's will. Smiley noticed that Cam didn't laugh with him as he did before Cuba or even during the war. It had become business.

At first, Smiley had stayed in the ranch house but then he had commissioned several workers to build him a three-room home at the edge of the cane fields. It was small, but adequate for his needs. He had a kitchen, sitting room and bedroom, and, alone at night sitting in the living room, he would feel contented. People had different drives, what he wanted was not what Cam wanted. He decided one night that there is no one in life like the other. We all go our own way till the grave, and with that knowledge he seemed to grow just a little harder.

Molly watched Cam as they strolled through the cane. He looked like the cane now. Tall, hard, filled with a sweetness. But hidden in the leaves and stalks were the tarantulas, the cane snakes. My cowboy, she thought, what happened to my cowboy?

The sun touched the top of the cane and Molly saw the workers stop their tasks and trudge from the cane. She noticed the cuts and gashes on their arms and legs and the fatigue on their faces. It was a wretched life for them, one without color or change, and she tugged at Cam's sleeve. "Let's go back to the house, Cam."

Cam, seeing the look on her face, turned and they began to walk back.

My home, Molly thought, my world. Inside there are no cane fields, no governments, no life or death, only my baby and my time. She hugged Cam's arm. Time, you have given me time and comfort, my love, she thought. What will happen to us I do not know, but you have given me comfort for now. They walked past the trudging workers and Molly did not see the look of hatred on their faces in the dimming light.

As they neared the house, they could see Smiley tossing Elizabeth into the air and hear her squeals of delight. Hearing them draw near, Smiley placed the child gently on the ground, where she immediately ran to her mother. "Elizabeth," Molly scolded, "you're going to be the death of your uncle yet."

Smiley laughed his light, open laugh. "Not that little one, Molly, but as his gaze went to Cam, his eyes showed there was something on his mind.

Molly, seeing the change in mood, began walking toward the house. "Well, time to clean this one up, and see what Bertha's cooking for dinner. Join us, Smiley?"

Smiley took off his hat and wiped his brow. "No thank you, Molly, not tonight, but I'll take a rain check."

Molly herded the child toward the house and when she was inside Smiley looked at Cam. "Trouble's comin', Cam."

Cam looked at Smiley and his jawbone tightened. "What kind?"

"The workers. Stable boy came to me today. Seems revolutionaries are in the hills and they have been sendin' people in to agitate the workers. They want the whites out, Palma killed and a new government put in. One that's for the people."

Cam turned and spit. "Same old shit," he grunted. "Damn people, don't they know it'll never change for them no matter who's in?"

Smiley looked at the sky. "It's always somethin', can't blame 'em, Cam."

Cam rubbed his head. "No, guess you can't. Arm the stable workers, carry your gun and hopefully nothing will come of this."

Smiley looked at Cam and could see the concern on his face. "It's comin' though, Cam. This time I can feel it. Like the day before the hill and we were all talkin' about the fightin'. You can feel it, somethin', somethin' in the air, something like blood."

Cam started to walk toward the house. "Blood. It follows me Smiley, even Roosevelt knew it. It follows me."

Elizabeth was playing with the yellow duck on the floor when Cam entered the house. He could hear the maid setting the table and smell the spicy smell of enchiladas. Molly beamed at him from the entrance to the dining room. He smiled back and did not show his distress. "A few minutes," she said.

He went and picked up the baby and sat in his chair. Elizabeth looked at him with her great blue eyes. "Daddy," she cooed, poking her finger into his lip. "Daddy," he smiled burying his face into her neck and blowing to make her giggle. They were playing when dinner was called, and Cam had forgotten about the talk with Smiley. That would be tomorrow. Tonight there would be love and sleep and dreams.

(13)

Juan Baca sat on the edge of the cot and looked at his wife and three children sleeping on their cots. His wife showed the toil of being married to a man who only knew cane for 32 years. His children slept in their rags, and although their faces were tranquil in sleep, Juan winced when he thought they had no hope but to be like him. A peon, forever to pick the cane, plant the cane, burn the cane, drive the cane. Long hours, sore muscles and little money. Promises. Promises is all he could remember. The whites were like the Spaniards, shipping the money back to their own country at the expense of his muscles. But it would end, this time it would end. The people, the people would rise up and kill the rich, fat ones and then there would be a life for his children and wife. Full stomachs and good clothes, and for Juan maybe a job in the army as a sergeant. They had told him that. In the new order he would be a sergeant and the people who owned the plantations would be cutting the cane and working all day.

Juan stood up from the cot and walked quietly from the shack. Outside in the darkness he was joined by three other faceless figures. "We go," he said gruffly. The four men walked in the shadows of the shacks and cut into the cane fields. They would be there. They had said so. They walked hidden by the cane for several minutes, then sat down silently to listen. Satisfied that they were not followed, they continued. Near the north end of the cane fields they stopped once more, but this time Juan whistled three times. From the dense undergrowth that grew next to the cane fields came two short whistles. The four men smiled at each other and watched as twelve men walked out from the brush. A short thin man walked up to Juan. They did not shake hands, nor did either of them smile. "What do you know?" The man said quickly, constantly moving his gaze from side to side.

"Sunday, there is a big party at Madrid's, all the big planters will be there, and the El Presidente.''

The thin man smiled a sharp smile that seemed to slash his face. ''Madrid,'' he spat, ''the American loving pig. What about food? Did you bring us food?''

Juan looked away from the man. ''No, there is no food.''

''It is your duty, your duty to give us food, next time we need food. We will be in touch. When the day is right we will burn the plantations and you will no longer work the cane fields.''

The group of men disappeared into the night. Juan looked at his friends and they began the walk back to the ranch. Food, food, he thought, there is not enough for my children, and he speaks of food. He does not work.

In the morning Cam called in Smiley and all the work bosses. The work bosses were hand-picked men in charge of different work gangs. Mostly big, mean men with foul dispositions, they kept the men in line. Cam looked at his six bosses and at Smiley. ''Word has it that there are bandits in the mountains, spreading trouble with the workers. You will be issued pistols and rifles. Keep your eyes open.''

The bosses smiled their large, dark grins. Bandits, what were bandits, kill them, hang them in the middle of town. They had known bandits all their lives.

Cam watched the men walk out of the room. He walked over to his desk. He liked this room. He had had it built the second month they were on the ranch. It was just one room, close to the house. A stark room, with no curtains or paintings on the walls, decorated simply with his books, a desk and the ledgers for the ranch. It was a sanctuary to Cam, a place that was completely his. He sat down behind the desk and pulled out paper and a pen. Writing slowly and deliberately he began:

Dear Mr. Johnson:

   Things are as planned, the losses that were presumed have not been as bad as expected. There has been little unrest in the area but lately there are more and more rumors about bandits. Some can be dismissed but I fear this may lead to trouble. (I only hope you with the power can keep the government in tune with developments over here and can protect us if necessary.) With the drop in sugar this year I wish to propose to you a few changes in the program. I would like to cut back on cane and lay some of the ground into tobacco. The tobacco over here is of superior quality and labor is so cheap that we can rival American tobacco. I would like your feelings on this as soon as possible as the cane will be burned soon and the land ready. All financial records have been forwarded to you for your inspection.

                                                    As always I am, Cam Stearns.

He sealed the letter and rose from the desk. Tobacco had been on his mind for months. Cane was good, it grew, but the market fluctuated and having all his eggs in one basket did not suit Cam. With tobacco there would be two crops. One to fall back on, and one to gamble with in the market. It would cost nothing, a few drying sheds, a few more workers. The profits could be enormous. The risk would be minimal with cane backing the first year.

Cam looked out the window. Bandits, he felt his stomach tighten, don't mess with me, he thought, or you'll end up dead.

Cam stood back and looked admiringly at the buggy, and the two matched white horses harnessed to it. It was beautiful. The deep-grained black wood shone like the night, and the stuffed red leather driver's and passenger's seats looked like they could be slept on. The driver smiled at Cam, feeling secure in his new white pants and brown shoes and his light pressed cotton shirt. Molly came from the house and Cam knew she would be the talk of the party. She wore a long, lace silk dress with a rounded low-cut bodice. A silk shawl fell from her shoulders and set off the double strand of pearls Cam had bought her on his last trip to Havana. Cam wore white riding pants tucked into spit-shined riding boots, and a light brown cotton shirt open at the neck. An open-weave round-brimmed hat sat lightly on his head. Molly was always impressed by the striking figure he cut, as Cam was aware of her impact on men, she thought of the hearts of the young ladies who eyed Cam. He opened the door of the buggy and she got in. He could see her excitement. Smiley stood holding the baby as they left. He felt happy for them, but he had seen Cam put the pistol and shotgun under the buggy seat earlier in the day.

The Madrid ranch was alive with laughter when they arrived. Men scurried to open the door of the buggy, while others led the buggies away. Mr. Madrid and his wife Carlotta greeted them at the door. "Welcome," Mr. Madrid said, shaking Cam's hand. Carlotta smiled, and was immediately taken with the blue-eyed, blond American wife. "Dear one, how the men will flutter tonight."

Cam watched as Carlotta led Molly away into the groups of people. "Women," Madrid chuckled, pulling a long tapered cigar from his pocket. "Come, let me introduce you to many men you have not met."

Cam looked around the large room. It was magnificent. Chandeliers hung from the ceilings and Persian rugs covered the floors. Everywhere maids ran with trays of drinks and snacks. The air was heavy with cigar smoke and talk. Women stood in dresses from Europe and America. Women who were unlike Molly, accustomed to their position in society. In the corner Cam noticed a short, stocky man with black hair combed back severely. He had small, dark, darting eyes that seemed to laugh and calculate at the same time. Madrid, noticing Cam staring, said, "a good man to single out, my friend. The one and only Estrada Palma, El Presidente of Cuba."

Cam looked at the man and the women around him, smiling and laughing at his conversation. He did not like the man at first glance, as there was a heavy and dense feeling about him.

"Come," Madrid said. "I will introduce you."

Palma watched Madrid walk toward him with the one-armed American. As the two men walked up to him, he nodded his head and smiled deeply. "El Presdente, this is Mr. Cam Stearns."

Palma shook hands and felt the strength of the grip of the man. Truly this was a man with which to go slowly. Palma was a great believer in what a man's handshake told about him. He did not introduce the women, nor take notice of them as he talked with Cam. "It is you, senor, who General Wood helped to get the old Marquez plantation. It is a beautiful rancho."

Cam looked at the man, he was shorter than Cam, but he could feel the power in this man. "Yes, it is beautiful."

And by reports, Mr. Stearns, your sugar grows well and your helpers are happy. I am told you pay them twenty-five cents more than the other plantations. This is good, you are for the people as I am for the people."

Cam smiled but thought, you lying bastard, the only people you are for are the people here. But instead he said, "no, Mr. President. I am for my family and the man I work for, Cuba is your responsibility."

Palma looked deep into the green eyes of the one-armed man. Truthful, but no tact, he thought. "Let me assure you, Mr. Stearns, I am for the good of Cuba and without the Americans and their plantations and businesses, there could be no free Cuba."

Palma looked across the room. "Excuse me please, an old friend I have not seen in months," and he left with the the women trailing behind.

Cam looked around the room and in the corner he saw Molly hemmed in by four Cuban men, each trying to outdo the other. He laughed to himself and continued his gaze around the room. It was surprising to Cam, he knew the faces and names of the men, but he did not know them personally. They were cane men like himself, tobacco men, men who ran the warehouses and the ships of Cuba. What Cam did not know was that he was one of the few planters not involved with the politics of Cuba. He picked up another drink from the tray of a passing maid and walked toward Molly.

Halfway across the room, he felt a grip on his arm. "Mr. Stearns," the face said as he turned. His eyes met the same green eyes as his own. The man stood several inches taller than Cam, and was broader in the shoulders. He was dressed in a white suit, and his tie was slightly off-center. His black hair was curly and unruly, and seemed to sprout out of his head in every direction. The man continued. "I know you don't know me, but I've seen you. Hood, Hood is the name. Bill Hood. I ship your sugar for you to Florida."

Stearns smiled. "I know the name."

"I knew a man you were in the army with. A Lieutenant Williams."

Stearns grew excited. "Where is the Lieutenant?"

Hood looked puzzled. "You mean you don't know? He died waiting for the boat. Yellow fever."

Stearns felt his stomach drop. "What?" he whispered. "Dead. He never got to Boston?"

Bill Hood looked at the man. "I'm sorry."

Cam looked into the room, and his gaze went above the heads of the milling people. There was the Lieutenant, a man who hated war, and who saw the exploitation of Cuba. A man who wanted nothing but home, and his wife and children. A peaceful man. He looked into the face of Mr. Hood. "I knew him well, he taught me how to read and write. He pulled me through this. And he pointed to his pinned shirt sleeve.

"He was a good man," Hood said, "we went to school together."

For the rest of the evening, Hood and Stearns talked and drank. They talked of Cuba and sugar, tobacco, the price of shipping and the automobile. "It's coming," Hood was saying at around eleven o'clock, "another revolution. I tell people and they don't believe me, but it is coming."

102

As he took a sip from his drink, Stearns saw four men in dirty clothes and carrying rifles run into the room. One stopped, took careful aim, and blew the brains out of a planter standing beside his wife. The wife, too shocked to scream, stood frozen. Others in the room began to scream, and Cam, scanning the room quickly for Molly, could not see her. He hurled himself over scrambling bodies, and before the assailant could move, Cam buried his drink glass full force into his face. The man screamed, his eyes disappeared forever, and dropped the rifle. Cam, seeing the other three pushing and slashing with their rifles through the crowd, picked up his rifle. The President, he thought, they must be after the President. He heard a shot from another room and saw a man fall backwards into the room where he was. The room was a swirling mass of people shoving for the door. He pushed and kicked his way toward the other room, and seeing one of the bandits, he fired and saw half of his face disappear. Three shots tore high over his head, and he held the rifle under his stub and worked the bolt with his one hand. A bandit ran into the room and fired indiscriminately at the crowd. Cam raised the rifle and shot him in the neck. The body flew against the wall, and low gurgling sounds could be heard as the man strangled to death on his own blood. Running back into the other room, he saw two large men with the last bandit between them. One man held his arm while the other yanked his head back by the hair, a quick blow to his adam's apple and the bandit slumped, twitching to the floor. Cam threw the rifle to the floor and began frantically to look for Molly. He saw her rise from the corner, from behind a woven chair. She looked dazed, but unharmed. He pushed his way to her and held her tightly. "It's okay," he said, as she sobbed into his shoulder. "It's fine, it's all over."

Mr. Madrid called into the room, "everyone please, out to the veranda. There has been an attempt to assassinate the Presidente, but it has been foiled."

He looked over at Cam. Cam led Molly to the veranda. "Bastards," he said under his breath, "bastards," and he swore an oath toward the bandits.

Outside women cried and men who had panicked and hidden tried to pull themselves back together. Immediately Palma came up to Cam. "Senor, I am forever in your debt. Your bravery is beyond reproach. Never, never in my life have I seen such a deed as you did tonight. To take action so quickly. It is above the normal man."

Madrid stood by Palma. "Mr. Presidente, I am so sorry, we did not dream we would need men guarding the ranch."

Palma's two bodyguards now stood like extensions of his own shoulders. "Nonesense, there is no blame, it is only bad that people had to die. I am sorry, my friend, it was your party."

Already buggies were heading down the lane. Cam took Molly and sat her down in a chair. "Cam," she looked at him, but she could not finish her thought.

"I'll be back, just relax, Molly."

Molly watched him leave. She had never seen a man move so quickly in her life. He had killed two men and blinded another. She sank into the chair and slowly the uncontrollable chatter of her teeth stopped.

Cam walked back into the house. The bodies had already been taken away. Mr. Hood stood by the window, sipping a drink. Cam walked over to him.

"Terrible," Hood said, "terrible. The rebels have no respect for the women."

He looked at Cam and Cam could see the respect in his eyes. "Come by the ranch any time, Mr. Hood. My wife would love to see you."

"Thank you, I will," Hood answered, "I will."

Cam left the room and called for the buggy. It was a slow ride home, with Molly asleep in his arm. The sky was moonless, and the stars were shrouded by the clouds.

Smiley heard the buggy and knew it was too early for the party to be over. He stepped off the veranda as the buggy pulled in front of the house, and he could tell something was wrong. Cam walked Molly into the house, and Smiley could see his concern for her. Smiley paced back and forth in the living room until Cam returned. "Bandits tried to kill the President," Cam mumbled, heading for the bar. He grabbed two glasses and poured two shots of whiskey. He walked back to Smiley and handed him a glass. "I killed two and hurt one," he told Smiley, calmly downing the drink. Smiley looked deep into the green eyes, and could see no fear or apprehension, only the embers of aburing hatred, and he felt a chill run up his spine.

Cam fell into the red stuffed chair. "Any bandits on this ranch, anyone seen walking or riding through with a gun without permission will be shot and the body turned over to the authorities."

Smiley drank his drink and did not speak. He had never seen Cam this cold, not even during the war. Although he had been a good soldier, unafraid and daring, he had never been cold, and the shooting and killing had never seemed to set well with him. But now, sitting in his chair looking calm and collected, Smiley felt the coldness that was a part of Cam.

"My family," Cam said, "no one subjects any person of my family to this," and he rose from his chair and strode to the bedroom.

Smiley sat alone in the living room for several minutes. He felt a change in his life, a different mood settle over the house. Nothing on the surface would change. Molly would still laugh, and he would still toss the baby, but there would be a quiet in the house now. A quiet somewhere beneath the din of everyday life.

In the morning, Cam was dressed and shaved as always. Inside the house he was considerate and jovial to Molly, watching her carefully to look for signs of nervousness or apprehension. They did not speak of the night before, and Cam stayed longer than usual at breakfast, talking and playing with Elizabeth. But once outside, he was curt to the stable boy who brought his horse, and meeting Smiley there was no good morning, just an order. "Bring in the workers and get the gang bosses. Tell Pedro I want to see him in my office. Gather all the others by the south cane field."

Pedro was Cam's most trusted gang boss. A soldier for many years and then a fighter in the resistance against the Spanish, he had been one of the many Cubans who helped the Americans during the war. He was given the job after a personal recommendation by General Wood, and he had proved both reliable and trustworthy. He had no family, so he was always ready to work without a grumble.

Cam looked out the window toward the cane. It was a beautiful June day. The breeze blew slightly and helped cool the skin. He heard the knock on the door and said "come in."

Pedro entered, his hat in his hands. He was a large man, with large, dark hands showing the signs of many years hard work. His large and swollen knuckles gripped the hat tightly. Already word of the shootings at the party had circulated throughout the fields. It did not take long for news to travel, and although the number of men Cam had killed varied, it was known that he had killed men.

Cam motioned for Pedro to sit down in front of the desk. Still standing, he said, "I suppose you heard about the party."

Pedro shook his head yes.

Cam sat down behind the desk. "I know there are bandit sympathizers here on my ranch. I want to know who they are. I want you to find out for me, use any means you have to, but keep it low-key. When you have the names, come to me and let me know."

Pedro's eyes narrowed. It was coming, he knew. Soon there would be killing and more killing. He looked at Stearns. "I will do it, Senor Stearns, you can count on me."

"Good," Stearns answered, standing. He eyed the pistol on Pedro's hip. "Keep your pistol handy. Only the gang bosses, Smiley, and I are to have guns. Without guns there are no bandits."

Pedro rose and placed his hat back on his head. "Cuba," he said as he left, "Cuba, she will never change. My people, they are a poor people, they do not understand that they cannot change life."

Twenty minutes later, Stearns rode to the south cane field and stopped his horse in front of the gathered helpers and gang bosses. He looked at each man without any expression on his face. The icy stare made the men's blood run cold. "There are bandits," he said, "some of you may be with them. If you are, you'd best leave my ranch. Any man caught helping the bandits will be shot and his body turned over to the government."

He watched the men, and as he turned his horse back toward the house, he said, "each man is to receive a twenty-five cent raise as of today."

Cam galloped his horse back to the stables. The stable helper, knowing his mood, was extra quick in grabbing the reins. Cam did not speak as he walked toward the house. If it's tough they want, then tough it will be, he thought.

He walked into the house and saw Molly sitting in her chair knitting. She smiled faintly as he came into the room, and Cam could see the fear in her eyes. "Are you well?" he asked, sitting down.

"I'm fine. Still a little shaken, I suppose. What a awful thing, Cam."

Cam rubbed his brow. "Killing is awful, Molly, killing and fighting."

He looked at Molly and thought of Lieutenant Williams and how he would talk about the killing, the war, and the exploitation. It was all the same, different countries, different races but still the same. The same banners and thoughts, the same givers and takers. It seemed so petty but here he was, ready to kill any man who got in the way of his ranch. He would post guards over the cane now. Some men would ride the fences of the ranch and other would be assigned to guard the house. Never again, he swore, never again will Molly be subjected to another ordeal like that. "I'll be going to Havana tomorrow, Molly. To see the bankers and talk to a few men about tobacco. Will you be all right?"

Molly looked at Cam. "I'll be fine, dear."

"Smiley will be here," Cam said, and all the gang bosses are armed. There should be no more trouble, but I have issued the bosses guns just in case."

Cam rose from his chair. "Well, I just wanted to see how you were doing."

Cam walked over to Molly's chair and kissed her on the forehead. Back outside, he went for his horse and rode off to find Smiley.

Smiley was overseeing the cutting of the southern cane fields. Men walked in rows swinging two-foot-long machets that felled the cane. Others followed, picking up the cane and stacking it, while still others gathered the bundles and placed them in large stacks. When the field was cut, wagons would come and the cane would be stacked twelve to fifteen feet high on the wagons. It would then be taken to the refineries where it would be processed into sugar.

Riding up to Smiley, Cam looked at the working, sweating men. "Don't burn this field when it's done, Smiley."

Smiley looked at Cam. "Tobacco?"

"Tobacco it is, Smiley."

It's about time," Smiley said, "one crop ain't enough."

He had never said anything to Cam about tobacco, it was not his place. But he was glad Cam had come to this decision. "Does Johnson know?"

"Not yet, I just wrote him, but he will soon."

"Taking it for granted he will agree?"

Cam looked at the men and their swinging machetes. "He will. I'm going to Havana tomorrow to buy some plows and disks. Watch Molly for me. She's still a little shaken. It was rough on her."

Smiley watched Cam ride away. You should watch her, he thought, and send me to Havana.

By sundown the field was half cut, the men had trudged back to their shacks and Smiley rode up to one of the gang bosses. He looked down at the man. "Tonight," he said, and spurred his horse into a gallop. The cooling evening air made his eyes water, and for a moment he was back in Texas, galloping across the open plain. His mother would have steak and potatoes and after dinner he would sit with the other cowboys and listen to the tales of the early west. His favorite had been the story of the Alamo and the bravery of the defenders.

It was dark when he walked into his house. Removing all his cothes, he went to the rain barrel beside the house, and pouring buckets of water over his body, he washed. Back inside, he shaved and put on clean clothes. He sat down in his living room, opened a bottle of whiskey and drank from the bottle.

At ten o'clock, there was a light tapping on his door. "Come in," his speech was slurred and his eyes were glassy. The young Cuban girl entered and quickly closed the door behind her. She looked about sixteen. Small, with firm young breasts. Her hair was long, and touched the top of her rounded buttocks.

Smiley did not get up. "Take off your clothes, slowly," he told the girl. The girl, remaining silent, looked into the eyes of the man, and she began to undress. She pulled the cotton blouse slowly over her head and Smiley saw the muscles under her breasts tighten and her large nipples seemed to dance. She pulled the

106

skirt slowly down over her hips and stepped out of it, naked.

Smiley stood and walked over to her. He took one of her arms and gently pulled her toward the back door. Standing by the rain barrel, he soaped up a sponge and began washing the girl. The soap-filled water ran in riverlets down her brown body. Back inside, he lay her down on the bed and took off his clothes. It isn't love, he thought, but that doesn't dull one's desire.

The train ride to Havana always exhilarated Stearns. Sitting in the first class coach, he would marvel at the countryside. The run-down shacks and the poverty never seemed to enter his mind, just the land and the lushness of it all. What a beautiful country, he would think. He never entered into conversation with the other passengers and most, seeing his stern expression, didn't bother to try and talk to him. In Havana he stayed in the best hotels, and during the past months he had learned how to eat, what to eat and what wines to drink. Although he had seen many fine women he did not bother with them. Other women never entered his mind. Aside from the small part of him he left open for love, the rest of Cam Stearns had become business. His daughter would go to a private college on the east coast. His wife would forever live in comfort and have the best he could afford. He would stay in the best places, eat the best food and ride the best horses. He did not need other women to talk about with the men, and besides, sex had never been a very strong drive for Cam. His drive to be prosperous and self-sufficient had always seemed to possess him.

In Havana he would buy the necessay equipment to plant tobacco, arrange for the seed, and look up Mr. Hood. Of all the men he had met in Cuba he felt he could grow to like Hood. There was something about him, something like himself, he supposed. That look in the eyes, or the way he stood away from the crowd. He did not know why, but he would contact him for dinner one night.

He had not thought of killing the two bandits since it happened. It had happened too quickly and he had been like an animal, quick to react and forgetful of the dead. It had to be done, and it was done. There was nothing more to think about.

The train chugged through the Cuban countryside and Cam reached into this pocket and pulled out a finely tapered black cigar. Lighting the cigar, he let the smoke roll in his mouth and blew it out slowly. It was the first cigar he had smoked in his life, and it was good. In Havana he would buy several boxes, and from this day forth people would see him with a cigar.

Bill Hood paced back and forth in his office. At times he wished he had never taken this job. Stearns walked into the office and saw the disarray of ledgers and paperwork piled high on the desk and in every available space. "Shipping," he laughed as Hood turned.

Hood saw Stearns and a large smile crossed his face. "Cam," he said, moving across the room and extending his hand, "good to see you."

"I came into town to buy a few things, and thought I would stop by and see you. How about lunch, I catch the train back tonight at seven, so I have a few hours."

Without hesitation, Hood grabbed his straw hat from the rack in the corner and the two men left the office.

Stearns was amazed at the number of ships in the harbor. "Different than a few years ago," he observed.

Hood looked at the ships. Sugar, tobacco, machinery, Cuba was on the move. The black figures in and around the docks moved in a steady flow like large, black ants. The docks were stacked high with boxes and crates of every description. "I know a good place, not too fancy but close," Hood said. "Cold beer, and fish. Just pretend you're back in the army, and not a distinguished planter."

The bar was several blocks from the docks. Men lined the bar who looked like dock hands, while other in suits sat at tables. The air hung heavy with cigar smoke and the place smelled of beer. It was hot and muggy inside.

They sat at a small table by the window looking out at the street. A large mulatto woman waddled to the table. "What you need?"

"Beer," Hood answered, "and fish."

She waddled back to the bar and Hood looked out the window. "Docks, not too friendly," he said.

Stearns looked at the man. He looked haggard and restless, not calm and rested as he had the night of the party. "Been a rough few weeks, Bill?"

Hood brought the beer to his lips and drank greedily. "Same old shit. Ships and more ships, lost cargo, stolen crates, insurance people always on your back, deadlines, bad weather, you name it. But the hell with me, how is it on the ranch since the trouble?"

Stearns drank slowly, eyeing the men at the bar. "Nothing, nothing lately. The wife seems to be okay."

"Good," Hood replied. "What else is new?"

Stearns reach into his shirt pocket and pulled out a cigar. "This," he said, "tobacco. I'm going to grow some tobacco."

Hood watched as Stearns lit the cigar and blew the smoke into the air. The two men stayed for several hours and talked of Cuba. Hood was under the general impression that there would be trouble soon. Rumor on the docks was that the workers were about to revolt. Men wore guns under their coats and kept rifles in their homes and offices. Somewhere there were agitators spreading leaflets and sending men to talk to the workers. Palma was the target, the people were already tired of his rule. There had been no change, the slums had not disappeared.

Stearns agreed, placing his empty beer glass down on the table. He looked at Hood. "It takes guns. Someone is arming them. Who it is must be found out. Without the guns and bullets there would be no bandits, no revolution."

Hood avoided his gaze. "Yes," he muttered, "but that's a big thing to do. Look at the coastline, a million harbors, a thousand small uninhabited islands to ship to."

"It's planters and shippers," Stearns said, "it's moneyed men who want more money. Men with millions to gain in the confusion and unrest in this country. Men who can buy influence and power during the takeover."

Hood saw the tightness in Stearns jaw. "They should be shot," Stearns continued.

Hood did not answer but looked quickly at his watch. "Well, friend, I have to get back to the office."

Stearns stood and shook hands. "Come out to the ranch, Bill, looks like you need a break."

"I will, I will," Hood answered, pushing his chair back to the table. "Good luck, keep your pistol ready."

Stearns laughed, "I always do."

Sitting at the table alone, Stearns ordered another beer and looked out the window. It was guns, somewhere among men he knew, it was guns. A deal, a small tax on the sugar and tobacco, a new order. He drank the beer and left the bar. Walking down the street, the thought of Molly and the child. For a brief moment a dark loneliness spread over him, but two men fighting in the street caught his attention and he quickened his pace and hailed a buggy for the train station. It had been a good trip. The tobacco seed would be on the way, and the bankers were more than happy with his profit. Several disks and plows were to be shipped with the seed to prepare the soil. Tobacco must be cultivated, unlike cane that was cut and laid in trenches. Stearns spit the cigar butt from his mouth and watched the hustle and bustle of Havana pass him by. It would be good to get back to the ranch and back to the country. Shipping and bars were not his cup of tea. He felt closed in and clammy.

(14)

Samuel Johnson sat in the leather chair looking out over Biscayne Bay, Florida. The sun sent red slivers of light through the large white clouds. He raised his hand and pointed at the windows, and a Black man hurried over and opened them. He loved the sunset here. They were like none in the world, peaceful. They seemed to give him a few moments of rest each day, which, God knew, he needed. This business of guns was becoming more than he had bargained for. What with the sugar, and the letter he had just mailed off giving Stearns the go ahead on the tobacco, he was amassing a great fortune. But, always, now there were the guns, and there was no turning back. He only wished there was some way out. Now there had been two shipments lost, supposedly delivered but never picked up by the right people. He hoped it was the Cubans themselves, but he had a feeling it was the Captain. After all the successful runs, maybe the greed was catching up to him. He would know soon.

The peaceful sunset would be no more when Juan Maldanado came. God, he hated to think of that man. A big, fat, greasy Cuban, runner of prostitutes and anything else that could turn a profit. He would never forget that day in his office. The money was gone, spent on all the wrong things. Oh, Johnson looked good, rings and clothes, a beautiful home, but the investors' money was gone, and he had no choice. It was the end. And then out of nowhere had come Maldanado with information that Johnson trusted with no one. A cunning, evil man, he sat looking at Johnson and said simply, "guns my friend, you ship them and your friends will not find out the bad news," and Johnson had jumped at the opportunity. He knew nothing, just the times and places where his ship should be. The burly captain he chose was a good man. A smuggler for years, he didn't care what the cargo was, as long as he got his pay. Johnson had pulled him in after slavery in Cuba was outlawed. "No more niggers," the captian had spat, "no more money," and he had been recruited. It had gone well for a while, General Wood took his bite, and Ramone his small percentage. But Johnson did not fully realize the character of Maldanado. Maldanado sold guns to anyone who wanted them, politics did not interest him. Now he was selling guns to the new revolutionaries who wanted Palma out, and Johnson was still in the middle of the trap.

Maldanado walked in and saw Johnson. He swaggered over to a chair and sat down with a grunt. Johnson forced a smile and waved for the waiter. The thin black man in black trousers and short-sleeved starched shirt walked over and bowed, "Gentlemen?"

"Rum," Maldanado grunted, Johnson shook his head no, and the waiter left.

"Unfortunate," Maldanado said, not waiting for formalities. "It is your captain."

Johnson felt fear surge through his body. Maldanado looked out the window. "Beautiful, no? The way the sea swallows the sun with no trace. Next week you will need a new captain, Senor Johnson," he sounded sinister. The waiter returned with the rum. Maldanado grabbed the glass with his fat hand. He gulped the rum and looked at Johnson. "Send your ship in two days."

He placed the glass back on the table and rose. "Good evening," he said with mocking eyes. "The new captain, you make sure he is trustworthy, or maybe next time it will be your turn."

Johnson looked out the window and shuddered. How did he get involved with this? It was turning into a nightmare. It had been easy to explain to General Wood his situation. Maldanado did offer a percentage of the profit, but then Palma was elected. How was he to know it would not end. Now it was guns for the people who wanted Palma out. And now the ship captain had stolen shipments. Johnson's nerves were on edge.

Smiley watched the buggy carry Cam toward the train station. He looks the part, he thought to himself, and the touch of bitterness in his thought frightened him. He looked across the yard and saw Molly and Elizabeth wave goodbye, watched them turn and walk into the house. The rest of the day he rode the fields and told the gang bosses that the cane would not be burned this time. Cut it off at the ground and leave the root. He left the fields early and took his usual bath behind the house. Washed and combed, he walked over to the main house and knocked on the door. Molly answered the door and smiled. "Come in, Smiley."

Smiley followed her into the living room and could not help but look at her back and dress as it moved around the curves of her body. She was the most beautiful woman he had ever known. Sitting down, Molly called the maid. "See what Smiley wants to drink."

"Nothing, thank you," Smiley said.

Smiley sat in the red stuffed chair and looked around the room. A regal feeling came over him, and he seemed to lose all the warmth he had felt for his small house. Here was a house, a beautiful woman, a child, and for the first time in his life he felt left out and used. Cam had everything, while he worked just as hard, and had nothing.

"Isn't it hot?" Molly broke his thoughts.

Smiley looked at her and the low-cut bodice of her cotton dress. Her blond hair always seemed to halo her face, and her blue eyes cut into his brain. "Hot as ever," he answered. He looked at her hands folded neatly in her lap.

Molly rose and walked to the window. "It's beautiful, isn't it Smiley? The green, and the color of the sky."

Smiley rose and stood beside her. "Yes," he said, looking out past the corrals and the edge of the cane left standing. "It is beautiful."

Molly turned to face him. "Stay for dinner, Smiley."

"I'd like that, my cooking gets a little old."

Molly laughed. "You need a lady, Smiley."

Smiley walked back to the chair and sat down. Elizabeth, up from her nap, ran into the room. "Oncle, Oncle," she giggled with glee. She ran and jumped on Smiley's lap. The child always filled Smiley with happiness. It was as though the world was no more, and the small bundle of joy and warmth crept inside of him. She was a beautiful child, and at times he felt she was his. Molly watched the two play, and laughed with the joyous cries from Elizabeth. "You two," she said, rising from her chair, "I'll go tell the maids to start dinner. Why don't you and Elizabeth go outside and play? She loves the stables."

Smiley picked up the child and hoisted her to his shoulders. "Come on, Elizabeth, let's go see the horses."

Elizabeth wound her fingers in his hair and they walked from the house toward the stables.

Molly watched Smiley carrying the baby toward the corral. She had not seen much of Smiley lately. What with the house and the baby, she only saw Cam for fleeting moments. She would see Smiley talking to Cam by the stables or riding off with him in the morning, but they had not had good long talks like before they came to Cuba. But seeing Smiley today, she noticed that he seemed older and graver. His smile was not as spontaneous and his jovial nature seemed to have hardened. We have all hardened, she thought to herself, from the bandits, the work. She was at times amazed at the change in her life, and some mornings when she woke up she felt as though she should be dressing and walking to the restaurant.

The last few days she had thought of New Mexico and of Poncho and his wife. She wondered how the children were and how the restaurant was doing. Today, standing by the window, she missed the sound of Poncho in the kitchen and the customers coming in the door. Life had been simpler than, in many ways harder, but the problems were smaller. Now, with Cam busy most of the time, she missed the association with other people and the small talk of customers as they ate and passed on the local gossip. She had not written Poncho, although the bank had received the draft for the payment on the restaurant. She told herself she would write tonight and tell them of Cuba.

The fear from the incident at the party had left her. She dismissed it as a bad dream, but still feared for Cam's safety, which she hadn't thought of before. He was a prosperous planter in a strange country. She could understand how the people of Cuba could grow to hate intruders in their land, that was only natural, but she knew Cam was a good man and was not out to purposely exploit the country.

The violence she had seen him display during the night of the party left her more shaken than the actual incident. He had been so swift and unafraid, as though there was a sleeping monster in him. A monster waiting and needing to kill, requiring excitement and blood to be fulfilled. The way he had acted so cold and unemotional after the incident, left her with a feeling of dread.

She did not confuse herself by trying to sort out the happenings of this life in Cuba, but turned more and more to her child and home. She placed more flowers in the windows and wrote notes to herself about things that she wanted to buy for the house. As the land was Cam's life, the house and flowers were Molly's. She could lose herself in each room, dreaming of rugs and paintings and making sure the house was neat and peaceful for Cam, when he came home.

Through the months she had discovered there were many things she did not know about Cam. Little of his childhood, except that he was raised on a ranch his parents had lost. She knew that his parents were dead that they had been poor, but little more. When she asked him about his early life in New Mexico, he would look at her with that certain look he gave people when they came too close to matters he did not want to discuss, and she would stop her questioning.

Molly turned from the window and walked to the kitchen. The maid stood over the long table, singing a soft song Molly had never heard. She was rolling tortillas, and flour covered her hands and apron. She smiled, seeing Molly. "Dinner good tonight," she said, "for you and the child."

"Make enough for Smiley too," Molly told her. The maid rolled the dough. "It is no problem, there is always too much."

Smiley pushed the empty plate away from him. "Delicious."

Elizabeth, already dressed for bed, was whisked away by the maid. Molly and Smiley sat in the dining room. "It's strange without Cam here," Molly said. "Would you like an after dinner drink?"

Smiley looked across the table at Molly and agreed. They rose and walked to the living room. "Gin and tonic?"

"Fine. Are you having one?"

"No, I don't think so," Molly answered.

Smiley sat in Cam's red chair. It would be easy to grow accustomed to this. Delicious dinner, fine house, a beautiful lady to look at and keep your house for you. Cam seemed to have everything going for him. Prestige, power, comfort and a home. Smiley once again felt the unfamiliar pang of envy.

Molly sat in her chair. "Well, how has life been treating you, Smiley?"

Smiley sipped his drink. "It's good over here, Molly," he said, hiding what he had just been thinking. "Cam has really made this plantation work."

He is a worker," Molly said, "driven, almost."

Smiley looked at Molly. "He's a very lucky man to have you, Molly," and Molly caught the gentleness in his voice.

"Well, thank you," she answered, disguising the small amount of alarm in her voice.

"I'd give ten years of my life to have what Cam has now, and he wants more."

"He wants a place of his own, Smiley, with you as his foreman, you know that. Cam will never be satisfied until he has a place of his own. Some men just aren't meant to work for others."

"And how about me?" Smiley asked, a tinge of bitterness in his voice.

Molly looked at Smiley, a little embarrassed. "Please, Smiley, don't. Your time will come."

Smiley set the glass down on the end table by the chair and stood up. "Thanks for dinner. I'd better be getting back to my house."

Molly walked him to the door. "Good night, Smiley," she wanted to reach out and touch his face. She watched as he disappeared into the darkness. Watching him walk away, she sensed a loneliness about him, and a strangeness that she had never felt.

———————

Captain Morrison pushed his curly black hair from his eyes. This load he would deliver. As of yet he had heard no report that Johnson was on to him. Two shipments of guns were delivered. If they didn't get them to where they were supposed to go, what did he know? His man, an insider in the bandit group took them somewhere. What he was telling the bandits, he didn't know, but the money in his account in St. Louis had jumped from the total take on two loads.

The ship bobbed peacefully in the calm water of the bay. His signal light had been answered and soon he would hear the sound of the oars as the boat drew near for its load of guns. He had sworn earlier he would make no more loads, but this paid even better than slaving, and the money was worth the extra few months. Soon he would just sail off with the last load, scuttle the boat on the coast of America somewhere where the authorities would find it, and settle in San Francisco. It was all going so well. He had more money than he dreamed of, and he could spend his last days in comfort.

The small wooden craft bumped against the side of the ship. Four men scrambled over the edge, carrying a small wooden box.

"Where's Alfonso?" the Captain asked.

"Sick," one of the men mumbled. "The guns?"

The Captain pointed at the crates on the deck of the ship. One man opened one of them and nodded his head in approval.

"And the money?"

A tall, thin Cuban handed the Captain the box. Holding the box, the Captain noticed a difference in weight from all the others, and he opened the lid. A look of sheer horror spread over his face, as he saw the open eyes of Alfonso's head staring blankly into his. A small cry began to emerge from his lips, when the roar of the shotgun blew his head off. The crew stood in shock as the Cubans lifted the headless body and tossed it in the water. Unspeaking, they lowered the guns to the waiting boat and scrambled over the side. "Stupid American," one said, "he did not know Maldanado."

They laughed as they neared the shore. This shipment was free. A gift from Malanado for the Captain's treachery.

It had been a long time since Stearns had thought of Roosevelt, although he had voted for him for President and was happy when he won. But here in Cuba, the United States seemed far away, even if it was only ninety miles. But sitting on the train, he had overheard small talk about Roosevelt. It seemed people were either for him, or violently opposed to his administration. Two men sitting across from him carried on a heated debate. "It's none of our business," one man said, "we are not guardians of North America. Look at last year. Venezuela owed money to Germany and England and Roosevelt warned them that if they used force we would have to interfere. He almost plunged us into a war over a country most of us don't even know exists."

The other man looked out the window in exasperation. "Don't you understand? We can't have foreign countries getting strongholds close to our borders. He did the right thing."

The man toyed with the end of his mustache. "No, never. He had gone too far."

Stearns smiled to himself. Good old Roosevelt, if there was trouble, look for Roosevelt. If nothing else he was no coward. Stearns made a mental note to write Roosevelt, although he doubted that he would receive an answer. It was strange how a man could have such a great influence on his life, and then never be in touch. President, Stearns thought, President of the United States, and he could see Roosevelt sitting in his office, making men jump and squirm and afterwards looking out the window and chuckling to himself.

Smiley sat on his porch and watched the lights of the main house slowly blink off. He watched Molly walk back and forth in front of her bedroom window. He did not mean to peek, but as he watched, Molly stopped by the window and began to undress. She unbuttoned the front of her dress and Smiley felt a great surge of passion sweep over his body as her breasts fell from their covering. Stepping lightly out of her dress, she stood naked, except for a thin white half-slip. Molly leaned her head back and ran her fingers through her hair, stretching her full, white breasts. She shook her head and pulled the slip from her hips. Smiley watched her naked white skin, glimmering in the light of the room, and he was nearly overcome with desire. Molly stood for a moment, looking out into the darkness, and then pulled the curtains. Smiley sat motionless on the porch, drained by the longing he had felt.

It was past midnight when Cam got to the house. He went to the bedroom and undressed quietly, watching Molly's sleeping form. Standing by the bed, he shook her gently. She rolled over, and seeing him, smiled drowsily. "Cam, you're home."

He leaned over and kissed her, running his hand over her warm bosom. He lay down on the bed and Molly curled into his side. For several minutes he ran his hand up and down her spine until he heard her breath deepen. Then, gently kissing her eyelids, he raised her nightgown and slowly kissed his way to her breasts. When he entered her she groaned with delight and as he climaxed her hips rose to take in all of him.

They slept late in the morning and Elizabeth was dressed and fed when they came into the kitchen. Smiley knocked on the door and could not help but show surprise when Cam answered. "Smiley," Cam greeted him happily, "come in, come in."

Molly came into the room and Smiley saw her and framed in his mind the picture of her naked in the bedroom window. Tonight he would wash the young Cuban girl and make love to her, but he would be kissing Molly's breasts, and feeling the warmth of Molly's thighs as she moved with his movements.

(15)

Carlos Galindo sat on a stump and wiped the grease from his hands. A small pig lay on a blanket of leaves while men cut chunks from the cooked body. It was safe here, high in the Sierra del Trinidad mountains. The lush overgrowth of the jungle rain forest was a perfect place for him and his men. Galindo watched his men file by and cut the chunks of warm pig flesh. Some of them were boys still in their teens, and others were old men, but all were united in their fugitive life. It was a hard lot of men. Men from the cane fields, men from the docks and tobacco plantations. They dressed in assorted remnants of army clothes, or the clothes of the peasants. But there was one difference. They all carried the newest weapons possible. New Spanish arms and a few new American automatic weapons. Tucked off from the camp in a crude hole dug in the ground and covered painstakingly with overgrowth, were over fifty thousand rounds of ammunition.

Galindo had hand-picked this select group of men. Men he had known growing up in his thirty-five years, and others he had heard of. Most had been in jail, and all were staunch enemies of Estrada Palma.

Over the past year his group had slowly grown until he had sympathizers in every corner of Cuba. First, proceeding cautiously, they had moved into the shacks of the planters and spread their propaganda, calling for armed revolt, and the need for food and clothing. Their call spread slowly, until now with the people beginning to lose faith in Palma, Galindo knew it would only be a matter of time until his men gathered for their push to power.

For years he had dreamed of this. Once in his early twenties, he had seen the El Presidente's palace in Havana, and the dream had begun. One day he would be there. A leader of his people. He alone would bring this nation to power. He would expel all foreign businesses and bring Cuba back to her people. A tall powerfully built man, with a deep resounding voice, he had no problem moving his followers. He ruled with an iron hand and took little, if any, insubordination. A traitor was shot without question, a man not able to keep up with the rest disappeared into the dense jungle. He had his most trusted men under him, each in charge of a squad of men who reported to him daily.

Already he had moved one squad into the rich land west of Havana, and another into the southernmost tip of the island. Weekly he received reports through runners of their success in recruiting men.

Three more gun shipments and he would have enough weapons for his purpose. With his men armed and the workers with clubs and knives, he would bring a new order to this land. It was his destiny, and it governed his every action.

He sat and watched his men eat. It was a powerful feeling to stand and watch the men devour his every word. They would move out to death or glory at his beckoning. Under him the resistance had grown and become strong. Under him the streets would be filled with blood, and one day he would stand at the top, the milling crowds of Havana screaming his name in admiration.

He rose from his log and walked through the camp. He nodded to the men as he passed them, some jumped to their feet and saluted. Those of the men who did not love him feared him, but Galindo knew that, at times, fear was a better mover of men than love.

Lying down in his tent, he fought the irresistable urge to begin. To order the workers to burn and destroy. But he knew it was not time. Six months, a year. He must wait, he must control his desire to blunder forth and conquer. He knew there was a fine line between victory and defeat, but he also knew he could not rule with only peons. He must spread his word to lawyers and doctors, planters and professors. It took more than a handful of men and a dream, it took brains, and Galindo prided himself on having brains. He had taught himself to read and write after the long hours in the fields. Sitting by a candle, the hum of mosquitoes around his head, he poured over the books. He had men who could read and write give daily lessons to his men. He raved on and on that education was the key to freedom; that words and books would control after the battles were done. But most of his men were simple people. Without him they would wander back to the plantations and work the fields, without him they were nothing. Strange, he smirked before falling asleep, "I, the lion, need the sheep as the sheep need me."

Antoinetta Saavedra cranked the handle of the hand printing press. She must finish soon. Already other students waited to pass out the pamphlets calling for the end of Palma and the expulsion of the Americans. She was a beautiful girl. Small, barely five feet tall, with long straight black hair. Her lines were straight, except for her large breasts that would have fit a woman twice her size. She had used her attributes well enough to seduce the editor of the college newspaper, and when the time was right, threatened him with telling the president of the college unless she could use the press. He had looked at the girl and consented. What would his wife say? The shame, seduced by a student. From here she ran off the pamphlets that appeared on the streets and on the docks.

To her there was only one love. Carlos Galindo, hiding in the jungle, his picture posted all over the cities by the government. Three thousand pesos for his capture, dead or alive. She would sleep with anyone she had to, but she would love only one man. She knew Carlos had other women, farm women who fell at his feet with admiration, but this was a war, and during a war life was different. There was only one rule. The means did justify the end.

Finished with the press, she looked with dark shining eyes at the stack of leaflets. Placing them in her large shoulder bag used for carrying books, she left the office. In the dark, on the campus, two male students walked up to her. One of them, taking the bag, smiled and said nothing. The other reached out and pinched her on the bottom. Antoinetta lashed out with her long nails, and raked the side of his face. The student yelled in pain. "I am not your whore," she spat in his face. She walked away from the two students. "Pig."

The student with the bag looked at his companion holding his face. "Do not play with her, friend. She is Galindo's lady. He will cut your balls off."

The young man held his face. "I did not know."

"It is good for you that you found out now."

The two walked from the campus. They had work to do. The pamphlets must be delivered. By noon they would be around the city, and it did not pay to tarry. Anyone caught with such propaganda would surely die before the firing squad.

(16)

Cam stood by the window of his office and looked at the bales of tobacco being stacked in the drying sheds. It was December 5, 1904. Elizabeth was now 4 years old, and was already quite the young lady. From the troublesome twos she had developed more and more into a look-alike of her mother. He blond hair, still alive with baby sheen, sparkled and bounced as she played. Although Cam bought her many toys, she was more and more drawn to the stables, and whenever there was time, she was allowed to ride the gentler horses.

The past years had merged in to one short moment for Cam. The tobacco crops had been excellent, outselling the sugar by two to one, and the care and time he took picking the better leaves for choice bales had paid off handsomely for himself and Johnson. He had doubled Smiley's pay, and more and more Smiley took complete care of the fields and hands as Cam was called into Havana for business meetings. It seemed as if, he always needed new machinery or had to have talks with buyers to assure them they would receive his crop.

Several rebel sympathizers had been discovered by Pedro and promptly reported to Cam, and they were rounded up quickly and turned over to the authorities. What became of them he did not know, he was just happy that they were found out. The rebel situation had somewhat died down over the past months. There were still incidents that occurred in various spots around the country, and a growing unrest against Palma, but there had been no major uprising. Word still circulated that the black workers on the docks and plantations would revolt, but Cam could not see how they could organize enough to not be taken care of quickly and efficiently.

Bill Hood had become a regular visitor to the ranch, finding a refuge from his hectic and never-racking job in Havana. He had started to drink heavily lately, and both Cam and Molly were concerned over him, but it seemed that no amount of talk could keep him from the bottle. It was as though he carried a deep dark secret that he could tell no one, and it was slowly eating him away.

The ranch now carried eighty workers and eight gang bosses. Forty men worked the cane, and forty the tobacco. Far more efficient railroad lines had been developed in the area and Stearns's sugar and tobacco found its way to Havana more quickly.

Cam had begun toying with an idea, to set up a cigar company in Florida with Johnson, but had not yet written him about it. It seemed reasonable to Cam that if they established their own company, they could regulate the price and so compete with any market in the states, and rake in enormous profits.

The Bay at Guantanamo had been completely finished and housed both army and navy personnel. It was a comfortable feeling to the American businessmen that the government kept them protected, and many had fallen into a false sense of security. Cam, though comfortable, had maintained rigid discipline and kept his bosses armed, along with himself and Smiley.

One event in the past months bothered him, though. A ship in Johnson's fleet had been stopped and searched by navy patrol boats, and eighteen crates of new, stolen weapons had been seized. Although Johnson had filed a theft report on the ship, therefore releasing him from all blame, Stearns still wondered at times. Johnson was a powerful man. Friend of many government officials, he was in a prime position to supply weapons. He had no proof, but it had left a sour feeling in his stomach.

The ranch was newly equipped with a telephone, which greatly helped in business, but it seemed to never work. He knew it made Molly feel more secure, and when he was gone on his trips to Havana he called every evening.

Cam stepped away from the window. It was his birthday, and looking in the mirror that hung on the door he laughed to himself. He was twenty-nine years old. The past five years of his life had been like a dream. Scanning the bookshelf that lined his office was like scanning the past five years. He read extensively in his free time. Westerns, history, the new psycyology books. His hunger for the written word would never diminish. Of all the happenings in his life, his ability to read would forever be a turning point.

Molly had wanted this birthday party for Cam. There was always so much to do it seemed that she very seldom got out. Bill Hood and Smiley and the Madrids were coming, and a lady who Bill had spoken about. "Maybe he's in love," Cam had said to Molly. "Every man should be in love," Molly had answered.

Molly was now twenty-five, and it seemed to Cam that she was more beautiful than ever. Although she took no interest in the ranch itself, the house was renowned in the area for its beauty. She had carpeted the floors with carpets from America. Paintings that Cam knew nothing about covered the walls. Photographs of their family filled in any empty places. She had commissioned a photographer to come to the ranch and spend a day taking photographs. Cam had complained the entire day, but now when he looked at the pictures he felt happy.

This year he had promised Molly that they would have a normal Christmas. In past years, Christmas had been a ragged affair, but this year there would be a tree and presents, and a big dinner. "For the girl," Molly had pleaded, and Cam, looking into her blue eyes, had consented. Christmas had never been much to him. As a child it was nothing. Just another day of work, until the afternoon when his

118

father would stop, and they would open a few gifts, mostly handmade, and then go back to work. He remembered once his father had bought a new dress for his mother, and opening the present his mother had begun to cry. He was too young to understand then, but now looking at his home, he knew how wonderful it must have been to his poor mother.

Cam walked outside in time to see Bill Hood and a beautiful dark-haired Cuban lady climb out of their buggy and walk toward the house. Bill was already sitting down and drinking rum when Cam entered the living room. "Well, you made it," Cam said, entering the room, and eyeing the slim woman sitting on the divan.

"How could I miss the most prosperous planter in Cuba's birthday?

Cam sat down and looked at Molly. Smiley walked into the room from the kitchen. "Beautiful," he drawled. "first time in years I've seen a cake like they make in Texas."

"Smiley!" Molly scolded, "keep your mouth shut."

Smiley feigned fright and sat down. "Me and my big mouth."

Bill stood up and said, "Everybody, this is Miss Linda Cortazar." Cam stood and shook her hand lightly. Molly seemed pleased, Bill had found a woman.

The Madrids arrived shortly, driven by their driver. "This hay machine is going soon," Mr Madrid grumbled, helping his wife down from the buggy. "I've ordered myself one of those new automobiles from the Americas."

"What type?" Cam asked.

A Stanley Steamer," Madrid said proudly. "Can you imagine movement without horses?"

"Call me as soon as you receive it," Cam said, "I'd like to see it."

"I know, I know," Madrid laughed, "then you will buy six of them."

Sitting in the living room the men talked about automobiles. Molly, seeing the boredom on Carlotta's and Linda's faces, quickly asked them outside, saying, "let me show you my flower gardens."

Madrid was saying, "they will have a tractor that will be practical in Cuba."

Tractors had been produced as early as the 1870's, but they were not practical for use in Cuba, because of the rain and mud. They were large steam-driven creatures. Horses had been the mainstay of Cuba, but Madrid and others saw the beginning of a new age. "It will come," Hood agreed, "gasoline powered tractors, able to do the work of forty men in less time."

Stearns sat and listened to the conversation. If tractors were in the future, he wanted a part of the action. He would contact Johnson and see what was necessary to set up a distributorship for tractors in Cuba. The first one gets the cake, he thought to himself. Tractors, and parts to fix them, would make a fortune in time.

The conversation lulled into the ever present talk of the rebels, and the slowly eroding power of Palma.

Molly, Carlotta and Linda walked slowly through the immaculately manicured flower gardens. During the first year in Cuba Molly had left the flowers to the maids, but now she alone tended the flower beds. Painstakingly digging perfect rows, she mulched and planted all the native flowers she could find. Large and small river rocks bordered the flowers, and set them off from the paths that wound in and around the house.

During all the seasons there were flowers, and there wasn't a morning that Molly could not stand from a window in the house and see the sprays of reds, blues and yellows. The ladies admired the flowers and talked of the latest dresses from America and the wonder of the automobile. "Simply amazing," Carlotta said, "a machine that moves by itself."

"For the life of me I will never understand," Linda entered the conversation whenever possible. She was a slim, dark-eyed woman who seemed alive and bubbling with life. The daughter of an important planter before the Spaniards, she was away in America when her father and mother were killed and the plantation burned. For several years she had walked through life in a daze, but the pain had subsided, and now she seemed eager to regain her lost time.

She had met Bill at a party for an important shipper in Havana and they immediately developed a mutual feeling for each other. At times she felt she loved Bill Hood, and could think only of him, but at other times, seeing the admiring looks of passing men, she questioned her thoughts.

She liked Molly, and was taken by her beauty. When she was introduced to Cam, she had felt a wave of passion run through her body and was glad they had left the room and walked among the flowers. But even here with the two women, she could not completely drive from her mind the green eyes and the upturned mustache that seemed to make his eyes pierce her soul. Of all the men she had known, she could not think of one that impressed her like Cam Stearns. She had heard the stories of Stearns, of his bravery and viciousness the night of the President's assassination attempt. So, when Bill had asked her to come, she had been more than willing to make the train ride from Havana and the short buggy ride from the station. She had pictured Stearns larger than he actually was, and with a more vicious look about him. More like a one-armed freak. But instead, she had seen a handsome, rather quiet man, and the fire had spread down over her breasts, to rest between her thighs.

Coming back into the house through the kitchen, the ladies could hear the men laughing and smell the foul odor of the cigars. "Cigars," Molly complained, "if anything, I just wish they would smoke those awful things outside."

Carlotta feigned a look of anguish. "Molly, it is impossible. It is like a little boy told to wipe his feet at the door."

The three men stood around the bar when the ladies entered. Molly carried a large white frosted cake with twenty-nine candles on it. They began to sing happy birthday, and Cam could feel the red rising from under his collar. He did not remember ever having a birthday party in his life. Elizabeth looked with wonder at the candles and ran and held Cam's leg. During the singing, Smiley glanced at Linda, and was impressed by her beauty. But behind her eyes and dark lashes and the small, thin cut lips he could see trouble. He looked at Bill holding her close to his side, and thought to himself, each man to his own poison, and he forgot about the Cuban woman from Havana.

After they had finished their cake, the men sat on the veranda while the women disappeared upstairs to look at a bolt of cloth Molly had received from the states.

"Did you hear Roosevelt won another term?" Hood said.

Cam looked at Smiley and both men smiled at each other. Cam had never written Roosevelt, and did not even think about the election. There had been men around for Americans to register for the vote but he had not been home, and anyway tobacco and cane were the only things on Cam's mind. Funny, he thought, so many things escape one in life.

"He won by two and a half million votes," Hood continued.

Cam looked at the glass of Kahlua in his hand. The last time he had seen Roosevelt was in Havana as Roosevelt stood on the deck of a ship. He was surrounded by admirals and generals who received small clusters of applause when they spoke. When it was Roosevelt's turn, the crowds had gone mad. The sailors and army men alike threw their hats into the air and it had taken some time to quiet the noise. Roosevelt, obviously moved, wiped his eyes with a handkerchief and stood silent for several moments. "You are my pride and the pride of our nation," he told the men. "Let us all forever live in freedom." And he had turned and walked into the ship. Cam had stood and looked at the emptiness he left behind, and it was as though a door had been closed in his life. From Roosevelt he had gained strength and courage to tackle life and not fear losing. Through his association with Roosevelt he had become a true man, and when he thought of him as President of the United States, he would always feel that if they met again one day, Teddy would smile and laugh his deep, boisterous laugh and shake his hand with the strength and conviction he always had. "See Cam," he would say, "see, it is only the heart and the will to succeed."

When Cam returned his attention to the converstation, Madrid was saying, "Roosevelt, he is a very great man. He knows there is no recourse now but for America to go forth and establish her power around the world. Have you heard what he did in Santo Domingo?"

Cam looked puzzled. "No," he answered, and he told himself he would order American newspapers and begin to keep up with more than his ranch.

"He has sent people in to take over the customs of the country to repay their European debt."

"Bully," Smiley broke in, "Bully for him," and he and Cam laughed at the inside joke.

"Also," Madrid continued, looking slightly confused, "he has been negotiating with Panama to buy a large cut of land that stretches from the Atlantic to the Pacific Ocean. He proposes a large canal that would connect the two oceans by a series of locks that would greatly save time and money in shipping. He is a man of action," Madrid said admiringly, "a true man of action."

Cam stood up from his chair. "To Roosevelt," he said, raising his glass.

"The power of your country grows with leaps and bounds," Madrid said, sitting down. "Your destiny had been spurred by the will of this man."

Cam sat and remembered the room at the Montezuma Hotel. "We are men of the same mold, Mr. Stearns," Roosevelt had said, "men driven to be what we are not, men to lead and in so doing to be led. It is not our calling, it is our destiny."

This ranch, the money in the bank, everything in one way or another was because of Roosevelt, and Roosevelt had never asked for anything in return. He wondered if Roosevelt ever thought of him in Cuba.

Smiley got up from his chair and walked into the house. He returned with a green wrapped package, which he handed to Cam. "Happy Birthday, Cam."

Cam looked at Smiley and opened the box. Inside was a new Colt 38. A beautiful pistol, with ivory grips and his initials, C.S., engraved on the outside of each grip. He picked up the pistol carefully and looked at the deepness of the blueing. "Thank you, Smiley," he said slowly, "thank you very much."

"Oh yes," Smiley said, going back into the house. He returned with a thin, hand-tooled belt that was surrounded with bullets. A holster hung from the belt, also hand-tooled in flowing flowers. Cam placed the pistol in the holster and could say no more.

Hood and Madrid eyed the beautiful set. Madrid gave Cam a box of cigars rolled especially for him in Havana, and Hood gave him a small gold clipper for cutting the ends off the cigars. "Thank you, thank you all," Cam muttered, finding it hard to speak his mind.

Madrid changed the mood by standing. "Well, let's shoot the pistol."

The four men walked out past the stables and set up a large board, on which Hood drew a circle the size of a silver dollar. One shot apiece. Cam loaded the pistol and handed it to Smiley. "You first, friend."

Smiley stood and took careful aim. The pistol kicked in his hand and a small dot could be seen slightly off center and to the right of the circle.

"Well done, well done," Madrid laughed, "but now watch this."

Madrid took careful aim and a dot appeared inside the left edge of the circle and high. He looked with satisfaction at the circle and handed the pistol to Hood. Hood, not accustomed to guns, missed the board entirely, to the amusement of the other men.

Stearns rested the balanced weapon in his hand. He looked at the circle and raised the pistol. It came to line like an extension of his arm. He squeezed the trigger and the small dot was directly in the middle of the circle.

Madrid faked exasperation. "I should have known."

Smiley watched Cam fire the pistol and for a moment he felt the same feelings he had held for Cam during the army days. The past year he had busied himself in the work and the raise Cam had given him, and kept the envy he felt at bay. He did not get close enough to Molly to stir the hidden feelings, and his life had stayed on an even keel. But he did not feel the old love for Cam until he watched him raise the pistol. My friend, he thought, I should be grateful.

Cam put the pistol in the holster and the men walked back to the house.

The women, hearing the shots from Molly's bedroom, had run to the veranda. Seeing no one around, they scampered back inside where Molly had grabbed a rifle and positioned herself by the door. Then they heard the men laughing and nearing the house, and she lowered the rifle in relief. Entering the house, the men saw her walk back toward the corner with the rifle. Molly looked at them seriously. "When you're going to shoot, you should tell people."

Carlotta stood in the corner, several shades lighter. "You inbecile," she yelled at her husband in Spanish, "such a fright you gave us."

Bill looked at Molly. "If you call holding a rifle being afraid, I'd hate to see you all really scared."

Later in the evening Bill and Linda were shown to their room and the Madrids, also staying over, were shown to theirs.

Cam walked into the bedroom. Molly lay in bed covered by a light cotton sheet. He undressed slowly and crawled into bed. Reaching over he touched Molly's naked skin. "Happy Birthday," she whispered softly as she moved into his side.

Linda Cortazar grabbed Bill as soon as they entered the room. Dropping the suitcases to the floor, she began to rub him through his pants. He tried to move, but the intensity with which she touched him soon had him standing with his arms around her shoulders. She unzipped his pants and pulled his swollen member out. Slowly kneading the flesh he could hear her groan. She lowered herself to her knees, and he could feel the slow, deliberate touch of her tongue. "Oh my God," he swallowed, as she took him into her mouth.

By mid-morning the guests had left and Cam sat in the office. He had written a letter to Johnson, and along with small talk about the ranch, he mentioned the idea of a cigar company. He told Johnson he would like an answer as quickly as possible concerning the matter. He also mentioned in passing his idea of a tractor distributorship in Cuba, along with a parts supply.

He was slightly disturbed this morning. Walking from the kitchen, he had met Linda. As he had stepped to one side, she had bumped against him and rubbed her breast into his shoulder a little too firmly for it to have been an accident. "Excuse me," he had said. Linda had only lowered her eyes and continued walking. Trouble, he thought to himself, and he felt fearful for his friend. Saying goodbye to Linda and Bill, he had seen the happiness on Bill's face, and he had felt ill at ease the rest of the morning.

Smiley had seemed like the old jovial Smiley when they met at the stables. He had worried Cam a lot lately. Smiley was subbdued, and never seemed to want to come to the house. His work was beyond reproach, but it seemed he was not the same person who could always lift Cam's spirits or make him forget the day. But today he had laughed and told a few dirty jokes to the stable hands. Cam knew that he was a hard man to get close to, but of any man alive Smiley should know this and never doubt Cam in his intentions.

Sitting on his horse about to ride to the fields Smiley had looked at Cam. "You know, Cam, it's almost nineteen hundred and five. Seven years since the war. It doesn't seem like it, does it?" and he had ridden off. Cam watched the back of the man he had known for so many years. Cam had never known a man so long. Sometimes he didn't know what he would do without him.

(17)

Galindo pushed the naked girl from his side. "Enough," he said gruffly. The girl reached and raked her nails slowly over his naked stomach. "Enough, I said," and he shoved the girl roughly from his cot. She landed with a thud on the ground, and grabbing her clothes she dressed quickly. The men around the campfire laughed as she came from the tent and disappeared into the jungle. "If nothing else," one muttered to his friend, "Galindo has fucked his way across Cuba."

Galindo came from the tent naked to the waist. He was a powerfully built man, and his muscles shown in the glow of the fire.

For eight days now he had camped with ten of his most trusted men in the hills ten miles from Havana. It was dangerous he knew, and each day brought a greater strain on him. But he must wait. Antoinetta would come, her message had been distinct. Meet me at the corner. The corner being this dense, mosquito-ridden overgrowth ten miles from Havana. She would never send such a message if it was not important.

Galindo grabbed a bottle of rum from a man sitting by the fire and took a long drink. He handed the bottle back without speaking and stared into the coals. The men had left him alone lately. A dark and vicious mood had settled upon him. Although there had been many raids, cutting phone lines and telegraph lines, derailing a few trains with their shipments of tobacco and sugar, Galindo had been in a bad mood. He had even kicked a man for no reason.

Antoinetta with her students had recruited many young men and women to the cause. Each week pamphlets made their way to the streets and shacks of the plantations. Although there had been many students arrested and tortured, they had never revealed any information, and the press still operated.

During their last meeting, after he had made love to her and she lay smoking in the bed, she had said, "there are many ready to die for you Galindo. Upwards of ten thousand people in Havana alone live for the day you tell them to start."

Galindo had reached over and touched her still hard nipple. "All in time," he said, "all in time. I need the military. Without them there is nothing, they will kill us with their tanks and guns. The soldiers will mow down the students like grass, and all the years will be for nothing. We are nothing but a fly without the army. No matter how many trains we derail, how many telephone lines we cut, they are repaired in a day and the Americans grow richer."

"I will get you the military," Antonietta had said, looking into the dark eyes of Galindo. "How are your peasant whores?"

He rolled on his back and laughed. "How are your students and professors?"

The next day Antonietta began carefully inquiring about the military. After several weeks she found a student sympathizer who had a brother who was a sergeant in the army. Luckily for the rebels, he also was dishonest, and looking for more in life than the trifling amount of money the army paid him.

First there had been the sergeant, then a lieutenant, then a captain in charge of many tanks, until soliders were carried over to the upcoming revolution. Babies, Antoninetta would think, lying beside the sleeping form of the army captain. So much power, one word and men will blow buildings apart at your command but because of these, and she would touch her breast, I have brought you over.

The captain and Antonietta had taken the train like any two young people on a Sunday trip to the interior. But after renting horses they had headed into the back country, and the picnic lunch they carried only served as an excuse to check the trail behind them. The last mile they had walked as quietly as possible and when a menacing "halt" split the night, Antoinetta said the password and they were escorted by three armed men into the camp.

Galindo rose, and Antonietta ran and hugged him. He looked suspiciously at the man with her, but said nothing. "My tent," he said and the captain, looking at the menacing stares of the men, was relieved to enter the tent. "What brings you?" he said bluntly.

"This is Captain Louis Rodriguez, tank commander of the third tank regiment. He has come to swear his allegiance to the revolution. He says with just a few days' notice he can surround the high command of the army in Havana and force the surrender of the commanders."

Galindo looked at the man with a stern glare, but then he let his face soften into a large, toothy grin. "My friend," he said, as he embraced the man, "It is good to find a man for the people."

The captain returned the embrace. "Colonel, after the revolution," he said cautiously.

Galindo nodded his head. "Of course, of course. Antonietta will be in touch. Now my men and I must move, it is dangerous here."

The two were escorted back to their horses to make doubly sure there had been no followers. As soon as they were gone, Galindo ordered the camp broken. "We will travel by night and leave this area."

He walked quickly through the night. Tanks, with tanks he could surround the President's palace and demand his surrender. With tanks he could fight the army and cripple the railroad. Time, time, he thought, soon, but not yet.

Now he would need politicians, and he had just the man. Senor Ramone, he thought with a vengence. Most trusted of Palma's aides. Now fat and jealous. Hiding his dreams of glory, always overshadowed by the pompous Palma. He would come. With promises of riches and power he would turn the government slowly against Palma. And when he had done his treachery, Galindo himself would shoot him. A traitor is never a man to be trusted.

Galindo stopped and looked at the stars illuminating the night. Surely the heavens were with him. These years in the jungle were for a purpose. He could see his face on billboards across the nation and hear his voice echo. The glory of Cuba would be his. Children would read of his bravery in school, and mothers would pray for his salvation.

———————

Theodore Roosevelt turned his swivel chair from behind the massive oak desk and looked out over the light of Washington Avenue. He rubbed his head wearily and glanced at this watch. As he turned, a knock on the door echoed through the room. "Come in," he said, rearranging a stack of papers on his desk. Two men entered his office, one a Cuban. The two men had been ushered into the White House secretly. There were only a handful of men who knew of Roosevelt's secret organization. A few very carefully selected men who ran a network of men in many countries around the world. Five in Costa Rico, eight in Panama, three in Cuba, sixteen in Venezula. Men who were in every walk of life, but all men dedicated to the United States. Roosevelt stood and shook hands with both men.

Mr. Arnold Stone was plump man of about fifty. A man who could have been anyone's happy grandfather, he was actually head of the intelligence network in Cuba. Working as an American newspaper reporter, he wrote articles that bordered on being trivia, but to those who knew, inside each article was coded message to the Commander in Chief.

Louis Rodriguez was a captain in the army. A dedicated man, and one who felt the future of Cuba lay solely in the hands of America. Rodriguez had important news. He had met Stone in a seedy downtown Havana bar and told him firmly. "I will speak to the President, and the President only."

Eight days of hectic maneuvering by Stone had arranged this late night visit. Rodriguez looked at Roosevelt. Roosevelt motioned for the men to sit down. He walked behind his desk and sat down wearily in the chair. Looking at Rodriguez, he said, "Well?"

Rodriguez looked at his hands and began to speak. "I have been contacted by the rebels, and after many months I was taken to meet the leader. His name is Galindo, as we all know, and he thinks I will bring my tanks to his aide when he gives the order for the revolution to begin."

Roosevelt leaned forward in his chair. "Go on."

"There are many students on his side. His most trusted aide in Havana is a woman named Antonietta Saavedra. By seducing a professor at the university, she has gained access to the printing press, where she prints all the leaflets that filter through the country. There are many groups affiliated with Galindo now. Men on the docks, men with the workers on the plantations. He will kill the Americans. He wants no one but Cubans controlling Cuba. He is a ruthless, resolute man."

Roosevelt looked at the captian. "Thank you, thank you very much. What you have told me will save many lives and insure the continued prosperity of your country."

The two men rose and were quickly escorted out a back door of the White House. Several hours later they were on a private ship for Cuba, where they would land without papers and be back to work without anyone noticing they had been gone.

Roosevelt walked toward the bedroom. Intelligence came daily from Cuba. He knew Johnson had been blackmailed into supplying ships for illegal gun running and that his main shipper in Havana, a Mr. Hood, was now being squeezed by Johnson. Since Johnson's ship had been seized, the guns that were being shipped were unloaded in Havana in falsely labeled crates. From there, Mr. Hood was meeting the rebles and exchanging the weapons for money.

Roosevelt had had Stearns checked out thoroughly, and found to his relief he was not involved. From the reports, Stearns was now a prosperous, hardworking planter in tobacco and cane. He had a child and his foreman was also ignorant of the deeds of their employer.

For now there would be no action. Specific army and navy personnel in Cuba would be alerted and men would be made battle ready. When it did start, it would end quickly. Roosevelt only wished a man could find and kill Galindo. Without the brain, there is no threat. He had discovered the actions of General Wood years earlier but Wood was an old man and retired, and he had left him alone. But now he would send a messenger to Wood with enough accusations that the old

General would tell Roosevelt the names he needed. When the time came, every bad apple would be weeded from the orchard. Roosevelt lay on the bed. Stearns, he thought, and a smile came to his face.

Retired General Wood sat in a rocking chair on the porch of his two-story sprawling Virginia home. In the acre or more front yard, his three grandchildren played. It was a brisk December day. The wind whistled through the trees, but the children were undeterred by the cold. The women were inside unpacking the stored tree decorations for the tree raising tonight. General Wood was old and comfortable.

An automobile chugged and spit up the winding driveway and stopped in front of the house. A man in his early thirties, Wood guessed, got out of the car and walked to the porch. "General Wood," he began as though he was Santa Claus, "I have a letter for you. I am instructed to let you read the letter and then hand you a paper and pen and an envelope. You will write your reply on the paper, fold the paper and place it in the envelope which you will seal."

Wood wanted to protest, but by the look in the man's eyes, he knew there was no use. He opened the letter the young man handed him, and read it. When he had finished, he said in a hoarse whisper. "The pen and paper please."

He wrote for only a few seconds, folded the paper and sealed it in the envelope. The young man placed the envelope in a leather folder. "Thank you, sir," he said briskly, and walked hurriedly back to the automobile.

Wood watched the auto disappear from view. "My old, dear friend," he moaned, "for all this time you have known."

He rose wearily and slowly from the chair and walked into the warmth of the house. His eldest daughter, mother of two of the grandchildren, looked at him lovingly from in front of the fireplace. "We are so lucky papa, so lucky to have such a beautiful Christmas."

The old General sat down in his chair. "I should have known, Roosevelt," he muttered half aloud, "I should have known."

Roosevelt opened the envelope and unfolded the piece of paper. In jerky, sprawling handwriting it read simply . . Senor Ramone. He set the letter down on his desk. It was hard to lose an old friend. One with whom you had served in a war. It was hard and it was sad. Roosevelt left his office and walked to the living quarters of the White House. The children would be there laughing and playing and his wife would be there. They would all be waiting for him to begin the tree. It would be a good Christmas this year, a very good Christmas.

Cam sat and watched Elizabeth's glowing face as she placed the assorted colored ornaments on the tree. Molly, dressed in a blue dress, beamed with love, seeing the child run back and forth from the box of decoration to the tree. Smiley drank his rum slowly and let the warmth of the house envelope him. "To Christmas," he said, raising his glass. "To Christmas and good friends."

Molly toasted her sherry and Cam his kahlua. They were together and it was Christmas. Bertha brought cookies from the kitchen and they all ate and went to bed filled with love and peace.

(18)

Estancia Martinez stood on the steps of the church and watched the milling crowd. For weeks, pamphlets had circulated around the campus calling for the demonstration against Palma. The turnout had been far greater than he expected. Well over three thousand students jammed the street in front of him. Stretched out sheets portrayed Americans strangling poor helpless Cuban workers. Uncle Sam, looming as a giant, trod on Cuba, while blood dripped from an open heart. Posters depicted Palma with his pockets bulging with money as he watched American ships sail from Cuba, the decks piled with goods. Other signs read, *Down with Palma, Out with America.*

The rally had begun at nine in the morning, with several hundred students chanting and singing. By noon, the mob pulsated like a giant ocean wave, and at two o'clock, it was a swirling, out of control mass of people. Soldiers with rifles and fixed bayonets began to blockade the city blocks around the students. A few brave men and women ventured forth from the safety of the crowd and threw bottles and rocks at the soldiers.

Soon the rally lost all remnants of control, and the windows and houses of the district came under attack from frantic students. Buggys and carts were overturned and the cry 'Kill Palma' shrieked through the streets. Estancia Martinez pleaded with the ones who could hear him to stop, but soon it was of no use as the mob lost all control and began to spill out into the neighboring streets.

The army officers, seeing the fires start, ordered the men to fire. Volley after volley of rifle bullets tore into the students. In a few short moments many students lay moaning and groaning in the street. Others lay twisted and contorted, a look of disbelief on their dead faces. The mob, once brave and boisterous, suddenly felt the fear of death and began stampeding in upon itself from all directions. Each wave of people met another wave closing in upon them, trying to escape the whine of the bullets. People fell and tried to stand, but were trampled by more and more feet. Screams of pain and helplessness replaced the cries for the death of Palma and the ousting of the Americans. Next the soldiers brought in the dogs and troops with helmets and clubs. Soldiers fell back and formed a corridor that let the crowd burst running down one street. As fast as the soldiers advanced the students ran back toward the university.

Three hours later the cleanup began. A hundred and seven killed by rifle fire, seventy-four trampled to death, and hundreds of superficial wounds.

Estancia Martinez hid in the cellar of his friends. They would search for him now. But his greatest fear was Galindo. Galindo would be very angry over the useless slaughter.

El Presidente Palma stood by the open windows of the palace and watched the last of the fires flicker away. He shrugged his shoulders and walked back into the room. Several generals and other military men paced back and forth in the room. Senor Ramone sat and toyed with the drink in his hand.

"Stupid, they are so stupid," Palma exploded. "Do they not understand that without America there is no Cuba? Without money there is no advancement, no hospitals. Dreams and dirty rebels hiding in the mountains do not cause change, only more killing."

Palma looked at the generals who had no answers. Ramone stood up. "El Presidente, it is nothing, do not trouble yourself, they were only students, just radicals with not enough life to understand the complexities of our country."

Palma turned sharpely to face Ramone. His dark eyes lashed out, "better we should have killed them all and torn their hearts out for the dogs. I want a detailed account of this and the names of the people who organized the rally. Another incident and I will place Havana under military law and make it a crime to venture forth during the night."

Palma looked at his generals. "This will not happen again. The next time, I want it stopped before there is time for trouble."

The generals looked at each other nervously after Palma had left the room. Ramone poured himself another drink. General El Diago Marquez smiled thinly at Ramone. In time, he thought, you will be El Presidente, and I, I will be supreme commander of all the military. It is good, he thought, to kill a few, it is good. Now they will know to wait for the right time.

Senor Ramone sat in the chair in his bedroom. He looked in the mirror that hung over the divan opposite his chair. "You will make a fine Presidente," he said to his reflection. Behind him he imagined the cries of joy from the people, and he could see Palma's face as he tried him and sentenced him to death. He would see him hang and then would have his body dragged through the streets of Havana. He finished his drink and walked to the bed. Galindo, he thought, with me you have the army, without me you will die like the pig you are.

Three days after the riot Galindo received the news of the killings in his mountain hideout. "Stupid, stupid," he raved on and on. "People dead for nothing, the army alerted, Palma now will sense the growing mistrust against him. There will be more soldiers combing the mountains for us." He walked hurriedly to his tent. "Tomorrow I will send for Martinez, and I will personally cut off his balls."

Antoinetta Saavedra played with the hair on Captain Rodriguez' chest. She bent her head and playfully bit his neck. "My captain," she cooed, "soon your tanks will surround the city to the sounds of the cheering of free Cuban people."

The captain reached over and squeezed her firm, mellon shaped right breast. He pulled her over on top of him and kissed her nipple. Antoinetta slid her thighs over him slowly and thightened the muscles of her vagina. Pumping ever so smoothly, she smiled with satisfaction when he came. "Like a soldier," she murmured, "hard, and strong like a soldier."

The captain opened his eyes and looked at the girl. You stupid little bitch, he thought, it will be too bad to turn you over to the authorities for them to take pleasure. I hope the revolution is far away so I will have many more nights like this.

(19)

Molly stood by the bedroom window and looked out toward the stables.

Smiley and Cam were standing by the corrals, engaged in what seemed to be a heated debate. She knew Cam was disgusted by the way he would talk and then look off toward the horizon. He had always had this manner about him. Once angered or disgusted, he would never look at the person talking to him.

She turned from the window and walked toward the kitchen. She knew she was pregnant again. Having missed her second month there was not more doubt. At times the news made her exceptionally happy. Elizabeth would have a brother. There was no question in her mind that the child would be a boy. But at other times, the thought of being pregnant left her empty and feeling alone.

The last months had been very good. Cam played with Elizabeth more and seemed to be around the house for longer periods of time. He had taken more interest in Molly and brought her presents whenever he went on business trips. She had a pair of exquisite diamond earrings, several gold bracelets and a tiny gold heart pendant which she wore around her neck at all times.

Cam had been more interested in lovemaking than he had at any other time of their lives. And though Molly on the outside did not appear to be a passionate woman, she and Cam both knew the intensity with which she made love and the warm glow it left around her. To her, sex was an important part of life. To Cam, until recently, it had only been an afterthought at the end of a long, hard day.

She wondered if news of the new baby would once again throw Cam into his work with less time for her. Sometimes she felt her desire to be pampered was selfish, and that she knew Cam worked hard and without his drive they would not live in the comfort they did. But at other times, she knew she needed the affection. More and more lately, even with the tenderness and love and presents Cam gave her, she found herself feeling alone and melancholy. It was as though she wanted to do something, something different, but she didn't know what.

Cam walked away from the corrals, obviously aggravated. Smiley had reported that twelve of the workers had left during the night. The word was out that rebles were in the mountains and all of the plantations were losing people. He would have to call Havana and have more men sent out.

The riot in Havana had left the plantation owners slightly on edge. Although there had been no raids on plantations or trains, everyone felt there was a large offensive brewing and all men wore their guns in the open and kept the corners of their homes stocked with loaded rifles.

Molly heard Cam enter the house and walk to the living room. He flopped heavily into his chair with a look of exhaustion. Seeing her, he smiled. "Men ran off last night. For the life of me, Molly, as long as I live here, I will never understand these Cubans. They would just as soon shoot each other as not."

Molly looked at Cam. "Every country is like that, Cam. Look at the U.S."

Cam smiled and his mood changed. "Life," he laughed, "that's all it is."

Bertha came in with coffee and pound cake. She cut the cake on the table, and gave Molly and Cam each a cup. Cam took a sip and set the cup down. "Cam," Molly said, "I'm pregnant again."

At first Cam sat as though he did not hear the words. Then slowly a look of comprehension spread over his face. Rising, he jumped across the room and picked up Molly. He had a way of grabbing her with his right arm, which was powerful beyond his size, and swinging her legs to where he held them with his stump. He kissed her on the neck.

Sitting her back down, he walked back to his chair. "Well, maybe a boy this time," and for the rest of the day he whistled and did his work with an aura of having received good news.

Molly, relieved the news-breaking was over, immediately felt better and the moods of isolation left, and did not return.

Bertha cupped her hands to her face, listening from the kitchen. "It is good," she said to herself, "many children, such a fine and wealthy family should have many children."

Cam broke the news to Smiley and Smiley shook his hand warmly. But that evening in his house, Smiley sat and felt very lonely. Although over the past months he had carefully screened his affection for Molly and ridden his inner self of his animosities toward Cam, he knew he loved Molly deeply, and the shell he placed over his feelings seemed to crumble with the news of the baby. It was as though in his mind Cam and Molly lived in a home that was a vacuum. They did not sleep together or talk. At night the lights went out and the house was a void until in the morning and Cam walked out of the house after hours of no life. Her pregnancy shattered this facade of existence, and Smiley felt himself more alone than ever. "It would be to my good to go," Smiley told himself. Although he loved the ranch and the outdoor work. It was times like this, thinking of Molly lying naked, her legs open to Cam, that seemed to plunge him into the depths of envy and despair. It was not like Smiley, and although he did not welcome the thoughts, he could do nothing to drive them from his mind.

Bill Hood watched from his two-story office as the Johnson ship Sleeping Sun was being unloaded. He knew the carefully stencilled crates were not what they were labeled, but were the lastest in American arms. Although Hood had not taken an active part in the gun business in the past, he was now thrown directly into the fires. The smuggling ship had been a close call for Johnson. Only his high official friends had arranged for him to back-date his notice of theft, thus saving him from scrutiny by the authorities. But Hood also knew that Johnson was not completely in control of the situation. He knew there were men or a man who manipulated Johnson. He wondered how such an important and wealthy man as Johnson could have gotten himself into such a situation.

Now Hood himself delivered the weapons and collected the money. It was a dirty business, and one he hated. The guns were for people who wanted to kill the planters who were his friends. The bottle had become more and more through the months a constant companion, and a flask he carried in his pocket seemed to be empty much sooner.

He had only seen Linda once in the last few weeks. Long enough to go to her house for two hours of animal love and return to the office exhausted. He had heard rumors she was sleeping with three other men, and although she denied the stories when Bill brought it up, he knew they were true. Lovemaking to Bill had become an outlet for his built up aggression. It seemed the more vicious he was with Linda the better she liked it. Her cries were like the cries of an animal, but afterwards she would stroke and rub his body and kiss him tenderly. The knowledge that she was not the love of his life left him bitter and remorseful.

The past few days he had wanted desperately to turn to someone and tell them of the guns. He had thought of Cam, but he pushed that from his mind. Cam would not be able to understand, and might kill both him and Johnson. The rebels, although never having touched Cam's plantation, were sworn and bitter enemies to him. No, he could not confide in Cam.

Cam talked on the phone to a banker in Havana. What with the price of seed, and a drop in sugar and tobacco, he needed a loan to replant this year. In the middle of the conversation the phone went dead. Cam slammed the phone down on the hook. "God damn phones," he cursed, walking from his office.

It was not until he was halfway to the house that he noticed the large, billowing black cloud of smoke coming from the direction of the Madrid plantation. It was odd, the cane had been burned weeks earlier. There was nothing that could cause such a cloud except trouble. He ran to the house and called to Molly. "Keep Elizabeth inside. You and the maids lock the doors and keep the rifles handy."

Running to the stables he ordered his horse made ready. Just then Smiley galloped into the area. He also had seen the smoke. "I'll be ready in a minute," he yelled to Smiley and ran back to the house, where he strapped on the pistol Smiley had given him. He picked up his rifle and threw a handful of shells in his pocket.

Molly and Bertha stood wide-eyed by the door. "It'll be okay, I'm leaving the bosses armed and outside the house."

Sitting on his horse, Cam ordered men to circle and guard the house. He and Smiley and four bosses started toward the Madrid plantation. It was only six miles, and it wouldn't take them long to get there.

Riding down the road, Cam noticed that there were no hands working any of the fields of the neighboring plantations. Entering the courtyard of the Madrid place, he saw the house enveloped in flames, and the bodies of Mr. and Mrs. Madrid laying in the once beautiful grass. The outbuildings were torn and shattered by bullets and several of the domestic help scampered toward Cam and the men, rattling the story in Spanish. Twenty or so men had attacked the house, dragging Carlotta from the home. They had each raped her, one after the other. Mr. Madrid had ridden in from the fields and they had held him and shot his wife through the head, and then cut his throat. Many of the workers had left with the men after running crazed and torching everything they could. People who liked the Madrids were shot, and several other women were raped.

Cam watched the house blaze and begin to crumble. A cold look like steel came into his eyes. He left Smiley with two men and he and the others galloped back toward his home. Riding down the road, Cam saw eight men with rifles run into a cane field. He unholstered his pistol and tore in the cane after them. A gutteral scream came from his lips, and the first bullet tore the back of a running man's skull off, two more shots and a man fell shot in the base of the spine. The other men circled and tore into the running figures on the ground. One boss fell from his horse, shot in the shoulder.

The brief encounter ended, and Cam saw two of the bosses jump from their horses and grab and hold a man between them. Cam leaped from his horse and

132

ran toward the man. He looked into the dark eyes of the captured man and lashed out at him with his pistol. "Shoot him," Cam ordered turning, and he heard the report of the pistol as he remounted and rode back toward his plantation.

Nearing the house, he noticed the cut phone lines, and as he rode into the stable area, he saw three men run behind the tobacco drying sheds. He pointed at two men who rode around one side. He heard a rifle shot, and saw a riderless horse gallop off into a field. Dismounting on the run he ran into the drying shed. Moving quickly through the piles of tobacco bales, he ran through the back door in time to see three men jump and throw the remaining gang boss to the ground. Cam fired three times quickly and two men fell. Seizing the opportunity, the gang boss drew his knife from his belt and drove it to the hilt into the kidneys of the remaining rebel. The rebel turned slowly and looked into the eyes of his killer, a low gurgle of blood bubbled from his mouth as he tumbled face forward into the ground.

Other men left to guard the house came running. Careful scrutiny of the area unearthed no more signs of rebels.

Cam ran to the house, and beating on the door he was immediately let in by a tearful Molly. Bertha stood in the living room holding a rifle. Elizabeth played in the middle of the floor, oblivious to the goings-on around her. "The Madrids," Cam said, holding Molly close, "they're both dead."

A low moan came from Molly which quickly turned into uncontrollable sobbing. Cam held her but did not speak, a far away look came into his eyes and a fire began to kindle in his heart.

Smiley did not return to the plantation that evening but stayed to watch the fire burn itself out at the Madrids and place the bodies in a tobacco shed that escaped the attack. Riding in early the next morning he left three men with orders to shoot anybody who came to ransack the plantation. Cam was already up and mounted when he entered the stable area. The two men did not speak for a moment. "I spoke with the workers," Cam said in a low monotone. "There will be no work today. The soldiers will be at the Madrids soon, and I expect a few will be here to hear my side of the story."

"How's Molly?" Smiley asked.

"She's fine," Cam answered, swinging into the saddle. "I'm going to ride around the plantation and take a look."

Smiley noticed Cam wore the pistol he had given him, and another tucked in his belt. Smiley handed the horse over to the stable boy who said nothing. Walking to his house the fatigue suddenly swept over him and once inside he fell into an exhausted sleep.

Cam trotted the horse slowly around the harvested cane fields. He could see the footprints of the workers who had come from the fields the previous day. In another field, he saw the footprints of a group of men who had stopped working and disappeared into the dense overgrowth that surrounded the fields. He dismounted and followed the trail slowly into the jungle. The men had walked in a single line and then stopped and gathered together. Eight different sets of boot prints led into the jungle for another quarter mile, and then back to the edge of another cane field where they blended into a trail that would lead directly to the

Madrid plantation. He knew that this was a prearranged spot, and that the other prints belonged to the men who staged the raid. Somebody is arming these dirty bastards, Cam thought. And that somebody is white like me.

He walked slowly back to his horse and rode back to the house. The workers milled around their shacks and disappeared into them when he rode by. He knew that he would get no information from them. Although they took no active part, he knew that they feared for their lives should it be known that they collaborated with a white man..

When he entered the house, he saw Molly, sitting in her chair in the living room, all the color drained from her body. Cam walked over and patted her tenderly on the shoulder. "There's nothing we can do, Molly," he said. "It's all over."

Tears ran down Molly's face, but no sound came from her mouth. Cam could not look at the pain and anguish that covered her face.

Bertha, subdued and quiet, came into the room. She placed hot coffee in front of Molly and stroked her head as though she were a child. Molly looked into Bertha's eyes and smiled faintly. "It is God's will," Bertha said with her Cuban mind.

Molly sipped the coffee while Cam poured himself a drink. Smiley knocked on the door in the early afternoon and Bertha let him in. He found Cam and Molly sitting in the living room silently. He looked at Cam who nodded toward the bar. Smiley poured some scotch and sat down. Molly did not acknowledge his presence, but just sat and looked out the window. "Soldiers are here," she said, in a faraway whisper.

Cam and Smiley walked out into the courtyard and watched as two men dismounted their horses. A dozens other stayed mounted with their rifles slung across their backs. The officers stayed for only a short while. "Too bad you didn't catch one alive," one said, mounting his horse. "But we will find one, and he will tell us where Galindo is."

Cam and Smiley watched the soldiers ride away from the ranch. "They'll find one, a pig's ass," Smiley snorted.

Walking back to the house Smiley asked Cam, "What will Molly do, Cam? She's taking this very hard."

Cam did not look at Smiley but answered, "Nothing, only time will heal this."

Inside the house the living room was empty. Molly was in bed and the child played by Bertha's feet.

Bill Hood read the paper and his mind began to spin. No, no it couldn't be, but the paper did not lie. The two-column headline showed photographs with the account of the attack. Peons told of the rape of Mrs. Madrid and the cutting of the throat of Mr. Madrid. They went into a lengtly account of the killing of the rebels by Mr. Cam Stearns and his men. The attack was spurred on in retaliation for the killing of the students in Havana, the report added.

Hood threw the paper against the wall of the office. Bile formed in the back of his throat and he wretched into the wastepaper basket.

Several hours later, sitting at his desk in a whiskey stupor, he took a pen and paper and wrote for several minutes. He sealed the envelope and placed it in his inside jacket pocket.

Riding the train the next day, he felt relaxed, and a peace of mind that he had not experienced in months surrounded him. By dark he was at the Stearns plantation. He saw only a few lights on in the house, but noticed Cam's figure pacing back and forth across the window of his office. He walked to the office and knocked on the door and entered after a rough "come in." Cam smiled faintly at seeing Bill. "You heard?" he asked.

Bill sat down in the chair. "I read everything in the paper. It's terrible, terrible, Cam, especially when it's so close to home."

Cam stood and looked out the window. "Some way, somehow I'll find them Bill, someone without a heart or a soul supplies those guns, and I will find them."

While Cam was still facing the window, Bill took the envelope from his jacket and placed it on Cam's desk. "Well, let's go see Molly," Cam said, turning and walking toward the door. "Maybe seeing you will cheer her up."

Molly, still pale but more composed, hugged Bill when he came into the room. They did not speak of the incident the entire evening, but talked of Elizabeth and the new baby. "It will be a boy, I'm sure of it" she told Bill. "A fine, handsome boy like his father, brave and just and hard-working." But then she added in a somber mood, "I only hope there will be no wars."

Shortly afterward she went to bed. "Stay with your friend, Cam," she said as she left. "I'll be fine."

The two men looked at each other after Molly had gone, and each sensed a weariness in the other. "Getting old," Cam finally said. "It's just a matter of time now. Love, children, fighting to stay alive and then one day the end. That's what getting old is, I suppose. Understanding there are no real winners, and we all die."

Hood sat forward in his chair with his head bent low toward the floor. "It's so useless and terrible," he said wearily.

Stearns looked at the slouched form. "Who is it, Bill?" Who controls the guns?"

For a brief moment Bill was taken off guard and Stearns sensed the change. He wanted to tell him, to lay bare the truth and take the burden from his shoulders, but he could only shake his head. "I don't know, Cam."

"It's somebody big, Bill. It's somebody on those docks that you know, someone you eat lunch with."

Cam paused and looked at Bill. "Listen, keep your ears open. There has to be a leak. And when the day comes that you hear something, you let me know."

He said with a vengeance Bill had never heard in his voice.

"You let me know and I swear I will see them all hang."

Hood managed a tone of neutrality. "It sounds as though you have taken on a personal vendetta, Cam."

Cam stood and walked to the bar and for the first time Bill heard and saw Stearns true feelings on the matter. Pointing to his stub, Stearns said. "You see this? My arm lays in this country somewhere, people I know died and were buried here. And I had a dream of a land where one could live and die minding his own business, being his own man. America has done nothing to harm this country. Our money supports it, keeps it, schools the children, but a handful of greedy, soulless people tear down what good men fought and died for. Greedy, wealthy men, who have nothing to do but play with their power, supplying the guns that destroy what good men have fought for. I do have a vendetta. A vendetta for the Madrids and a vendetta for the people who have turned my wife's night into nightmares, and vendetta for those who have destroyed my dream."

"It will never end, Cam," Bill said, "catch one man and another will take his place."

"I know," Cam answered, "but maybe another man like me will catch him."

Stearns gulped the drink. "You know where the guest room is. I'll see you in the morning. Sorry for the bad company," he apologized.

"I understand," Bill answered.

Cam walked to the bedroom slowly. He knew now that the ranch and the land would never be the same. No matter how much people would make light conversation, no matter how much the children would romp and play, there would always be fear. Gone were the peaceful nights sitting on the veranda watching the stars. Gone were the conversations with Molly about the years and the ranch. The dream was shattered.

Cam once more stood over the dead body of the man who had hurt his mother. A cold, icy feeling filled his veins and a curtain closed in his mind. He stood by the edge of the bed and looked at his sleeping wife. So peaceful you look, he thought. But he knew only in her dreams would Molly find peace, only in the confines of sleep, until the rebels were dead.

Bill poured himself another drink and walked to the veranda. He stood and looked up into the dark sky. It would rain soon. After years in Cuba he knew the feeling when the rain was about to come. It would rain and in the morning with the first light everything would be fresh and sparkling. But he knew it was too late for him. All his life, the years of school, the striving to find a decent-paying job, were all wasted because of this. All he should have said was no, no it wasn't for him and been fired. He knew many men, he had good credentials and was known for his honesty. He could have had a job in innumerable places. But he had nodded his head meekly and said yes, because he was afraid. The money was too good, and he was afraid of a life without money. He set his empty glass down on the floor of the veranda and walked out into the night. A fine drizzle began cooling the land, but he was oblivious to the freshness. Several hours later he returned to the house. Changing his clothes, he sat in the guest room alone, very much alone.

Molly was up and dressed as usual when Cam came into the kitchen. The aroma of coffee filled the air and she bustled around keeping Elizabeth out of mischief. Bill sat nursing a cup of coffee. Cam looked at him disgustedly. "Bill, you're going to have to keep off that booze. You must have stayed up half the night with the bottle by the way you look."

Bill rubbed his hand through his tosseled hair. "I know, I keep telling myself."

Molly set the eggs and ham in front of Bill and smiled meekly at him. "Eat, you'll feel better."

Cam sat down and marveled at life. Each day so different, so unexpected. Molly set his plate down and sat down herself with only coffee. "It's a beautiful morning," she said, and as Cam watched her and listened to her he felt his love flowing through his heart. "The air is so fresh, and my flowers are sparkling."

Cam ate quickly and rose from the table. "I'm going to see the workers, and try to get some more men."

Bill picked at his food. "I think I'll head back to Havana."

"Oh, Bill," Molly pleaded, "you came out for a rest, you should stay."

"No," Bill persisted, "I should get back and stay on top of things. It's been so busy I just haven't had time to relax, and just this one day has done wonders for me."

He stood and shook hands with Cam. "Be careful, Cam," he said with a concerned tone to his voice.

"Well, Molly will see you off, Bill, please watch out for that booze."

Cam walked out and down to the stables. Smiley's horse was already saddled and Smiley busied himself attaching a rifle scabbard to the saddle. Cam noticed the new repeating lever action rifle. "Nice," he said, "when did you get that?'

"I ordered it over a month ago. 25/20, holds fifteen rounds. How's Molly, Cam?"

"She's a strong woman, Smiley."

"I know," Smiley answered, swinging up into the saddle.

Cam and Smiley did not see each other for the rest of the day. Smiley rode and felt like he was in Texas. His eyes scanned the trees and jungle for any movement. The workers felt the never ending gaze of the rider with the rifle and pistol, and whenever they looked away, soon they would see Cam with is pistol. Neither man smiled, only said a few words to the gang bosses and then were off again. There would be no repeat of the Madrids here. Whoever tried to assault this plantation would lose many men and the dead ones would be luckier than the unfortunate ones that would be caught alive.

When Cam returned to the house Bill was gone and Molly sat reading in her chair. She smiled when he entered, but did not get up and kiss him as was her practice. He walked over and kissed her on the forehead, and Molly looked deep into his eyes. "Those poor people," she said, and Cam could see the sadness that seemed to take the glow from the blueness of her eyes.

Bill Hood was back in Havana by four in the afternoon. He was in the office by six. Sitting in the office he looked out over the docks and watched as the day shift slowly plodded by, being replaced by the night workers. It was a wretched life for them, he knew. Working twelve hours a day, barely making enough to eat and yet they came, each day, silently moving black and brown men, their eyes filled with hate. Forever caught on the bottom, from government to government, no out, no dreams, only the dreams of brave and reckless bandits and revolutionaries who came and went with the wind. He knew he could never live as they did. Watching his children beg and steal, murder for a few dollars, pawing through people's trash for discarded clothes and shoes. One day they would boil out from the docks and burn and kill everything and everyone in their path, and the soldiers would come and kill them by the hundreds and push their bodies into holes that they would dig on the edge of town. It would happen, it was as predictable as the sun and the moon.

He sat down heavily behind his desk and looked at the ledgers and papers around the office. Ledgers for men who had millions, men who drove the new automobiles and sent their children to Europe for schooling. Men who paid more for horses than they paid living, breathing men to load and unload their ships. He sat and he remembered Williams, the dead Lieutenant Williams, Cam's friend. How ironic, he thought. All the days of college, sitting and talking, sharing their dreams. They had both been peaceful men, dreamers he supposed, not ones for war or hate, simply wanting to live and let live.

Bill opened the drawer to his desk and looked at the pistol. He picked it up slowly and looked once more out toward the docks. The men lifting the crates and cursing them did not hear the shot. There would be no alarm until the next morning when the secretary would find Bill's body, stiff and cold in his brains and blood.

_____

After dinner Cam kissed Molly and excused himself in order to go to his office. He had a few papers that he wanted to go over and a letter to write to Johnson. He was in his office several hours before he saw the envelope tucked into the edge of the writing blotter, It read simply . . . Open upon my death. Bill Hood.

Stearns did not comprehend its meaning, and in a moment of non-understanding, he placed the envelope in his top desk drawer. "Too much booze," he mumbled to himself. It was not until he left the office and was walking back to the house that a feeling of dread crept over his body and a chill made him shiver. He would call Bill in the morning and make sure everything was all right. "Please don't do anything rash," he said to the sky. He knew that the girl had been cheating on him, but he felt sure that Bill would not be one to do anything stupid in a fit of jealousy.

He told nothing of the letter to Molly as they prepared for bed. He wanted to touch her and feel her passion grow, but while Molly had been smiling during the days, he felt a distance about her now and a dread as though there was no more joy in her body. Only a complacency toward life, the passion was gone. Oh, there was beauty and a peace that come with living and surviving, but no passion that comes with dreams and hope. She was only slightly over two months pregnant, so there was no reason for the physical side of sex to be hampered.

Cam lay in bed and soon forgot about Molly, his mind restless and worried as more and more he thought of the letter with the strange inscription.

His sleep was slight this night, and for the first time in many months he dreamed. A dream that left him tired and edgy in the morning.

He was on the cliff, and although he did not see himself, he knew he stood on the edge. His mind was young and alive, and his heart light and happy. Ice covered the river below, and crows circled, riding the updrafts and turning their wings quickly as they played in the wind. Three crows circled over his head slowly, ever so slowly coming closer to him, until he could see the small red circle around their eyes. Then suddenly they vanished, and it was warm, Cam and his sister ran and laughed behind the wood pile. "Oh, Cam," she cried, falling and skinning her knee, and Cam stopped and ran to her and picked her up gently. She looked at him, her young eyes filled with love and adoration. "Will you always protect me, Cam?"

"I will always protect you, you know that."

"I know," she said, making a bigger fuss over her knee than necessary. "I know, I know you're not as mean as the other kids say."

The crows appeared again and they circled, mere dots on the face of the white icy clouds. Cam felt but did not see his face cold and blue from the wind, and as the dots had been but mere specks, one fluttered and set his wings, and his face, with gaping beak and closed eye, plummeted toward the ground. It flew faster and faster until it was a black line from the sky to the earth, and it hit and lay at Cam's feet, a thin trickle of rose red blood on the snow.

Cam began to run. Away from the cliff toward the path that led to the house, but upon reaching the house panting and afraid, with tears streaming down his face, there was no ne inside. Only emptiness, with no fire in the wood stove, no sister on the bed and no scolding from his mother to take his boots off before coming in the house.

And then he was awake, and the sound of the rain hitting the window came to his ears. He looked at the bed and Molly was not there. He rose and looked at the room with the white walls and the dressing table and chair with Molly's perfumes and makeup, and the wardrobe with his clothes and boots, and he was alone. Alone save his reflection in the mirror.

Molly had risen early and dressed quietly. She had accepted the death of the Madrids, but the past few days had changed her. She would continue to be the gracious and courteous lady she was, loving and devoted to her child. But her greatest joy would be the early morning, when the house was silent and the birds sang in her garden. She would lose herself in the color and the sky. Here with the flowers there was a sanity in the world. The neatly placed rows of flowers held no malice nor did they need understanding. She would see a flower toppled during the night and her heart would feel the same amount of pain as when she heard the news of the Madrids and other tragedies. Her house would always be filled with flowers, flowers in the windows and on the table. It was her world, a world she gradually began not to share with anyone. People visiting the ranch would not be invited to see the paths and rows upon rows of flowers. Cam would see her bending and pulling, see her lips move as she talked, and he would wonder what she was thinking and saying, but he would never be invited to walk among the flowers. Here Molly found peace, time and a simplicity that forever would fight the truths of life, its only goal to bring color and joy to the beholder.

This morning she sat in a wicker chair and looked out upon her flowers. What earlier had been only a few rows now covered forty yards in either direction and wound in circular and straight paths. It was not a planned, laid-out flower garden, but one which one added on to according to one's mood. At times the paths were straight with yellow and red flowers, but at other times they were circles with flowers in the middle. One lone chair sat in the very middle of the garden, and here Molly sat. She held her hands over her stomach. "I will love you as I love my other child," she said to the rising sun. "I will love you as I love my husband, but I will not give you my heart, little one. Your own heart you must protect and look after."

Cam stood by the window and looked at his wife. Maybe the baby will help, he hoped.

After breakfast in his office Cam received a phone call from Bill Hood's office. He put the receiver down slowly and looked at the empty chair where Bill had sat the day before. Remembering the letter, he opened his drawer and cut the envelope open with a thin knife. It began:

I suppose I am not man enough to face you, but you must understand you are one of the few men in my life I call a friend, and I would hate to see our friendship die. There are many things in a man's life that are mistakes. I pray you find in your heart the power to forgive me mine. Without details as to how or why, Cam, I must tell you that for the past several months I have been in direct contact with the rebels and in charge of seeing that they are delivered weapons.

With this Cam's stomach fell, his mind reeled and cried no, no, not you, why in God's name, why?

I know that Mr. Johnson has been blackmailed into supplying ships and crews to deliver the guns. The confiscation of his ship made it impossible to run the risk of detection by use of another boat, so the large cargo boats have been used with falsely marked crates. Mr. Johnson in reputation is beyond reproach. You must stop this, as I know after the happenings of the past weeks you will try with all your might to do. Mr. Johnson is not to blame, so do not hold hate for him in your heart. I know there is a man, a man I have never met nor do I know his name, who pulls the strings on Johnson. I do know for a fact Senor Romone, who you met with General Wood, is in direct contact with the rebels. The rebel's name is Galindo. I cannot live with myself, Cam. There is no way I could ever make up for my actions. The best to you during your life. My hopes to your wife.

The letter was not signed. Cam sat and let the letter fall to the floor. All energy left his body and his mind went blank.

He never told Molly of the letter, nor did Molly know of Bill's death until she happened across the clipping from Cam's newspaper. She fell into a state of shock, and spent three weeks in the hospital. During this time, Cam completely forgot the ranch and stayed in a room in Havana. He did not call Smiley or inquire into any aspects of work.

In time Molly would recover from her nervous breakdown. But for several months she was but a ghost, moving through each day as in a dream. With no sign of emotion, neither joy nor grief, she spent the hours in her garden digging and watering the flowers. Elizabeth was forgotten, but was filled with so much love by Bertha and Smiley and Cam's attention that she lived happily and noisily around the house. Molly recovered one day when standing in front of her mirror naked, she noticed the protrusion of her now bulging stomach, and it was as though a light went back on in her mind. There is more than me, she realized, and when she walked into the room with Cam and Elizabeth they both knew Molly was back. Cam did not stand or run to kiss and hug his wife, he only smiled deeply into her once more sparkling eyes as she stood before him and said, "Cam, the baby, it will be soon," and she walked to her chair and sat down and laughed, "yes, it will be soon."

Elizabeth, seeing her mother smile for the first time in months, ran over and hugged her legs. "Elizabeth, Elizabeth," Molly cried, tears streaming down her cheeks, "how beautiful you are."

Her small mind confused, Elizabeth looked at Molly and said, "why Mommy cry?"

Molly looked at Cam and Cam could feel her love and relief flow across the room. "Because I feel, Elizabeth, because I feel."

The next day the house was alive and singing. The grey, cool, subdued days were over. Cam smiled a lot, Bertha worked in the kitchen and Molly busied herself around the house. She looked at the flower garden once as Cam was leaving the house. "It's lovely, isn't it Cam?"

Cam looked over her shoulder into the garden. "It's beautiful, Molly."

Estancia Martinez sat in the dirty bar and looked over the backs of two bar women. Two men looking like dock workers came into the bar and sat on either side of him. One man, in his early fifties, looked at Martinez and through a heavy beard said. "The rain is early this year Senor, no?"

Estancia, knowing the code, finished his beer and stood up from the bar.

"Not so early that it won't help the cane," he said, and left the bar.

Several minutes later, the two men walked out of the bar into the street. On the corner four blocks away Estancia waited. Walking and paying no attention to Estancia standing on the corner, they passed him and walked a few more blocks to a waiting carriage. Estancia followed, and ducked into the carriage as it passed. The two men did not smile. "He waits," one said, his face not visible in the dark. Estancia felt his stomach tighten, and he watched the faceless flow of people as the fleeing carriage passed.

Galindo, shaven and dressed in the clothes of a railroad engineer, sat in the bar and looked out the window. He saw the carriage pass, then stop and the three men got out. He paid his bill and walked out into the night. Walking up to the three men, he held out his hand. "My friends, it has been so long."

The men embraced and patted each other on the backs and began walking down the street. "To a good bar, the beer in there is like rat piss," one said. "I know a bar where the women are not fat and the beer is not water."

Arnold Stone watched the men disappear into the night. Intelligence had known where Martinez was for seven weeks. A whore, badly beaten and not paid, had willingly told everything. The Chief of Police, one who knew the value of a few dollars, soon knew the house where Martinez was hiding. Stone had waited patiently for this day, it must be something big, he thought. And now, seeing Galindo, he knew his hunch was right. He went home and typed his story for the Florida Star. Roosevelt would read the paper and know the details.

Once the four men felt safe, they darted into the alley and ran for several blocks. Looking back, they hailed a passing carriage and rode to the train station.

After nearly two hours on the train, Galindo saw the flashing light. The men jumped from the speeding train and ran into the cane field. By sunrise they were high in the mountains and swatting the mosquitoes.

Martinez was nervous. Galindo had said nothing to him during the entire time. But soon he would. "Sleep," Galindo had said and disappered. He would not sleep forever, and Martinez knew Galindo was not happy about the useless killing of the students.

More than ninety men that Martinez had counted moved in and around the well fortified camp. All had modern, new weapons and all wore more than ample ammunition.

He had done well, in the last year, Martinez thought. He had never been in the field, a student raiser, he had never experienced the life of a true revolutionary. But now, wanted and on the run, he knew he had better get used to the idea.

Galindo, unknown to Martinez, had been in town for three days before he was contacted. Knowing that if there was ever trouble he should go to the Gato Negro each evening and wait for two hours, he had done so. It had taken months before the contact was made. But to see Galindo in town meant there was something in the air.

Galindo had ridden a cane cart to the edge of town. The first night he was shuffled from house to house. Changing into the clothes of a wealthy Cuban businessman, he went directly to Ramone's home. Ramone let him in, after he was stopped by the security. "What better way than under the tiger's nose," he often said.

For several hours they talked. Ramone assured him that he had the generals, what few he did not have would quickly surrender. Ramone knew about the tank captain. When Galindo began his assaults against the railroads and telegraph poles, Ramone's generals would take over the military. What force was required would be backed up by tanks, and the palace would be surrounded. Palma would surrender and the revolution would be over. Galindo would become premier, setting up a temporary military rule which would conduct a "Democratic" election. Ramone would be elected El Presidente, and Galindo appointed to a high position.

They both agreed that the tank captain should be killed. Galindo informed Ramone about the situation with the guns, and the death of Hood. Ramone took no active part in the distribution of the guns. There must be a new man, a pick-up man, a place for the guns to be stored until the actual fighting, Galindo told Ramone. Galindo now had over six thousand men scattered over Cuba. Workers, dock hands, students, professors and the army, even the President's best friend.

Galindo laughed to himself as he walked quickly away from Ramone's large home. "It is time, my star fills the sky. The streets will sing my name, my people's blood flows for freedom."

Two days later, General Marquez and Senor Ramone sat watching the thin, long-legged cocktail waitress approach with their drinks. "The time is close," Ramone whispered. "Be careful and wait for my word."

The General leaned back in his chair and sipped his brandy. "The brandy is good, no?" "Better than it has been in a long time."

Galindo walked from his tent followed by two large dirty men. Both were unshaven, and wore green army pants, boots and tee shirts. Around their middles hung ammunition belts, and thrown lazily over their shoulders were two rifles, American 45/70's.

Galindo stood over the sleeping form of Martinez and kicked him in the ribs. "Get up, you stupid fool," he bellowed, "It is time to talk."

He grabbed the half-awake man by the neck and dragged him to this feet. Martinez held Galindo's wrists, and felt the power of the arms and the death-like grip on his throat. "Please, please, it was not my fault," he pleaded, "the crowd would not listen, I called for them to stop, I told them it was not time."

Galindo looked into the terrified eyes of the man he held between life and death. Without a word, he slowly loosened his grip and stood back from the petrified man. He turned sharply on his heel. "Issue him a rifle and a belt of bullets," he growled to one of the men beside him. "Put him in the jungle by the path."

Martinez hid behind the trees and the undergrowth which was carefully tucked around the guard post. He scanned the jungle around him, and felt relieved and very lucky to be alive.

(20)

During the three weeks Cam had been in Havana with Molly, Smiley had slept little. Constantly on guard, he rode day and night around the ranch. The workers who deserted had been replaced by trusted men who had worked for the Madrids. The Madrid ranch would lay fallow now. Smiley knew little of the family, whether there were any sons or daughters. The estate would be settled in court, and if no will or family was found, would be placed on the auction block by the government. Identical to the Stearns ranch, except for the destruction of the home and outbuildings, it would take little work to construct another home and buildings. If it did come up for auction, Smiley hoped he could persuade Cam to talk to Johnson about purchasing it. The two properties combined would be a substantial holding, one of the largest in Cuba, able to regulate and control prices. With Cam in power, Smiley knew all dealing would be fair and on the up and up.

Smiley felt comfortable in the position of sole man in charge. For three weeks the ranch ran smoothly, and Smiley rose from his few hours of sleep exuberant and ready for the day. He started several workers on projects to fix up the shacks, and had given the hands an extra day off. He would suggest to Cam that he institute a program that would give clothing to the workers and a school with a teacher solely to teach the chidren of the workers. With eighty workers, there were many children, and they needed a school. Chained to the fields, Smiley knew there must be change, or other incidents like the Madrids' would forever plague the area.

With the return of Molly and Cam and the weeks of tension that followed, Cam talked little and Smiley knew better than to bring forth his ideas. Cam looked at the construction on the shacks and only mumbled, "good idea."

But with the sudden recovery of Molly, Cam's mood changed and once again he seemed to pour himself into the ranch.

One afternoon, sitting on the veranda during a heavy rain, Smiley approached Cam with his idea for the school, and Cam immediately applauded it. A week later, a school was under construction and word had been sent to Havana inquiring for a school teacher to fill the position. The workers were told about the new school, and also issued new clothes, both of which were met with many smiles and looks of gratitude. Cam also set into action a program that twenty head of

143

cattle would be shipped in, and a beef ration would be given to the workers, along with beans and flour.

Within a month, the school was completed with a room for the teacher connected to the back. Twenty head of cattle were confined to a small section of the property on the western edge of the plantation. Both Cam and Smiley reveled in the sight of the cattle, and they spent their free time riding and roping. Sometimes Molly would ride out, and watch them replay a part of their childhood. Both men knew cattle, and the mooing of the cows in the morning was a sound that they dearly loved.

Mr. Alvarez Baca, riding an old appaloosa mare, came to the ranch early one afternoon. He was a small man, about five foot two, with tiny, dark, beady eyes that darted in all directions, and with a haughty air about him.

Covered with mud, he walked briskly to the door, set his suitcase down, and announced to Molly when the door was opened, "I am the teacher, show me please where I am to live."

He was a dedicated man, not young, but through the weeks he became a part of the household, eating his meals with the Stearns.

He had been born in Havana poor, but through work and effort had received his teacher's certificate. He praised the Stearns' for their program, and would go on and on about the progress of the children in the school. "You are kind and gracious, senor," he would say to Cam, "these children have been given a chance at life through your generosity."

The workers threw themselves into the work now. No other workers on the island had as nice living conditions as they did. Before, they had been a quiet, slow-paced lot, but now with clothes, food and a school for their children, they looked with gratitude at Cam and Smiley.

Molly was a blond angel, helping out many days in the school, and Elizabeth, who before had been distant with the workers' children, began to disappear for hours, playing hide-and-seek and other childrens' games.

Johnson wrote a letter inquiring about the additional expenses that were not planned, and Cam wrote him about the program that had been initiated. Johnson said nothing of the matter again.

It was not until Molly was in her seventh month that Cam called Smiley into his office one afternoon and showed Smiley the letter that Bill Hood had left him. Smiley read the letter and looked at Cam with searching eyes. "What should we do, Cam?"

"I want you to go to Florida and see Mr. Johnson. You will pretend to be going on your own accord, simply in the states to see your sister. By no means is Johnson to know that I have any idea as to what is going on. Tell him Hood confided in you, and that you will take his place in handling the guns. That you will ship the guns to the ranch and secure them and hand them over to the rebels. For a fee, of course. Use whatever story you need to convince him of your loyalty. If it works, we will then see what happens and make our moves as they develop. Molly knows nothing and will continue not to know anything. The only people who will be involved are you and I."

"When do I leave?" Smiley asked.

"Whenever you are ready. I will write Johnson and tell him you are coming to Florida to see your sister who is on vacation. Once there, contact him and approach him with your plan. It's getting close, Smiley. There are happenings all over the country. More demonstrations, more train tracks destroyed. Workers from many plantations have disappeared. They are moving into the jungles. Professors loyal to the government talk of more and more unrest on the campuses. It is only a matter of time."

Smiley rose and walked toward the door. "I know, Cam."

Roosevelt read and deciphered the daily articles in the paper written by Stone. Through trusted men he alerted the forces on Guantanamo. At the first notion of complete revolt, the forces would be on the move in twelve hours. Ships would steam to Havana and landed forces would march and secure American-owned mills and plantations. He wrote and had delivered to the post office a letter to Cam Stearns. It was time, and he knew he could trust Stearns.

Since the death of Hood, Johnson had not seen Maldanado for weeks, but late one afternoon he arrived in the office. "Have you a trusted man yet?" he asked.

Johnson shook his head no.

"Find one. The shipment is ready. There are only two more."

Johnson did not know how Maldanado received his information, but he seemed always to know all of the moves of the people with which he dealt. He was a very powerful man who moved in his seedy world alone, but in full control. Maldanado enjoyed seeing the powerful men of countries squirm. He lived alone with no wife or family, a man with no ties to anything except money. Surrounding himself with trusted men, he had the ability to pull up the garbage on people and use it to his advantage.

His one weakness, which not even his closest confidantes knew, was his love for little boys. But through careful and secret meetings, his lusts were satisfied through a rich madam in Key West who supplied the young tender morsels. If at times they were hurt and bleeding, there was never a confrontation. The money was good.

He strolled leisurely down the streets of Key West and watched the Palm trees sway in the breeze. Soon there would be no more need for the guns, and he would disappear. Already, informed sources had told him of the growing unrest in Mexico, and a man of his talents would be greatly needed.

Adjusting his white straw hat, he watched two small boys play in the gentle surf. His mind roamed over the young round buttocks of the children in their wet swimsuits.

It was with interest that Johnson read the letter from Stearns. He would be happy to see Smiley, having only spoken to him in passing, while they were on their way to Cuba many years ago. Funny, Johnson mused, how I have never been to see the plantation or the docks.

A week later, Smiley and Johnson sat in an expensive restaurant discussing the politics of Cuba. After several drinks, Smiley came directly out with it. "Bill Hood told me everything. I will take his place."

Johnson tried not to look alarmed, but a red flush spread across his face "Does Cam know?" he stammered.

"Cam knows nothing, nothing at all," Smiley said with confidence. "Send the guns, I will personally oversee their delivery."

Johnson felt his nervousness disappear. Here was the man, a trusted man by Stearns, but really only a man like every other man, greedy, looking for fast and easy money.

"But I need ten thousand to start," Smiley added.

Johnson didn't bat an eyelash. "Come by the office in the morning. I will give you the details and the money in cash."

Smiley returned to his hotel room, feeling good that his mission had been successful. The bellboy located the woman he wanted within an hour. A small woman with large breasts knocked on his door. Smiley fondled and eyed the woman's flesh the entire night. "You can't imagine what it's like to see large tits," he told the girl as she undressed. The girl giggled, and turned out to be very proficient in her profession.

Upon his return to Cuba, Smiley contacted the owner of the Black Cat Bar. A small Cuban with darting paranoid eyes, he whisked Smiley into the back room. Without preliminaries, he spit out his words in a flurry. "I will pick up the weapons, you will not see nor meet anybody. The money will be counted and given to you when I come for them."

Smiley did not know the man's name, but in time he would.

As he told Cam the story of Florida and Johnson, and about the man in Havana, Cam sat motionless and said nothing. A slow fire kindled in his heart and he felt the steel jaws of his trap begin to close. "Good, good."

Smiley reached into his pocket and handed Cam ten thousand dollars in hundred dollar bills. "A gift from Johnson."

Stearns looked at the money. "Keep it, it's yours," he said.

Smiley, flabbergasted, looked at the money. "No," he said after a moment, "Put in in the safe. For cattle one day, you and I and cattle."

Cam, recalling the original dream, smiled at his friend. "So many complications. A dream begins to seem like such a small thing."

Smiley looked into the eyes of his friend and boss. "You must hang onto that dream, Cam. You must."

Three days later, Cam received a letter in a plain brown envelope. It was addressed to him, and the return on it said Mr. and Mrs. William Brown. He was puzzled. He knew no Browns. But as he began to read the letter, his senses became acutely alive.

Dear Cam,

Time flies and soon we die. It has been many years I know, but rest assured you have always been in my thoughts. Many things develop during one's lifetime, and I am happy for your success in Cuba. Know that I have kept up with you, even though I have been lacking in personal contact. I have a matter of utmost importance and direly need men I can trust. You are such a man, although you are not forced to partake in this venture for me or for your country if you do not wish. I will understand, but if you will, please contact a Mr. Arnold Stone in Havana. He will fill you in on all details and be in contact with me. I hear you have a beautiful daughter and your wife is now expecting your second child. I pray it is a boy. One with your honor and character.

I am yours, T. Roosevelt

146

Cam put the letter on the table and looked out the window to where he could see Molly's flower garden. His mind raced back through the years, and he could see Roosevelt in all his glory and power parading in front of the men on his white horse. He remembered the chills that raced up his spine whenever he saw Roosevelt. He returned to the letter, and taking a match from his pocket he lit the letter and watched it burn.

That night at dinner he informed Molly that he would have to go to Havana for a few days. Molly was large now, and Bertha had told the family it would be soon, a few weeks. Soon another little life, she had said.

Molly did not suspect anything out of the ordinary, although she had thought Smiley's trip to Florida strange. She dismissed the matter with her thought of the child to come. Men, they were strange creatures, and she was not one to meddle in their affairs.

Cam had never uttered anything about his activities, and more and more was a good and kind father to Elizabeth and a loving husband to Molly. They had already decided that the boy would be named Cam Stearns, Jr., and lying in bed at night, feeling the baby kick and fight for life, they had already sent him to Harvard and watched his law firm prosper.

Arnold Stone sat typing at his desk. God, I wish I was back in the east today, he thought, stopping the article and looking out the window. Here it is October, and it's hot and humid. Rain and more rain. How I'd love to be sitting and letting that good old Chesapeake wind whip across the water with the cool spray hitting me in the face.

The secretary entered the office. "A Mr. Cams Stearns to see you, Mr. Stone."

Stone stood and watched the man enter. He was everything that Roosevelt had said he was. He shook hands and sat back down, motioning to a chair.

Stearns sat down. "The one arm becomes you." Stone said.

Stearns, without emotion, answered, "one grows used to many things," then he added, "Roosevelt asked me to see you."

Stone looked at the man and quickly judged him. Being a reporter he had learned through the years to capture, in a glance, the makeup of people. Here was an unafraid, and calculating man. And Stone sensed immediately that here could also be a dangerous man. A man who could kill one minute and sit down to dinner the next.

Stone pulled a bottle of Scotch out of his desk. "Scotch, Mr. Stearns?"

Stearns nooded his head yes.

The formalities out of the way, Stone plunged right into the heart of the matter. "Unknown to all but a few men, I and several others are here because of Roosevelt. Working with contacts in the government and other key positions, we report to Roosevelt any activities or news which might endanger our position in Cuba."

"Our?" Stearns broke in.

"The United States." Stone answered

Stearns nodded.

"We happen to know that your boss, so to speak, a Mr. Samuel Johnson, has been blackmailed into supplying transportation, his docks and warehouse for the illegal shipment of weapons for the rebels. We have a main source in the rebel camp right now. We also know Galindo has contacted Ramone who is Palma's most trusted friend. Student plants and other sources have told us that the revolution is close at hand. We feel confident that it will be put down without problem, but it is important that we take control of the next shipment. Mr. Roosevelt wants your help. He knows you know Johnson."

Stearns held out his empty glass. Stone poured him another drink. "Ironic," Stearns said, sipping the Scotch. "I already have."

"You've what? How?" Stone sputtered.

"I was going to contact Roosevelt myself, and then his letter came in the mail." Stearns explained to Stone about the letter from Bill Hood and the mission from which Smiley had just returned. Stone was flabbergasted. "Why, may I ask?"

Stearns said coldly. "Because they should be killed and their bodies left in the jungle to rot."

For the first time, Stone saw the hatred in Stearns' eyes, and he pursued the matter no further.

"Get this information to Roosevelt," Stearns said. "My friend has already made contact with the man here in Havana who will pick up and pay for the weapons."

Stone watched Stearns leave his office, and shook his head in amazement. Here was a man who was going to take on the rebels alone. He and his friend, in order to kill as many as they could.

Stearns walked down the streets of Havana. It was a bad time, even the air carried the feeling of dread and death.

The train ride back to the plantation was slow. Stearns did not watch the countryside or listen to the conversation of the other passengers. Soon he would have, in his possesion, the man responsible for the guns, and he did not know if he could control himself.

Driving the buggy the last miles to the house Stearns relaxed. During the train ride it had poured rain all the way, but now, close to home, the sky was clear and the setting sun sent red slivers reflecting off the fields. It is so peaceful at times, Cam thought. Brief moments of our lives when there is no tomorrow or yesterday, When the color radiating off a flower or a bird taking wing is all that there is to life.

At times Cam did not feel like a young man anymore, even though at thirty-one, he was in the prime of his life. His muscles were toned, his body supple, but he felt as though his mind was old and alone. His wife and child, though he loved them, seemed more and more to be pushed into the background of his days. It seemed to Cam that he had been born alone, and until Molly, had moved soundlessly through a vacuum, keeping his thoughts and dreams to himself. Even in the army, although he felt a part of something, he had not comprehended his life. Then there had been Molly and the first years, laughing, working so hard his nights were but dark nothingness. But now his mind was as before. Not wanting to think of the rebels, not wanting to think of the guns, but unable not to because of the burning hate that overwhelmed him. No one knew the full extent of his drive to exterminate the rebels. The ranch, his wife and child were like images in front of him. Touched and talked to, but never fully grasped. There was no all-emcompassing love that took away the fears of the world, there were no dreams that compensated for the pain and suffering. There was nothing logical or moral except tiny portions of one's life that atoned for the innumerable sins of living. Cam now would look at the ranch, and although it was dear to him, it did not fill him with joy or warmth. He set out upon his tasks with a grim determination, he longed more and more for time alone. Time to sit and not think, be or work. But to sit and let nothing enter his mind, let his brain and his body rest.

He had gone so far the past years, from murderer to Rough Rider, to wealthy plantation manager. According to his accountant he was now worth close to a half million dollars in hard cash. It had seemed too quick, the transformation. He could not look into the mirror now and feel like Cam Stearns, the broke cowboy or Cam Stearns, the broke army sergeant. It seemed like an eternity, since then. He slept in a comfortable bed, his house was filled with books, fine furniture and works of art. His wife and child wore the best clothes. He walked and breathed and bore the trappings of a man used to the comforts of life. But the money did not stop the need to fight, the need to be cold and cunning.

Sitting in the buggy, he understood for the first time that what he had sought through the years was to be more than just an animal. He knew there was no God. On this there was no debate or question in his mind. There had been too much proverty, too many days alone, for there ever to be a God, but he felt there was a bond between men that should prevail. Men should be able to live to their potential without fear of shooting or killing.

He thought of Molly and the love that had consumed him when they were first married. Theirs was a comfortable life. She was pleasing and gracious, and even though her passion was gone, she was still alluring. But now he realized they were two separate people, people bound together by a child and a child to be. Sleeping and waking together, but living two different lives, and this knowledge made him feel more cold and alone than ever.

Cam thought again of Roosevelt's words. *"There are people bound to be different, leader of by no choice, men marked by blood. Their lives are not their lives, their dreams only the calling of the knowledge they possess. You and I, Cam Stearns, we are such men. No matter what life brings to us, we will always be alone."*

He thought of Smiley, a man who had been through everything with him, and although they had shared so much he did not really know Smiley. He knew Smiley liked women with big breasts, and he liked his eggs over easy. He knew his quick smile and his slow temper. But these were only the external things of the man. Cam did not really know Smiley, and who he really was.

Cam drove the buggy into the stable area and rang the hanging bell for the stable hand. Walking to the house, he noticed the lights on. He was weary and depressed, and hoped his mood would pass.

Entering the house, he saw Smiley sitting in his chair looking nervous. Bertha walked toward the bedroom with towels piled in her arms. She did not look at him. Cam walked in and Smiley rose. "She's in labor, Cam," and Cam could see the worry on Smiley's face. "It happened a few hours ago. She was in the kitchen with Bertha and she fell to the floor in pain. Her water broke right there. Bertha helped her to the bedroom and Mr. Baca is in there."

"What's Baca doing in there?" Cam said angrily, heading for the bedroom.

Smiley grabbed his arm. "He has delivered many babies. The phones are out, so we can't call a doctor. We have to sit and wait, Cam."

Cam looked at Smiley and at the hall to the bedroom. He flopped into the chair. "My God, Smiley, must there be a fight to all things?"

Smiley walked to the bar and brought Cam a scotch. He did not speak, there was nothing to say. For two hours both men sat and said nothing. The only sound was their footsteps to and from the bar. The living room hung heavy with cigar smoke. Twice Bertha came from the bedroom, but said not a word, only returned with basins of warm water.

Several hours passed, and Cam felt dread build up in his heart for the first time in many years. He looked at Smiley and Smiley could feel the unspoken emotion of Cam, but he could only look away from the pleading eyes of the man. Cam let his head fall into his hand, and he could feel the tears begin to well up in his eyes. The last time he cried was when he was a child for his sister.

Just then, the door to the bedroom burst open and Mr. Baca stepped from the room, his shirt sleeves rolled up. He walked briskly to the living room and straight to the bar. Looking totally self-satisfied, he drained a double shot of rum and walked over to Cam. "Senor," he said, holding his chin high and his thin shallow chest out, "you are the father of a fine child." And then he slapped Cam on the shoulder, which was completely out of his character, and began to laugh. "He has balls too, senor, two of the best little balls I have ever seen."

Cam leaped from his chair and shook Mr. Baca's hand vigorously. "Thank you, thank you," he cried, and he ran to the bedroom. Baca's words trailed after him. "She is tired, not too long."

Baca then turned to Smiley, who felt the anxiety drain from his body in waves. Sitting in Cam's chair, he crossed his legs. Baca said, "the first baby I delivered was in a buggy."

"If you were prettier, Baca," Smiley laughed, "I'd kiss you."

Molly lay, drawn and exhausted. Cam could see the strain on her face and feel the dampness of the sheets. She smiled faintly at him and held out her hand. "A little boy, Cam," she said, kissing the small head of the baby in her arms. "Look, Cam, he has green eyes just like you."

Cam looked at his wife and the miniature hands of the baby. The little eyes were scrunched up into tiny wrinkles. He knelt beside the bed and buried his head in the covers and wept. Molly stroked his head gently and turned her head toward the baby. She was asleep when he stood up. He bent over and kissed the child on the forehead and walked out into the living room. Baca, Smiley and Bertha stood around the bar. Baca stood, moving from side to side, his words were slurs. Bertha giggled and sipped the rum slowly. Smiley hugged Cam and both men laughed. "See?" Baca laughed, "two tiny little bitty balls," and he fell over backwards.

The children laughed and pointed at the unshaven and untidy teacher the next morning in school. After an hour he dismissed the class and slept the rest of the day and night.

Cam helped Elizabeth dress in the morning and took her with him on the horse. He held her close to him on the front of the saddle and marveled at her fine features. It was as though he was seeing his daughter for the first time. He rode and showed her the cattle and the caltivated tobacco fields. They laughed at the birds and a field mouse that darted in front of the horse. "You have a little brother now," he told her.

Elizabeth smiled. "I know, Daddy, it's because Mommy and you love each other."

"You must be nice to him, and help your mother with the baby."

"Oh, I will," Elizabeth said, in a ladylike manner.

"You have all the grace of your mother," Cam said, kissing her on the back of the head.

"Daddy," Elizabeth said, looking concerned, "will your arm ever grow back?"

For the first time in a long while, Cam threw his head back and laughed long and hard. "No, little one, it will not grow back."

Elizabeth's fifth birthday passed, and it was the first week in December before Molly was out of the bed and beginning to show signs of recovering. She fussed over the baby and played with him, and the crib was set at the foot of the bed. Many nights Cam would rise to hold and speak softly to the child, and Molly would look at the darkened form, seeing a gentle side of him that she knew no one else ever saw.

A week before Christmas Smiley received a letter from Johnson. On the fourth of January, four large crates addressed to the Stearns ranch would be unloaded and placed in a warehouse. He would pick them up and secure them, contact the bar owner and receive the money. The money would be deposited in the bank of Havana to the account of Mrs. W. Ringley.

Smiley and Cam read and reread the letter. Cam called Stone. Stone said he would be out the next day. Cam informed Molly that they would have a house guest. Mr. Arnold Stone, who was a reporter for the Florida Star.

Sitting at the dinner table the next evening. Molly was fascinated by the man. "A reporter," she said. "I know you must meet many exciting people."

Stone smiled. "At times it can be very dull."

Stone was impressed by the Stearns house, and was taken by the charm and tact of Molly. "You have a fine home and a lovely wife," he told Cam when they were in the office after dinner.

Then he abruptly changed the subject. "You should take delivery of the weapons. Bring them here and contact the man in Havana. As soon as that is done, we will take over. But the weapons will not be delivered. Under no circumstances shall they be delivered. Roosevelt has a plan that I know nothing of. I only know I have explicit orders not to deliver the weapons."

Stearns sat and played with his mustache. A habit he had when he was deep in thought. "When Smiley receives word, I'll call you."

"Call and say you are ready with the story on the mill," Stone said. "If I'm not in the office, leave the message with my secretary."

Business settled, the men walked back to the house.

Smiley had sat and said nothing during the conversation. He saw the intensity on both Stone's and Stearns' faces. It was coming, and it was dangerous.

Molly served coffee and cookies and talked and laughed through the evening. It was seldom that new faces were at the ranch, and she found a diversion from her day to day life. Not a word was spoken of the rebels.

Climbing into bed that night, Molly hugged Cam and kissed him on the chin. "I love you, you know, don't you?"

"I know," Cam answered, running his hand down to her bottom.

She pulled him down on top of her and entwined her legs around his waist. "Please, no babies this time." she said.

"God, I hope not," Cam mumbled, trying to undo with one hand the buttons on her nightgown.

"The biggest disadvantage of one arm. Buttons," he said, "especially yours."

———————

Cam and Smiley stood and watched the wide eyes of the children as they crowded around Mr. Baca. Mr. Baca passed out the large paper sacks of candy to the outstretched hands. Each child was also given a package wrapped in bright red paper. The girls received dolls and the boys ball mitts. Several bats and balls were in the corner of the school room.

In the afternoon, packages of clothes and new shoes were given to the hands and each worker, men and women, received ten dollars.

When the sun set, two calves were roasted over an open fire and the entire ranch ate. The workers sang and danced, and Cam felt a warmth that he had never known at Christmastime. Sitting and watching Molly serve food with Smiley beside her, he thought to himself, it's another year, and we are still together. This ranch will never fall.

Elizabeth ran up to her father, stood for a moment out of breath, and then ran off gleefully, followed by several Cuban children laughing and playing. Unlike himself, Elizabeth was already speaking both English and Spanish. Her interaction with the workers' children had started her, and with her young mind the words came without effort. Cam had never had the desire to learn, simply trusting in his bosses to translate for him.

Mr. Baca stepped briskly in and around the eating, milling people and looked at Cam sitting. He felt a great deal of gratitude in his heart. "You are a good man, Cam Stearns. I pray your family is blessed."

Bertha held the baby and all the workers' wives laughed and cooed at the tiny form. They were speaking in Spanish, so Cam did not understand what they said, but they were happy and smiling, and whenever they looked at him, he smiled back at them.

Smiley finished serving food, and seeing couples dance a lively Spanish dance to the tune of several men playing guitars, he grabbed Molly's hand and they began to dance with the others. Molly laughed and Smiley laughed as they turned and twirled around the yard. The tune over, everybody clapped and another song began. Molly ran over to Cam. "Dance with me, Cam."

Cam sat and looked bewildered. "I don't know how."

"Who cares?" she said.

"Well, okay," Cam said, rising slowly. Molly took his hand and placed her

152

other hand on his shoulder and they began to turn and twirl slowly and stiffly. Soon the serious look on Cam's face softened and the twirls became easier. He forgot the eyes of the people and he began to laugh. His head thrown back, he laughed and twirled and soon he even sang.

Late in the evening, Mr. Baca gathered the children. He brought out chairs for Molly, Smiley, Cam and Bertha, and placed the rest of the workers in a group behind them. Calling the children, he stood them in rows according to height. Turning to the people, he said first in English and then in Spanish. "A gift from the children."

He turned and looked at the rows of brown faces and the one white face, Elizabeth's. He raised his arm and the youngsters began to sing. *"Silent night, Holy night, all is calm, all is bright, round yon Virgin, Mother and Child, Holy infant so tender and mild, sleep in heavenly peace, sleep in heavenly peace."*

The young voices captivated the entire group and when they finished, Mr. Baca bowed deeply.

Cam felt a great tenderness that he had never before experienced.

Molly began to clap, and soon all the people applauded. The children stood and lost their nervousness. Cam and Molly rose, and Cam taking Elizabeth, Molly, and Cam Jr., shook hands with Mr. Baca, and walked to the house.

They had left Smiley talking to a young Cuban girl in her early twenties.

Inside the house, Bertha whisked Elizabeth away to bed and Molly walked to the bedroom with the baby. Cam stood and watched the people from the window. It was happy and peaceful and the laughter filled the night for many hours. Molly came from the room and placed her arms around his waist. "That was nice of you, Cam," she said.

"What?" Cam answered.

"The presents, the party."

"They're people," Cam answered slowly.

Molly remembered years earlier how to Cam they had been just like cattle, born to work and slave. "Yes," Molly answered, resting her check on his shoulder, "they are people."

In the morning, Mr. Baca in a dark suit, Smiley, Bertha, Molly, Cam and the children gathered in the main house and opened presents. They laughed and played, and at noon had a large meal.

Mr. Baca, sitting in the living room after the meal and sipping rum, stood with tears in his eyes. "It is beautiful, no, the people and you, it is beautiful. My dream is fulfilled."

Bertha walked over to him, and her large, squatty form picked up the little man and hugged him with all her might. Setting him back down on the floor, she kissed him on the face, with a loud, smacking kiss. "You sentimental old goat," she said in Spanish, "you are a good man."

Mr. Baca dried his eyes and the rest of the afternoon he followed Bertha around like a puppy dog, laughing and talking with her.

A week later, Bertha moved in with Mr. Baca behind the school house. In the evenings they could be seen, Mr. Baca with his small arms moving constantly as he talked on and on about school, children, and the stars. Bertha would listen and look at the small, caring man, and her heart was filled with love. At night he would lie with his head on her large breasts and listen to her heart, and she would stroke his head with a gentle movement of her fingers. "Marry me," he said one night.

Bertha said into the darkness. "No, we are old now, so let us just enjoy this time together. It is short."

Baca never asked her again, nor was it ever mentioned by Cam, Molly or Smiley. "This would be a scandal back in the states," Molly laughed one morning to Cam, watching Mr. Baca kiss Bertha goodbye on the steps of the school house.

Cam sipped his coffee. "This is a new land, a new world. Hopefully it will grow to know people and let people lead their own lives and be governed by their hearts."

_____

The new year came with Mr. Stone coming from Havana. There was dinner and a few drinks and everyone sang Auld Lang Syne. "to peace, and no war," Molly toasted after the song, "to a new year."

Everyone looked at Molly and toasted, and then threw their glasses into the very seldom used fireplace.

On January fourth, Smiley received the coded letter from Johnson. He left the next morning and by evening had signed for the crates of harnesses and equipment parts. Standing by the train watching the crates being loaded into the cars, he felt his blood grow cold. Christmas is over, he thought, let the children play and sing.

He walked into the Black Cat bar, and he and the owner went to the back. He found it hard not to grab the man by the throat and strangle him. "Five days. I will meet you by the railroad sign before the main entrance to the ranch. Bring the money."

The small Cuban smiled his tiny smile. "I will be there."

_____

Samuel Johnson walked briskly into the bar at the Mutiny Hotel in Biscayne Bay, Florida. One more shipment and it would be over. Maldanado had said that. This dirty business would be over, and he could get back to his life. As he entered he only glanced at the striking woman who sat with two men in the corner.

Juan Maldanado entered several minutes later, and was very amiable and gracious as they said. "When you receive the money and it is in the account. I will be back in touch."

He rose and walked out the door. He did not notice the two men and the lady rise and follow closely behind him, nor did he notice the Ford that followed him through town. Walking up the steps to his house he heard only the laughter of two men and a women as they rode by.

_____

Roosevelt looked admiringly at the young dark-eyed brunette. "Lovely, lovely," he said to her. "If I were only younger," he chuckled.

"Mr. President," the girl feigned shock, "your wife would kill us both."

"I know, I know," he kidded, "but what an exciting way to go."

She noticed his black eye. "What happened?"

"Boxing, nasty blow to the eye, but it will be fine."

The girl crossed her shapely legs, outlined by the long dress. "His connection is Maldanado, a wealthy, independent gun runner. From what we can find out, he has supplied guns for many years. He first contacted General Wood. We know

Ramone does not know him, he thinks Johnson runs the show. Johnson is caught in the middle."

"There is nobody in the middle when it comes to death and destruction," Roosevelt broke in. "The shipment is already in Cuba and the man with the money has been contacted. Where do the guns come from?"

"Stolen," the woman answered. "From what we can gather they are stolen. Each shipment can be traced back to arsenals all around the country, slowly finding their way to Florida and into Cuba."

"When the next shipment is on the boat to Cuba, you know what to do."

The woman stood up. "Lovely, lovely," Roosevelt said again.

She flashed a bright smile. "If only my husband was like you."

The room empty, Roosevelt touched his eye. He could see nothing with it. Only the doctor knew, and he was under strict orders to tell no one. No one must know he was blind in that eye. No one, not even his wife.

Arnold Stone and four men hid in the cane and watched the wagon slowly stop at the railroad crossing. Cam Stearns crouched on the other side of the road with a lever action rifle. Three men sat on the wagon as Smiley rode up. "Follow me," he snorted into the dark. They rode for several hundred yards where Smiley stopped and dismounted. Wading into the cane field, followed by the three men, he pried open one of the crates. "Here you are."

One man looked at the new rifles. "To get rid of you whites," he said.

Smiley looked at the man and said nothing except, "the money."

The man looked at the two others, then walked back to the wagon and returned with a set of saddle bags. "As you requested."

Smiley took the money and walked out to the road. Throwing the saddle bags over the horse, he rode back to the railroad crossing and into the cane. Dismounting next to Stearns, he smiled a cynical smile. "Soon."

Presently the wagon could be heard creaking down the rock road. As it crossed the railroad tracks, two shots rang out and the horses fell dead. Stone stepped out of the bushes and shot the man closest to him in the face. The man lurched forward onto the bodies of the horses. The two others scrambled frantically over the back of the wagon and jumped to the ground. Smiley met the man who had muttered "to rid my country of you whites," shot him and watched him fall into the wagon. The other man ran toward the cane. Shots from Cam and the others tore his back to ribbons and he fell. They gathered the bodies and tossed them into the back of the wagon. The dead horses were disconnected and mounted horses put in their place. They took the crates to a tobacco barn and unloaded them. They buried the bodies on the old Madrid ranch in shallow graves. Cam and Smiley stood by the crates. Neither man spoke, but each could sense the other's feelings. "Now for the big man," Cam broke the silence.

Two days later Smiley deposited the money in the bank. Johnson, checking on the deposits, felt relieved.

Maldanado appeared in Johnson's office nine days later. "Tomorrow," he said, toying with the box of expensive cigars on Jonhnson's desk. Johnson sat back in his chair and said. "Then, it is over?"

Maldanado took a cigar out of the box and placed it in his pocket. "Yes, then it is over."

Maldanado walked around his home dressed in silk pajamas with a burgundy bathrobe. His personal butler entered the room. "A Mrs. Blakesly to see you, sir."

Maldanado looked at the butler. "I know no Mrs. Blakesly."

Maldanado walked and looked through the secret peep hole that looked from his study into the adjoining waiting room. He saw a tall, statuesque brunette with a dark blue dress and a large matching handbag. Satisfied that he was in no danger, he walked out of the room behind the butler. Mrs. Blakesly smiled at him. "I have a message from Johnson," she said.

"Johnson does not know where I live, my dear," he answered.

He watched as her hand reached into the large handbag and his face, with its sneering grin, suddenly realized the danger. He took several hurried steps toward the lady, but it was too late. The small dark-handled pistol exploded twice, and two red dots spurting blood appeared in the middle of his chest. Maldanado clutched his chest and his mouth moved but emitted no words. The butler ran into the room in time to see the lady calmly and deliberately stand over the prostrate figure on the floor, and place a well-aimed shot into the temple. The body jerked, she then turned and looked at the butler, and pointing the pistol at his head, shot him between the eyes.

Four men walked into Mr. Johnson's office, pushing past the secretary who tried to stop them. Johnson stood, hearing the rude intrusion. "What is the meaning of this?"

"Police, you are under arrest, Mr. Johnson."

"For what?"

"You know," a tall, well-built man in his early forties said. "You know damn well."

Johnson felt the cold of the steel around his wrists and saw his life disappear before him. He was crying and his nose was running as they led him from his office in the back of the bank and out past the wide-eyed and astonished people.

Several hours later, the ship bound for Cuba was boarded and the crates were confiscated. There were no arrests, as the men and captains knew nothing of the illegal contents of the crates.

Johnson was thrown into an individual cell and his clothes taken and replaced with a blue jumpsuit. He had called several attorneys, but as yet there was no bond. Early in the morning on the fourth day of his captivity, he was taken from his cell, walked briskly to an upstairs office and placed in a straight backed chair in front of a desk. He looked around at the green painted office and the cracked pine wood desk. Hearing the door open he didn't bother to turn around. It was not until Roosevelt was in front of him that he gasped, and once again began to cry. Roosevelt sat down heavily behind the desk. "You will be found guilty, Sam," Roosevelt said without emotion, "and you will die in prison. There is no need to play dumb, I have you."

Roosevelt took out several sheets of paper from a briefcase he carried. "You will sign these and I will see what I can do for you during your imprisonment. I cannot get you off, nor do I wish to, but I can make your prison time easier."

The papers were pushed across the desk to Johnson. He read them quickly and looked with grief and astonishment at Roosevelt. "Mr. President," he pleaded, "I cannot."

"Oh but you can," Roosevelt said, handing him a pen, "you can and you will."

Johnson looked at the unmoving and cold eyes of the President. He signed the papers quickly and his head fell toward the floor.

Roosevelt rose. "You are a disgrace to this country, and the blood of many men rest on your soul. I only hope God sees fit to forgive you, and you die with peace in your heart."

The door shut and the room was empty. Johnson stood and looked at the drab office. It was over.

———————————

Cam sat on the veranda and looked carefully over several dried tobacco leaves lying on the table. He rubbed and stretched the tobacco and then lit a match and burned a hole, raising the smoldering leaf to his nose and breathing deeply. "Good, good," he said to Smiley, "the best we have ever grown."

Looking up from the veranda, he saw Arnold Stone and another man who he recognized as a banker from Havana riding in. They dismounted and walked to the veranda. Stone smiled. "You know Mr. Bradshaw, of course."

"Of course," Stearns said, "he sends the money to the states."

Bradshaw shook his hand warmly. "Lovely, lovely ranch you have here, Mr. Stearns."

"It's not mine," Stearns responded.

Bradshaw only smiled.

Sitting down, Arnold took a deep breath and looked around the ranch. 'I'd give five years of my life for a place like this."

Smiley looked at Arnold seriously. "I'd give ten."

"How about a drink?" Cam asked, and he stood and called into the house for Bertha. "Rum, please, Bertha!"

"Oh yes," Stone said, reaching into his inside pocket. "I have a letter for you, and Mr. Bradshaw also has something for you."

He handed Stearns an over-sized envelope. The letter read:
Dear Cam,
    Thank you for your cooperation. Once more you have proven your love for your country and concern for free people. I hope all is well and you continue to prosper. I fear I grow tired of public duty, and feel I may soon retire. I have heard that the hunting is grand in Africa, and have already planned a long and restful vacation as soon as my term is over. My best to your wife and your daughter and new son.

                                                                    T. Roosevelt

Stearns smiled and folded the letter back in the envelope. He did not notice the banker opening his briefcase and shuffling some papers. "Now, Mr. Stearns." he said, "If you will sign these we can get down to a more enjoyable aspect of this ride and see your ranch."

He handed a stack of papers to Stearns. The first page read: "I, Samuel Johnson, being of sound mind and body, do hereby relinquish to Cam Stearns my plantation."

And it went into section markers and recorded deed numbers. It continued, *"this property and everything on this property from this day forth shall be duly constituted his legal possession."* And the letter was signed by Johnson, with an empty line for Cam's signature.

Cam looked at the banker in astonishment. He handed Cam a gold pen. "Well?"

Cam signed the paper and looked at Smiley. He started to hand the stack of papers back to Bradshaw, when Bradshaw said, "there's more."

"Also, I hand over to Mr. Cam Stearns my fifty-two percent holdings in the Johnson sugar refining mill, and my sixty-seven percent holdings in the tobacco shares."

Cam signed the papers, bewildered. "Why?" he asked.

Stone sipped his rum. "Don't ask me, Cam, I just work here."

Mr. Bradshaw took his pen back, "you keep those. I have the copies on record in the bank. In a few weeks I will mail you a complete and detailed list of all your holdings and your net worth as of now. I will say though, Mr. Stearns, that, along with the personal cash you have saved, you are now a very wealthy man."

Smiley looked confused as the men talked. After several minutes he could take it no longer. "What's goin' on, Cam?"

Cam looked at Smiley. "Johnson gave me the ranch."

Smiley arched his eyebrows and began to laugh, long and hard.

Sitting around the dinner table that evening Molly only said, "that's very nice of Mr. Johnson." She had no idea of the enormity of the transaction.

Cam stood by the flower garden late that evening and looked out upon the darkened ranch. "Mine," he said, "it's mine."

He did not sleep that night but lay staring into the dark, trying to believe what had happened.

Samuel Johnson was never to go to prison. The arrest, the total ruin, the rejection that came from his business partners, was too much for the man. They found him dead in his cell from a heart attack, and his burial received only a small mention in the obituaries.

———————————

Senor Ramone paced back and forth in his study. The Galindo camp reported that there had been no delivery of the shipment of guns. There was something wrong. He did not know exactly what it was, but he knew it could be big trouble.

Galindo sat in his tent, instructing his lieutenants. "In three days the attacks will begin. Flores' men in the south will blow the main tracks running north and south. Desidario and his band will attack the army base outside of Trinidad. We will bring our forces into Havana, gathering the students as we go. Here we will join with the army loyal to our side, and bear down on the Presidential palace with the tanks that will join us. When the Presidente surrenders we will telegraph all points."

The runners for the other rebels departed and Galindo dismissed the other men.

Antoinetta Saavedra sat in the corner of the tent. She watched Galindo. He truly was a man of the people, strong, brave, and one that would bring freedom to the masses. Through his power and foresight Cuba would forever be independent, not needing the aid of foreign countries.

Galindo looked at her. "Soon, my love, my face will appear on all the streets, people will shout my name and in Cuban history I will be known as the man who freed Cuba and chased the foreigners from our soil.''

Antoinetta stood and began unbuttoning her army shirt. Galindo walked to her and pulled her close to him. He picked her up and lay her down on his cot. Unbuttoning her pants, he pulled them from her long shapely legs. Standing looking at her naked form he laughed, ''tanks because of your beauty, my love,'' and he quickly undressed and fell upon her.

The men outside the tent heard the moans of the two. ''Even before the fighting, he fucks,'' one grumbled. ''What better time,'' another answered, ''soon maybe we die.''

Three days later the peace of Cuba was shattered. Three hundred men under the leadership of Flores swept down out of the jungles and attacked the main railroad station in the southern part of Cuba. Quickly overrunning and startling people, they set up for the defense of their position.

Desidario's band attacked the army base and quickly breached the outer wall. Galindo, his men and Antoinetta began storming down the streets of Havana, killing many whites as they went. They were soon joined by club-waving dock workers and frenzied students.

General El Diago Marquez, hearing of the attack, contacted the tank leader, Louis Rodriguez. ''Gather your tanks,'' he ordered the captain, bursting into his office.

The captain storm. ''It is time.''

The General turned to storm from the office. ''Soon we will be the government.''

Before he reached the door Rodgriguez blew his spine away. He would not die, but for the rest of his life he would be a crippled imbecile, forever destined to a wheel chair and the sight of the clean white walls of a hospital.

Rodriguez called Stone. ''It has begun,'' he stated simply.

Mustering his men, they quickly started the tanks and began to storm through the streets, headed for the growing mass of rebels and sympathizers.

Galindo's confidence grew as they penetrated deeper and deeper into the city. Entire blocks went up in flames, the docks were ablaze and all around him the crazed followers grew. Looting and destroying all in their path, they slowly wound their way toward the palace. Meeting little resistance, they advanced quickly.

''Look, they come, they come,'' he heard Antoinetta's voice above the noise of the rifle fire. A great cheer went up from the people. He had promised tanks, and here they were. The men began running and waving as the first of the tanks rounded the corner. It was too late when Galindo saw the trap close, tanks circled the mob and with a wave of Captain Rodriguez' hand, the great destructive machines poured out their deadly fire. Small canons brought in behind the tanks were quickly set up and also fired, machine guns spit their trail of death. In the first volley, Rodriguez saw the beautiful body of Antoinetta disintegrate. The trained rebels and mob were slaughtered.

After fifteen minutes the firing stopped, and all that remained was the smell of powder and a few dazed people, walking blindly through the smoke. Galindo was found alive with one leg and hand gone. Rushed to the hospital he lay in critical condition for several weeks.

With the severe crushing of the rebels in Havana, the army's might was thrown against the other rebel leaders in the country. Forces from Guantanamo joined in the fighting, but it was little more than a maneuver. Rebel leaders were hanged and placed in downtown squares where people gaped and childen stared with curiosity.

After the battle, Ramone was the first to reach the palace. Estrada Palma stood looking out of his window at the fires that burned on the edges of the city. "El Presidente," Ramone said, "you are well, praise the blessed Virgin."

Palma turned and looked at the man he had trusted for so many years. "I am sad for you, my friend, and for my self."

He pulled the cord beside his desk and four armed men entered the room. "Take him away," the Presidente said.

Ramone struggled, "my Presidente, what have I done, what have I done?"

Palma did not answer nor turn from the window.

(21)

Galindo languished in the hospital until one morning his dead body was found on the ground below his room. The official announcement said that he had jumped to his death, unable to live with the pain and suffering he had brought. No investigation was ordered.

Palma, thinking the revolution was thwarted, recalled his troops, but immediately after the troops were off the streets, mob violence spread across the land. Dock workers and field workers overpowered authorities, burned and destroyed in a mad frenzy. Without leadership, they destroyed their own homes, and had no goal to their destruction except the disillusioned hopelessness of their lives. Many mills and plantations were overrun by the workers. Stearns' ranch was not touched, nor did any of his workers leave to join the mobs. At one time, when a neighboring ranch was set on fire by a mob, forcing the owner to flee for Havana, Stearns' workers circled his ranch without orders, and stopped the mob from entering.

With his country completely out of control and his army and government in shambles, Palma, under the Platt Amendment, simply handed Cuba over once more to the United States. Charles E. Magoon was sent in by Roosevelt and placed the land under Civil Military Law. Ship after ship load of American troops poured into the country and the rioting stopped. The country fell once more into a forced complacency, much like a vicious dog on a leash.

The planters and ranchers relaxed with the army men on patrol and the bandits dead. It had been short and bloody, with many mills and ranches destroyed, but once again the American dollars flowed and the workers worked, and it would take no time at all to rebuild a few weeks of destruction.

Palma stepped down with no ceremony and was never heard from again. Many thought he went to Mexico, some said to Costa Rico, but to the general public it was never discovered. A considerable amount of Cuba money disappeared with him, a reported twelve million dollars.

Stearns discovered that his net worth was now slight over two million dollars. He immediately sold his share of the sugar mill and tobacco distribution and placed the cash in several banks in the United States. He now had two and a half million dollars in hard cash and a ranch free and clear. Telling Molly over dinner of his worth, she could not comprehend the figures and it left her slightly dizzy. Cam ordered two automobiles, both the just-produced Model T Fords. He added to the tobacco sheds and imported a dozen Arabian horses, ten mares and two stallions. "I will have the best horses in Cuba," he stated, watching the beautiful animals being unloaded. He made Smiley a new deal and drew up a contract where Smiley received ten percent of the crop and forty thousand dollars a year, with opportunities to invest his money in horses or crops from the ranch. Smiley added to his home, bought shares in the animals and re-did his wardrobe. With his blond hair and blue eyes, he now was the picture of a misplaced dashing cowboy. He had a custom made silver inlaid western saddle, wore boots hand made in Texas, and a western hat. Smiley, looking like a rich ranch owner and Stearns like a wealthy Cuban plantation owner made quite a contrasting pair. But a new, warm friendship seemed to grow between them. Smiley's words were listened to, and the men spent long hours going over the tobacco and cane. They started a program of crossing their tobacco, and enlarged their cattle herd to a hundred head. The workers were given a fifty cent an hour raise, and Mr. Baca was given an account for the needs of the school. They had the latest textbooks and desks. The school on the Stearns plantation rivaled any in the country. Stearns began to give many parties. There were many army officers and navy men with their wives on the island now, and Molly loved the parties.

It was a grand time in Cuba after the fighting in early 1906.

(22)

Mr. Charles E. Magoon stood, his hands held lightly behind his back, and gazed out over the city below him. It was August and he felt uncomfortable standing in his light suit. Turning from the window, he returned to his desk and sat down heavily. "Paper work," he muttered angrily to the walls. "God, would I love to get out of this hell hole for a while. A few days on the Stearns plantation, sitting on the veranda and sipping a few ice cold bloody marys would sure do the trick."

The thought of the beautiful Molly crossed is mind and he picked up the phone. He waited patiently for the operator to connect his call and fiddled with his pen.

"Hello, Stearns plantation," cracked over the line.

"Cam, this is Charles Magoon."

Cam sat in his office and ran his hand through his hair. "Charles, how are you?"

"Tire and hot and sick of this office."

Cam laughed. "Well, why don't you come on out to the ranch for a few days, and bring your wife."

"I was hoping you'd ask," Magoon answered. "We'll be there in two days. Tell your charming wife hello for me," and he hung up.

Stearns stood up from the desk and walked toward the house. It had been peaceful the last months. Now with the military everywhere to be seen there had been no burning or rioting. Magoon, under the tutelage of Roosevelt, had quickly and efficiently shut down the resistance. There had been three months of trials for rebels and government officials involved with the revolution, and all were tucked neatly away in the foul jails of Cuba for many years. New programs had been put into action to bring more money into Cuba for schools and roads. If after the war there had been an influx of American business now it seemed every other face in Havana was white. There were many sputtering and coughing automobiles adding to the congestion, and a new bank opened every week.

Stearns stopped in front of the house and looked admiringly at the two matched Model T Fords parked there. He and Smiley fussed and fumed over the new gadgets. Molly and the children loved riding through the countryside on Sundays. He wiped the polished black fender with his hand and walked into the house.

Molly sat fussing with Cam Jr. "Hold still," she scolded, wiping his face with a wet rag, "I swear all you can do is get into the dirt."

Cam Jr., seeing his father, broke from his mother's grasp and ran to Cam. Cam picked him up and rubbed his tossled head. Molly rose from her chair, looking exasperated. "He becomes more like you every day. Hard headed, stubborn and always into something."

Cam sat the boy back down on the floor. "Charles and his wife are coming for a few days," he said. Molly smiled. "Good, it's been a while since we've had company."

For several months after the fighting was over, Cam and Molly had given a party almost every weekend. The new government people, new businessmen, army and navy personnel. They were lavish affairs, with fine imported wines and elaborate meals. The ladies dressed in the latest American fashions and the men in open necked shirts and light airy pants and jackets. But then one evening when the guests had all gone, Molly looked at Cam and said, "let's not have any more parties for a while, Cam, I'm tired."

Cam looked at Molly through the haze of cigar smoke still in the room. "I'm glad you spoke up first. One more party, one more low-cut gown and my mind might burst. Not that I mind looking at all the pink bosoms, mind you, it just gets a little tiresome."

But now, the sound of another voice and a woman to talk to instead of the ever present chatter of cane and tobacco would be a pleasant break for Molly. Cam sat in his red chair. Life had been good, a mixture of calm, peace and contentment had finally surrounded him. With money in the bank Cam did not think about his children's security. He did not think about the next meal, or even worry himself about the crops for the season. The plantation could lose many crops and still Cam would be wealthy. More and more Cam thought less of the plantation itself. Smiley, through action alone, had gradually taken over the overseeing of the workers and bosses. He watched the crops, the cuttings, and checked the tobacco. Cam worked from his office to Havana setting up accounts, and negotiating with buyers. Drawn into the social whirl of Havana with the aura of mystique that surrounded him, Cam enjoyed the lazy afternoons sitting in the fine bars and restaurants. He could always feel the thoughts of others as they met him. He knew that tales of his killing the rebels circulated through the ranks of the social class. But it did not bother him, it set him apart in most cases from the others. He had no law degree or business degree. But his stunning green eyes and sandy hair, and the killer in him, gave him his own niche and presence. Through hard work and diligence he had acquired a deathlike approach to business. He sold, he did not con or play any games. People accustomed to the soft-sell wine and dine approach to business grew to like Stearns. He quoted a price and that was the deal. He took what the market would bear. He had grown accustomed to the comfort of his position. Never would he use his power for anything except the welfare of his family. He would never lose the simple roots of his childhood.

What at first had posed no problem now, at many times, left Cam troubled. There had been women he knew fancied his attention, and with word of his success with the plantation there was not a party or a gathering that there was not at least one woman who sought to stand and talk with him. Laughing and joking, they would eye his fine features. There had been one exceptional lady in Havana, the daughter of a rich shipper he had met through Mr. Magoon at a dinner. After a quiet evening Cam had driven the lady home in his new Model T. The night, the stars, and the naked arms of the woman had intoxicated him, and it was only with a frail will that he did not accept the invitation to her room. But even to this day, there were times when Cam would think about the young dark haired girl and feel the passion grown within him. With Molly he was relaxed and happy. Theirs was a wholesome house. The dark happenings of the near past had been shelved like so many books, and Molly's eyes seemed to glow. There was never a mention made of the Madrids or Bill Hood. It had happened, but it seemed to have not.

Molly, given her own expense account for the care of the house, proved to be quite frugal and meticulous in her purchases. Although she was not one to waste or spent foolishly, she bought fine clothes, good food and added to the splendor of the house. Each week Cam would see a new vase or painting. The house was lavish, but taseful. Good enough, but not so rich and luxurious as to be uncomfortable. Cam had never scolded Molly for her expenditures. She still had Bertha and Mary as maids. Mr. Baca lived happily with Bertha and taught school religiously every day.

One night, sitting on the porch of his house, Smiley saw Cam and Molly walking through the flower garden. Like a cloud, he lost the intense feeling he held for Molly. "I am a child," he said to himself. "She is like my sister."

And Smiley once again became calm and relaxed, not locked in mortal combat with his emotions whenever he was around Molly. What with working all day with little or no comment from Cam, he enjoyed the power. He liked the way the men and the boses looked at him when he rode up. He made his decisions quickly and without hesitation. The men listened. He sat and was one with Cam. Life was good. He did not envy Cam his home or his wife now. He was young, wealthy enough, and free of all ties.

Elizabeth was drawn more and more to the horses and rode whenever possible. Molly watched her one day and, in passing, metioned to Cam that maybe she should have lessons. The next week a man from Havana arrived, stayed for three weeks and taught Elizabeth the basics of English riding. Now at random times the instructor would arrive and give her more lessons and tell her what to work on for his next visit. Elizabeth was a happy, bubbling child, content with few friends except the Cuban children, but already the childhood ties were dying. The Cubans went from school to the fields, few would leave the plantation. Elizabeth went from school to the stables and the fine home with beautiful clothes. Although the Cubans on the plantation had it much better than their co-workers around the country they still did not have, by any means, a life of leisure. The old ones sang praise and relief, the young ones' minds already looked to the future.

Cam Jr., turning a year old, was the joy of Cam's life. He did not lavish gifts upon him, and as with both children he was strict. One could tell, watching Cam look at the boy, that he was as proud as a father could be. Cam Jr., never a child to laugh and play boisterously, was prone more to playing alone and in a quiet, subdued manner. It was as if his mind had already come to grips with the world, and he toyed with the problems that would face him during his life. He loved his father, and his face would light up with joy whenever Cam came into the room. Cam would sit looking at him and think, how different it is for you, little one, and feel amazed at the separation already present between himself and his son. There were so many things in life that were lonely. The distance of it all, he would muse.

All in all it was good for Cam Stearns and his family. It was a full life, rewarding and comfortable. But, in other parts of Cuba, it was a quite different story.

(23)

Roberto Alvarez longed for the sea, at times so much he would dismiss the duties his father had ordered him to do. Tucking the shoe shine box beneath a pile of garbage in an alley, he would run to the docks of Havana and look past the many ships with their ant-like parades of people and stare transfixed out upon the sea. His thin body would seem to gain strength, and he would dream of the large fishs trapped in his nets and the smile of his mother piling the cooked fish upon the table. When he was young, six years old, his father would wake him early and they would take the tortillas and cold fish from dinner the night before and walk to the fishing boat. His father was a quiet, tall, well-built man with hands torn and twisted from a life of pulling in the rough coarse nets. Sometimes it would be hours before his father would talk. Patiently heading the small wooded sailboat into the wind, tacking the reefs, he would say, "it is time, Roberto," and they would strain and pull the net with its sparkling fish into the boat. With each fish Roberto would marvel at the flashes of silver and the gaping gills as they thrashed on the deck. But his father would only work, unsmiling. Each pull as if it was just another pain he must endure. One day he said, "you will not work like a dog, someday we will eat meat and chickens and your sister's will dress right and not have to work like the dogs they make of us."

Roberto's father did not understand his son. Roberto loved the work and the fish, the smell of the ocean and the way the wind caught the small, patched sail. He loved the old, and many times patched, little ship which he called Little Sister. Neither the rags he wore for clothes nor the hard work troubled him. He dreamed of nothing but fishing and the ocean. He was proud, and boasted of his father to the other children. "My father is a fisherman, the best in all Cuba."

But the fishing had ended. One day his father did not wake him with the dark, and when Roberto woke to the smell of tortillas, his mother looked at him and said, "Your father is gone, he will return, but I do not know when."

He had been confused but not alarmed, but later in the day he saw Juan Ortega and two men set sail on his father's boat. Running back to the palm-thatched hut, he said to his mother. "The boat, it is being stolen."

His mother looked at Roberto and said with sad eyes. "Your father sold the boat, Roberto. He has gone to the mountains to fight for the people."

Roberto did not understand, and was not to understand until the day when his father returned. His face was blank, showing no life. "We have lost," he said, "Galindo is dead. There is no new world."

And then Roberto heard the tales of the mountains and the fighting. The scream of the bullets and the cries of the dying men and women.

Two weeks after his father's return, they loaded their few belongings onto the cart and behind the swishing tail of the ox, they traveled to Havana. Roberto hated Havana; with its garbage and rat infested houses piled so close to one another. There was no fresh smell of the ocean. No glistening fish being unloaded into the boat. His father rose early and went to work on the docks, loading and unloading the great ships each day. His sisters did washing and ironing and mended rich people's clothes, and he, with a wooden box his father made, went around the city shining the shoes of men dressed in fancy clothes.

By the ocean with the sea winds and the gulls, he had not known that they were poor. But, here in Havana, it took only a few months for Roberto to learn of his lot in life. He would stand on the street corners and see the automobiles and carriages ride past him filled with rich men and women. The other people, his father called them, smiling, smelling of good food and comfort. And he would go home to the one room with the laundry hanging and the small dirt-covered mattresses they slept on. His life had changed. No more did he run on the beach with the other near-naked children and play with the sand crabs or sand fleas. Instead, he ran with the other boys of his neighborhood and fought the boys from down the street. He was bullied by the older boys. He learned to use a knife, and to run through the alleys from the other boys who would take his pennies and nickels he had earned from shining shoes. He learned to steal from the fruit vendors and bread bakers, and even from the large stores with colored cloth and shoes. He would steal, and his mother would cry, "my son, my son." But the fruit was eaten and the cloth sewn into clothes for his sisters. His father would come home and sit at the small table eating his food in a dream, then he would sleep and be gone. At times his father would not come home for days, and when he did he would smell of rum and dirt from the street. Once his father had come home and screamed at his mother, "We are pigs for the white men," and in these drunken stupors Roberto would hear again of the fighting in the mountains, and of the heroic people who had tried to fight and change the lives of the real people of the land. And with this, Roberto in his young heart and mind began to hate. He hated the city, the smell of the city, he hated the cars, the carriages and the fine stores, but most of all he hated white men and women. He hated men with the shoes he shined as he smiled up into their well-fed faces. The ladies with the smiles that looked at him and quickly turned their gaze, as if to say, you poor little boy. He hated them all. There would be days when his hatred would consume him, and he and the other boys would throw rocks and break windows, and paint dirty words about the Americans on the walls of the shacks. But, at other times, his hate would be so unbearable he would run to the docks and the ocean and sit. "Why, my father, why?" he would moan, "let us return to the sea and the smell of the fish. Let us return where we will still be poor but we will work for ourselves." But his crying did not change his life, nor that of his mother and sisters.

Then one day his father came home and he was not drunk. And although he was not happy, he seemed to be relieved. "I have a new job," he told the family. "A job by Guines. We will leave soon."

They had packed their few belongings, tying the clothes in balls, and walked to the train station. Roberto had seen the trains, but, inside he marveled at the seats and the smell of the train, and at the conductors who came for the tickets. He ate his food and watched the country roll by. It was like a dream, a dream that did not end until the train lurched to a stop and his father rose. "We are here."

A tall, wiry white man met them at the station. He smiled at Roberto, but Roberto did not smile back. He talked to Roberto's father in Spanish, and they walked to one of the fine American cars Roberto had seen in Havana, and, to his surprise, they got in. His mother, his father and two sisters sat with their scant belongings. The white man started the vehicle and they drove down the dusty road. There was cane, tobacco, pigs and cattle. Men and women worked in the fields. It was not the ocean, and there was no smell except of the land. The car stopped and the white man helped his mother out of the car. He spoke pleasantly and the family followed him into a three-room house. It was a house like Roberto had never seen. The roof was tin, not palm, and it was clean. There was a room to cook and eat in, a room to sit in with chairs, a sofa and a table, and a room to sleep in. His mother touched the cleanliness of the house and smiled, and the white man left. "He is a just and fair man," his father said. "Mr. Stearns owns this plantation."

Roberto did not understand, but seeing his mother sitting on the porch that evening resting, and his sisters talking with others who lived in houses like theirs, he felt a change. In the back of his mind there was a stirring and a calling. The next day his mother took him, clean and washed with his sisters to a small square building where children played and hollered outside, and with stern words told him, "you will listen to this man. If I hear of any mischief from any of you, your father will beat you and so will I."

These were unusually strong words for his mother. Mr. Baca stepped from the building and rang a bell. Immediately the children formed into lines and marched into the school. Roberto and his sisters stood, perplexed and afraid. Mr. Baca walked down the steps of the school and said to them. "Come, this is the day of your new life. Inside I hold the wonders of the world and the key to unlock your minds."

He whisked them inside, holding the hands of Roberto's sisters, and introduced them to the children. Roberto had never seen a room like this. The desks were in neat lines, the children were clean and their clothes were not patched. On one wall there was a board that one could write on and erase what was just written. And there were books that the children could read. There was a smell here, a smell of turpentine and cleanliness. Once inside, he was to find there was no foolishness, or one suffered the swift smack of the small rod from Mr. Baca.

After the school day ended Roberto stood in front of the building and watched the children. They ran and laughed, some of the boys came and talked to him, and his sisters walked back to the house with other girls. There were no fights or having to run from older boys.

Arriving at their house, he was surprised to find a white woman sitting in the kitchen with his mother. She smiled as he came into the room. His mother looked at him. "Roberto, this is Mrs. Stearns."

Roberto looked at the blond, white lady and his dark eyes showed apprehension. Molly looked at the handsome lad. "Hello, Roberto," she said, and held out her hand. Roberto shook her hand and looked at his mother. He wanted to tell her of the school, the smell, the books, but his mother pushed him toward the door. "Play, Roberto, play and meet the other children."

Mrs. Alvarez looked at Molly after Roberto was gone. "My son, I love him dearly."

That evening the family sat at dinner and there were beans, corn and meat on the table and tortillas, at least a dozen. They ate and then his father laughed and went into the other room. From the other room he brought out pants, shirts and shoes for Roberto, three pair of each. And for the girls there were dresses, and then he went back and brought to his wife two dresses. His wife did not speak as she looked at the new clothes, but sat and ran her fingers over the material. "We get beans, flour and meat from the cattle. There were pigs and chickens for the people too, and fifty cents more than other workers in all of Cuba. You must pray for our good fortune children," his mother said, "and you must always remember that there are good and bad people from all countries and of all colors."

Roberto did not understand. But that night, lying on the clean mattress and hearing the sleeping of his sisters, he was relaxed and at peace. Before sleep overcame him he dreamed of the ocean and stars over the ocean. Before the house awoke in the morning he was up and dressed and looking out the window toward the school, with the turpentine smell and the books.

Charles Magoon and his wife Mary sat on the veranda and looked out over the cane fields. Elizabeth rode her horse around the arena and took the low hurdles in stride. "Splendid," Mr. Magoon said, "a good life for a child."

Mary sat and watched Cam Jr. play in the grass. Cam rode in from one of his few excursions into the fields and saw that the company had arrived. He walked briskly up to the porch. Mr. Magoon rose and shook hands warmly. "Quite different from the government life, eh?" Stearns laughed. Mr. Magoon sat back down. "If any man besides Roosevelt had asked me to come here and run this government I would have told them no, but it was Roosevelt, so here I am."

Cam sat down and Bertha came from the house and handed him an iced tea. "Well, the government is for men like you," Stearns said, savoring the tea, "me, I'll stick with cane and tobacco."

After a few moments of silence Stearns asked Magoon, "how long do you think you'll be here, Charles?"

"Oh, a few years at least," he sighed. "A few years to get Cuba back to a some sort of self government, weed out as many of the thieves as possible and then I can go back to the states. But I fear it is endless. Just because one revolt was put down doesn't mean that is the end of it. The people are poor, and they will continue to be poor. They are leaderless right now, but there will be others."

Cam looked at his son playing in the grass. "I suppose you're right, there will be another leader, another fighter with hopes and dreams. There are no easy answers."

Molly turned to Mary. "And how is Cuba for you, Mary?"

Mary wiped the perspiration from her brow. "Fine, I suppose, but, I must admit, I miss the states."

"It takes getting used to," Molly said. "But it is a good life."

Cam watched the workers come in from the fields. He had noticed several new faces among the children, and supposed they were the children of the new men Smiley had told him about. Cam rose, "if you will excuse me I will clean up and get ready for dinner."

"We're already settled in," Magoon answered, "take your time. I'll sit here and enjoy the quiet of the country."

_____

Roberto Alvarez had seen Cam Stearns several times. The first time riding by on a large white horse. He noticed the set jaw and pinned up sleeve and through conversation with the other children he soon learned the history of Cam. The war, the rebel fighting. In Havana he could have hated this man, this man with the daring look about him, the fine horses and saddles. But here he could only look at him and picture himself upon the great horse, his hair blowing in the wind. He could only look and marvel at the thought that the house he and his family lived in, the large beautiful hacienda, the stables and barns, the drying sheds and all the animals belonged to this one man.

One evening, sitting on the porch of their house, Roberto looked up at the stars and listened to the crickets and he thought, it is most important in one's life, one must be true to oneself and just. We are all people. And he remembered standing with Mr. Baca as he watched with fascination the large round globe turn with the different colors and patterns that were mountains and valleys and oceans. He remembered Mr. Baca saying "in all this world here we are, a tiny island off the coast of North America and here," and he circled his hands, "around the globe are people and places we will never see. People who like you and I get up in the morning and go to work. Isn't it amazing?"

Roberto had been truly amazed. The small piece of ground he stood on was but one tiny chunk of the earth, and there were children like himself who were red and black and yellow and talked differently but all dreamed and played just like he did.

One morning Mr. Baca sat in the kitchen while Bertha cleaned off the table. "That new boy, Roberto, the thin young man with the darting black eyes. He is a smart child, inquisitive, bright. Of all the children I have taught there is a glow in him."

Bertha turned and looked at the small teacher and she saw a look she had never seen on his face. As if through this one child there was a hope, a desire to perform beyond the ordinary. The type of man a teacher would say with pride, pointing to a photograph on his wall, "I was his teacher."

After several weeks Mr. Baca saw the unquenchable thirst for knowledge Roberto possessed. He loved all the children, all the faces, but Roberto had something about him, something that placed him beyond his age. Not a toughness learned from the streets, but a quiet look that seemed to decipher life and send him into the future. Mr. Baca began going out of his way with Roberto. While the other children played during recess he would talk to Roberto. He told him of Cuba and its history. The years of slavery and the land under the Spanish rule. He told him of the war and how Cuba had been under the Spanish, and how when he was a boy in Havana, much like Roberto, poor and alone, he worked hard to go to school. He told him of the Stearns and Smiley, and made up stories of the United States. Mr. Baca had always wanted to go to America and he told the boy his dream. He told it so that Roberto saw the large buildings and the throngs of people, the prairies with the Indians and the gold in California. But he would always tell him, "there are no real winners, Roberto, it is always a lonely struggle for justice."

Roberto would look at him and say nothing, but one day, standing on the front steps of the school, he looked at Mr. Baca and said, "there is an order, Mr. Baca, there is a true and just way to life, we must only find it."

Mr. Baca watched the boy walk from the school and his mind was alive and filled with joy.

The children in bed, the Stearns' and Magoon's sat around the living room drinking coffee. "It seems so very complicated," Molly said, "the United States came here and expelled the Spanish. But, although we have built roads, put in telephones, built schools and hospitals it seems we have done nothing."

Mr. Magoon looked at Molly, "there have been great changes, Molly."

Molly looked at Magoon. "I have been other places Charles, I have seen the workers of other plantations, I have seen the dock workers and the fruit pickers of Havana. Cam and I have sailed down to the port of Santiago. It is the same, the people are devastated. I know there are large plantations like this one, but how many help the workers like Cam does? It seems all the help is just a token, while we truly reap the benefits of this land."

169

Mr. Magoon shifted uneasily in his chair and looked at Cam. Cam smiled, "my wife is strong willed, Charles."

Magoon sipped his coffee and chuckled, "Molly, if I could answer your question I would gladly, but, my dear, I don't know. I really don't think there are answers now, the world is so troubled and complex that I think we go through our lives trying to catch rainbows, mired and befuddled by time and history and always trying to repair the mistakes of others while we, ourselves, blunder on."

"I suppose so," Molly conceded, "but it is sad."

"It's always been sad," Mr. Magoon added.

Cam sat and listened to the conversation, but his mind did not ponder the questions. Man could not help everybody, with luck and work hopefully you ended up in comfort. Fate, destiny, calling, and you were forever poor and lost to the world. He did not know. Fate, after much thought he finally called it, either you made it or you didn't, that was all.

"You're so cold at times," Molly would tell him, "rational, cold, and unfeeling."

Cam would look at her, "to the rest of the world, I suppose, but I love you and the children," and Molly could not answer. Cam had the traits of success. Cold, calculating and hard working. Beyond the land of his plantation there was no other world. No lives, no loves, Cam only cared here in this house and in the fields.

Mary looked at Charles. "My dear, are you ready for bed?"

Charles downed the rest of his drink. "I suppose. Cam is going to show me the plantation tomorrow, and I should get some rest."

Mary slid the dress down to her feet. Kicking it off quickly, she took off the half slip and the brasier and slid under the covers. Charles moved sluggishly around the room. His large round stomach fell over his waistline. He was not a charmer. More sluggish than anything else, he sat down and grunted with his pants. Mary looked at him. He is a good man, she thought. She remembered the days when he courted her. His long wavy black hair, which now had become a few white hairs in a sea of pink skin. How he would ride the buggy for two hours to get to her house and how for months her father had stood on the porch and told him he could not see his daughter. But he would still come, and finally one day her father spit a large gob of tobacco onto the ground and looked up at Mary's window. "A feller here to see ya Mary. You'd best come on down," and he had walked from the porch to the barn without shaking hands with Charles or saying hello. Not until after they were married and Charles was a young lawyer in Augusta did her father tell him one day while visiting from the farm, "I always liked you boy, but my Mary wasn't gonna go off with some fancy dan unless he cared enough to make the trip more than once."

Yes, he was a good man, perhaps too good for this appointment as acting Governor of Cuba but, he would handle it with good will. Charles crawled into bed. Mary placed her arm across his chest. "Good night dear," he said yawning, "I love you." Mary curled up into his side and they slept.

Cam and Mr. Magoon drove down the road of the ranch. "I will never cease to be amazed at the cane," Magoon shouted above the noise of the Model T engine

"Sugar and more sugar, sugar as far as the eye can see. It reminds me of the miles and miles of corn in Nebraska and Iowa."

Cam stopped the car by a well-tended white board fence. "These are my beauties," he said proudly, pointing to the ten Arabian mares that galloped away from the car. All ten ran, their ears forward, tails sailing behind them, and came to a stop in a small cluster on the far side of the field. "A Mr. Booker ordered them for me, all the way from Egypt, the purest strain of horse on the face of the earth."

All of the horses were white except one, which was coal black. "Soon I will start breeding them to the stallion that is kept by the house."

Mr. Magoon looked at the fine beasts. "How much are they worth, Cam?"

"Fifteen thousand dollars apiece."

Fifteen thousand dollars, Magoon thought to himself, he had worked in government his entire life. Always an assistant to somebody, digging through law books and answering letters. Helping his bosses through countless pitfalls in their lives. And he had never made fifteen thousand dollars in a year, until now. Cuba had been his best paying job, twenty-seven thousand. Not quite two of these animals. "Simply amazing, Cam, amazing."

"I think that myself," Cam answered, "every time I see them," and he chuckled "Life, it will never cease to amaze me. A few years ago I would have never dreamed I would be standing here looking at two hundred fifty thousand dollars worth of horses, let alone own them."

Mr. Magoon heard the irony in Cam's voice. He like Cam. Of all the planters and businessmen that he met in his capacity as governor he like Cam the most. He would never forget sitting with Roosevelt over dinner, and how Roosevelt went on and on about this man Cam Stearns. His New Mexico background, excluding the brush with the law, his bravery under fire, and how he had taken on the rebels. When Magoon first met Cam they had immediately felt a tie of friendship. Cam was not open with many men, preferring to be silent and cautious, but with Mr. Magoon he had been open, and they had quickly become friends. They very seldom talked of business or politics. In each other they found a man to be just themselves with. Somenone with whom to relax and smile and drink one too many drinks. There had been no one in Cam's life like Magoon since Bill Hood, and he like the company.

The afternoon breeze began its trip from the ocean. Soon it rustled the cane and Cam and Charles stood watching the horses in silence, "It's beautiful, Cam," Magoon finally said, "It's too bad this country is so often in turmoil. If all men could stand, and view the world like this, it would be so much easier."

Cam looked at Charles. "True," Cam said, "but it never can be."

The Magoons caught the train back to Havana in the morning. Cam returned to his office and books, and Smiley continued his overseeing the ranch. Life was a gentle pattern, only changed by the weather.

Two days later, Cam stood by the corral of the stallion and for the first time he noticed the young thin Cuban boy gazing at the horse. Roberto looked with wonderment at the fine white stallion. The stallion pranced around the corral, his nostrils flaring and his eyes rolling wildly in their sockets. He had never seen such an animal. It was far better than the ocean or the sails of the ships. In his mind he could not communicate the thought but the horse was free, even in its cage it was free, free and wild like nothing he had ever seen.

Cam watched the boy, and for a moment he was standing by the loading shoot in New Mexico. He was fourteen years old, and the two year old filly snorted and pranced in the shoot. Cowboys ran other horses into the shoot and the door of the train car banged open. Men hollered and cussed at the dust-throwing animals and soon the horses snorted and glared from between the wooden slats of the train car. He had stood and watched his horse, his filly, her eye looking madly out into the day, and the train had started and slowly pulled away. He could hear the horses stomping on the hard wooden floor of the train, and the nervousness that surrounded them. It was to have been his horse, he had fed her and halter broken her, but they were poor, and the money was badly needed. Cam blinked his eyes, he had all but forgotten that day long ago. But now he could taste the dust and smell the horses in the hot afternoon.

The boy's spell with the stallion broke, and he looked across the corral and saw Cam standing there. He felt a flash of guilt for no reason, and for a moment he and Stearns locked eyes. Cam was startled, looking at the eyes of the boy. Although they were dark, they were his eyes, hard, cold, searching eyes. He looked at the boy and slowly a smile crossed his face and he waved. Roberto raised his hand slowly and waved, then darted from the corral. Cam turned from the corral and walked toward the office.

Roberto ran to the house and into the kitchen. "Mother," he said, winded, "have you seen the stallion? It is so beautiful. One day I will have a horse like that."

His mother, busy with the laundry, did not speak. It was not good to dream past one's position. She had learned this early. A devout Catholic, she went through life passively, silently enduring the hardships. "Go find your sisters," she said, "soon your father will be in from the fields and we will eat."

Life was good for Roberto and his family. There were no knife fights, no running from the other boys. His father did not become drunk and yell the night away. But at times Roberto would look at his father coming in from the fields, walking slowly, his large weatherbeaten features so much like the earth, and he would feel perplexed. Here on one side, lived the white family with everything one could want in life, and on the other side lived men and people like his father. Happy with a small shred of comfort. He did not understand or comprehend the enormity of the riddle. His father would walk by Roberto and every day he would say, "what did you learn in school today?" And even before he walked to the back of the house to bathe from the rain barrels, they would sit on the porch and Roberto would tell him all they had talked about in school, and his father would smile. "It is good, it is very good," he would say, rising and stretching his tired arms and legs. "To be able to learn is very good."

Roberto's sisters, being older, sixteen and seventeen, were more interested in the boys, and did not have Roberto's appetite for school. Their mother prayed each night that they would be virtuous and not succumb to the fire she knew burned inside them. She did not know of the loss of their virtue in Havana. Both sisters had slept with many men and had taken money for it. They never were caught or found out, but it had happened. And now in school on the ranch, it was hard for them to think back as children. They liked the ranch, but both enjoyed the hustle and bustle of the city and the look of fine women. Both in the quiet of the night had spoken often of the day when they would return to Havana. "Our mother," the oldest daughter would say, "praying to those statues, it is all for nothing. This is what will bring us to good fortune," and she would touch her breast and push them from the sides with her hands so they stuck out like two overripe melons. "For people as we are there is only one way to life. While our bodies are young we can be as we want."

Roberto never knew of the thoughts of his sisters.

(24)

Michele Diangello stood in the shadows several paces from the corner. It was hot, and the street lamp swirled with the sounds of the insects. He looked across the street and saw the four other boys playing. Returning his gaze down the street, he waited patiently until he heard the familiar clatter of the horses' hooves on the brick road. As the wagon neared the street lamp, he ran and thumped heavily into the horse. Falling to the pavement, he began to moan and cry, "my legs, my legs."

The driver, seeing the flash of the boy, jerked the horses to a halt, and the enclosed wagon came to an abrupt stop. Wrapping the double reins quickly, he leaped from the wagon. The round young lad lay in the street, crying and clutching his legs. The men bent down and tried to quiet the thrashing boy. "I didn't see you, I didn't see you," he stammered, trying to control the child. The four boys across the street quickly stole into the darkness and slipped into the back of the wagon. One, with chain cutters, deftly snipped the chain holding the wooden doors together. Another jumped into the back of the wagon and began passing out the racks of clothes. The man caught up with the thrashing boy, and heard nothing else until he heard the sound of feet running. Catching a glimpse of the clothes, he ran after the boys. Drawing near to them as they disappeared around a corner, he lengthened his stride. As he came around the corner the last thing he felt was an excruciating pain that sent him lifeless to the ground, his skull crushed by the swinging bat. A large lad of fifteen looked down at the man. "Hit 'im too hard, George," one of the boys said. "He's dead."

The boy threw the bat down beside the still twitching body. "Next time I'll be more careful," he spat, and they began to run.

Michele, watching the young men run down the street, got up and ran the other way. It had worked as all the others. His plans never failed. Slowing to a walk blocks from the scene of the crime, he smiled to himself. Tomorrow they would meet at the small run-down apartment and distribute the clothes. He was fifteen years old, and wealthy for his age. A bright boy from a middle-class

173

neighborhood, he spurned his parents and the children of his class to lead a gang of tough kids from the slums. His brains and their viciousness had led from small, dime-store candy heists to a lucrative trade with businessmen for hot clothing and other items he and his gang stole.

One day this town would be his. Philadelphia, with its smoke and dung smell. Its poor and rich. He would control the streets like the mayor and the governor controlled the city and state. He would wear rich clothes and have diamonds and jewelry. People would pay him. Everybody would pay him. He broke into a run for the remaining block to his home.

Michele's father looked up from the newspaper as he came into the house. It was a comfortable home, a large, two-story white wood. It had many windows and lace curtains. His father watched the boy run up the stairs to his room and returned to his paper. "Young fucker," he scoffed, "one day those boys will be the death of you."

Michele kicked off his shoes and sat down at the desk in the corner of his room. He opened his math book and began working diligently on his homework. He was a bright lad, straight A's in school. Always clean and dressed neatly. He hated dirt, he hated working with his hands or seeing dirt under his fingernails. Always well mannered and obedient in school, the teachers, when they scolded the other children, told them they should be more like Michele. Michele closed the math book and took the small thin blue book from inside his secret hiding place behind his bookshelf. Eighteen hundred dollars he had. Each heist, each job, was carefully written down. His take, the money he paid out. Money spent in setting up the caper. It was all neat and well planned.

At dinner his father looked at the boy. "Been over on ninth street with the trash again?" he said, shoveling mashed potatoes onto his plate. Michele did not answer. His mother sat down and looked at her husband. "Leave the boy alone, dear, let him eat," and she smiled at her son. She knew he was a little wild, but he was a good boy, such a clean and handsome boy. Michele smiled at her and neatly put potatoes on his plate. He was not a slob like his father. He would not work his life away for coal like his father. The plant, the work, the tired back, sitting and growing old in a dream of being comfortable. For him there would be wealth. In his young cunning mind the stage was set. There was no one, no one who could stop him, especially not the police.

(25)

The years 1906 through 1909 were tranquil years in Cuba. American businessmen poured more and more money into the country. Shipments of tobacco and sugar doubled, and even during the 1907 fall in the stock exchange, all managed to weather the storm.

In 1909, with the country in seeming peace, Charles E. Magoon went back to the United States, and Cuba once more held a national election. General Samuel Mendosa took office shortly after Magoon's departure, and Cuba seemed once more to be on the road to independence and a democratic govenment.

Magoon was happy to leave Cuba. His wife was ailing, and was bothered by the heat and humidity. He went to St. Louis, where he lived for seven more years and died a tranquil old man in his sleep.

American forces no longer walked the streets, and the base at Guantanamo again represented the only American forces on the island.

For several months, Mendosa's reign ran smoothly, until gradually pamphlets again began to circulate in the streets of the towns and a new wave of anti-Americanism began to spread across the country. Located solely on the campuses with no rebel leaders terrorizing the trains and shipyards, it was a sleeping menace, with the Americans watching the newspapers for the first report of violence. There were scattered riots on the docks by workers, but they were quickly and efficiently put down by the Cuban military. Americans once more traveled armed, and houses hid weapons in each room. Although Americans were cautious, there was no widespread alarm. The United States government had shown that they would send troops at a moment's notice, and most businesses except those poorly run did well and prospered.

The time passed quickly and quietly for Cam and Molly. The children grew, the cane grew, and the tobacco grew. Cam dismissed his ideas of a cigar company and a tractor plant and stayed with his two crops. He worked more and more with his horses. Breeding to his original mares, he sold four and kept four of the new stock. Molly felt the days go by one by one, but steeped into the country life, she would have to look at the calendar to know what day it was. Smiley did not change nor did he wish to change. On a trip to Havana for Cam, he had met a young lady from Boston. Her father, a shipbuilder, was on vacation in Havana and had brought her with him. Smiley noticed the smiling brunette while eating dinner at the hotel, and not being one to hesitate, he sent a note to the girl via the waiter. He asked her if she would like a drink. Reading the note, the girl smiled and blushed slightly and looked over at him. Her father, a plump man with a double chin and a humor to match his size, laughed and invited Smiley over. "Sit down, sit down, my boy," he said through his double chin and large sideburns. "So you are one of the multitude," he went on, "falling at the feet of my beautiful daughter."

Smiley looked at the man and laughed deeply. "No, sir," he drawled, putting on his best Texas accent, which he had almost lost over the years. "It's just that I was sittin' here and I looked over at your daughter's face, and what could I do?"

Linda Wright was her name, and her father was Bill. "Just call me Bill," he said. They had an enjoyable evening. The conversation was kept decent for Linda, but she was not a shy girl, and seemed genuinely interested in the blue-eyed ex-cowboy who worked on a plantation. Bill talked of ships and sails and the new steel and laughed and eyed the young man approvingly. After the meal, he pushed his large frame from the table. Smiling at his daughter and Smiley, he rose. "Well, I'll let you two young people be alone, I have a book I've been dying to read. Back in the states I never have time for anything but ledgers and boats and all those business things.''

He winked at Smiley and patted his daughter on the hand. ''Not a word of this to your mother, rest her backward heart, if she hears I let you run around with a worthless misplaced cowboy while we were in Havana, she'll have both our skins.''

''Don't worry, Daddy, I'll never tell.''

The rest of the evening Smiley sat enraptured. Linda talked and laughed, told him of Boston and the sea and the gulls. After an hour or so, they went into the bar, and Smiley sat looking at the girl and thought, he had never enjoyed a woman's conversation before except Molly's. To Smiley, women were only good from the neck down. If they were suppose to be good thinkers and conversationalists, then why did they have tits and fine legs? But Linda was different. She had been to college and was very opinionated like Molly. He found himself outclassed in almost every subject of conversation. ''Guess I don't keep up much with the world, Linda,'' he confessed, after her oratory about Europe and how there would be a war within a few years. Smiley looked at Linda and he could see her moving daintily through the social circle of Boston, drinking tea and having parties on the lawn. Linda was infatuated by Smiley. Having never been west of Mississippi, she pleaded with him until he told her about Texas, Indians and the army. She looked at him and thought of her husband-to-be. An educated, well-mannered man, schooled at Harvard, from a very good family, but he seemed so boring and drab compared to this wild-eyed misplanted cowboy.

Smiley walked her to her suite, which she shared with her father, and stood by the door looking at the beautiful lady. In desperation, he asked her if she would like to see the plantation. ''Oh, yes,'' she answered, ''I would love it, but I will have to ask my father.''

''Ask him to come too.''

She seemed relieved with that, and invited Smiley into the room. Her father sat reading a book and smiled at them as they entered. ''Daddy, Smiley has asked us to see the plantation, let's.''

Bill looked at the girl and Smiley, and turned his gaze to the window. For a moment his mind wandered, and he remembered years earlier, engaged to Linda's mother, he had gone to Virginia to see an old school chum of his, and his sister had been there. They had a whirlwind affair. Breakfast, lunches, dinners and late night walks, and they had parted. She was married to a senator now, and they met often. It had been a grand happening in his life. Deceitful, he confessed to himself, but now, in old age, a lovely memory.

He looked at this daughter. ''You go, Linda, I would like to sit and rest and read my book.''

He looked at Smiley. ''I'm sure your young cowboy is a gentleman.''

In the morning Smiley picked her up after calling Cam and telling him about the girl. ''Sure, bring her out,'' Cam laughed. ''She can use our guest room.''

The car ride out to the ranch was delightful, the girl marveled at the cane and the tobacco. As Smiley helped her out of the car in front of the Stearns house, Molly looked at Smiley with a gleam in her eye. ''My dear,'' she said to Linda, ''we are delighted.''

For two days, she stayed in the guest room in the Stearns house. Riding with Smiley during the day and the two of them sitting in the house at night talking. She fell naturally and comfortably into the house. The last night of Linda's stay, she and Smiley walked slowly around the moonlit flower garden. "How beautiful," Linda exclaimed. Smiley stopped and turned Linda to face him. "You're beautiful." he said, and he kissed her on the forehead. She stepped lightly away from him and her gaze looked deep into his eyes. "I can't Smiley, I'm engaged."

"I know," Smiley answered.

The next day as the train pulled away from the station, Smiley waved at the fading form. He was quiet for a few days and neither Molly nor Cam saw him, but soon he was at the house and never again was Linda's name spoken.

Teddy Roosevelt sat in the large, overstuffed chair and looked at the lights of New York. He rubbed his left eye wearily and reached for his Scotch. The eight years had gone by so fast. Now, no longer President, he felt without direction for the first time in years. All his energy, his waking moments, had been for the country. One obstacle after the next, he had moved forward without hesitation. But now, sitting alone in his study, he was afraid. Afraid of being alone or afraid of being useless, he did not know which, but a fear crept over his body. He thought of Cuba, Panama and Latin America, the Japanese and all the hostilities in the world. After all the years of public service, he wondered what he would do now. His body, soft and little too plump, no longer moved like his mind. Later in the evening, he stood up from his chair. "I'll go to Africa, by God," he spoke out loud, "I'll go and hunt, and get outdoors. Do these old bones good, by God."

He went to bed smiling. Of course the press would know, and the country would follow his hunt as if they were there. "Bully," he snorted, falling into bed. "Africa, it has loins and elephants, zebras and gazelles."

He closed his eyes and sleep blanketed him. He was growing old, but there was time, time and life, time to be his own man and not a leader. It would be good, it would be enjoyable. The hell with politics, the country would grow and prosper without him. It was no longer his responsibility.

(26)

Cam parked the car in front of the offices of Rogers and Smith. They had handled his crops ever since the twist of fate with Johnson, and had done a good job. Deftly avoiding ruin in the fall of 1907 they were, as far as Cam knew, honest. Cam walked up the stairs to the building. It had been a good year. The tobacco drying in his sheds was the best he had ever grown. The sugar crop, although down slightly, would not cut any noticeable profits for the year.

He was happy today. In a few days Elizabeth would be twelve years old. The past years since 1909 had flown by. The children were healthy and happy. It was hard to believe the speed with which his life was passing, what with the children so large and becoming young adults. Elizabeth was already quite the young lady. Several months earlier he had been sitting on the veranda watching Elizabeth ride, and he noticed for the first time the young budding breasts that were forming on her chest. Not one to grow sad at the passing of time, he had chuckled to himself. But a few moments later, when Cam Jr. walked into the yard covered with mud from head to foot from hunting frogs with the other boys, he saw the green eyes and the disheveled brown hair, and he felt somewhere in the past years he had missed something. It had been too fast. There had been many things going on in the world that seemed to take Cam's time and energy, and he had missed the days when his children must have grown inches at a time. They were walking, talking people now, not small infants to be played with and coddled. Their eyes were open and their lives were advancing into an uncertain future.

He walked into the oak paneled outer offices of the establishment. The young secretary smiled at him and said. "Sit down, Mr. Stearns, it will only be a short while."

Stearns sat down and began glancing through the magazines that lay neatly on a low coffee table. More news about Taft, whom Cam did not like. His passive attitude, his lack of drive, filled Cam with moments of loud talk and vehement preaching as to the glorious days of Roosevelt. He was glad Roosevelt was getting back into the picture again. He had followed his trips to Africa and his tally of trophy animals. And then he had followed closely Roosevelt's re-emergence into politics. It would be close this year, Roosevelt's campaign covered the country. But from what Stearns had been able to gather from conversations with people who traveled to America frequently, Roosevelt drew a harder line than many Americans liked. Soft, soft, Stearns muttered, the country is growing soft. The name 'War Monger' began to be attached to Roosevelt. The more Roosevelt talked, the more resolute he became about Germany. Germany must be controlled as her war machine grinds away. Steps must be taken now to curb her power before all of Europe is thrown into war and America along with her. Although Stearns would vote for Roosevelt he knew Roosevelt would not win. There were new leaders now, new thinkers, they did not stand on a hard line, but sought more and more to appease the growing American prosperity. They did not know of war or dream that a nation would even think of trying America's might.

The secretary looked over at Stearns reading. "Excuse me, Mr. Stearns, but did you hear that a man named Schrank tried to assassinate Roosevelt?"

Stearns looked at the young lady. "What?" he said, his eyes narrowing.

The lady saw the alarm in Stearns's face. "A saloon keeper named Schrank walked up to Roosevelt and at point blank range shot him."

Stearns stood up. "Is he dead?"

"No, the bullet hit his glasses case, and it hardly harmed him at all."

Stearns sat back down. He shook his head, "Roosevelt, you lucky bastard. I bet you tell the story well."

He picked up the magazine again and began to read. Turning the page, he thought he heard a shot some distance away. Listening carefully but hearing no commotion outside, he passed it off as the ever present backfire of a car. But several moments later, he heard what he knew were scattered shots. Running to the door and looking out he saw the street in a mad frenzy of rushing and shoving people. Cars honked and horses galloped through the throng. Looking toward the docks, he saw large billows of dark smoke ascending into the sky and the sound of more gun fire. He ran back into the office and yelled to the secretary, ''tell everyone to stay inside, there's trouble on the docks.''

He reached for and reassuringly felt the 32 caliber pistol he always carried in his belt. Rogers and Smith with two nervous looking clients came from their offices. Samuel Rogers said, ''what is it?''

Cam stepped back outside and looked down the street. He saw several hundred Blacks beginning to pour into the street. He immediately knew what had happened. The dock workers had rioted. Starting at the docks they were now beginning to attack the merchant section of town. Already two buildings on either side of the street were beginning to flame. He saw several bodies kicked and hacked where they lay. ''Everybody out,'' he called into the building, ''out and into my car.''

They scampered into the car, and fortunately with one crank it started. Stearns saw three or four men break from the mob and begin running toward them. Putting the car into motion, he grabbed his pistol and fired six quick rounds at the men. He saw two men clutch their bodies and fall, and the others stopped. Leaving the mob behind, he saw the terror in the secretary's eyes as he placed the empty revolver back into his belt. Near the center of town they passed soldiers hurriedly moving toward the mob. It would be over soon, the soldiers would put a swift end to the riot.

Stearns stayed at Mr. Rogers' home for two days. He called the plantation and found to his relief that there was no trouble there. But immediately after the call Smiley armed the bosses and carried extra round for his own weapons. He had Molly put rifles in every room of the house and all the children were not allowed outside of the yard to play. Molly moved quickly, loading the guns. It had been a long time, but now the cold feeling of dread again came upon her.

For two days the fighting continued, one group of rioters would be dispersed, only to have another group appear on the other side of town. What at first had been dock workers only, soon became students as well. But in either case, the soldiers waded through the mobs. Cutting and shooting, they soon ended the hostilities. Houses were locked tight and the streets were deserted.

When peace finally settled over Havana the people began to slowly poke their heads out of their houses and cautiously moved around the town. Entire sections of the city lay in ruins. Stores gutted by fire and riddled by rifle slugs were surveyed, damage appraised, and the slow, dirty job of rebuilding began again.

The next morning the newspaper carried the account of the damages and dead. Three hundred and seventy-four rioters had been killed, mostly dock workers, but many young students. Cam read the paper slowly. He felt the old familiar tight feeling in his stomach, and he knew the peaceful years were drawing to an end. Besides accounts of the riots, the newspaper also covered the growing unrest in Europe. Roosevelt was right, Germany was flexing her muscles. Looking out the window of the Rogers home, Stearns felt the old feelings return. He saw for a moment the rioters running toward the car and the slugs in slow motion leave his pistol and pierce the bodies of the two. He had killed again, and he would know the feeling even more in the future.

Leaving Havana and driving toward the plantation, he did not relax until he was in the country. Here there was no burning, no bodies on the street. It was cane, tobacco, horses and cattle. The birds flew in the sky. Molly ran to him when he got out of the car, and the children stopped playing in the yard and watched their mother hug their father and cry. Cam held Molly. "It's fine, Molly, it's fine," but he felt the dread she felt as they walked to the house. He knew Molly covered her fear well, but he also knew it would not take much to shatter her tranquility.

Within a week American forces were back in Cuba and forced control was once again in effect. This time the United States did not place an acting governor in power. General Mendosa kept his rule, but with the power of the United States behind him, he began a swift and bloody cleanup. Each day new bodies were found in the streets. Bodies that Mendosa's intelligence office had confirmed were rebel instigators. They were found and shot by well-trained assassins for the government. There were no trials for those not caught in the riot, only a gutter on the street, their life's blood dark and drying in the morning sun.

Several weeks after the riot, Roosevelt was defeated in his bid for the Presidency. Stearns was not surprised, but in the excitement he had forgotten to vote. He knew Roosevelt would take the defeat badly, and he could see his old friend, moping around his home.

Stearns had never heard from Stone after Roosevelt's term as President had ended. He would never know that Roosevelt, confiding in Taft about his men in all the Latin American countries, would be rebuffed and all the men would be recalled and warned sternly that there must never be a public word of their activities. Roosevelt had fumed and yelled, "there must be intelligence, there must be," but his cries were drowned out by Taft. With intelligence, the riots might have been avoided, but with none, there was no way to follow the activites of the anti-government people and prevent them from planning it and spread their tentacles without interference.

Elizabeth's birthday came and passed with no further trouble. Slowly the rifles loaded and placed in the rooms of the house were placed back in the gun cabinet, but kept loaded and ready.

(27)

Mr. Baca sat smiling on the veranda. Cam walked around the veranda and said nothing for a while. Then he stopped walking and sat down. "It's a strange thing you ask of me, Mr. Baca," he said. "One that I have never thought of before."

Mr. Baca put his drink down on the table and looked at Cam. "Mr. Stearns, if I were not so sure, if I did not know this in my heart, I would never ask of you such a thing."

"I know that," Cam answered.

Mr. Baca had kept the plan to himself for over two years. Not even telling Bertha of his idea, he had watched Roberto Alvarez carefully. Giving him more work than the other students and filling his mind with subtle hints until he was sure in his own mind, he then laid out his plan. He would approach Mr. Stearns and tell him about Roberto. He would beg and cry, pull out his hair if necessary. If only Stearns would send the boy to college. Stearns could contact the proper people to get Roberto accepted. Baca knew that without Cam's help, there would be no college for Roberto. He did not tell Roberto of his plan, nor would he, if Stearns said no. But he knew Roberto dreamed of college, of the books and the classes filled with so many young minds. He dreamed as Baca dreamed. It must be. He would even relinquish some of his wages back to Stearns if he would only help the boy go to college.

Stearns sat and looked at Baca. The little man's eyes were pleading. He looked away from the teacher and out toward the school where children still played and their laughter rolled in his ears. "Didn't the boy have two sisters?"

Mr. Baca nodded his head. "Yes, but they have gone back to Havana. I have heard nothing about them."

He did not know, nor did the family, that for two years the daughters would work the streets, selling their bodies to soldiers and sailors. Living in a rundown, rat-infested apartment, they would save their money and on Christmas day, 1910, set sail for America, where in years to come they would have eleven beauty parlors scattered over Miami, Florida. Both would live to be old ladies and die in middle-class comfort, long out living their husbands.

Stearns stood up from his chair. "Go and get the boy and bring him to my office."

Mr. Baca sprang to his feet and half-walked, half-ran toward the Alvarez house. Stearns watched the aging teacher and smiled to himself. "We have been together many years, Mr. Baca. If nothing else, for that I owe you something."

Roberto glanced over the college history book Mr. Baca had given him. It was a beautiful book. He would read it slowly, savoring each page like a fine meal. History, to know where you came from, to be able to correlate one's life with the life of all the world. It was fascinating.

At first, Roberto's father had been proud of how hard Roberto had studied. But then, Roberto seemed to be obsessed with learning, and his father had grown worried. "He is not a man, I do not think," he had told his wife. His wife looked at the man with whom she had suffered through so much. "He is a man," she said, "he is a man with passions for other things besides women."

Her husband looked at her and said nothing. But he watched Roberto. Watched him study and read and noticed how he did not spend time with the other boys. He did not crave to hunt frogs or fish the rivers. He didn't seem to be interested in anything but reading and studying. Sometimes his father would catch him as he stood in the evenings and watched the sun dip over the corral of the stallion. He would see the stallion prancing and the red of the sun settle over the horse and his son.

Then, one evening sitting on the porch, as he watched his son by the corral, he looked at his own hands and the cuts and scratches on his arms, and he thought, the mind also wears scars and bruises and also becomes calloused. It is the same.

With that, once again he would come home from work and sit on the porch and ask Roberto to tell him of school. One day Roberto told him, "I must go to college, some way, if I have to work in Havana for years to go. Mr. Baca says he can get me a job in Havana, and if I save and save, maybe in time I could go to college."

Roberto's father looked at him and saw that soon his son would be gone like his daughters. He held back a tear that formed on his rough and pitted face. "If it is your dream Roberto, you must follow it with all your life and your breath."

Mr. Baca burst into Roberto's house. Roberto looked with astonishment at the normally subdued, quiet school teacher. "Roberto, Roberto, you must come with me," and he grabbed the boy as Roberto stumbled to rise. Pushing him out the door, talking rapidly, he began to steer Roberto toward Mr. Stearns office. "Talk to the man, do not be afraid."

"Talk to who?" Roberto stammered.

"Mr. Stearns."

Roberto felt his stomach fall and his face flush. He had never talked to Mr. Stearns. He had watched him and envied him, but now he would talk to the man who controlled his family's lives. Mr. Baca looked at the boy as they stood at the door to Stearns' office. He patted the boy lovingly on the shoulder. "You are a man," he said, and he left.

Roberto took a deep breath and knocked on the door. Stearns answered the door and looked at the Cuban boy. He was handsome in some respects, but more plain than most. A full head of dark hair, medium-sized shoulders that ended with short-fingered hands. He was clean and tidy. "Come in, Roberto," Stearns said. Roberto entered the office and sat down in the chair in which Stearns motioned. Stearns walked over and sat down behind his desk. He did not speak right away, but observed the boy. He judged he was a strong lad, quiet, unafraid, around seventeen.

Roberto looked at the man and glanced around the large room. Shelves and shelves of books. Rifles hung on the walls. He looked at the large, dark desk. It was an impressive room. Much like Mr. Stearns, Roberto thought. Straight, quiet, but daring. Stearns took a cigar from his desk and lit it slowly. Looking at Roberto through the blue haze of smoke he said. "So you want to go to college."

Roberto was dumfounded. Stearns, seeing Roberto's surprised expression, said "then Mr. Baca did not lie, he has told you nothing." And he continued, "so tell me, why do you want to go to college?"

"I want to be a teacher. I want to fill people's mind with new thoughts. I want to be able to make people see their dreams."

The words tumbled out of Roberto's mouth. He was not really afraid, but it was a kind of fear that made him speak. "You do not know what it is like, Mr. Stearns, seeing your father and mother work to death. You would not understand."

Cam looked at the boy, but did not tell him of New Mexico and his youth. He only said, nodding his head, "perhaps."

"If I go to school and get a good job, then my mother and father can live and not work for once in their lives."

Cam turned in his swivel chair and looked out the window and said, "I will send you to college. I will pay for everything, but in the summer you will work here for me. And when your school is over, wherever you go, you will pay me back one-third more than whatever my total cost was for your schooling."

Stearns looked at the boy. "You may go and tell Mr. Baca I would like to see him."

Roberto rose from the chair. He looked at the man he did not know. He wanted to thank him, to shake his hand, something, but Stearns sat there impassively smoking his cigar, looking straight into Roberto's eyes, and all he could do was move backward to the door, open it, and leave without a word.

Cam butted the cigar and looked at the walls of his office. "You would not understand, eh? Oh yes, but I do understand, boy, I do understand."

He did not feel particularly happy or gratified with what he was doing for the boy. But he thought of that day with Roosevelt in the Montezuma hotel. It would not be right to not help.

Mr. Baca sat in the chair in Stearns office. Stearns looked at the man who had delivered his son. "I will draw up a contract for Roberto. You will be in charge and see that he does well. The first time his grades fall, or he steps out of line, I will no longer assist him."

Mr. Baca rose, and standing by the door, he looked at Stearns. "It is a strange life, Mr. Stearns, but it is also, at times, a very wonderful life."

He stepped out into the sunshine of the day and smiled as he walked to his school and to his house in the back. Who would have known, he thought, who would have known.

Cam rose from his desk and walked toward the house. Dinner would be ready soon, the children would be smiling and playing in the kitchen, helping Bertha set the table or being a nuisance. He stopped and looked back toward the workers' house and the school and thought, "Roberto, I know more than you think."

(28)

Early in 1913, with the riots ended and tranquility once more in Cuba, American troops again returned home. The entire population of Cuba and North America was suddenly brought to the realization of the great restlessness in Europe. Newspapers carried the day to day developments of the power in Europe. Roosevelt more and more spoke up for a quick and decisive action to firmly align our country with Great Britain. He called for a buildup of the navy and support for all nations who opposed the Triple Alliance. Germany, Austria and Italy had formed an alliance which simply stated that they would oppose each other's enemies. Great Britain, feeling the buildup of Germany and fearing the

183

loss of her rule of the sea, quickly signed alliances with Russia and France. Europe was now divided into two power blocks, with all the other smaller countries siding with one or the other. For many years, Europe had been divided in her interests. Colonies in other countries, new markets for greater industrial output, had put the major nations at odds with each other. Each country had dreams of world dominance and each attempted to spread their flag around the world.

Cam Stearns felt drawn to the unfolding difficulties. He would fume, reading the newspaper, and at times would grow so disgusted he would fling the paper at the wall. The United States lagged far behind. The new President, Wilson, did nothing but pray that the difficulties would go away. Roosevelt, from his retirment home, sent out a steady barrage to the newspapers calling for an upswing in military development.

Molly would watch Cam and marvel at his temper. One day after breakfast Molly asked him. "Will there be a war, Cam?"

Cam looked at his wife. "I think so, Molly. There can only be so much unrest before something blows the lid off."

Molly looked out the window. "Will Smiley go, Cam? He is five years younger than you."

Cam did not answer, he had never thought of Smiley and the war. He would not go, there was no doubt about that, the army did not need one-armed veterans. He looked back at Molly. "I suppose he would go Molly, if the country called him."

Molly stood up from the table. "The hell with countries," she said, language very severe for her, "the hell with war and power and colonies."

Walking away from the table she half said to herself, "my son will never go to war. There is no cause large enough to die for and lay with other dead soldiers on foreign soil."

Cam dismissed the incident and the questions, and didn't think about it again until one day, while working with a young colt, he turned and saw Smiley watching him. He stopped and walked over to the fence. "Great looking colt," Smiley said, watching the young, sleek animal bound away. Stearns looked at the horse's tiny legs. "He's going to be a fast one, real fast."

"How about a beer?" Smiley asked.

"Sure," Cam agreed. Sitting on Smiley's porch the men talked about the cane crop and the tobacco. Small idle chatter, until Smiley set his beer bottle down and said abruptly. "If there's a war Cam, I'm gonna go. I wanna fly one of them new planes the army's been talkin' about."

Cam looked at Smiley. "A plane, why those things are just toys for men. They're only good for carnivals and side shows." Cam remembered the show in Havana, the two planes flying overhead with men walking on the wings. The children had loved the show and he and Molly had laughed, there were banners and flags and booths selling sandwiches and beer. It had been a fine day. Smiley had been strangely silent after the show, he had gone and looked at the planes, had run his hands over the wings and stared inside the cockpit. Cam had never thought of it, but ever since the show Smiley had kept all the articles he could find on planes. He had pictures and stories of longer and longer flights, photographs of the new Russian planes with four engines. One afternoon reading the paper, Smiley had read where the army was testing planes for military use, and the writer had speculated that if they proved to be of use there would be a new branch of the army formed. Airplanes could go far behind enemy lines and bring back vital information about troop movements and buildup.

Smiley looked at Cam. "No, Cam, they're more than games, one day they'll fill the skys. Now they're like the first ships, but one day they'll be like the metal ships that tamed the ocean."

Cam looked at Smiley and laughed. "Well, if it comes to that, Smiley, you're your own man."

"I hope it doesn't, but if it does, I wanna fly. I'm young enough, and what with my army record and all, it shouldn't be that hard."

Cam sipped his beer. "The world is changing every day, seems the minute we have something that we think will make life easier, another more sophisticated model turns up. Maybe you're right Smiley, maybe one day there will be airplanes all over the sky." And rising, he laughed, "but I sure doubt it. Hell, we can't even keep the damn cars running on the ground. How are we supposed to keep airplanes in the air?"

He did not tell Molly of his converstaion with Smiley. It would worry her, and Cam knew that she didn't need that.

(29)

Since the death of Bill Hood and the revolution, Molly had kept herself insulated from the world. Enjoying the moments of social whirls and parties, she was content to live on the plantation with little more than occasional outings with Cam. On the outside, people meeting her would feel at ease and caught up in the demure and confident bearing of Molly. What they did not know was the fear that she lived with each day. The fear that was recently rekindled by Cam's near brush with death in Havana and the growing momentum for the world to be at war. She knew Cam would not go, but she feared for Smiley, who she knew would go at the slightest mention of America being involved in the war. Although people did not see this in Molly, it had become the driving factor in her life. At home, safe within the confines of the plantation, she was at rest. The fear was still there, but only slightly tangible and easy to control. Even Bertha did not sense Molly's fear, but although they had never talked about it, she knew Cam sensed an uneasiness in her and she tried her best in front of him to be brave. It seemed that he was so brave, unnerved by life and unfeeling to her plight. But she never was to realize the complete understanding that Cam had of her. Molly immersed herself in the children, they were showered with love, but by no means spoiled or pampered. Even with the maids, each child had duties and the duties were done with only slight protest allowed, and none if Cam was in the room. The children in turn loved their mother, while at times, they feared Cam deeply. He had thrashed them more than once, and each time it had been painful.

Molly's interests did not extend much beyond her garden. Besides occasionally helping Mr. Baca with the school, grading papers, or having an occasional talk with the workers' wives, she lived, breathed and was the house. For several years Cam had tried to persuade her to have other interests, but he had finally given up. People were people, a life was a life. It was not until they had the car that she even rode completely around the ranch. The car rides she enjoyed, the feel of the wind on her face, it was a safe object of the home, all steel and shiny. Riding with Cam and the children, she loved picnics by the river and the sound of the birds on those lazy days.

Each day was a different day to Molly, each day her mind would travel to some other world in her home. It was not a bad life for Molly, she knew there were no answers and she fought the fear that came over her. She knew there had been wars and would be wars, and no matter how important or how grand she would feel, she was just a small tiny dot of mankind. She supposed, at times, that this feeling of insignificance made her afraid. But she went through the days hiding her fear, hearing the stories of war and living in a world where often her husband was feared to be violent. She smiled and laughed and hugged the kids. And she ate, until now her face had a round, rosey look, round so that when she smiled her face seemed to beam. Her hips and arms had rounded. Cam would look at her and laugh, "my little butter ball."

But he did not mind. When occasionally, Cam would make love to her, it seemed to him that the extra weight made Molly softer. Molly was not offended by Cam chiding, but would only smile. "You know how it is with us Swedish stock women, our ancestors carried water buckets, big, strong women."

Cam and Molly's life together had been mostly free of arguments. There were a few, but usually it was Cam exploding over some happening in the world. Only once had Molly screamed at Cam and rushed to the kitchen breaking plates. He had punished Elizabeth too harshly for Molly's mind. She threw dishes and broke bowls for several minutes. Going back into the living room, she saw Cam standing there with a look on his face she had never seen before. He told her, far too calmly, "this is my home, my will prevails."

Never again did she make comments to Cam about discipline unless they were alone.

This was a home with trees, the flowers and life. Molly could live anywhere in the world with a home making her insulated from the world except for brief moments. Alone in the world, Molly knew she would perish. Gone was the strength of New Mexico. Too many deaths in her life, too much struggle. She accepted her easy life, enjoyed the food, the wine and the fine clothes, and prayed that each day would be the same as the last.

Roberto Alvarez walked quickly down the marble corridors of the college. The awe he had felt in the first few weeks was gone. Now he hurried to his class, his mind already going over the history lesson he had read three times. Havana was different now, different from when he was a child here, different to him, alone. He knew the shack they had lived in still existed, that the alleys with the rats and the garbage cans were still there, but here there was no dirt nor people dressed in rags. Here was learning and argument. Here were all the factors of life, all thought out, played over, talked about and discussed. In these walls were the leaders of tomorrow and the new rebels. Some would die by fire, others would live to be old and wise. The campus was a teeming, breathing, living, heartbeat of the city. Roberto had already been given a small, undergound, revolutionary hand-book entitled FREEDOM. Reading it at night he had felt the old hatreds for the white men, but sitting on his comfortable bed hearing the noise of the other students in the dorm, he could not hold the hate in his heart. There was no absolute, one could not blame every American. A new thought could not be based on the simple assumption that white Americans were the cause of all the country's ills, that Cuba under Cuba would be new and different. Roberto thought of Stearns. The students must call for change in government, there must be new incentives and higher wages, help for the old and for the sick who could not help themselves, but most of all, there must be a democarcy like in America. A democracy that paved the way for people. There must be a hope. But Roberto had no time to be political. His mind craved for more knowledge and he bore into his books, keeping the students who talked of revolution and the pamphlets in the corner of his mind. In spare moments he deciphered the cause, and slowly built in his mind thoughts about what would be correct and proper for his people.

But of all the wonder that the university had proven to be, he knew he would never forget the day he caught the train to Havana. Mr. Baca and his mother were there. His father was working in the cane. Mr. Baca smiled and walked like a banty rooster, struting beside Roberto. Roberto who would go to the university. His mother looked at her boy and was proud. She hugged him as he was about to board the train. "You are a hope, Roberto," she told him, "you are a hope, go with the Virgin Mother."

Mr. Baca had shaken his hand vigorously and said nothing, but Roberto saw the pride in his eyes. He would not fail his family nor Mr. Baca. He would not. And he would not give Mr. Stearns the satisfaction of his failing. He would study and work and one day he would give him the money. All in clean, new American dollars with the one-third over, and he would stand his equal then, he would not owe him anything.

During the months Roberto had been in school he had received one letter from Mr. Baca. Mr. Stearns had arranged for Roberto to have a spare time job from Rogers and Smith. He would be delivering legal papers for them.

In Roberto's fifth week of school, he met Carmella. Walking down the hall he had heard his name, and looking around, he saw a small girl. He recognized her immediately as being a pretty girl in his history class. She walked over to him through the traffic of hurrying students. "May I talk to you?" she asked.

Roberto looked at his watch. "I have a few moments before my next class. Walk with me."

"It is my history, Roberto, it is very hard. I was wondering if you would help me in the evenings sometimes."

Roberto looked at the girl and smiled. "Of course, tomorrow night. Are you at the girls' dorm?"

"Yes."

"I will come by and get you."

For two weeks Roberto was dilligent in his tutoring of Carmella but then one evening he looked at her and said, "you know, you are really beautiful."

She giggled and he laughed. From then on, they began to talk. They would take long walks around the campus, talking of birds one evening or war the next. Neither of them were rebels. She was the only child and daughter of a hard working grocery store owner. Roberto told her about himself. Neither Roberto nor Carmella neglected their studies. He would come to her dorm, they would walk and talk, and then they would go back to their studies. But one evening, sitting at his desk, Robert looked away from the math book out the one tiny window and knew he was in love.

His first year in school Roberto was in the top ten for marks in the freshman class. Arriving back at the plantation, he was greeted by his parents, Bertha and Mr. Baca. They had a dinner of roast chicken and two bottles of wine that Mr. Baca had bought. After the celebration, Mr. Baca looked at Roberto. "You have made me proud, Roberto," he said quietly, "tomorrow Mr. Stearns wishes to see you."

Roberto watched Mr. Baca and Bertha walk to their home. "You will never be disappointed in me, Mr. Baca."

Then he looked over toward the Stearns home. "Nor you, Mr. Stearns, nor you."

Cam had never once thought of Roberto during the past year. More and more his mind was on the growing hostilities in Europe and the foreign policy of the U.S. in regard to their hostilities. Roosevelt vehemently expressed his view that the U.S. should side with the allies, but Wilson continued his policy of total noninvolvement. But now with the happenings of the past months, Cam knew that the United States would be forced into the war and Smiley would go. It was only a matter of time. Germany had declared war first on Russia, and then on France and then, moving its troops into neutral Belgium, the English had declared war on Germany. There were too many ties and common interests for the United States not be drawn into the war on the side of France and Great Britain. Articles in the newspapers proclaimed the numerous atrocities performed by the advancing German soldiers. The Germans had already severely defeated the first Russian army, and had rushed swiftly through Belgium. Striking into France, they were not halted until fifteen miles from Paris at the Marne River. Over a million and a half men took part in the battle, and the casualty counts were staggering with four hundred fifty thousand men dead, and over two hundred thousand wounded. Cam did not understand the causes or reason for the war. He knew that the allies were drawing the sympathy of our country. He also knew that the entire European continent was at war. He read the newspapers religiously. The Russians had defeated an army of the Austro-Hungarian Empire. The Turks had sided with Germany and attacked the British forces. The more the war progressed, the more Cam could not determine who exactly was on who's side, and he pinned a large map of Europe on his den wall and followed the events of the war like some distant General.

In late 1914, Smiley came to his office early one afternoon. "I'm leaving, Cam," he said, sitting down. "If you would write to Roosevelt, I know he can get me in the new air corps."

Cam nodded his head. "I'll do that, Smiley."

He wanted to ask Smiley not to go, but he did not. He wanted to look at Smiley and talk about the years, but he did not. He only looked at the man and remembered and was sad. Sad because he would have liked to go with him, to sit once more in the tents and talk as only men talk, not about tobacco or cane, or all the complications that came from this living, but about women, love and home. He watched Smiley leave his office and he looked at his arm. No matter what, no matter his bravery, he was still only half a man, not able to be whole to the world. He walked from his office slowly and watched the sun dip behind the distant hills. The sky was red, like blood, and Smiley's form could be seen disappearing into the sunset.

Stearns eyed Roberto impassively and looked over the transcript of his grades. Laying the transcript on the desk, he said, "good, very good, it seems you work very hard."

Roberto smiled at Stearns confidently. "It is not easy, Mr. Stearns, but I do work."

"How about the rebel newspaper, Roberto, do you know who prints it?"

Roberto's smile did not fade. "No, Mr. Stearns, I do not. I only go to school. It does not interest me."

Stearns watched Roberto's face intently, but could see no sign of deceit. Oh well, he thought to himself, it was worth a try. But he would try again, and maybe next time he would find out a few names, enough names to inform the authorities and nip the growing movement in the bud. Stearns looked out the window and back to Roberto. "You will be in charge of keeping my books. Your math is very good, far better than mine," and he added, "I never went to school. Everything I have learned has come from doing everything wrong."

Roberto looked surprised. "Don't be surprised," Stearns said, "I am probably not at all what you think I am, Roberto."

For the first time, Roberto felt confused about Stearns. He believed Stearns to have been born wealthy, sent to a private college in the states, and gone to war for the excitement, but now he did not know, and he looked closely into the green eyes that seemed to bore through him and puzzle him at the same time.

Stearns stood up from his desk. "You will start tomorrow. Come here in the morning and I will explain everything to you, then you will be on your own. I will move another desk in here so you will have a place to work. Now go and relax, your parents must be very proud of you. I know Mr. Baca is beside himself whenever he talks about you and school."

Roberto rose from the chair. He looked at the man who had changed his life, and could say nothing. Stearns watched the boy go and reached for paper and pen. He sighed deeply and began to write.

Dear Mr. Roosevelt,

It has been a long while since I have been in communication with you, but I follow you around the world through the newspapers. I see you have not lost your flair for the pass. It is too bad about the election, but your years as President were many and your accomplishments great. My life on the plantation has gone smoothly. My wife is well and the children seem to become wiser with each day. The crops have been good and since the last uprising in Havana everything seems to be running with the wind. I must admit to you now that I am not one to ask for favors and I never have. My life and the lives of all my family and friends have been shaped by your will and the trust you have shown in me. But putting all that aside, as you know, I have had the same foreman since I came to Cuba. He also served in the Rough Riders under your command, and was instrumental in the dealing with the rebels. He is a brave and thoughtful man and will not sit idly by while our country is about be be plunged into war. He wishes for reasons beyond my understanding to join the army air corps and become a pilot. He sees a new era in the air which I do not see. He asked me to write you and see if you could arrange for him to be placed in the air corps. I know it might prove difficult, as he is not a young man, but a man cannot be judged by his age and he is hard as nails, having lived outdoors all his life. If this is at all possible, I can promise you he will place his entire being into becoming a good pilot. My best to you and your family. May your luck hold true and keep your glasses in your pocket.

I am yours respectfully, Cam Stearns

Stearns placed the letter in an envelope and frowned.

(31)

Michele Diangello walked confidently across the stage. Taking the diploma from the dean, he smiled graciously. College had been easy for Michele. Easy enough that it had not interfered with his rackets nor the businesses he had established in Philadelphia. He owned, already, two night clubs and several buildings in the slums that he had converted into apartments. The apartments were filthy. The rats and mice and garbage vied from the corners with the people. But they were profitable and easy to maintain. What had started out as a small time group, heisting various merchandise, had now blossomed into a large operation. A week before graduation he had opened a clothing store in Chicago which could handle all the clothes his men hijacked in Philadelphia. He had heard through reliable sources that several of the large established crime families on the east coast had mentioned his name, and that they were impressed by his success and style. Michele walked from the graduation ceremony and breathed the night air deeply. Looking around, it took him several moments to see Nancy. She saw him and ran to his side. He held her lightly and laughed. "Well, that's over, now on to bigger and better things."

They walked through the milling people and drove off in his new Ford. Michele had met Nancy in his second year of school. Her father owned several wholesale stores in Philadephia and also in New York. Nancy nor any one of the people he associated with in college knew of Michele's business. Thinking he was a rich kid, they never questioned his new cars or expensive clothes. He gave large parties and made friends with the best students of the campus and those with the weathiest parents. Although the people he assoicated with never were close friends, they all saw in him a drive beyond the one they possessed to become wealthy and powerful. He gave Nancy pearls and jewelry, and for her birthday this year he gave her a mink stole. She had been flabbergasted, but he brushed it off with a simple, "it's nothing, don't worry about it."

She did not know that it had been from the latest shipment of stolen furs and had cost him nothing.

As they drove slowly down the road, Michele pulled the girl close to him and Nancy raised her head and kissed his neck. He let his hand fall and slowly rubbed her small, compact breast.

Stopping in front of a two-story brick house, they walked up to the door and entered. The house was in a middle-class section of Philadelphia. Decorated smartly with stolen merchandise, it sat among the cottonwoods and other homes, and was, to the untrained eye, nothing but a comfortable home. It was Michele's house. Here he held his parties and brought his girl. Here he met with his men in charge, and discussed heists and strategies. Everyone thought he rented the house, but in truth he owned it. One of the benefits of loan sharking. It was simple. Either a ball bat or the house, the owner had been told, and eyeing the circle of men around him, it had been the house. As he left, Michele had told him, "your family, I hope they live long."

Two weeks later, the man had been found dead beside the highway, the apparent fatality of a hit and run.

Michele closed the door behind them and looked at the girl. He held her lightly by the neck and kissed her. Looking into her eyes, he slowly began to unbutton her dress. Running his hands over her breasts, he helped her step out of the dress. He pulled her panties down and unfastened her bra. Picking her up, he carried her up the stairs and lay her on his bed. Michele undressed, and as he stood looking down at Nancy, he smiled. Nancy would never get over his strange smile. It was not a friendly smile, nor a happy smile, more a crooked sneer, as though he had something on someone. She looked at the small, knotty muscles of his chest and the way the muscles of his stomach blended into his thighs. He was not a gentle lover, but he brought her to wild passions. Lying on top of her, he kissed her eyelids and made his way down between her breasts. Nancy's thighs rose up to meet his stomach, and he slowly inched his way down past her navel. She moaned as his tongue flicked out.

When she awoke in the morning Michele was not there. There was a hastily written note on the dresser. "Back in a few hours. I'll take you to lunch."

Nancy stretched naked in front of the full-length mirror on the closet door. Her breasts were still rosy and her thighs still burned. She looked into the mirror. He mocks me, I know, but she fought the idea and went to the bathroom. Someday I will know, she told herself, someday I will know what is behind those dark, cold eyes.

Michele sat in the restaurant and drank his coffee slowly. "Fucking war," he spat, "I'll be damned if I go to some fucking war for a bunch of Europeans I don't even know."

Two men slightly older than Michele walked in and sat down at his table. Both men were dressed well, their suits were not as expensive as Michele's but immaculately pressed. The young waitress smiled as she walked over. "Coffee, just coffee," Michele told her. All the men watched her as she walked away. Michele chuckled, looking back at the men. One of them said, "we have a man who works security for Black Brothers. They have a new warehouse filled with suits and coats and a cooler section with over three hundred fur coats there now. A few dollars and a light tap on the head for our man, and he will have seen nothing."

Michele looked at the man. "Good, we'll take it directly to Chicago. The furs we'll keep here and see what I can come up with. It might be possible for me to arrange a very important buyer for them, one who could handle all of our goods from now on."

The men smiled and drank their coffee.

Michele left the restaurant, but then turned and walked back in after his friends were gone. The restaurant was empty and the owner gone. The girl stood alone in the corner. Walking over to her, he leaned over and whispered in her ear. She took his hand and led him to the back. Putting her hands on the cutting board table, Michele pulled her panties down and lifed up the back of her dress. He unzipped his trousers and held her breast from the rear. The girl lowered her head and pushed her rear into him. He plunged into her quickly and was done in a few moments. Zipping his pants up, he reached into his coat pocket and handed the girl a twenty dollar bill. "Any time, Mr. Diangello," she smiled, "any time when the boss is gone."

Michele patted the girl on the rear and laughed. "Maybe someday you and I can work something out. You do have other friends who like to do this, don't you?"

She smiled, "a few."

Michele straightened his jacket and glanced at his watch. Plenty of time. He would pick up Nancy and eat lunch and still have time to see Angelo.

Jo Jo Jones, his real name unknown, looked at the men around him. Working class men with work clothes and boots, they were a rough lot. Jo Jo remembered when he had been like them. Working, doing anything to get ahead, but now, now with Michele, he no longer worked for a factory or a grocery store. He ran the machine. Michele did the thinking, and he ran the machine. Jo Jo was a large gorilla-like man, every part of his body hairy from the backs of his hand to the coal black mop of hair on his head. His eyebrows were like small bushes and his mustache hid his mouth so it was hard to tell if he was smiling or not. No wonder people did not like to get into trouble with Jo Jo. He had clubbed men to death for nothing, and for a few dollars he would cut a person up and feed them to the ducks at the park. Michele had taken his raw strength and shaped him into a new man. He wore new clothes, drove a new car and saw women. In exchange, Jo Jo was loyal and trustworthy. There was nothing too small or too large for him to devote his attention. This job would be their biggest to date. It was important that there were no slip-ups. The watchman was married to Jo Jo's sister, and the men had been told that if they hit him too hard they were in for it. Two ice trucks were arranged for moving the stolen goods. The furs would be in one, to be taken to the house where Michele lived. Jo Jo was the only one of the men who knew about Michele's house. The other would go directly to Chicago. "Okay, we'll all meet at the corner of third and fourth streets at ten o'clock tonight. Be there," Jo Jo said.

The men left in small groups. Jo Jo lit a cigar and ran his hand through his hair. It would be easy.

———————————

Angelo Salvadora owned a butcher shop. For years he had owned the shop. After arriving in this country from Italy, he moved to Philadelphia and opened his shop. It was a clean shop and honest. But for all his hard work and honesty, it had been a hard life for Angelo, with his wife and her incessant nagging, and his children. For years it had been hard to make ends meet, but then with the marriage of his oldest daughter to the son of the Don of Philadelphia, Angelo's life had changed. Suddenly important people wanted his beef and lamb. His little shop prospered, and within several years he had three butcher shops. He enjoyed his life now. He bought his wife enough dresses, makeup and perfume to keep her quiet, and spent his time doing odd jobs for his daughter's husband. Having only met his father once at the wedding, he did not really care to know him better, because he knew it was dangerous to get too close. He had known Michele since he was a small boy, and was surprised when Michele had approached him one day out of the blue. Angelo's dark eyes had quickly calculated the esteem and money he could make with Michele. All he had to do was connect his son-in-law with Michele and take his cut.

It had taken weeks for Angelo to get up the nerve to approach Carlos Dimitri, and minutes more for him to gain the courage to tell him his proposition. Sitting in Carlos' large, expensive home with his bodyguard in the room, Angelo kissed his hand and sat in the chair Carlos motioned to. Carlos was a large man, fat from good food and wine. Although jovial on the outside, people who knew him knew that he could kill a man as easily as he could shake his hand. Born into a position of power, he was confident in his power.

Angelo told him of Michele and how he was a smart young man looking for an outlet for stolen furs. Carlos, fiddling with a gold watch, listened carefully and then consented to a meeting at a place of his choosing. Angelo left the house cheerfully, feeling his pockets fill with his small percentage of the deal.

Michele dressed carefully, putting on a new suit and straightening his tie in front of the mirror. He smiled at Nancy. "This is an imporant day for me," he told her. "This man can help me expand my clothing stores."

Michele knew that in time he would marry Nancy. Already he saw the future.

He did not want to be with the Black Hand, as they were called, but their power in the Italian communities was unquestioned. Nothing, no store nor business worked without their approval and help, and so, his dreams needed their influence.

Michele stood up as the three men walked to his table. Carlos sat down and nodded his head and the other two men obediently took another table facing the door. "I am Carlos Dimitri," the man said, holding out his hand, the large diamond on his little finger sparkling. Michele kissed his hand. "It is my pleasure to meet such a renowned man."

He saw the look of satisfaction on Carlos' face. Michele began to uncork the bottle of Banti wine he already had on the table. "A small glass of wine?'

Carlos nodded his head. After the wine was poured, the two men eyed each other and toasted to a profitable future. Setting the glass back down on the table, Carlos said casually. "Angelo tells me you have a business offer that will interest me."

Michele held back his excitement and said calmly. "I have a group of friends who deliver to me expensive furs, but as I am a man of little significance, I have no outlet for items as expensive as these."

"Your store in Chicago is no good?" Carlos broke in.

Michele did not show alarm. "Your research is very good. No, these are too expensive, and might cause scrutiny from the wrong people."

Carlos looked at Michele and smiled. He liked Michele right away. They were the same, both immaculate dressers, both hungry for power. Both knew it took important people and money to gain one's long-range dreams and both saw an opportunity to widen their connections. "When it is time, contact Angelo and tell him the beef steaks were not so good this last time. I will come to your house and see if your wares are as you say. Is there anything more?"

Michele sipped his wine. "Yes, I wish to open a whore house and I need your protection.

Carlos poured himself another glass of wine. "Fifteen percent, and tell me when you open and where. It will be no problem, the police will not bother you."

The two men talked for several hours after that, drinking another bottle of wine. They talked of the war and women. When the sun was setting and the streets filled with people, Carlos rose from the table. Michele rose and kissed his hand. "Go with God," he said. Carlos did not answer. Passing the table where his bodyguards waited, they rose and followed behind him. Michele drained his glass of wine and waved for the bill. Paying the check, he walked to his car. He felt nervous and comfortable at the same time.

The two trucks moved slowly up to the locked gates of the warehouse. A young security guard came to the gates. Seeing Jo Jo, he cut the chain with chain cutters. Jo Jo walked with him to his night shack. He tied his hands, asking how his sister was. "Fine, fine, Jo Jo. Not too hard on the head please, just enough to look good."

Jo Jo took the butt of the pistol and cracked him hard enough for the blood to ooze out of the wound. The unconscious form sprawled on the floor. He bent over and listened for his breathing. "Sorry, brother-in-law," he said. In forty minutes the trucks were on the highway. One with suits and coats and ladies' dresses bound for Chicago. The other to a dimly lit street where the fur coats

194

were placed in different trucks.

Michele paced nervously until he heard the trucks in his driveway. He and Jo Jo unloaded the furs into the basement. An hour later they stood and laughed together. "Beautiful, beautiful," Michele said.

"How did the meeting go?" Jo Jo asked. Michele smiled, "we're set. Start lining up the girls. We're going to need a few."

Carlos had paid cash for the furs. One-third their value, a nifty twenty-seven thousand. Within two weeks, Michele had twenty-five girls working the streets, with a protected hotel where they took their customers. Fifteen percent of each trick went into a box which was picked up once a week. The girl from the restaurant ran the business and was told her tits would be cut off if the books were wrong. There was no cheating, Michele knew better than that. There was time and the world, his word must be good, his reputation must remain unblemished. Only through good business would he stay on the good side and live to be an old man. He was no fool, and knew better than to test his fate.

(32)

Teddy Roosevelt rubbed his tired good eye and replaced his glasses. He cursed his bad eye, and looked once again at the pile of letters on his desk. He signed and reached randomly for a letter. Scanning the envelope, his mind retraced the years and he opened the letter and read quickly. "That should be easy enough, my old friend," he said out loud. But then he chuckled. "Stearns, my friend, you are wrong about the airplane. I feel it will have a far greater effect on mankind than even I imagine."

Roosevelt had followed closely the development of the airplane. He had been skeptical at first, but now he felt it was of the utmost importance to develop an airplane for military use. Already other countries, mainly Germany, were developing airplanes. Why does it always take a crisis for this country to see the light? He mumbled to himself, jotting on a notepad to answer Stearns and make the necessary arrangements. He rose from his desk and stood by the window. His retirement was driving him nuts. He felt old, unused, his drive to form a military unit which he would command in Europe had been shunned without so much as a debate. A war raged and would engulf his country, and he must sit like the old man he was and do nothing. Glancing at his watch, he saw it was close to dinner time. He fought the boredom within himself and walked down the stairs. He could smell roast beef and potatoes and hear laughter coming from the kitchen. Standing at the bottom of the stairs, he stopped to catch his breath. Tired, always tired, he grumbled, and he made a mental note to see a doctor soon. There must be something they could give him to make him feel better.

Cam had not mentioned Smiley's wanting to join the air corps to Molly. He did not want to worry her needlessly, and he hoped it would prove to be a momen-

195

tary infatuation. But on the day he received the letter from Roosevelt, he felt uneasy as he opened it. The letter was not typed but written in large, sprawling handwriting.

Dear Cam,

It was with pleasure that I received your letter. It is often I think of you and the Rough Riders especially now that I have more time to dream and vegetate. One day I must come to your plantation and look for myself at the changes in Cuba. It seems very strange that I have never been back there. I would like once again to visit Kettle Hill. Old warrior's dreams. Concerning your friend, all has been taken care of. He should report to Ft. Sill, Oklahoma, where he will be placed directly in the pilot's school. There already are great advancements in the airplane and I must confess I see a future there that far outshines what we imagine. I pray Smiley does well, and I know he is a brave and courageous man. I also wish for the smell of war. It seems so inappropriate that I must remain here, while so many men train and prepare for war. But such is life, I suppose my mind is stronger than my body. Besides boredom, all is well with me and the family. Life continues and we struggle through. Take care of yourself, Cam.

As always, T. Roosevelt

Stearns looked up from the letter and felt sad for Roosevelt. It must be hard for such a man to stand and watch the world go by. Reduced to a distant rumble in the background. A monument to his people, slowly being eroded away by time.

Cam stood up from his desk and walked to the stables. He saw Roberto Alvarez walking toward the office, but he did not wave, Alvarez had proved to be a reliable man. The books were meticulously done, the figures correct and neatly columned. Stearns' books had been hop-scotch affairs, but Roberto had redone all of them, until one shelf was lined with expenditures and the other with profits. Everything was categorized. Stearns had even begun to like the boy.

"My horse," Stearns called to the stable man, and within ten minutes he was riding toward the lower cane fields. Smiley would be overseeing the burning today. The cane had been good this year. Tall stalks, so abundant that thirty part-time workers had to be hired to haul in the load. Smiley saw Cam approaching. Cam rode up. "Is everything on schedule?"

Smiley grunted and wiped his forehead with the back of his drenched shirt. "Goin' good, real good."

Cam looked at Smiley and their gazes locked for a moment. "You're in, Smiley, you have two weeks to report to Fort Sill, Oklahoma. There you will be placed in flight training."

Smiley did not show any excitement. He looked at Cam and at the workers starting the fires through the fields, and he felt the hot muggy air that he had grown accustomed to. Then he looked back at Cam. "Thanks," he mumbled, and he trotted his horse off. Stearns turned the head of the white stallion and drove his heels into the flanks of the beast. They bore down the road toward the corral and Cam wanted to go forever, out past the corrals and over the mountains to the ocean. But, pulling back on the reins beside the corral, he jumped off and walked briskly to his office. Roberto looked up quietly as he entered and returned his attention to his books. Stearns walked to his desk and sat down. He reread the letter from Roosevelt and turned his chair to look out the window, where he remained until the sun kissed the ridge and the crickets began their nightly song.

Molly, after thirteen years of marriage, knew Cam Stearns well. For the past weeks she knew he was keeping something from her. She knew he was troubled. She also knew he felt strongly that the United States would be pulled into the conflict. The casualties that she read about in the paper were staggering, and she thought sometimes how strange that at the same moment she was cutting a flower or watching a child play, men were killing each other by the thousands. There were reports of terrible new weapons such as the agonizing gas that left men dying in twisted, tormented knots. After dinner, and when the children had gone to their rooms, Cam looked at her and said, "Molly, Smiley is joining the Army Air Corps."

Molly was devastated. She looked at Cam and said nothing, while slowly a look of dread spread across her face. Cam sat in silence.

When they drove Smiley to Havana to catch the boat to Florida, Molly was stiff-lipped and quiet. But when Smiley was another face on the crowded deck of the ship, she began to cry. Smiley looked at the two figures on the dock and waved. He was excited, but he was also sad. It was a new life now, and he knew he may never see this land again or hear the laughter of Molly or the voices of Elizabeth or Cam, Jr. He stood as the island disappeared from view, and then walked slowly to his cabin. He lay on his bunk and slept.

Once in the states, Smiley's heart quickened the closer he came to Oklahoma. It was good to be back in the United States, good to see the plains and the cattle. But after three days in the army, he wondered if he really had done the right thing. He had forgotten the discipline, and was not used to being told what to do. There was the haircut, the dog tags, the running, exercises, more running, until in the afternoon there were two hours of training. Every day after reveille he would look out from the drab brown barracks and see the lines of airplanes. They were beautiful machines. Stretched fabric over wood. He would watch the advanced classes leaping into the planes and hear the roar of the engines as they spit fire from their exhaust. He would watch wide-eyed as the planes slowly gained speed until they crept from the earth, their wing tips fluttering until they stabilized and gained altitude. It was a tremendous sight, better even than the grace of a horse in gallop. Each day Smiley ran, and worked, and practiced in the dummy cockpits. He shut his mind to the shouting of the instructors and to the harrassment he and the other men endured. Soon he would have his wings and his bar. The class consisted of eighteen men. All except Smiley were in their early twenties, brash, daring young fellows. They drank and cussed and dreamed of women and the war. At night, limited only to the barracks and its yard with weights and a basketball net, they talked of home and girls. The feeling of war was as Cuba, the talk was the same. Nothing had changed except the circumstances and the development ofnewer and far superior weapons. Slowly Smiley began to become the leader of the group. After ten weeks they made their first flight. Smiley sat feeling the air from the engine rush past his leather, helmeted face. He adjusted his gloves and looked at the other men. With one wave of emotion they held their thumbs up and he pushed the throttle. All the days of practice, the days of riding behind an instructor, and he roared down the runway. Down and up and away with the clouds. His mind raced as he watched the world below him whirl by as he skirted the clouds and passed the birds. He was alone and wild and free. The engine purred and he alone controlled his world. Back on the ground he stood and looked at the dull finish of the fabric bird and patted it lovingly. "My sweet lady," he said, "the demon of the sky."

During what little time the men had off from their rigorous schedule of exercise and flying, Smiley would look upon the rolling hills of Oklahoma and he knew that to the south was Texas and his home. Smiley had never talked much about his home, not even to Stearns. He had found his escape from home when he joined the army.

Smiley's father had been a large, mean man, proud of his slaughtering of the Indians. He treated everyone around him like dirt except Smiley's mother. She was the one person in the world who seemed, as Smiley was growing up, to have some slight control over the angry man. Smiley had left Texas and never looked back, except for the brief moment in time when he left the army and Colorado. He wondered what his life would be like now if he had gone back to Texas and not New Mexico. All he knew was that it would have been different. He did not think of Cuba often, and as of yet had not written. He told himself he would write, but with the flying it seemed he either didn't have the time, or he didn't have anything to say. But he felt in his heart everything was fine and that the plantation was running as smoothly as ever.

Of the eighteen men who had originally started the class with Smiley, eleven were given their wings. After the graduation ceremony, the men were allowed off the base for the first time. For two days they drank, laughed and chased the young, Oklahoma farm girls. Back in the camp they were mustered out early in the morning and told there would be a briefing after breakfast. Colonel Sigmore, in charge of the unit, would address the men with a French officer whose name no one could pronounce. "Some French fucker," the Captain had said, and he was gone.

The men ate slowly, feeling a slight regaining of their senses after two days of fun. "Wonder who the Frenchie is," Sam Brown said between gulps of black coffee. Every man knew France was already in the war, and that they had their own flying men in the sky. Sitting in the barracks, they had talked about the war and the exploits of the French and British flying squads. All the men felt they must enter the war, and each day the newspapers told of the battles and the advancements and defeats.

After the initial advancement of the German troops, the war had settled into a dog-eat-dog existence. The trenches and their horror could not be lived through the newspapers, but the pilots all agreed they would rather fly through the air than sit with the mud and the rats on the ground. They were a happy go lucky group of men, afraid of nothing, finding pride in the fact that they were the first in what they knew, which with all certainty, would become one of the greatest turning points in the history of man, the ability to fly.

Colonel Sigmore entered the small cramped room. "Sit down, men," he said lightly. The stiff backboned men sat down ad focused their attention on the colonel. "War is changing," the colonel began. "Never before in the history of man have we stood on the brink as we do now. New weapons, tanks, machine guns, the toll of mens' deaths is amazing. We here are the first of what will become in time the greatest fighting force in history. We are a beginning, and what we do and accomplish will affect the lives of every man, woman and child in this country."

He looked over the men slowly, weighing his effect upon them. "As you know," he continued, "we have been slow in our approach to the airplane, while the European countries, Germany, England and France, have gone on with full government support. The French and British already have hundreds of airplanes in the sky. Their pilots are courageous men, flying out past enemy lines, braving the ground fire from enemy troops and bringing back information."

The men barely noticed the small, neat, pencil-mustached form sitting in the chair behind the colonel. "We have special orders from the Commander in Chief that will be further explained to you by Colonel Boudreaux. Men, I would like you to meet Colonel Boudeaux, Commander of the Lafayette Escadrille of the French Air Corps."

The men applauded as the French colonel stood up. His dark eyes smiled as he looked at the men. "It is my pleasure," he said, bowing deeply. "As you all know, we French have been fighting for several months. Our planes fill the sky. I have been given permission to enlist, under the guise of aides, pilots from the United States to return to France and join our air corps. Pilots who volunteer and are accepted will fly with us on our operations. I know this country is not at war," and he added, "as of yet. But it will come, I promise you, gentlemen, it will come and those men who join with us share in the glory of being the first of their kind to do battle. I have watched you men secretly for several weeks, and although your planes are slower than ours, it will take no time for you to master our faster airplanes. I am here to beseech you to come with me and wave the banner of freedom your country stands for. There will be no newspaper accounts of your deeds. It is strictly a volunteer mission. But you will have the knowledge that you were the first to stand up for your country and the rights of free men around the world."

The French colonel bowed again, and sat down. The men were perplexed. To fight for the French as volunteers, what if America did not go to war? Colonel Sigmore addressed the men. "Those of you wishing to volunteer for this duty submit your names to the Captain. Within a few days you will be notified and called to my office. That is all, men. As of now, you, the second graduating class, have no further assignments. I am waiting for official word as to what our capacity will be in this peacetime army. The new class of pilots will be in your barracks this afternoon. Make them feel at home, gentlemen."

The Captain stood and dismissed the men, and they filed from the briefing room. Sam Brown walked beside Smiley. Brown and Smiley had become good friends through the weeks. Brown was from Virgina, as young, well-bred, educated, dashing man, he had been a disgrace to his family. Not content to live out his life running his father's extensive business interests, he had barely made it through college, more interested in the women and sports. His family had been somewhat disappointed in his choice of a military career, but his father had said to his mother, "at least he will be gone from here."

He was lean like Smiley, quicker to anger mainly because of the eight-year difference in their ages, but a fun-loving, hard drinking man with no cares in the world. Marriage did not concern him nor did a life of lavishness between business meetings around the country. "I'm all for going," Brown exclaimed, "let's go show those Germans a thing or two."

Smiley laughed, not caught up in the fever. If this country was at war, it would be different, but to go and get killed for another country not his own did not appeal to him. "But what if we don't enter the war?" Smiley said.

Brown looked at him in amazement. "We will get into the war, can't you see that, Smiley?"

Smiley shook his head. "No, Sam, I don't see."

The men sat in small groups discussing the matter when the new class arrived. They laughed, seeing the new faces. The new men joked in returned and looked out the windows at the small line of airplanes. Smiley stood and held out his hand to the men. "Rickenbacker," one said, shaking his hand vigorously, "Eddie, just call me Eddie."

"Now, that's a fine pilot's name," Brown joked, merriment in his eyes.

Rickenbacker looked at Brown. "I'm going to be the best pilot in the army." and he said the word with such conviction that Brown stopped smiling.

"Quintan Roosevelt," another man said. "Hell, you're Teddy Roosevelt's son," Brown said. The man nodded his head meekly. "I'll be damned," Smiley broke in, "I served under your father in Cuba."

Roosevelt smiled, but said nothing. It must be tough, Smiley thought to himself, to be born the son of such a man. To be cursed all one's life to live up to the expectations of a father like him.

The rest of the afternoon was spent telling the new men of the weeks ahead, the running, the pushups, the terrible temper of the captain. All the new men listened with interest except Rickenbacker, who sat on the his bunk and shined his shoes. That night, Smiley sat down and for the first time he wrote a letter to Cam. Now that the training was over, he found himself thinking of the plantation and the children.

Dear Cam,

Sorry I haven't written since I left Cuba, but, to say the least, my time has not really been my own and I must say I've been caught up in the excitement of it all. You wouldn't believe the feeling, Cam. Being in the air and looking down at the earth as so few men have in the world. The country and the cities are so different from the air, I can't express the difference. My comrades are a jolly lot, 'devil may care' types from all over the country. Of the eighteen men who were in my class, eleven of us made our wings. Guess what? Today the new class arrived and Roosevelt's son is one of the men. Small world, isn't it? He seems a bright sort, but I cannot but feel he truly does not want to be here, but feels pressured by his father's reputation. I do not know what will come of us now. The country is still

200

not in the war and seems to go out of its way to stay neutral. I know if Roosevelt was President we would be there, but only God knows what will happen now. There are several men in my class who will be going to Europe under an agreement with the French to fly in their air force, but I will not volunteer. As long as this country is not offically at war it is not my fight. Those of us not volunteering for service in Europe will receive our orders soon. What they may be I would not know, I only hope there are women close by. Say hello to everyone for me. Tell Molly and the children I miss them dearly. How is that lovely Elizabeth doing? I trust all is well for you. I have read nothing in the newspapers about Cuba, so I guess there has been no unrest or rioting. Write me soon and tell me of all developments in your lives.

I am your friend, Smiley

Within two weeks orders had arrived. Of the eleven men who graduated, five received orders to join the French. The others would start a goodwill mission across the country. Flying from one state to the next, they would put on air shows and slowly indoctrinate the people as to the potential power of the airplaine. The ones going to Europe were given a farewell party with much drinking and toasting to their bravery. Smiley, watching Brown board the train that would take him east and to the waiting ship, felt a momentary loneliness. "Be careful," he shouted above the roar of the train. Brown looked out the window and held his hand out with the thumb up, and the train was gone.

Two days later, the six pilots took off for a flight to Dallas and the beginning of their tour. It was a grand feeling to Smiley. People in the fields would stop and look toward the sky and the pilots would dip their wings in salute. "Look at that, paw," he could hear the children say, "look at those men."

In the air there was no thought of the world, no cares or desires, only the sound of the engine and the freedom of the wind. With each stop they were addressed by mayors of cities. Flying upside down and barely above the ground, they could see but not hear the reactions of the watching crowds. Back on the ground, they were wined and dined by the better families, and more than once escorted by the lovely daughters. It was a relaxing time, a joyous time. They were the first of a breed of men that would dominate the skies. It was novel, it was enjoyable, and the ladies, in whose eyes they were the bravest men in the world, were free. Whatever town the men were in they were constantly told of the exploits of the Americans serving with the French. For a year the men traveled around the country. Flying, laughing and sleeping with the women. It was endless parade from party to party.

At first, the reports of the pilots in Europe told of the numerous scouting missions. The German pilots would fly by the allied pilots and each would wave. But then came stories of small arms fire from one plane at the next, and then early in 1915, the development of a machine gun that fired through the propeller changed the outlook forever of the airplane.

It was quiet when the Colonel left the room, after telling the men of the devastating toll the machine guns had taken on allied planes. Flying in groups, the German pilots had swarmed in on a squadron of French planes. The French had waved and shot their rifles and pistols, which before had never really taken any toll, but this time the German planes nosed high into the air and came down behind the allied planes and with their machine guns opened fire. What had been fun and games suddenly became death and destruction. One allied plane managed to limp back to base and the dying pilot told of the machine gun fire before he succumbed to a frothy mouthfull of blood. The Colonel was silent for a moment. The man was Sam Brown, the first American pilot killed in the war. There would be no mention of him in the papers, no military honors except to his family. He was officially classified as having died in a training mission with the allies.

The men seemed to change after this, they knew the government had not appropriated the funds to further develop the airplane, but now they spoke always of the need for more money for the development of faster planes with firepower. They began to talk about bomber planes. They heard of the planes flying behind enemy lines with sacks of bombs that the co-pilots dropped from the cockpit, but more and more they wanted planes that could carry large bombs under the fuselage that could be released by a lever.

The pilots added to their show. Besides formation flying and low flying, mock dogfights were performed, with planes spiraling and twisting to get into position to destroy another aircraft. Back on the ground, they would look at each other and say, "I got you," or "good maneuver, my rounds went over your wing."

Although the planes were not equipped with mock guns, and although the men knew their planes would easily fall to the enemies faster than the newer models, the men, in their own way, prepared for war. But as the months passed, the men grew disgruntled by the reports of the war. It seemed to the country that they were just airborn clowns, flying from town to town putting on shows. Their planes were in disrepair, and already every man had made forced landings in fields. They looked at the photographs of the German Fokker and the French Nieuport, which would do a hundred fifty miles an hour, and they looked at their tiring ninety mile an hour planes, and they were angry.

But in 1916 their lives changed. Flying a show around Dallas, the men were told they were going to Columbus, New Mexico where a Mexican bandit had raided and killed American men and women. They would support the army under General Pershing in pursuing and punishing this Poncho Villa. Now they would go to war, their country had been invaded, and Smiley lay in his bunk dreaming of the fighting. But after four weeks of futile flying, dust clogged engines, and no part to fix the already battered little planes, they were recalled and sent once more to Oklahoma, where they taught the new pilots. It was tedious to Smiley, instructing the new men, flying the trainers. It was boring, and he more and more thought of Cuba and dreamed about when his time would be up and he would return. He did not know at the time that soon the country would be plunged into war. If he had, he might have fought his boredom, and kept his mind alert.

In April 1917, Wilson read his war message to Germany. On April 6, the United States officially declared war on Germany, but did not make a formal statement that the United States was behind the allies. From the beginning, Wilson had attempted to keep America out of the war. Even after several of our ships were sunk by German U boats and information was gathered that Germany

202

was trying to per-suade Mexico to join them against America. It was only after several more sinkings and the armed of American merchant ships that war was declared. Immediately programs were started to get the military machine rolling quickly. Six hundred million dollars were allotted to the air corps. A selective service program was initiated for men between twenty and thirty. Gasoline was rationed and people were implored to save food and hot meat on certain days. It was a feverish time, and a time when most Americans were shocked to find that they were indeed a part of the world, and could not expect to remain isolationist in the midst of a world war. Roosevelt filled the newspaper with oratory on how the sad shape of the country was due to Wilson and his conservatism. Overnight, from being a nation watching the world fight, the United States was turned into a fierce fighting machine.

Smiley was terminated from his position as instructor and he and every available pilot were ordered to France, where the Americans formed a squadron under the Lafayette Escadrille. Eighteen hundred pilots were hurriedly trained, mostly on the east coast, and what once had been a small group of men volunteering to fight and barn storm around the country, became a large fighting force.

Smiley, with his tenure, was made a captain and a squadron leader. Sitting on the ship watching the New York skyline slowly disappear, he thought of nothing. It was war, and they were off to France. Events had happened so quickly that he had not even written Cam. He knew only one thing, he was deathly afraid of threat of the U boats. He would rather die a hundred deaths than drown in the cold Atlantic. Each night of the voyage, he stood by the rail, looking out into the darkness, straining his eyes for the telltale white tail of the torpedo. The days were long, filled with practice alerts and life boat safety. The men under him were a good lot, young men, trained in a few months for what should have taken close to a year. Soon they would fill the sky, these brave Americans, some to die, some to return home to their parents and wives. All to be faceless figures in the planes flying over Europe.

On the sixth day at sea, Smiley ran into Quintan Roosevelt. "Roosevelt," he called, "long time."

Roosevelt still looked reserved, but he smiled and shook hands warmly. He had been transferred to Maryland after his graduation and had been instrumental in the increase output of pilots. "You couldn't believe it," he said, "no breaks, one class to the next, if he could take off and land, he was passed."

"Army," Smiley snorted, "Who's your squadron commander?"

"Rickenbacker," Roosevelt answered, "remember him?"

Smiley nooded his head. "Yes, I remember him. The one who's the best pilot in the world."

Roosevelt looked at Smiley seriously. "You know, he just may well be. Damned man, I think he was born with feathers on his skin. I've never seen anyone fly like him."

"Well then, he's a good man to be under," Smiley said.

While life on board ship for the sailors was an endless chain of guard duty or KP, to the pilots it was time to play cards, look at the ocean or be officer of the night. The army brass looked at the young pilots disdainfully, eager to send their armies head first into the Germans. There was no war except on the ground. The navy to carry the men to the war, and the army to blood and guts it to victory. Pilots were children, fighting individual battles in the sky, glory boys. Because of this, the pilots did not associate with the other officers, finding it much easier to be with their own men and talk about the French planes.

After eleven days, Smiley sat down by Rickenbacker at dinner. "Eddie," he said, "glad you could make the party."

He could tell by Rickenbacker's drawn face that he did not take well to the ocean, but Eddie smiled. "Get me in the air," he snorted, "and off this water."

Both men laughed, Many men had spent days ill, but now most had gained their sea legs and were able to hold down food, as long as they didn't overdo it. "Heard you fly like the wind," Smiley said. Rickenbacker smiled. "Let's hope we all do."

The men sat in silence for the rest of the meal. Rising, Rickenbacker looked at Smiley. "Stay alert, friend," and disappeared into the sea of green men standing in line to dump their trays.

Smiley looked at all the men around him. Most were as the pilots in his squad. Between twenty-one and twenty-five years old, young, bright, shiny faces, dreaming of the battles to come and of the hero's welcome back home. He was suddenly struck by the grandeur of it all. This was no Kettle Hill. During all the time Smiley had trained and flown around the country, the war had been going on with fronts that spanned across countries. He sat and looked at the men and he was afraid. The world was shrinking. He would soon be in France, a place he had never seen nor knew anything about. He would be there, flying over fields and cities that had been there long before he was alive. His bullets ripping into men he did not know.

Rising from the steel table, he stood in the tray line and it was here he decided he must have children. Children to tell his story to, someone to know what he had done. Death, the threat of death surrounded him and all the men with their living, breathing tissue and their red blood. They were going to death behind a song and a banner. Walking to his hammock, Smiley recovered his composure, but he felt the longing for children and a wife burning deep in the back of his mind.

(33)

Although Cuba was never to be affected by the war like the United States, the war crept into all families. Either concern over brothers or fathers in the war, or concern over a friend's son, there was never a time the war was not on one's mind. The Stearns never had to think about days without meat, because they had their cattle. Sugar was at a high, and tobacco remained relatively stable. Molly was thankful that Cam Jr. was still a boy, but looking at him at times, she would wonder, what war will you see, my son. Cam followed the details of the war religiously. His world map marked the armies for the allies and the Axis. Guantanamo was alive with movement. Ships steaming in and out twenty-four hours a day. There were rumors of submarine sightings that spread like fire through the island, but all in all, the war was not in Cuba.

The Cubans thought nothing of the war. But with the money of Cuba controlled by Americans, and the shift in their interest to the war, it gave small groups of radicals a time of a little control and thought and they began to spread more leaflets and books calling for the ousting of the Americans. Several graduates of the university began a training center for people loyal to the cause. Here was taught weapon use, living off the land, and instruction in the latest in radios. Radios, used initially from ship to ship, were now becoming an integral part of the army. Already large, bulky units were in operation in headquarters. Smaller receivers kept the tides of battle and movement in constant command with the brass. Several of these had fallen into the hands of the new Cuban rebels and were guarded with their lives. Communication would become the major breakthrough in all phases of military life.

The students who attended this school saw only one way to rid their country of the American vermin. Violence. Power was given and taken in only one way. For the years of the war rebel camps scattered all over the island trained and placed back into society several thousand people. Unlike the earlier guerilla warfare, run by ignorant peasants, these were educated people. People mainly from the cities. Many were managers and salesman. They trained and spread the word of their discontent. They did not burn trains or attack warehouses. They did not call for riots in the streets. They would wait until the right time. They must be strong, and they grew stronger every day.

After Smiley departed for the army, Cam once again rose in the morning and rode the plantation. He talked to the bosses and watched every aspect of the ranch. He marveled at the vastness of it now, from the men working the cattle, to the cane and tobacco, to the men hauling the food for the workers and the constant rebuilding of fences and barns. He had forgotten all these aspects of his life, shut in his office, left to comfort and good cigars and wine. He knew the ledgers and the aspects of the market. He could judge the tobacco as it came off the wagons and knew the price of cane before the paper was out in the morning, but he had forgotten the smell of the fields and the sweat of the men.

Roberto Alvarez proved to be a bonus to the plantation. He alone knew the exact goings on about the ranch. For weeks on end Stearns would not even ask for an accounting of the monies. Cam trusted him, and knew he worked diligently. He did not go out of his way to become Roberto's friend, nor did he invite him to his house, but he trusted him, and in Roberto, Stearns saw a promise for the future. By the outbreak of the war, Roberto would graduate from college with a teacher's certificate and under the prompting of Mr. Baca, would stammer to Stearns one day, "I can be a good lawyer."

Stearns looked at the lad for several long moments and said, "I'll see what I can do."

Within the month Roberto was accepted to law school. "With work, in two years you can be back here," Stearns told him. "when the time comes, I wish first chance at hiring you. I need an attorney, a man I can trust.''

Roberto told the news to a fidgeting Baca and they sat around the rest of the evening with Baca going on and on until the glasses of wine caught up with him, and Roberto went home relieved.

Elizabeth and Cam Jr. did not really ever comprehend the war. They knew that Smiley was in Europe flying airplanes, but in their young minds they could not fathom the immensity of the war nor the effect it had on people's lives. Elizabeth was an accomplished English rider, and Cam had looked to the east coast for a college for her. Unlike many, Cam saw the approach of the equality of women, and he wanted his daughter to have a jump on it. Cam Jr. grew and remained a shy lad. As when he was a baby, he preferred to be alone, spending hours by himself around the plantation. He watched the flowers and the trees and he loved the sound of the rain as he stood by the river. Birds with their heads moving rapidly in their search for bugs, interested Cam Jr. for hours. He liked to be with his mother more than with Cam, and spent time in the kitchen with Bertha. He would ask her questions as she cooked, and knew how to make bread and tortillas and many other dishes. Cam began to feel apprehensive about Cam Jr.'s behavior, and started watching him when he didn't know he was being watched. Sometimes Cam Jr. seemed more like a girl than a boy. But he did not seem to be effeminate, and Cam breathed a sigh of relief. Cam would not force his son to be what he was not. If the boy was quiet and loved the outdoors, he would strive to help him develop interests along these lines.

Roosevelt had established the National Park Service, and Cam had told his son about the rangers and supervisors who worked in the parks. Cam Jr. had loved the idea, and sent for many books and pamphlets about a career in the Park Service. His life was planned. It was hard to believe his children were so big. Elizabeth at seventeen was no longer a child but a budding women. Cam Jr. at fourteen, made Cam shut his eyes and try to visualize where the time had gone.

Molly would never discuss the war, and Cam would say nothing to her about it. There was an occasional ''Bastards got it,'' which she soon dismissed. She told Cam, ''I wish not to hear about the war until it is over.''

Although she worried about Smiley, she did not show her fear. But her steps were quicker and her pace around the house hurried. She kept her hands in her lap and her fingers were never still. Sleep was an escape, a dark world where her dreams were unremembered and her body and mind disappeared into nothingness. Her children, she was happy to see, were not interested in the war, content to keep their interests on their own lives. It was a great relief that Cam Jr. did not wish for toy guns or tanks to play with. He was a good boy, and she saw the growing inquisitiveness in his eyes. He was a man who would be content with deciphering the living part of this world, not one to wish to maim and kill, not interested in conquest or world power. He would live his life quietly and unobtrusively.

Molly had seen the changes in Cam. Now after the years of wealth and being used to being a man of distinction, Cam had ridden himself of his riding boots and britches, his open-necked shirts and finest tapered cigars. He wore cowboy boots and pants, the boots too large, in order to allow for circulation in the damp

206

climate. His trousers were loose and of a blue material almost like denim. His shirts now were any shirt he found, the sleeves rolled up and more often than not, he wore no hat. Seeing him around the plantation, one might have thought him to be one of the workers. But driving to town, he would always be the image of the gentleman. But even Cam knew that this was but a facade. One day, standing in front of the mirror, he looked at himself and began to laugh. "Money doesn't make you what you're not," he told his reflection.

All in all, it was as most times on the plantation, quiet and tranquil. The sun set and rose, and there was no gun fire, no deadly gas moving across the land. Everyone was healthy and the war was just a story across the ocean. The dead were mere numbers to be written down and recorded, and one's life was not judged by whether or not the bullet or grenade or screaming artillery shell would take you, when the sun rose.

(34)

Michele Diangello greeted the war as nothing more than another opportunity in his life. The growing fascination with the automobile and drastic cutbacks in gasoline for personal use opened up an entirely new field for Michele to exploit. Averaging a hijacked gas truck a week, he put more cash into his pocket. Stations in and around Philadelphia and other major cities were sold the gas at half price. It was never recorded, but paid for willingly. As the war continued, gas became more and more a valuable commodity. His clothing stores were prosperous, and every valuable shipment his men took was immediately sold to Carlos. Jo Jo more and more became a part of Michele's life, as a constant negotiator between Michele and new buyers, and keeping order among the men. Michele knew that without Jo Jo he could not operate, and unlike the other men who drew straight wages, Jo Jo received a percentage.

Jo Jo was a perceptive man. Although born on the streets and tough, he was not a fool. He did not aspire to be a boss of a group. He knew that when the final shakedown came, it was always the boss who went, the other men of the group usually being integrated into the new group. If he played his cards right, he could live a full life and make a good living. He had a wife and two children. At first encounter, he gave the impression of a small store owner. Polite and considerate to his wife and children. He did not play with the whores like Michele did, nor did he frequent the better restaurants, leaving oulandish tips. Money that he made was counted, wrapped carefully and kept in a safe in the floor of his home. Unlike Michele, he did not like the Italians nor see a need for their assistance in distributing expensive merchandise. He would have just kept with the medium priced clothes, the gasoline and the girls. In dealings with the Italians he saw only trouble. The Black Hand, as they were called, who controlled all aspect of Italian life, were backward old men to him. Living like old Roman throwbacks. Kissing the ring, and hugging each other in mock affection. He saw in them only two-faced people who controlled by fear and violence. Jo Jo at heart was no longer a man of violence, but when minor reports of thievery within the group happended, he was swift and forceful in finding out the truth. Several men had their hands broken, but were not expelled from the group. A man once caught and given the fear of the Lord proved to be a better man than before. Jo Jo knew of his inventory going down to the penny. The heists gave him a secret joy, and were planned so well and executed with sure professionalism that there had never been any trouble. The one job he hated was delivering the fifteen percent to the Italians once a week from the whore house. He hated the air of the men he met, their mock superiority, and he planned in his mind how each of them would go if Michele ever needed them to disappear. "Meatballs," he would mutter to Michele, "old, greasy meatballs, squeezing their own people so they can live in mansions."

Michele, half-Italian by birth, did not care for the full blood himself, but through them he saw a means to his own end. Thriving on protection and small-time loan sharking and gambling, they were nothing to him. It was their political connections he needed, and he saw in these old men with their large mustaches and gaudy rings the beginning of a power that would sweep the country. With his dreams and their money there were riches beyond the imagination to be reaped, some within the knowledge of the law, and some without. He would look at Jo Jo and laugh, "meatballs, yes, fools, no," and that was the end of the conversation.

Michele married Nancy in the Spring of 1917. The wedding was an expensive affair. Over three hundred people attended the Catholic Mass. Nancy's father gave them a new car. There were two baskets full of money, clothes, pots and pans. Slipping away from the reception, Michele looked at his beautiful bride. Life was good, he had money, a fine home, new cars and a beautiful wife. Everywhere they went they were looked upon admiringly.

When the army started drafting men, through a stroke of luck Michele saw the man taking the filled-out forms. He was a frequent visitor to his whore house. Stepping quickly out of line, he spent the next week watching the men who frequented the house. Finally the man showed up. A short, squat, balding Greek, Michele quickly pulled him to the side. After several minutes of contemplation, the Greek, being a prudent man, smiled and slapped Michele on the back roughly. As he left the establishment, Michele told the girl working at the door, "for the Greek, anything he wants, on the house, one girl or two."

The girl obediently made the entry and Michele Diangello was never to see the army. He told Nancy that he failed the physical, as his heartbeat was too weak. Although in her heart she did not believe him, she was relieved, nevertheless.

For the many months they had dated, Nancy had often wondered exactly what Michele did. She knew the way he lived, with the expensive gifts, were not feasible on the profit of two stores in Chicago. Several weeks after the wedding over breakfast, she looked at Michele. "Michele, what else do you do?"

She was rosy and happy after several hours of lovemaking. Michele looked at her and said nothing for several moments. Then, in a voice that chilled her bones, he said, "never ask me any questions about what I do."

She had been silent the reminder of breakfast and silent when Michele left the house shortly afterwards. From that moment on, her life seemed to change. Nancy had always been a well taken care of child. She knew she loved Michele, but as the months passed and he was gone more and more from the house, and came home tired and grouchy, she wondered if he loved her as much. She knew he loved his money, and everything he placed around himself, but more and more she felt like an ornament, just another of his possessions, to be looked at and admired by other men like a fine race horse. She felt, but did not know for sure, that Michele had other women. Sometimes at night, rubbing against him, her hands exporing his body, he would fail to stiffen, and she would stop her approaches and lie there, her eyes staring into the darkness.

Through the months she began to see her future. She would be like her mother. Children, a nice home, tea with the ladies, never really understanding the world of her husband. Content but stifled. And she began to grown discontent and irritable. Michele, in his businesslike manner, did not see the changes coming over Nancy and even if he had, might not have been able to curb the storm that was brewing.

(35)

In France, Smiley was to come face to face with the true nature of war. On the ships that carried the American troops to Europe, there were over two thousand young pilots. The United States armies were brought together to fight together, and were called The First Army. The pilots were separated and stationed in many areas around France. Most became the Lafayette Americana and supported all phases of military action. The men, hearing of the beauty of France, the quiet, small towns and the grandeur of Paris, were appalled by the countryside and Paris. The terrian was pock-marked and despoiled, everywhere were wounded and crippled soldiers. The economy was in shambles. The one-legged, one-armed and blind veterans were left to beg on the streets and sleep around flaming garbage cans.

The front was a world within a world. Trenches filled with shells of men, whose nights were nightmares and days an endless daze of attack and retreat. Soon the pilots lost the look of young, bright, brave men, and became more and more a somber and drawn looking group of people. From the air one could get a true picture of the devastation and the horror of the trenches. The trenches ran for miles in long, ugly, grey slashes across the land. Germans on one side, allies on the other. The land between, a smoldering, lifeless landscape. With each assault and repulsion came white flags and the frenzied gathering of the bodies from either side. Men ate with the rats, lived in their own excrement and fought, day after day. The sky was constant drone of the airplanes, days of endless bombing missions. Time to fly out, drop the loads of death, and fly back to be refitted and regassed and once more back to the air. The planes would strafe the trenches, pouring the machine gun shells into the exposed men. Smiley would see the men running like frightened deer into the bunkers that studded the trenches. He would see the faces of men as the slugs tore into their bodies and they lay sprawled in their death poses. In no way was this war like Cuba, with fifteen thousand men, moving through the countryside, and devastating the enemy in a few months. Soldiers told tales of months in the trenches, the attacks that left thousands dead and dying. The groans of the men between the trenches. Each day became another day to fly and deliver the airborne death. There were many battles in the air with German planes. The diving and coughing planes swarmed in the air like tiny, winged devils, and men in the trenches would bet sacred cigarettes or canned food on first one, than another pilot. Word traveled among the troops of the exploits of Eddie Rickenbacker, the allies' number one ace of the war. In only a few months he had sixteen kills and three dirigibles.

It was a powerful, ugly feeling that gripped the men. Even flying over the trenches, dipping the wings in salute, one could smell the stench of the waving men below, and feel the lice that infested their bodies. In several attacks there had been more than eight hundred planes in the air, leaving such a toll of destruction of the earth that Smiley wondered if the land would ever again be green, or frequented by birds or any living thing. He began to hate the war, the airplanes and the men in the trenches on both sides. And then he began to examine his own motivations for coming here. But through it all he loved the flying. At times, sent out on reconnaissance, there would be no sudden attack from a German plane through the clouds, and for some unknown reason the tired enemy on the ground would not take pot shots at the American plane. During these times there would only be the sound of the engine and if Smiley concentrated on the sky and not the shell-shocked earth below, he found moments of release. He wished his plane would fly forever, never again to touch the earth. Lost with the clouds in some great eternal sanctuary of the sky. But these moments were few as the allies readied for their push against the German forces.

The war to the pilots was not a war of advance and retreat, although they had to move their bases frequently from the bombing attacks of the Germans. Their perspective from above gave them a day to day report on the struggles in the trenches. Pilots shot down and lucky enough to be picked up by friendly forces gave report of the ground battle, and swore on their lives they would never want to fight on the ground. "My son will know to be a pilot," one pilot said. "Those men on the ground are worse than lice."

Through the months Smiley became a solitary figure, not wanting to know the men in his squad for fear of the pain he would feel if they were killed. A quiet, sullen man on the ground, he gave his all in the air, twisting and maneuvering his plane in battle, flying cover for those limping back to the lines. Other pilots were mere faces in leather helmets, not human beings. He did not write Cam or Molly, though at times he would sit down and begin to write, be usually could think of nothing to say. As the time passed, he began to miss the plantation more and more. Spending hours thinking of the Cuban girls he had slept with in his house and visualizing the cane and tobacco. He would smile, thinking of Elizabeth, and knew now that she was a full-fleged young lady. At times he would allow himself to think of Molly, and his mind would fill with her naked form standing in front of her window. Her breasts outlined by the moon, and Smiley would begin to feel lonely, a deep, bone-chilling lonely. If he died there was no one, to mourn him, no wife, no children.

The pain of loneliness engulfed him one foggy morning as the mechanic rechecked his plane for his brief mission of dropping a load of bombs. Climbing up and out of the fog, he did not scan the horizon as he knew he should. It was these few moments that enabled the German plane to use the clouds and suddenly appear behind him. He saw the holes in the fabric before he even realized that the enemy was on his tail. A quick dive and a bank to the left was not enough, and the machine gun bullets tore into the fuselage. He was spinning, and the smoke was engulfing him and it was dark.

Smiley woke and slowly moved his aching body. A tree had somehow saved his life, catching the tail of the airplane and spinning it sideways, so the collision with the ground was a series of skips and not a headlong plunge into death. It was dark, and although Smiley felt blood on his face and arms, he knew he was in reasonably good shape. He knew he was only several miles behind enemy lines, but he also knew German forces would have been alerted that a plane had been shot down, and would be looking for him. It was rather a hopeless situation. Men shot down behind the lines were usually never heard of again, and presumed dead or as well as dead, as a prisoner of war. He heard the scraping of heavy boots and tried rising, but found his left leg would not move. He felt no pain, but try as he may, he could not move the leg. Resigning himself to the fact that there was no use struggling, he rested for a moment against the fuselage of the twisted airplane, and remembered the Indian lady patiently spooning the deer broth into his mouth, and the sullen chief who sat in the corner of the tepee and watched him slowly gain strength.

Through the darkness Smiley saw a large figure standing before him and the rustle of branches as two other men ran to the figure. He could not understand what they were saying, but the three men hurriedly picked him up and bore him through the fields. He knew this area well. It was once beautiful rolling farmland, filled with barley and wheat and fruit trees. He winced in pain as the men carried him, but said nothing.

After several hours, the men stumbled into a bombed-out barn. Hurriedly moving the dirty hay that covered the floor, they uncovered a trap door. Two men clambered down, while one helped Smiley down the narrow shaft. The door was closed above, and he could hear the men hastily arrange the straw around the floor and leave the barn.

It was not until the two men sat him in a corner that Smiley adjusted his eyes to the candlelight of the room. It was a large room, surely as large as the bottom of the barn. About thirty by forty feet. Along one wall was stacked canned goods and various German and American weapons, what were obviously found and horded. Along another wall were cots and various remnants of blankets, upon which sat several children and five women. The women looked at Smiley and walked over. One of the men walked to a small stove, kerosene by the smell, and poured large steaming mugs of tea. He brought one to Smiley, and handing it to him was roughly pushed aside by two women, who with deft hands ripped the material of his trouser leg and, talking softly in French, looked at the large ugly gash that went from his knee to his hip. They washed the wound in cold water, bandaged it with some rags and left.

With the risk the men had taken for him, Smiley was surprised when no apparent interest was shown in him. The men fell on the cots and were immediately asleep. The women, in their long wool dresses and sweaters, did the same. Smiley pulled his jacket tighter around him and shortly felt the anxiety leave him. He looked at the sleeping people and with this etched in his mind, he slept. They were French, he knew that, but wondered what they were doing here.

It was cold and damp in the barn basement when he woke. It was daylight outside, judging by his watch, which still miraculously ran. He watched as the cold, stiff people awoke and began to move about. The children were not allowed to speak, in case a German patrol happened to be in the area. It would not take long to find the hiding place. The two men looked at him and smiled and brought him warm tea, heated by a candle under a tin can. He nodded and sipped the tea, feeling the warmth spread down his throat. The men walked away and sat down at a small table in the middle of the room and Smiley could see they were going over maps. He struggled to his feet and limped to them. Smiley quickly discerned that they had maps of the trenches, and picking up a pencil stub, Smiley drew in the new locations of the trenches and the ground lost by the Germans. The men smiled and spoke something in French and pointed to a spot on the map. He gathered this was their position, no more than two miles from the German front. This place must be crawling with Germans, he thought. This barn, a burned out remnant of someone's farm. He then knew how perilous their position was.

December was cold and rainy, and the barn, although partially destroyed, would seem an inviting refuge from the weather to passing German troops. He turned from the men and looked at the women, and saw that none of them were young, but all were strong, farm women with deeply lined faces. They smiled at him and he smiled back and limped over to his corner. The day passed as such, little movement, little talk, much looking at the map.

Then at eight in the evening, Smiley watched as one man opened several cans of food, and passed them out to be devoured quickly. Another can was opened and fed entirely to the children. The little girls, five or six years old, sat on the dirt, their light faces covered with dirt, and ate the canned peaches happily. Each took the can silently, grabbed one sliced peach with a short and stubby finger and passed the can to another. In this way the can was shared and afterward, the sweet sugar syrup was drunk.

At ten o'clock, there was a sudden sound of boots on the ceiling. Then three knocks, and the French relaxed. A man fell to the ground from the hole above, leaving the trap door open. After a few sporadic sentences, the women tightened their clothing around them and tucked in the clothes of the little girls. The men looked at Smiley, who rose to his feet. One man started to help him, but Smiley shook his head no. The men took only the weapons by the wall, one went out first, then the women and children, and then Smiley, followed by the last man, who carefully covered the trap door with the hay.

The tattered line of people inched through the countryside. At times the leader would stop and all would do exactly what the person in front of them did. If the lead man fell to the ground, they all fell, one at a time. If he froze and did not move, all froze and did not move. At times they moved through trees inches at a time, the voices of German sentries around them. Smiley moved his leg, gritting his teeth. There is no pain, he told himself.

It was not until four in the morning that Smiley realized what they were doing. A path lay, cut through rolls and rolls of wire. They walked until there was no more wire. All around hung a strong acid smell, and smell of urine and feces. After agonizing minutes, the lead man began shouting in broken English, "American pilot, American pilot." Smiley heard the scuffling of men and the sound of banging weapons. "Don't shoot, don't shoot," he yelled, "Americans."

Figures appeared around them, dragging them the remaining yard to the trench. Thrown to the bottom of the trench, the French men, women and children, and Smiley lay in a heap. A Frenchman beside Smiley looked deep into Smiley's face and smiled a toothy smile. "American."

The women rose slowly, clutching the little girls tightly to their sides, and several sobbed softly. Smiley stood and looked at the open-mouthed soldiers. "Would ya look at that Percy," one said, "fuckin' Frenchmen."

Smiley held out his hand and helped the others up. Turning and looking at the soldiers he said in his best Texas drawl, "I'm Captain William Stone. Take us to the Commander."

"A Frenchman and a fuckin' Texan," the G.I. laughed.

"Yes sir," the other man answered.

The trenches were cut into the ground, braced in spots by beams and brick. The line of French stepped through the soldiers. Most looked momentarily, then returned to the small fires that flamed on the ground and the tin of coffee and tea.

Colonel Shafter sat in the command bunker and shook his head. "Well, you were certainly fortunate, Captain," he said. That day they sat in the bunker and listened to the sporadic firing that went back and forth during the day. When evening came, he and the French were put in an ambulance and taken to the rear. As they rode, they watched the slowly parading line of men to and from the trenches. They were a sad, torn, tired lot.

The ambulance stopped in a small village Smiley knew was only about six miles from his unit. Here he got out and watched stone-faced, as the group of French men, women and children disappeared into the milling throng of soldiers and people. He limped into the two-story brick house that was now a hospital.

For a week, he would sit in the hospital and look out the window and the incessant rain, and think of the men in the dark and the walk through the enemy lines. The courage of the people filled him with a feeling he did not understand, and reporting back to his unit, he eagerly sat in his plane, with the familiar smell of the gasoline and gun oil, and visualized the German plane in his sights and the men running on the ground from his death fire. They were the enemy, they were the people that sent families fleeing from their tranquil farms. All he would see would die, and on his first mission out, he scored two kills and strafed the enemy line with his remaining rounds when coming back in.

He became loud and boisterous back in the barracks, and the spirit of the men under him rose. They sang and drank excessively and flew their planes into any battle, bringing their fire into heavily infested enemy concentration. "Catch Rickenbacker," became the battle cry. Smiley had fourteen kills and two dirigibles, Rickenbacker, at last count, had nineteen and three dirigibles.

For several months the fighting in the trenches had been sporadic. Each side braced for the coming onslaught. Finally the German troops started a last-ditch effort to capture Paris. After weeks of bloody fighting the allies held, and the retreating German army was laid to waste. Plane after plane strafed and bombed the cut-off, supplyless men. Day after day, until the roads were littered with the dead and the burning vehicles.

Two weeks, later, Germany surrendered, and what had been a land of war, overnight became alive. People crawled out of their holes. Soldiers wiped their eyes and cleared their minds of death and killing and looked at the torn and twisted land. Women wept and men began the slow walk back to their farms. There were many dead, many family members who would never be officially called dead, but missing in action. The war was over, and an entire world limped back home.

Smiley was transferred to Paris. He sat in an office with other officers who were billeted together. Some marine, some army, all with different stories, all somber, but slowly regaining the thoughts of home and family. "You know, it's been impossible to think of the wife," a marine lieutenant said one night, "wife and kids, sitting there looking at the rat gnaw on a body in the field, the stench of the gas and the nose of the rifles, always the rifles. You would have gone insane."

During this time, there were many women. Bright, alive French women, women with long, graceful necks and small, firm breasts. The best women in the world, all the men had to agree. "They'll do anything," a colonel from Georgia told Smiley one night. "Now, if I can teach my wife that, I'll have something," but then a moment later he said, "she'd wonder where I learned it."

Smiley loved the night life of Paris and for a few weeks of his life, he forgot about everything. There was no Cuba, no America. There was only Paris, the wine, the food and the women. All lonely, tired women, who were not thinking of the rest of their lives, or who they would marry, but only who they would dance with, laugh with and love. It was a grand time, but an all too brief time.

In May of 1918, Smiley received his orders. New York and discharge. He sat in his office and looked out the window at the neatly parked airplanes, and he thought of the French women, and then he looked out past his world and he saw Cuba and the blue ocean and his house. The world waited and Smiley was ready to leave.

_____

Cam hadn't paid much attention to the fact that Smiley did not write, although he knew Molly longed desperately for a letter. He knew that if he was killed he would know, so as long as there was no letter, Smiley was fine. The day the armistice was signed, Mr. Baca, Cam, Bertha and Molly stood in the kitchen and toasted the victory. It was not a solemn affair, they did not witness first-hand the particular ugliness of this war, but it was over. Cam looked forward to a letter now from Smiley, telling them when he would return. Cam had not hired another man to take Smiley's place. This he would never do. Once a week Smiley's house had been cleaned, and his clothes washed. Everything was as he had left it, the plantation, his house, everything except the children, who had grown and matured. Smiley would walk into his house and it would be as if he had been away for the weekend. There had been no war, no France, no French women. It had all been like a dream he had dreamed one afternoon, sleeping by the river.

(36)

Smiley watched the outline of Havana. It had not changed. It was still dirty and cramped and the docks swarmed with the same plodding, tired, dissatisfied men. He felt good, relaxed from his trip. Dressed in a light, airy tan suit, the warm muggy air engulfed him. Back to Cuba, Smiley thought, as he stood on deck and watched the large ship slowly dock. The tie-down ropes attached, he took a cigar from his pocket, lit it and walked casually toward the ramp. His mind did not race with joy, nor did he show any excitement at being home. He had not written Cam and Molly to expect him. After so few letters during the war, there was really nothing to say, and now Smiley knew the familiarity he felt for the ranch had changed. No matter how vivid the vision of the houses and the fields, it would be, he knew, a different place, strange faces different from the old workers he had known. Three years had passed, with only ghosts for memories. Smiley had wanted to write to them, it would have been nice to come home to a party with champagne. But it would be nice this way also. He would ride in, dismount and knock on the door.

It was not until Smiley was on the train and watching the miles and miles of cane and tobacco pass that his heart began to race and he felt a nervousness building inside of him. And then it was as though a fog had lifted from his mind and a haze from his vision, and he saw around him more clearly than ever before, the full reality of it. The war was over, the hidden fear, the many French girls whose naked breasts and thighs had slowly absorbed the paranoia.

He looked around him at the various well-to-do Cubans and the American growers smoking cigars and talking loudly in the corner of the car. He was home. He was home from the war.

Smiley sat in the taxi, his first realization of change. An old Cuban with a run-down Ford met the train. A dirty, toothless old man who loved the sputtering automobile, he whistled and sang between short fast bursts of Spanish. All Smiley could catch was that General Mendosa, El Presidente, was a blood-sucking pig.

The sun was perched on top of the drying sheds when the old car pumped and sneezed into the main gate of the ranch. Smiley told the man to stop, and paying him double, stepped out on the Stearns plantation. He could see the fresh foot-prints of the men going back to their homes. He walked slowly and breathed deep the air, his suit was dirty and stuck to his skin but he did not mind, it was a good feeling. Ahead he could see the outline of his house and the workers' quarters. On the edge of the night, he heard the horses, snorting across the corral at each other. Far off could be heard the faint sound of one of the workers strumming his guitar on the porch. Mr. Baca's school loomed ahead, and off to the right, next to the garden, he could see Cam's and Molly's house. Several cars were parked in front, and he could hear the deep happy laugh of Molly. For a brief moment his throat became dry and he caught his breath, trying not to cry. He stopped in the center of the plantation, and was impressed by the order of the layout, the neatness of the buildings. How every building seemed to want to be, a needed, stately part of the machine.

Smiley walked first to his house. Everything was spotless, his freshly laundered clothes were in the closet, the furniture shiny and dust free. He ran his hands over the clean walls and walked out onto the porch. He looked over toward the Stearns house, and then through the window he could see Cam walking back and forth, obviously disturbed about something. He was talking, his one arm slashing the air with each word. In the kitchen he could see Molly talking to Bertha. Both were laughing about something. Two women and two men sat listening to Cam. Upstairs the lights to the children's rooms were on. With a gasp he saw Elizabeth standing in front of the window. She was a thin, shapely girl, her blond hair long and falling around her shoulders. Smiley could make out the outline of her womanly body. Lord, how time had flown.

Smiley went back into the house and noticed for the first time the new addi-tion, a bathtub and toilet. In the kitchen there was running water and an ice box. He chuckled to himself. Taking off his clothes, he washed and put on the Levis and shirt that were in this closet. He looked at his boots, and they felt foreign as he put them on. Standing in front of the mirror, he placed in his mind the old Smiley.

Cam felt the anger within him grow. For the past months President Mendosa had begun a blood bath. Students, dock workers, any man, woman or child thought to have said anything against the government was systematically picked up, held without bond, given no trial and then shot. Mendosa, a friend of the Americans, had come under fire from the American government. But what with the entrenched businesses and plantations, he merely shrugged off their comments and continued his bloody and violent regime. Only by the genocide of all possible rebels could his power be insured. A short, thin, intense man with small dark eyes that seemed to move constantly, he surrounded himself with cut-throat military generals and an undercover police force that melted into all phases of Cuba. To this date, there had been over seven hundred executions. People in power applauded his actions. People in the universities became more and more underground and prayed and waited for the time a new leader would rise to lead them.

They did not know it, but an obscure army sergeant named Batista was slowly and patiently building his forces. A resolute man, with large ambitions and dreams, he spread his work well under the noses of the army and the secret police.

With each execution, Cam became more and more enraged. This land was not fought for and helped by the United States for it to become a home for dictators who, at their own whim, killed those who opposed them. In every country one should have the right to voice one's opinion. "You watch," Cam said heatedly, "all this will lead to another revolution, a bloody one at that."

Molly came in from the kitchen, with Bertha behind carrying coffee and cookies. Mr. Baca looked at Cam. "This is a volatile country, Cam. As long as I have been alive, there has been blood and more blood."

Cam looked at Baca exaspered, saw Molly with the coffee and sat down in his chair. "I suppose it's all violent. Here, Europe, America, it doesn't really matter, it just seems to me that it is all so unnecessary."

And then, changing the subject, "How is Roberto doing in school, Mr. Baca?"

Mr. Baca smiled from ear to ear. Everyone knew Roberto was Mr. Baca's pride. "Fine, fine, he will be a great man, a man of peace and learning who will help this country in many ways. He is the new way."

Molly looked at Mr. Baca. "Hopefully his education will be enough to temper the guns. I do not know if I fully believe the pen is mightier than the sword anymore, from my experiences in life."

Cam jumped when he heard the knock on the door. No one ever came to the house without first calling. It could only mean trouble. Molly's and Mr. Baca's eyes followed him as he went to the door. "Who's there?"

Smiley answered, "It's me, Cam, I'm home."

Cam opened the door and for a moment he stood and looked at Smiley and said nothing. He just stared at the man he had worried about, thought about so many hours over the past years. Then, with his normal reserve, he held out his hand. "Smiley, welcome home."

Smiley stepped into the house. Molly ran to him and hugged him, the tears streaming down her face. Mr. Baca stood, silent and then began to cry. "Senor Smiley," was all he could say, and he sat back down. Molly fixed Smiley a drink.

The remainder of the evening the talk was subdued, interrupted with stories of the past. Once again there would need to be a focal point of mutual interest to rekindle the friendship. Time had passed, everyone was different. But the plantation was complete once again.

———————————

Roberto Alvarez ran his hand down the flesh of Carmella's stomach. "There is nothing more fine in the world than your stomach," he whispered into her ear. Carmella laughed, sitting up from the bed. The morning sun shown through the off-yellow curtains. "Roberto, you lie so well. A man, just a man, and in a few years after we are married and my stomach is fat with your child you will tell your mistress that."

Roberto kissed her on the cheek and rose from the bed. "Another semester and I will be out of this place. Then, a year after that, I will pay Mr. Stearns back, and you and I can have a place far better than this run-down little apartment."

Carmella rose from the bed, her young supple body breathing in the day. "Roberto, one day you will be a great man, or you will die young. You and your dreams. Haven't you been in Cuba long enough to know? Do not dream, live your life, each day to each day."

Roberto patted Carmella's bare behind and pulled her to him. "Good, then get back into bed and I will not go to class."

She pushed him away playfully. "No, there is always a dream."

The years for Roberto were good. His law school was almost complete. Digesting the books as though they were food, he went from class to class, never losing interest or becoming bored. Carmella, although playful and vivacious, knew the importance of an education.

Here in Havana, working part time as a dancer in a club, and with Roberto working for Stearns' accounting firm, they had an apartment, food and decent clothes. She kidded Roberto often about his drive, his dedication and belief that he would change Cuba, but she did not ridicule him.

Already Roberto knew his political beliefs, which he had carefully thought out. A benevolent dictator, a man of utmost character and regard for human life. A man not encumbered by congress or government. Able to give immediate orders and have them carried out without delay. Cuba needed such a man. A man not greedy nor filled with the lust for power. But most important of all, a man tied with the United States. Regardless of Roberto's younger feelings about the Americans, he realized now that they were a country with which to be allied. A democracy with many problems, they were still the only power with a heart. A giant, able to crush all her enemies.

It had been a shock to Roberto when he realized that his father had been wrong to fight with Galindo. The dreams aside, Galindo had been no more than an uneducated peasant, lashing out with no control at a system he had no knowledge of, nor the capability of running.

And now General Mendosa. To Roberto he was the epitome of injustice. The people starved, while he rolled in his riches. The army was nothing but an execution squad. He could understand the United States' concern over Cuba, but he could not understand how the United States could tolerate Mendosa. The people were in fear, the students demonstrated for his ousting. There must be a new man, a man of the people. Not a man only for himself, killing all those who spoke against him, ready at any moment he felt his power waning to leave the country with untold millions of hoarded money. Money rightfully belonging to the children who starved in the streets and the old who begged on the corners.

More and more Roberto grew to admire Stearns. A man of few words but with strong conviction. A man who lost his arm for pursuit of freedom. A man like Stearns would bring joy and life to Cuba. A hard man on the surface, but a deep thinking, dedicated man. It was such men with vision that would change Cuba, men like Roberto, educated men, men who through luck had left the streets.

Roberto finished dressing and grabbed his books from the table. Carmella still stood naked by the window. He blew her a kiss. "This afternoon, senorita, if there is time I would like to see you like this once again."

Carmella turned and tossed her dark hair. "Go to school, Roberto."

Roberto walked through the dirty crowded streets. He was late to meet Fernando. It had taken months before he had begun attending the secret meetings. Not even Carmella knew of his ties. A new breed of people printed the pamphlets. A group dedicated to Cuba, not caught up in the fury for revolution. They slowly took control of the radicals, calling for change through peace. They moved within intellectual circles. They did not strike the revolutionary people with long-range views, nor short, immediate burts of gunfire that would end in only one way. Maybe they were dreamers, time would tell, but for now there were no shootings, no bombings, no railroad derailments. But Roberto knew that although the violent side of the movement was pacified, they kept their weapons well oiled and cleaned for the day they would be called.

Only last week a new name had popped up at the meeting. A Batista, an unknown army sergeant from the country. Reported to have worked many jobs, a man with vision and tact, a true man of the people. Batista was beginning to make his move for the presidency. Tonight, this Batista would be at the meeting. Roberto only hoped he was a true man, or he and his assoicates would be arrested and shot like all of the others preaching the downfall of Mendosa. It seemed so strange. The world was no longer at war, but in Cuba the war was just beginning.

The garbage laden streets only made the rain more bothersome. Walking the alleys, Roberto and his friend Fernando tried to miss the puddles of liquid that flowed from the piles of garbage. Stopping at every corner and looking back, they made their way for over thirty minutes before they were sure there was no one following. Satisfied, they back-tracked and relaxed, walking to the small, cluttered apartment. Knocking twice, Fernando said, "bread for your mother," and the door opened.

Inside, thirty people sat close together. All were familiar to Roberto. All were students like himself, except for one, who was a professor of science. A tall, medium-built man stood in the corner smoking a cigar. Roberto looked at the man and immediately felt the power he possessed. From the death-like stare of his eyes to the curl of his snarling lips, here was a man searching for more than peace and tanquility. Roberto and Fernando sat in the knot of people. Most, like Roberto, were non-violent, though others teetered from side to side. If peaceful resistance did not work they would fill the streets with blood once more. Again and again, if necessary, until their people were free and the ills of the country were healed.

The students were strangely quiet this evening. There was no boisterous talk nor the smell of marijuana nor glasses of rum. Each in their own way seemed to be transfixed by the presence of this army sergeant who sneaked through the streets like themselves and longed for power. They were nervous.

Eyeing each student separately, Batista did not move from his corner until he was sure everyone knew him as an outsider. Then he casually ground the cigar into the floor and began to speak. With his first words the quiet room became hushed. "I am Fulgencio Batista. Many of you here do not know me, but one day Cuba will call my name. Through me your children will be as no other children of Cuba. Through me there will be schools and hospitals and a country where all our brothers shall live without the fear of rats in the room or empty stomachs."

Batista's cold eyes scanned the room. "I am not an educated man like you. I was born in a small fishing village and saw my sisters become prostitutes and my mother die in rags. My father drank himself to death. I have worked on the docks and cut the cane, my back has ached from the tobacco and my stomach has suffered from the lack of food. But through the years I have held onto a dream, a dream of our people and our country. A dream that at night blankets my sleep. And I knew that in this country there were people like me, people who dreamed as I, people with a vision. Tonight we are but a handful in a damp, rat-infested room, but in time we will fill the streets and our cry will spur the people. I come to you as a lowly sergeant in the army. I come to you as a brother, and ask your support. The time draws near, already the country calls for the blood of Mendosa. He is a pig, living and growing fat off the agony of our people. He bends to the Americans, giving all and what is left, he puts in his own pocket."

Batista clenched his fists in front of him and looked at the students. "When I am Presidente, there will be no pilfering of the money that belongs to our people."

He relaxed his features and reached into his pocket and lit another cigar. Looking once more at the students, he said calmly. "I am here seeking your help, without you, I am nothing. Through me there is a voice, a hope."

The students looked at the man, there wasn't one among them who would not follow Batista. Soon his name would filter through the streets. Never in print, but always on the lips of the people, his fame would grow until the right moment.

Leaving the apartment, Batista walked slowly down the wet street. A car pulled up beside him and he looked cautiously at the driver. Satisfied with his safety, he got in, and breathed deeply. The army private looked at him and smiled. "Now it begins, senor," he said.

"Now it begins," Batista answered, looking out the window of the car.

The car sped through the streets and back to the drab army barracks. Inside his small room, Batista looked in the mirror and laughed. Behind him he looked at the army shirt with the sergeant stripes on the sleeve. "A sergeant now, a king later," he said to his reflection.

Roberto and Fernando walked down the deserted streets, not speaking. Both were entranced by this man, Batista. Never had they seen such a man, his presence alone made one stop and think. He was one of those men who is born to lead. To have people live out his dreams and fantasies without being conscious of why they followed happily in his tracks.

Standing at the corner where Roberto's apartment was, Fernando said softly. "He is the man we have needed, Roberto, now in our lives we have a chance."

Roberto looked at his friend. "Words are but words, my friend, and often a flowery voice is but the seeds of deceit."

Feranado laughed. "Roberto, Roberto, you will see, we will all grow to love this man, he is the answer for Cuba."

Carmella looked agitated when Roberto entered the apartment. "Late, very late," she said coldly. Roberto reached around and held her close. "Never too late for you."

"Where have you been, starting a revolution?"

Roberto looked at Carmella, then walked to the table and placed his books on it. "Not me, revolutions are for brave men. I am but a young aspiring attorney, not a brave man of the jungle."

Carmella laughed and moved to his arms. "Well then, my young attorney, I remember the words of this morning."

She stepped back and undid the loose dress she wore. Stepping out of the dress she stood naked, and Roberto turned down the light. "That's what I like about you, you're never serious, and never angry when I return home."

Carmella pulled his face into her breasts. "When will you marry me?" she asked, holding the back of his head. "When I can afford not to live in a dump, and I can dress and feed my children," Roberto said from between her breasts, "not until then."

<hr />

Smiley was amazed at the changes in Elizabeth and Cam Jr. Elizabeth knew she was an attractive girl now, and at times Smiley felt uncomfortable, sensing that certain movements and actions were intended for him. Over the past weeks Elizabeth had found a way to be wherever Smiley was, asking for help or brushing her full breasts into his sides as if by accident. Smiley had at first paid no attention to the matter, but as the incidences mounted, he began to feel nervous around Elizabeth. Not that he would not love to bed the young girl. She was beautiful, but she was the daughter of Cam, which could lead to many complications. To Cam and Molly, Elizabeth was perfect, but to Smiley, having been away at war, he saw in her a very shallow and spoiled girl. Her mannerisms were quick and curt and her disdain for everyone around her made Smiley marvel at how such a person, treated so well her entire life, could be so selfish. Her one love was the horses, but to the stable hands and workers she was rude and discourteous. In front of her father she was more subdued than she was with others. One day after an outburst of profanity and anger at a helpless stable boy, Smiley looked at Elizabeth and said, "you shouldn't act that way, Elizabeth, it wasn't the boy's fault."

Elizabeth turned sharply on her heel and lashed out at Smiley. "He's just a lousy, stupid Cuban. What does it matter?"

Smiley had been so shocked by the remark that he could say nothing. He just looked at the girl he had tossed on his knee and who used to call him uncle. Now he looked at the tall lady. Blond hair like her mother, with Cam's green eyes. She was thinner than Molly, and her features more chiseled, but unlike Molly, who radiated grace and charm, Elizabeth radiated sex and mischief. Already men followed her with their eyes, not out of admiration, but with dreams of her body. As she walked her hips moved seductively, her eyes bore into men, and as she talked she had a habit of flicking her pink tongue against her lips. Cam and Molly, in their love for her, did not see her habits. She was their daughter, young, feeling her oats and becoming a woman, but to others it was a perplexing and troublesome problem.

Cam Jr. continued his pursuit of nature. Already he dreamed of going to the United States and following a career in the outdoors. The University in Salt Lake City, known for its approach to conservation, was on his mind, and already he had mailed letters for their catalogs and entrance exams. A good student, he loved to read and delve into the world of knowledge. He was a bright, quiet lad, needing few friends and little interaction with other people. He was Cam's pride and joy. Deep, smart, non-violent, he was unlike Cam in so many ways. In him

Cam saw a boy he wished he could have been, and at times would sit rehashing his life and wondering how different things would have been if he had not been born in New Mexico.

Batista walked around the small but well furnished apartment. Loosening the buttons on his army shirt, he moved to the bar and poured himself a glass of gin and squeezed a lime into it. Adding salt, he sipped the drink, returning to the middle of the room. He sat down in a comfortable stuffed chair and breathed deeply. In all his life this place was the only place where he could relax. Here in this apartment with the smell of lavender and the small, dainty figurines and lace doilies.

He had met Lillian months ago. A white woman teaching school to American children, she immediately fell in love with him. Soon he was telling her of his plans to be Presidente, his dreams as a child. Over the months she became part of his drive and destiny, and when after days or weeks he needed rest and respite from his world of treachery and danger, he came here. Here where he smelled the lavender and loosened his shirt and drank gin. Lillian would kiss him at the door and then go to her room and clean up. As always she came from her room dressed in a provocative nightgown.

She was an average built woman, not pretty nor ugly. Long features that seemed to all be in place. Batista loved her blond hair, and loved the sight of her naked with the tones of blond between her legs.

Lillian walked over smiling, and sat on the arm of his chair. He ran his hand over her buttocks and smiled into her blue eyes. "It is hard trying to take over a government," Lillian said. Batista closed his eyes. "It is hard," he mumbled. "The army, the students, the men of the docks, it is hard and treacherous in a country as mine, filled with American politicians trying in vain to model our behavior."

Batista did not worry about the information the school teacher knew. He had learned through the months much about this Lillian. She was a sexually oppressed woman from the midwest. A small town girl who ran away from home to find more than pigs and cows. In New York City, she became a teacher. Here she sided with Blacks and women's suffrage. Devout in the belief that people should be free and unoppressed, she gladly accepted a position in Cuba as a teacher. In Cuba she saw poverty beyond her imagaination, and weekly wrote letters to American representatives calling for the ousting of Mendosa and the return of an American to run the country. In her belief, only her country could change the tide of Cuba.

She met Batista informally at a party for political figures and American businessmen. She had bumped into him in the punch line, and immediately fallen for his dark eyes. In two weeks they were lovers, and in two months she was his confidant. Through her, Batista knew the only way to gain control of Cuba was with the help of the United States. And although Lillian was plain, she had slept with a broad segment of the American community. Batista had never let on that he knew she slept with many men when she mentioned her acquaintances with American businessmen and consulates. Now, through sly probes and causual talk, Batista knew the United States was growing tired of Mendosa. In time, he knew they would supply his followers with weapons. Thus the United States could avoid more intervention in Cuba, which the country would not stand, having just come out of a war. And Batista, with promises of full cooperation from the Americans, would rule with power.

Lillian took the drink from Batista's hand. She stood and smiled at him. "Come, come my love, I have the medicine your body needs."

Batista followed Lillian to her room.

At precisely two a.m., the army car stopped in front of the apartment. Batista stepped from the shadows and looked at the driver. He climbed into the car. The driver did not smile nor look sideways, but drove straight down the middle of the narrow street. Nearing a bar, he slowed and stopped by two men dressed as peasants. The two men looked nervously around them and jumped quickly into the back of the car. Alonso Ortega smiled at Batista, a large, toothy smile. The corners of his fifty-year-old eyes wrinkled as he smiled, making him look both foolish and dumb, which he was not. "It is done," he said softly, "the arms and ammunition are safely in the jungle."

"How many?" Batista asked gruffly.

"Four thousand rifles and a hundred thousands rounds of ammunition."

Batista smiled. "Good, it is good. How many men lost?"

"None," Alonso answered. "Four soldiers were killed, though."

"Four less we will have to kill," Batista laughed, and for the first time during the ride the driver looked at Batista and smiled. The raid on the munitions dump had been planned for months. Finally, everything was in readiness, and it had been done while Batista was with Lillian, safe in her lavender smelling room.

Stopping in the center of the road, the two peasants jumped from the car and the driver gunned the motor. It was dangerous to be seen with the wrong people as Mendosa's spies were everywhere. One word to the wrong person, one wrong move, and they all would be in jail and their bodies thrown to the buzzards in the morning. Now in a few days Batista would know for sure if the time was right. A very important American was to be contacted.

Batista was sitting at his drab desk on the base. Going over more papers for men to be executed, which had become a daily task, when a small, thin American entered his office. Batista glared at the man and was surprised when he did not look at all distressed by Batista's manner. Sitting down confidently, he lit an American cigarette and exhaled slowly. "Sergeant," he said casually, "you aspire to be a great man."

Batista began to stand from behind his desk. "Sit down, sit down," the man said. "I am here with orders from the President of the United States. And the first of those orders is that you sit there and listen before doing something rash."

Batista looked at the man and sat down slowly. The man puffed on the cigarette once more and reached into his jacket pocket. "The day and place are written here. Look at it and burn it, and be there. If you know what is good for you."

(37)

During the early part of 1918, with Wilson firmly entranched as President and the country out of the war and enjoying the peace and tranquility, Roosevelt wrote President Wilson. Roosevelt was appalled by the turn of events in Cuba, but he knew that the President was in a very delicate situation. Now that the country was out of a war, there was no desire for any more hostilities. The country would not send troops off to Cuba as they had for Roosevelt. It was Roosevelt's belief that there must be an intelligence force in every country the United States maintained as its own.

Through writing Wilson, and having friends talk to him, a meeting was arranged, and one fine spring day Mr. Wilson, followed by two security men at a respectful distance, met with Roosevelt in a park in Washington. Both men talked about the war and the weather for several moments until Roosevelt became very serious. "Mr. President," he said, "I am a sick man. I feel my life energy leaving me every day, but I need to see one last thing for my country. We must place trusted men in the countries where we maintain an interest to look out for our needs and help in any way possible with the governments that work for us and want us to help develop their nations."

Wilson looked at Roosevelt. "Once a fighter always a fighter, Mr. Roosevelt."

Beginning to walk again, both men were caught at once by the beginning of spring. The budding trees seemed to smell of good tiding and the robins darted among the fresh sprouting green grass. "Would you ever have dreamed, Mr. Roosevelt," Wilson said, "that our lives would lead to such complicated matters?"

Roosevelt looked at the budding trees. "No, never in my wildest imagination. I remember as a boy, as a weak and sickly boy, having the drive to be someone, someone strong and brave, a leader. And now, after the years, the wars, the fighting, I must confess I am a little awed by it all."

Wilson looked at Roosevelt and stopped walking. Roosevelt turned to face the man with the burden of a country. The guards stopped discreetly and watched the trees. "Teddy," Wilson said slowly, "I already have men in our possessions, trusted men, not always legal men but men sworn to our country."

"How about Cuba?" Roosevelt asked.

"Cuba also, Teddy."

Roosevelt smiled and took a deep breath. "Good, good. I've had nightmares that you'd be another Taft, content to sit and let the world pass us by, believing in all the fairy tale stories that speeches and parades and flags make up. But I see you are a true man and know the realities of our life on this Godforsaken planet. I have a friend in Cuba. A Mr. Cam Stearns. He is a trusted man, although an independent transplanted man of the west. He will do what he says he will do, and for this country he would lay down his life."

Wilson etched the name in his mind. The two men shook hands. "The best to your family, Teddy," Wilson said. Roosevelt looked at the President. "I envy you, oh, how I envy you."

The two men parted. One walked briskly toward his security officers, and the other slowly watched once again the buds of the trees and the early robins. Nearing the car, he felt the familiar fatigue spread through his body and the humming in his ears.

———————

Batista pulled the white straw hat firmly onto his head. Entering the bar he looked reassuredly at the men on each corner. He would not be taken. If that were the case, he would run and hide in the mountains and let fate carry his soul.

The bar was filled with Blacks and Cubans. It was loud and dirty and smelled of sweat and cheap beer. Adjusting his eyes to the darkness of the bar, he saw the thin man who had come to his office standing and waving to him. Nearing his table he noticed another man, middle-aged, balding, with large, stooped shoulders and very large hands. Batista came to the table and the large man, without standing, pulled a chair for him to sit. "Sit, Sergeant," he said in what Batista knew was a southern American accent. Looking at Batista, he held out his hand. "Vandall, Joseph Vandell, Louisiana."

Batista shook the man's hand. "I knew you would come. Phil and I had us a little bet, twenty bucks he owes me. He said you wouldn't come."

Vandall laughed, and then his eyes narrowing, he abruptly stopped laughing and looked at Batista. "You are a brave man, Senor," he said in fluent Spanish. "Your dreams and desires are large. I am here to help you become what you wish to be."

Batista looked at the man. "I represent the United States. I have been instructed and ordered to help you in any way possible to become Presidente of this country," Vandall continued.

Batista started to speak, but was interrupted. "There is no need to speak, no matter what you say, I know the truth and maybe I know more about you than even you. I also have contacts you would never reach by your Lillian or your students or the few generals for your daring dream. I happen to know there is already in motion a plan for the ouster of Mendosa and the placing in of a man who is not in the interest of my country. Knowing that you well know the need for our support and the continued good relations of our two nations, you are our man. Therefore, from this day forth our contact will be Lillian."

Batista looked at the man in amazement. She was an American spy, an agent, but through her this had all been possible. Batista looked at the table and said quietly. "You seem to be very well informed, Mr. Vandall, and you do your work very well."

Vandall laughed. "I am a single man, at times very bored, and I find the work exciting and fulfilling. There are no distractions. I happen to know you have many weapons now, due to your friends the other night. We feel that within a year you should be in office."

Batista leaned back in his chair. Vandall stood and Phil, shaking Batista's hand, said seriously. "I pray we never meet again. Good luck with your dream."

Batista sat dumbfounded for several moments and then he rose and began to laugh. When the men at the corners surrounded him he was laughing. He did not speak to any of the men, but was dropped off at Lillian's, where he spent a happy and carefree evening in the arms of his confidant.

Joseph Vandall opened his mail slowly. He was a slow, meticulous man, a man who could stand and watch a building for three days without complaint. For months he had written and requested more men. The country was about to explode, and there were not enough men to keep the lid on until it was supposed to explode. Reading the coded message carefully, he smiled to himself. The Stearns plantation, Mr. Cam Stearns, and his foreman, William Stone.

Smiley walked along the edge of the small winding stream that flowed around

225

the southern cane field. The elephant grass sprouted profusely. It was Sunday, and the men were not working. He was restless today and not in the mood for sitting in the house with Cam and discussing horses or tobacco.

It was November, almost Thanksgiving, and for the first time in his life, Smiley was homesick. A brief, overwhelming sadness surrounded him. He never talked about his parents to anyone. For all anybody knew, there was nothing to talk about. Years earlier, during the war, Cam had asked Smiley about his folks. Smiley still remembered the white lie. My mother and father loved each other. Yes, it was true his mother had ridden out by train and stagecoach to marry his father. But they were two hateful people, he with this Germanic temper and she with her Swedish snobbery. And when he left the ranch for the Rough Riders, Smiley never thought about them, until today. Today he wondered if they were still alive, and if they both still fought, cussed and bitched at each other.

Smiley was engrossed by his thoughts and did not see Elizabeth swimming in a small pool of the stream until he was by the bank. Elizabeth laughed and Smiley, startled, looked at the naked young lady standing in the pool, the roundness and whiteness of her breasts in the water. "Are you hot?" Elizabeth teased.

Smiley began to walk away. "Swim with me, Smiley," her voice called, "swim with me."

Smiley turned and began to speak, but looking at the girl he slowly closed his mouth and began to take off his shirt. Elizabeth laughed and splashed the water with her hands. Standing naked, he walked into the water and stood for a moment looking at the nineteen-year-old eyes. He stroked her back and then moved his hands around to her breasts. Elizabeth smiled. "In the grass, Smiley, in the grass."

Smiley walked quickly away from the pool. He had not said goodbye to Elizabeth after he made love to her, nor had he uttered a word during it. Afterwards, she had the same laughing, taunting expression she had when he stumbled into the pool.

Smiley did not see the sky nor the birds nor the fields. He walked to his house, engulfed by the pale skin of Elizabeth and the round, young red nipples. But sitting on his porch he watched Cam walking to his office and dread filled his body. If Cam ever found out about this day, one of the two men would die.

Joseph Vandall drove slowly through the countryside. To the left and to the right of him lay the Stearns plantation. He noted the well-kept fields and the brisk pace of the Cuban workers. Driving close to the house, he was impressed by the orderly layout and the touch of simplicity that made the ranch not so forbidding to people of a lower class. Joseph had not called Cam nor written him a letter. It was best that there be as little contact as possible with him. No matter what the depth of his patriotism is he might not feel right in actively taking part in a coup of a government.

Vandall himself would do whatever the country needed. Assassinate, kidnap, or bomb. There was no moral side to the issue to him. His country was his God and his mother. A strong-willed southern man, born and raised working a poor black-dirt farm, he was simple but resolute, and one-sided in all his thinking.

Vandall had throughly checked Stearns' background. He knew all the facts of his life except about a period of several years before he joined the army. There seemed to be no information about this period. But, from the army on, Vandall knew the most minute details of Cam's life. He also knew that he was a dedicated man, devoted to his ranch and family.

Stopping the car, Joseph watched Molly walk toward him from the flower garden. He was immediately taken in by her smile and sense of security. "I'm looking for your husband," Vandall said. Molly eyed the man and felt no apprehension. "Good guess," Molly smiled, "I am Mrs. Stearns, And you sir, are?"

"Excuse me," Joseph answered, "Joseph Vandall. Sorry to drop in unexpectedly like this, but I must see your husband."

"Well, come in and have some coffee. He will be here shortly. He rode out with the foreman to see the horses. One of his arabian mares is foaling today."

They walked to the door. Vandall was impressed by the neatness and order of the home. Molly laid the flowers that she was cutting on the table. "Bertha," she called. The round Cuban lady appeared from the kitchen. "Coffee, please."

Pointing to the sitting room, Molly said, "make yourself comfortable, Mr. Vandall, my husband will be here soon. Please excuse me for a moment, I must get these flowers in water, or they will die. It won't be long."

Vandall sat in the room and looked at the photographs of the family. One could know a man without meeting him by just sitting in his home. Bertha came into the room with a silver tray and two cups of coffee. Setting the tray beside Vandall, she smiled. As Vandall was pouring the coffee, Molly came back into the room with some yellow marigolds in a vase. "Marigolds all year long, even in December," she said. "I don't think I will ever get over that, no matter how long I live in Cuba."

Vandall poured Molly's coffee. "Mrs. Stearns, all the years I have lived here, I will never really think of December as being anything but cold."

Molly sat down. "Looking for tobacco, Mr. Vandall?"

Vandall sipped his coffee. "You are a shrewed woman, Mrs. Stearns. Tobacco it is, and I hear your husband grows the best tobacco in this province."

Just then the door opened and Cam walked in. He did not see the stranger, but said to Molly, "a stallion, we have another stallion."

Then, seeing Vandall, Cam eyed the man with caution. Vandall noticed the hesitation and listed it in his perceptive mind. A cautious man will always be necessary, a man who runs into tight situations with too much vigor is a dead man, or a man destined to many years in jail. "Cam, this is Mr. Vandall. He is here to see you about tobacco."

Cam was about to ask Vandall why he didn't just see his broker, but Vandall was smiling and extending his hand before he could get the words out, so instead he took his hand. "I had a few horses as a boy," Joseph drawled, "nothing' like yours, though. A stallion must be worth a pretty penny."

Cam sat down while Molly went to get a cup for his coffee. "No way to tell yet, but possibilities," Cam replied.

Molly brought Cam his cup and then excused herself from the room. "I told Mr. Baca I would help him decorate the school for the Christmas party this afternoon, so if you gentlemen will excuse me, I will be off."

When the two men were alone in the room, Vandall looked at Cam. "Lovely wife sir, you are a lucky man."

Cam smiled but said nothing. "What type of tobacco are you interested in, sir?" Cam, eyeing the large, strange man. Vandall knew there was no point in beating around the bush with Stearns, so he said directly. "I am here because President Wilson sent me. You were recommended to him by Teddy Roosevelt, who, I understand, is a friend of yours.

Stearns looked at the man and placed his cup gently on the table. "There has been no trouble in Cuba, sir."

Vandall looked at Cam. "But there will be, Mr. Stearns, and that is why I am here."

"Well then, let me show you to the guest room, and after dinner we will go to my office and discuss the matter further. Now is not the time."

Cam looked at his reflection in the mirror. He was puzzled. There must be trouble of some kind, but it was strange that he had heard no word of the matter. There had been no riots or burnings, nothing during the past months to disturb the peace. But now, comes a man not looking like a tobacco buyer at all, a man who didn't even smoke, and how could one buy tobacco if one did not smoke? Cam had read about a munitions dump being attacked and a large amount of rifles and ammunition being stolen. Maybe it had something to do with that. Whatever it was, Cam knew one thing. If it involved Roosevelt it meant trouble in some way, and was something that Roosevelt considered important. He wondered how Roosevelt was. The years had passed, and all the good intentions of letters and contact seemed to have been neglected.

Smiley and Cam talked and laughed about the stallion. Mr. Vandall, between some small talk with the men, was drawn to Molly. Elizabeth was bewitching, but after a cordial hello, he tried to ignore the girl, seeing trouble in her eyes. It did not pay to get involved with this family, not by thought or sight or manner. One could get strangled in the pitfalls of life, and Mr. Vandall was not a man to deliberately add complications to his life. Women were women, pretty creatures with whom to be polite. For sleeping, he preferred whores, because they involved no commitments and no names.

Vandall sat across the desk from Stearns. He looked at Cam but Cam said nothing, waiting for him to speak. Taking a breath, he began. "I am a member of an intelligence program started by President Wilson. Working with other people planted in this country in key rolls, we try, without the common knowledge of the people, to help maintain the interests of America. It has come to our attention over the past months that there is a planned coup by several members of parliment, who, if the coup is successful, will try their best to drive the Americans and their possessions out of the country and take them over for themselves. As you well know, this is not good for the country, or for people like you."

Cam looked passively at the man, unspeaking.

"We also know there is a man in this country who has started his own climb to the presidency. He is not a well-known man, but he is resolute and has all the credentials to make a good leader of the people. He came from a poor family, and has slowly worked his way into a small amount of power without bringing notice to himself by the authorities who surround Mendosa. Mendosa, as you know, although he is indifferent to the United States, is an animal, and must be removed. In fact, it is only a matter of time."

Stearns looked at the man and slowly lit a small, black cigar. "What does this have to do with me, Mr. Vandall?"

"We need people. The pay is not great, but men of character and strength are needed. Mr. Roosevelt suggested your name. We were hoping you would join and help us in any way possible."

"In other words," Stearns said, "a spy, and other things."

Vandall looked at the man. "It's not a pretty business, sir. It's a dirty affair, this behind the scenes work in politics. This is a young nation, and there are few people accepted as you are in all ranks of life in Cuba, from the planters to the government officials. You have been active before in the inner affairs of Cuba."

Stearns broke in, "only when it affected me or my family and this ranch. The rest of Cuba is Cuba's business."

"It's everyone's business, Mr. Stearns. It's everyone's."

"So all you need is a nod of my head and a promise that I will follow orders?"

Mr. Vandall nodded his head. Cam rose from his desk. "I will think the matter over. Give me an address where I can contact you in Havana, and I will let you know. I feel it is in both our best interest not to call each other, or even let on that we have met."

"I will be off in the morning, Mr. Stearns. I thank you and your wife for your hospitality."

Both men walked to the house in silence.

Cam lay down on the bed as softly as he could. Molly rolled over and faced him in the dark. "Who is that man, Cam?"

"A tobacco buyer trying to make it rich."

Molly turned her face toward Cam in the darkness. "Try again, Cam. He doesn't even smoke."

Cam put his arm around Molly. "Sleep well, my love, he is a very strange tobacco buyer."

Cam tried to sleep, but he could not get his conversation with Vandall out of his mind. He decided he would not wrestle with the matter just yet.

The dinner with Vandall was extremely uncomfortable for Smiley. Elizabeth's eyes followed his every move. No matter what the conversation or the moment, Smiley could not retreat from the young beaming face. He would avoid her gaze, but drawn to the seductive smile, he would secretly scan her young, vibrant form.

After the dinner, Smiley walked to his house, his mind filled with guilt and regret. It would have been so easy to have left the girl, why did it ever happen? She was an animal. There was no grace or kindness to her lovemaking. Her movements were strong and deliberate, roughly grinding her body into his. They had lain exhausted when it was over, their bodies glued together by their sweat. He was not even the seducer. He had been pulled into the arms of his best friend's daughter, a girl half his age.

Smiley sat in his house and swigged the Bacardi directly from the bottle. God, there were so many women, why this one?

The last days of December drifted by. Cam did not approach Smiley on the matter of Vandall. Instead, he drove to Havana, and meeting Mr. Vandall as planned, he told him he would have to think the matter over more fully, and he would get back to him after Christmas.

In the last few years Christmas had become an important part of the year for the Stearns family. The school party had become a tradition, with the children singing, and there was always a large barbeque. Elizabeth and Cam Jr. still decorated the tree, and Cam and Molly seemed to draw closer to one another. Although they were close, the years moved them into more a feeling of comfort than a deep, burning love. Sometimes Cam would think about life alone without Molly, and he knew that his life would not change. He had many hours to sit and contemplate his life, and more and more he would sit in his office looking out over the corrals, and travel in his mind the old paths of the ranch in New Mexico and feel the old feelings of wander and need. Each Christmas he would think back to the Christmasses with his parents and his sister. He supposed he was getting old.

The conversation with Vandall left Cam perplexed. Before the war, Cam would have already said yes. Yes, without hesitation or fear, willing to kill rebels and think nothing of it the next day. But now he did not feel the hate rising, nor the need for their demise. His life was a comfortable routine. There was breakfast, lunch and dinner, and small conversations with Molly each day. There was the tranquility of looking at the flowers and the sun setting in the evening, with the sound of the dogs and the chickens and the neighing of the horses. But nowhere was there a desire to kill or cleanse Cuba. Cuba had been good to him, good to all around him, and Cam did not believe it was his business to control the destiny of Cuba. He felt that there was no economical way for Cuba to rid herself of her internal poverty without American aid. Before he would have taken it for granted that he could play an integral part in the changing of Cuba, but now he realized he was only one of the thousands of Americans comfortable in Cuba. Still, there was Roosevelt in the back of his mind. Roosevelt felt strongly enough to recommend him. Roosevelt, without whom there would be no Cam Stearns, the Rancher, no plantation with children and servants, no Arabian horses nor land that one could retreat to. Beyond the fence and the gate with the sign reading simply, Stearns Plantation, there was no world, no world that would change the remaining years of Cam's life. Even in America, Cam and Molly and the children would be comfortable. He sent money to the banks regularly. Already he had over five hundred thousands dollars sitting in cash. It was a most perplexing situation for Cam. He knew his son would not wish to run the plantation after his death. Cam Jr. was not a man of the soil, he was a man of thought and solitude, a lover of the outdoors. He was not resolute enough to be a farmer, nor hard enough to control workers. Elizabeth would be off to the United States and college in April. Her life was about to start on its own path. Cam saw in her the wildness in him when he was her age. Of the two children, she was most like him. In her eyes he saw the burning for life, a destructive kind of intensity that gripped her in the past few years. He saw in her full body a ripe young woman who would go far, but who would have little regard for many people. He only hoped that she did not enter into the real world too confident, and allow herself to be ruled by her desires only to be used by men much smarter than she. He had noticed a change in her recently. Watching his daughter, it was difficult to find any little girl left in her. He saw the looks of other men and knew their thoughts, but he hid his inner suspicions about Elizabeth from Molly. Molly had grown to avoid any and all confrontation with reality. Her life was a bubble, filled only with good things, and in her children she would never see any wrong.

1918 drifted into the past. Molly, beaming around her home, planned the meals and the school party. The children had trouble concentrating on studies, and each day another decoration appeared in a window or on the wall of the school.

For Molly, 1918 had been a good year. Her children were grown. Elizabeth, young and beautiful, would be off to America to attend a private college and win the heart of some young man. Cam Jr. in another year would also be off to America, and perhaps in a few years, ten or fifteen, Molly and Cam would return to the mainland. It was funny, but neither Cam nor Molly had visited the United States since they had lived in Cuba. There was really no reason to do so. The restaurant was long ago paid off, and neither of them had any living relatives.

Smiley was back from the war, but he was not the same man that went to war. He was colder now, more somber like Cam. At times he would be the old Smiley, joking and laughing, but these were brief moments. He still worked as hard as ever, but the war had taken something from him. A little joy, a little love, Molly did not really know, but he was different, and she felt sad about that.

Her life with Cam was peaceful. He was not taxing nor overbearing. It seemed except for brief encounters during the day, small talk and a few parties, they really didn't see each other that much anymore. They moved around the house, seeing the same things, doing the same routine every day, but doing it separately. But they did love, and it was good.

Molly stepped back and looked at the tree. Cam, Smiley and the kids laughed and sipped sherry. Bertha and Mr. Baca were in a serious mood, contemplating what their lives would be like if they had met much earlier in life. Molly smiled. It was a good year, they were alive and well and home together.

Lillian ran her fingernails lightly down the large protruding stomach of Joseph Vandall. Vandall smiled. "You are still the best."

Lillian sat up and Joseph watched her large breasts sag. Reaching over his naked body she took a cigarette from the end table. Lighting it, she blew the smoke playfully in Joseph's face. "Our little revolutionary has not been by lately."

"He will be," Joseph answered. "With your thighs and blond hair, there isn't a Cuban who could stay away for long."

Lillian laughed. "At least my line of work has kept me well bedded these many years. God, sleeping with American consulates, police. I should write a book."

Joseph raised his eyebrows. "Just kidding, love," Lillian said, between puffs on the cigarette.

Joseph reached out and cupped her right breast. "Life on One's Back, by a lady spy. This spy business gets a little out of hand, I must confess."

Rising and kissing her on the neck, he stood up from the bed and began dressing. "So soon, my love. Tell Batista that I will meet him at the same place as before on the twenty-first of January."

Lillian ground the cigarette into the ashtray. "Joe," she said, looking at the large man dressed and heading for the door. "Yes, Lillian?"

"Are you going to have to kill him?"

Joe looked at the naked woman sitting on the bed. A pang of sadness gripped him, but he suppressed it quickly. "He won't die, Lillian, I promise you, he won't die."

Lillian pulled the sheet over her and looked at the ceiling. Two large tears formed in the corners of her eyes. Yes, she had left her small town home, looking for the world. Now after all the men, the secrecy of her life, at times, especially Christmas, she thought of the snow and the people of her home. All down-home country folk, simple people who did not dream life was a terrible back-stabbing ordeal. Full of corn and watermelon and chicken, they went through each day in a dream. Lillian would lie in bed and dream she was running through her home town naked, yelling "looking at me, the bruises, the touch of men. This is your real life."

But now she thought of the tree, and the snow glistening in the moonlight and her parents sitting with her aunts and uncles around the table piled with food. She looked at the ceiling and thought of the warmth of her home when she was a child, and she began to weep. Soft, quiet sobs that only the walls heard.

Three days after Christmas, Smiley lay in bed. It was late and he and Cam had stayed up drinking punch. A warm blanket covered Smiley, and his mind remembered a parade of French girls that he had known in Paris. At first he thought it was a dream, when he thought he saw a young girl with a flowing nightgown standing by his bed. She smiled down at him, and began to move the sheet. With a start, Smiley felt the hand slide down his stomach. He grabbed Elizabeth roughly and jumped from the bed, pulling her with him. Shaking her violently, he began to scream at the girl. "No, never again, do you understand? What we did was wrong, wrong."

He flung the girl to the floor and stood over her. Her eyes bore into him. "You bastard, what do you know about wrong? You like it, didn't you?"

She stood up and walked toward the door. "I hope my father kills you."

Smiley ran and grabbed the retreating girl. He dragged her to a chair and threw her across his lap and began to spank her, hard, until her sobs became audible. Stopping and gaining control over his anger, he took her to the door. "If your father ever finds out, he should kill me, but you remember one thing, Elizabeth, if anyone ever finds out what we've done, it will distroy your mother and father. You're going to have to find out there's something more in this world than your ass."

Smiley slammed the door behind her as she left. He sat down in the chair in the living room, still shaking from his outburst, and looked into the night.

Elizabeth lay in her bed, her eyes open, staring into the darkness. "You bastard," she said aloud, "you no good little bastard, I hate you. I hate you."

(38)

Teddy Roosevelt could feel the stiffness of the sheets, which was strange as around him were the Black Hills, and he was sitting on his paint horse. It was a beautiful day, the small powder puff clouds drifted lazily over the mountains. It was one of those glorious spring days. The first day when the jacket may be discarded, the wood left unchopped. He felt the air stroke his neck, and all sadness left his heart. Below him, nosing around for the green shoots of spring, were hundreds of cattle. Mean, quick tempered mountain cattle.

He felt the familiar pain in his arm and he awoke for a brief moment. There were people, too many people, all standing and looking at him. But he did not know why they were. The smell was clean, too damned clean. Not a mountain-air fresh, but a sterile, scrubbed clean. He would have to get out of here.

There was a knoll. A small, unobtrusive rising of the ground. Roosevelt stood and looked out over the rolling countryside around him. Ahead he knew the Spanish waited. Waited for his men and his voice commanding them. Somewhere a Spaniard who he did not know would aim at him, and either fate or good shooting would settle the meeting. The muggy Cuban air was oppressive, a hot, sticky substance that made one irritable and cranky. To his right the Rough Riders camped. Good men, he thought, my men, my sons. This is our greatness, the willingness of our sons to do battle, without this we are nothing. He stood and he wondered how the children were. Before battle he always had these periods of grief that came over him. The death of his wife, the loss of a child, each moment blanketed him. And then as it came it would pass, and there would be nothing but the men and the rifles and the cannon. The smell of powder and the feeling that once again you have defied the Gods. The test, the ultimate test.

The two doctors looked around the room. "There is nothing we can do, Mrs. Roosevelt," a middle-aged doctor said. Mrs. Roosevelt did not cry, but turned to the gathered friends and relatives. "I would like to be alone with Teddy, please."

The doctors and people filed out, the finality of the moment upon them. The lady stood over the man on the hospital bed. She smiled and patted the folded arm. Drawing a chair close to his side, she sat, and watched.

"Remember Kama," a voice said. Roosevelt squinted his eyes. "These eyes, man," he bellowed, "come closer, come closer."

It was Mr. Roft, his African hunting partner. "Kama," Roosevelt answered. "The guide. God, what a man. Track anything alive, little more than a midget, but afraid of nothing. What a place, Africa, the grandest land in the world. So big, unexplored, the last land in the world still a mystery."

"Remember the lion," the voice said.

"The lion, do I ever remember. It was glorious, shooting the lion. He was like me, resolute, determined. But the elephant, I would never shoot another one. It was there I caught this damned dreaded disease you know, Mr. Roth. This disease that is killing me."

He chuckled. "Seems a pity, really. My life, starting out so weak to become

233

strong, and then to die weak. No glory in life, Mr. Roth, no glory."

Mr. Roth's face loomed before his eyes. "No glory, Teddy. Another life, a life like all the rest."

Roosevelt smiled at the image. "Oh well, it's been a good show, I suppose the world will jolly well go on without me."

There was his wife. He smiled and felt her hand on his arm. What a strong lady. He tried to lift his arm to touch her face, his lips moved.

Mrs. Roosevelt closed her eyes and held back the tears. She stood and walked to the door. Looking back once, she closed the door quietly behind her.

Cam and Molly sat on the portal. It was a damp, drizzly afternoon, but beneath the portal the light breeze was cool and refreshing. Molly said, not looking at Cam. "The children are nearly grown, Cam."

Cam did not know why, but lately Molly kept her mind on the children and how they were almost grown. "Yes, Elizabeth will be in America soon," Cam answered. "The college in Boston is a good one. She will be surrounded by the best of Boston society. It will be a good opportunity for her."

Molly sighed. "But so swiftly, Cam. I find it so hard to fathom the time."

Cam stood and walked over to Molly's chair. He leaned over and kissed her on the forehead. "Even we get old, Molly."

Molly smiled up into his eyes. "Cam, you are so brave, I wonder at times what I would do without you."

Cam laughed. "You'd move to America, buy a nice house and become the most popular widow on the block."

"Cam, you are so damned practical."

Cam sat back down and picked up the newspaper. He looked at it only very briefly, then very slowly folded it back up and placed it on the floor. Molly noticed the peculiar look on his face. "What is it, Cam?"

Cam looked at his wife, the grief written on his face. "Roosevelt is dead, Molly, Teddy Roosevelt is dead."

Cam rose and walked through the drizzle to his office. He stood inside and looked at the rows and rows of books, the polished desk. He smelled the ingrained smell of tobacco in the wood. It seemed to Cam that no matter what, Roosevelt had been with him every day of his life, sitting in the back of his mind influencing ever decision Cam had made. Now he was gone. Cam walked to his desk and sat down. He sat very stiffly, trying to hold back the tears that rolled from his eyes.

Joseph Vandall breathed deep the steamed shrimp. "One thing about Cuba," he joked to Cam, "the sea food. Delicious. If it wasn't for the humidity and the rain, I'd love this place."

Cam watched the large man, stuffing the shrimp into his mouth. "How much does this job pay, Mr. Vandall?"

Joe wiped his hands on the napkin and looked at Stearns. "Finally down to the brass tacks. It's fourteen thousand a year, Mr. Stearns."

"I will help," Stearns answered. "Whenever you need me, I will help."

Vandall nodded his head. "Good, good, we need good men."

Changing the subject, Joe looked at the bottle of Barcardi on the table. "What

234

do you think of the drive to outlaw liquor in the United States?"

Cam shook his head in bewilderment. "The way the world is now, it doesn't surprise me in the least."

"I know what you mean," Vandall agreed. "Tellin' a man he can't drink is like tellin' a bull to leave the cows alone. More trouble, world loves trouble. I'll contact you through the mail, Mr. Stearns."

Stearns stood. "My foreman, I haven't mentioned anything to him. I'd rather leave it that way."

Vandall noded his head, smart, an intellligent, safe, man. This man could be used in many ways. But Joe thought to himself, watching the tall, one-armed man leave the restaurant, this may be a bad day for your mind, Mr. Stearns. In time you may be as simple as me, with so many lies and deceits, before long the truth is not needed.

The ride back to the ranch was slow and lonely. Cam felt as he had when he rode through the desert after escaping from jail. He knew there was a new world, a world he would play a part in, but he was afraid and apprehensive. No one must know, not Molly nor Smiley, only Vandall. It must be this way. Cam was alone, locked into his secret. _____

Smiley felt relaxed. For a week he would be in Havana. The two trucks Cam ordered for the ranch were on a different boat than they had been told, and instead of going back to the ranch, Cam told Smiley over the phone to stay in town and have a little vacation. The first night Smiley rented a room in the Havana Royale, a small, quiet hotel with a nice bar and show. It was a quiet place, for newly-weds from the States and older couples looking for relaxation.

Smiley needed the break, after the episode with Elizabeth, he felt uncomfortable and nervous around the ranch. It had become impossible for Smiley to looked Cam in the eyes. Enough so that Cam had asked Smiley if he was feeling well. "Tired, just tired," Smiley had mumbled in reply.

It seemed that no matter what, Elizabeth's eyes were always on him, walking, or riding. He would turn, refreshed for a moment, and she would be there, with her haughty, glaring look. There were her ripe bosoms and young, vibrant thighs. There to haunt him, to remind him of his transgression. The days dragged for Smiley. He dreamed of April, and the day Elizabeth would be on the boat for the United States. Then and only then could he rest, but he knew it would never end. The summers, the vacation periods she would return. Return to move past him, swaying her hips ever so slightly. Moving her arms in such a manner as to outline her breasts.

Smiley sat down on the bed and rubbed the weariness from his eyes. He ate dinner in his room and went to the bar shortly before midnight. A few drinks by himself, and then a good sleep. Then maybe tomorrow he would try to find a woman. A nice, fine, American woman. A school teacher or widow on vacation. Cuba was filled with such women now. Women who for a week or ten days, wanted to forget their lives and make small talk with some halfway handsome man.

Smiley sat at the bar. Two men with two beautiful women sat at a table close to the stools. As he sat down, he did not acknowledge them, but in his mind's eye the memory of the women were etched. They were rich ladies. The men were happy and full of joy at their good fortune. The bartender smiled broadly as Smiley sat down. "Mr. Stone," he said, "you are in from the plantation."

The two men turned and looked at Smiley's back and glanced at each other. Smiley looked at the bartender. "Pedro. It's been a long time, since before the war."

Pedro laughed. "The work, the sugar, the tobacco. It became too hard. My brother, he got a job here, and then one for me, and I moved."

"Beats being a gang boss, I suppose," Smiley said. How is your life now?"

Pedro poured Smiley a glass of brandy. "Not too bad, life is good, More and more Americans come, more money. Now that the United States has outlawed liquor, more and more people come just to drink."

Smiley sipped the brandy. "Another law for our Godfearing country. Get us out of one war and start another one within the country."

"Never fear, Mr. Stone, here there will never be prohibition."

Smiley drained the brandy. "Well, good seeing you, Pedro. The best to you."

Smiley lay in bed and watched the shadows on the ceiling. After all the years, the battle, the fighting and the good life, he felt terribly alone. His days came and went and he was still alone. He slept deeply and did not dream.

Michele Diangello smiled at Nancy. She was beautiful in her new dress. The glances of the Cuban men filled Michele with pride as they walked around town, and here sitting in the bar, she was gorgeous.

Jo Jo felt the hand of Sally tighten on his. She smiled at him. All the years they had been married, and she was finally on a vacation with Jo Jo. Life had been good for them the past years. The war had come and gone. His relationship with Michele had been good. She knew the men did many things, not all legal, but she did not pry into her husband's business. The children were well clothed and well fed and she was treated warmly. She had new dresses and every year they were still together.

It had been a surprise when Jo Jo asked her to come to Cuba with him, Michele and his wife. They would vacation for a few weeks by driving through the country, and seeing a few shows. Time away from Philadelphia, and the rain and the noise.

During the day the two women were left to themselves. Shopping or sitting by the pool, they talked small, unnecessary talk. Sally saw the worry and anxiety on Nancy's face. "What are they doing, Sally?"' she asked one morning. Sally shook her head. "I don't know, it is none of my business. If the day comes when I want to know what a man does all the time, I will want to go back home and live with my mother."

Life was good for Nancy, although there were no children. Michele did not want children. Their life was lavish. They lived in the best neighborhood of Philadelphia. The oak trees were old and magnificent. The grass was neatly kept by the gardener. Nancy's every whim was taken care of. She had her private maid, and a chauffeur for the car. She dressed in the latest fashion and could choose from many fur coats. But she worried. The clothing stores, the other small businesses Michele maintained, she knew from bits and pieces of information, they were but fronts for many enterprises Michele controlled. She did not know of his girls, nor his heist ring, nor his activities in gambling, but she knew the extravange with which they lived could not be afforded by a small chain of clothing stores. There had been a few confrontations over Nancy's insistence on knowing about Michele's business dealings, but they were ended quickly with much emotion by Michele. He would yell and scream and avoid the issue, until finally Nancy no longer brought up the subject. But she would go through his billfold, his pockets, gaining a small thread of information here, a bit there. There were always strange men coming to see him. Men who, although polite and well dressed, were sinister looking men. Men who did not speak of clothing or ship-ping, but waited patiently until Nancy left the room, and talked behind the locked door of Michele's study. Nancy knew she loved him, but it was an annoyance, to know she would never know the complete truth.

The two couples sat in the bar and talked into the night. It was a wonderful vacation. The ladies were rested and smiling, and Michele and Jo Jo had learned much. More than they had ever wished in their wildest dreams.

Jo Jo thought back over the past months and he smiled to himself. Michele had burst into the restaurant. He sat down anxiously, not his usual calm, composed self. "This is it, Jo Jo. This is it. The Volstead Act. Soon everyone in this country will want booze. We have to start now. It could mean a fortune, a fortune larger than we've ever dreamed."

And now, months later, here they were in Cuba. Looking, looking for sugar and liquor. Sugar to supply their own stills, that would sell the liquor directly to the organized underworld figures. Let the big boys make the big money. Provide a service, Michele had said, a service to whoever wants to pay. No competition, just a commodity. Liquor would not be a problem. Every Cuban they talked to would be more than willing to meet boats in small, secluded coves. Filling the small ships to the maximum with Cuban-made Bacardi, the liquor would be high risk, expensive to buy, expensive to ship, and expensive to distribute. But sugar, sugar bought in a foreign country, loaded in cladestine spots and shipped to the United States would be more economical.

Michele lay in bed staring into the darkness, Nancy's nude form beside him fast asleep. He played back the evening. The man at the bar, the tall, thin man, a sugar grower. Here was a possibility. A possibility that, like most aspects of life was not planned, but which might lead to large rewards. Closing his eyes, he ran his hand over the bare skin of his wife. Life was good, very good and full of surprises.

Smiley ate his breakfast slowly. It was good to sit and eat with no plans for the day. A tranquil boredom surrounded him. Maybe his mood was due to the ranch. Ever since Elizabeth, he had grown tired of the ranch. Each day seemed to be a chore. A drudgery of time and lost motion. The work, the smell of the fields, it was all the same, day in and day out. At times he would think about the war and flying, the tightness of the muscles and the overcoming of the fear. He ached for something, something out of the ordinary. He did not crave money. He had more than he had ever dreamed of. But there was something lacking, a missing segment of his life that not even women or love could satisfy.

He was absorbed in these thoughts when the two men walked to his table. He did not recognize them from the night before at the bar. "Mr. Stone," the younger of the two said, "may we join you?"

Smiley looked at the man and his friend and smiled. "Sure, be my guest."

The men sat down and Smiley noticed their expensive clothes and the gold rings and watches they wore. Michele spoke first. "I couldn't help but overhear the bartender last night. You are a planter, Mr. Stone?"

Smiley looked at the man. "Yes, I own a plantation." He did not know why he lied, perhaps it was the expensive dress of the men, the fact that he did not want to feel inferior. Michele continued. "Just by a stroke of luck I am in Cuba looking for sugar. Perhaps we will be able to work something out."

Smiley looked at the dark eyes of the man. "Perhaps, one never knows just what life will lead to."

"Dinner tonight then, Mr. Stone? Our two wives have a friend of theirs traveling with us, who would love to have an escort."

Smiley looked at the man. "Pretty?"

"Gorgeous," Jo Jo answered. Smiley, sipped his coffee. "Dinner then, why not? I have a few days till I'm due back at the plantation. It would be enjoyable."

Smiley walked away from the table. Michele looked at Jo Jo. "We have him, Jo Jo. We have him. Now to find a girl."

Jo Jo laughed. "That's easy. Tell the bellman we need an American girl. We'll tell the ladies it's Mr. Stone's girlfriend and try to stay clear of conversation about America."

Michele and Jo Jo sat in the room. The ladies were shopping and would return in a few hours. A gentle knock on the door. Michele stood. "Come in."

A medium height girl entered the room. She was blond, and looked like she was just out of college. She smiled as the men looked at her. "Hey, nothing doing, two guys wasn't what I was told. I may work, but I don't work two guys."

Michele looked at the girl. Peeling two hundred dollars from his wallet, he handed it to the girl. "You go buy some nice clothes," he said, then grabbing the girl, he dragged her toward him. "And tonight, for the man you are with, don't come on like any street whore, understand? And if you do, I'll cut your tits off."

He released the girl. She looked at the money. "I understand," she answered.

"Good, be here at eight tonight."

Standing by the door, Jo Jo looked at the girl. "Be here."

The girl turned and walked out the door. Two hundred. For two hundred, she would be there.

Smiley spent the afternoon lazying around his room. It would be nice to see an American girl, very refreshing. Dinner, a few drinks, a little dancing, and who knows what else? He did not think of Elizabeth or the ranch. The afternoon was spent day-dreaming of the American girl.

Batista listened with interest to the man in his office. The man, who ran several small fishing boats, and was a confidant of Batista's, talked slowly. He was dressed as an army private, a disguise he wore when he came to talk to Batista on the army base. Batista puffed thoughtfully on the cigar. "These two men who are asking people about sugar and rum, do they seem rich?"

"Very rich, senor, very rich. They also seem very shrewd."

"Did they say what they wanted with the sugar?"

The man shrugged his shoulders. "It is not my job to ask what they want. They went to several people and then to me, because of my boats. They want me to ship the sugar for them into the Florida Keys where their own boats will unload the cargo into their holds for the final run into America."

Batista smiled. "This is indeed a stroke of luck, my friend. Maybe the two American's can be convinced that they should do business with us. The money, we need the money, with money we can do many things. I want you to put the word out. The next time the two men are seen, hold them for me, politely please, and send for me. I would like to talk to these men."

The man rose. "It is done, Sergeant."

Batista sat at his desk. He knew this would happen, because the United States, in its rush to be perfect, was trying to outlaw liquor. He laughed. "These Americans, they are like children in so many ways."

Smiley was at his best throughout the evening. He lit the lady's cigarette and laughed at her jokes. The entire evening the conversation centered around Smiley. With dinner and wine, and then after-dinner drinks and dancing at the Club Jetty, Smiley was feeling wealthy. He had promulgated the lie about owning the plantation. The men and ladies seemed absorbed in his stories, from the Rough Riders to the war. The two men were especially interested in the shipment of the sugar, and the prices.

Smiley was intrigued by Michele and Jo Jo. They were important people. Not people who worked each day, dirty and sweaty, but people who worked and told others what to do and went home to their big lavish houses. During the evening, Smiley began seeing himself driven around the country by his private driver, with maids cleaning his home, and fine women on his arm. He would be his own man. Dancing with Ruth, Smiley did not know her last name, he became enraptured with her light green eyes and the soft, delicate color of her skin. "You will walk me to my room when we get back to the hotel," she teased. Smiley smiled at the girl. "Your wish is my command."

When they all returned to the hotel, Michele and Jo Jo quickly whisked their wives away from Smiley and Ruth. Smiley kissed Ruth on the forehead by her door. "Come in, Mr. Stone." she said, "for a nightcap."

Inside her room, Smiley watched the girl sit down. She had exquisite legs, the new fashions for women were much to Smiley's liking. The long dresses were replaced by short, just below the knee cuts. To his surprise, Ruth dimmed the lights and standing before him, she began to undress. Her eyes teased him. "Do you like what you see?"

Smiley watched the girl undress completely and then he pulled her to him. He kissed her neck and breathed deep her perfume. Running his hands down her breasts, he worked to her thighs and stroked the dampness of them firmly. Ruth began to pant and squirm in his arms. Her hands worked quickly and efficiently on his shirt and to his zipper. She squirmed and molded her body until she took Smiley in her mouth. Inching down to the floor, she was on her knees between his legs. For several minutes she manipulated him at will, then she stood. "Let's go to bed, love."

Smiley removed the rest of his clothes on the way to the bed.

In the morning, laying beside the still sleeping Ruth, Smiley looked at the girl. She was more than a simple girl from the States. This one had been around. He felt uneasy looking at her, but he could not put his finger on the reason why

For two days the three couples toured Havana. Each night Smiley and Ruth frolicked in bed with wild abandon. Then on the third day she was gone. Michele met Smiley in the restaurant and told him Ruth had to leave. There was no good-bye. But Smiley felt no love growing for the girl, and only shrugged his shoulders and looked at Michele. "It was good while it lasted."

Michele eyed Smiley and sipped his coffee. "Mr. Stone," he said, "I am looking for sugar. Sugar not in the usual way."

Smiley looked at the man.

"I need sugar to run my stills in the United States. Do you understand?"

Smiley leaned back from the table and smiled. "You aim to supply those poor bastards who will want the booze."

Michele laughed. "That's right, Mr. Stone, and to do that I need sugar. Sugar bought here, but not loaded through the docks. Sugar taken to points where Cuban boats will take it to sea to be loaded on my own ships. I will pay double market price for such a service."

Smiley looked at Michele. Double market. Lord, he could arrange for sugar and make a killing. He could make more money than he had ever dreamed of and be like Michele and Jo Jo. Maybe be could even buy his own plantation. He did not think of Cam nor the years, he only thought of the vision he saw of himself. A power within himself, not second fiddle to any man. He could make enough to be gone, away from the ranch, away from Elizabeth, a new beginning. He looked deeply into Michele's eyes. "You pay cash, Mr. Diangello?"

Diangello nodded his head. "Of course, cash when the boat is loaded."

"Well then, how will it work?" Smiley asked.

"Jo Jo will contact you. You get the sugar, stockpile it, arrange for transportation and when Jo Jo contacts you, he will know where the boat is to be loaded. He will pay you."

Smiley reached into his pocket and took out a pen, writing his address on a napkin, he handed it to Michele. "When you are ready, write me here. Upon receiving your letter, I will start gathering the sugar."

Michele handed Smiley an envelope. "Here. Here is ten thousand dollars. Hold it until you get the letter."

Michele stood up from the table. "It has been a pleasure, Mr. Stone. We will be in touch."

He began to walk away when Smiley said. "O yes, Mr. Diangello, how much money was that hooker I was with?"

Diangello looked at the man. It would be of no use to lie. "Too much, Mr. Stone, too much."

Smiley answered, "she was good, very good."

Michele and Jo Jo sat at the small dockside cafe. It seemed that it had been easy, too easy. The three large tough-looking men standing in the corners of the room did not divert their attention from them for more than a moment. "So sorry," the small, dark-eyed Cuban told them, "sorry you must sit here and wait. There is someone who would like to speak with you."

When Jo Jo began to protest, Michele spied the three large men and held him back. Jo Jo looked at the men menacingly, but the men remained, standing and watching. There was no use, whatever was in store for them would happen.

They sat there for several hours, until Batista entered the bar, flanked by two men. He walked directly to the table where Jo Jo and Michele sat. "Sorry for the delay, my friends," Batista said, smiling, "but my men were told to hold you. I trust it was not difficult."

Michele looked at the man and the army uniform with the sergeant's stripes. "My name is Batista, Sergeant Batista, and you are Michele Diangello and this is your friend Joe."

Batista sat down and looked at the two men. "It has come to my attention, Mr. Diangello, that you and your friend have been looking for sugar and rum. What you intend to do with it is of no concern to me, but I am here to tell you that on any successful shipment of sugar from Cuba, there must be a small tax. For my family, you understand. There is very little that happens in Cuba that I do not know about. You see, I am an inspiring man and make it my business to surround myself with truthful people. My men have watched you for weeks. So you see, for a small fee I can guarantee the sugar will reach the boats wherever you load them."

Jo Jo was fuming. These Cuba fuckers with their slicked back greasy hair and their two-bit smiles. He would like to take this one and shove his pistol down his throat.

Michele looked at Batista and lit a cigarette, not offering the Cuban one. He exhaled slowly. "It is a good bargain, senor," he said, "one that I can find no fault with, as long as you are a man of your world. My partner here, Joe, will contact any man you designate when he comes to Cuba."

Batista pointed to a man standing in the corner. "When you come, come to this bar. Within a few hours, my friend Rafael here, will be in contact with you. The sugar is your business, where you get it, how you get it, but the tax, that must be paid. Let us say, twenty cents on the pound. But we also can supply all your needs, so if you wish to buy, inform Rafael here, he will take care of everything."

Batista rose from the table. "My pleasure, gentlemen, it is my pleasure."

Michele watched the man leave and the guards in the corners settle back to their drinking. He looked at Jo Jo. "When in Rome, do as the Romans."

"I don't like that pig," Jo Jo said, through clenched teeth. Michele looked at Jo Jo. "Me either, but there's something about that man, something, he's going to be more than an army sergeant in his life, Jo Jo. Mark my words, he will be much more than an army sergeant."

_____

The Cuban driver followed Smiley with the new trucks. He drove slowly, In all of his life Smiley could not remember Cuba as being so beautiful. Everything seemed greener than green. He drove, deep in thought, the ten thousand safely in his boot. For once in his life, Smiley felt life was smiling on him. He went over the deal with Diangello a thousand times in his mind. The figures were staggering, the profit amazing. Six months, a year, he could amass a fortune in cash. Smiley decided the safest way for him to acquire the sugar was to steal it. Refined sugar was left by the boxcar, sitting for days. Stored for months sometimes, waiting for a price increase. During this time many boxcars could be emptied. There were no guards. Who ever heard of stealing sugar in Cuba? Cam would never know of his dealings. It would be neat and simple, and one day Smiley would disappear with his money.

Batista walked quickly. He was late, a habit he did not relish. Being late, he would lose face, and he did not want to lose face with Mr. Vandall. Lillian had even instructed him not to be late. Entering the park, he saw Vandall standing by the bench. People milled and strolled about, the hot, muggy afternoon air settling around them. Eyeing Batista, Vandall walked toward him. "I have a car over here, shall we?"

Batista noted the crisp, businesslike tone to Vandall's voice. Once in the car and driving down the street, Vandall spoke again. "Within three months there will be a coup by members of the government. We shall let this happen. Then, several days after the new government has established themselves, fat and comfortable in their new victory, you will start your revolution and make yourself President of Cuba."

Vandall handed Batista a small sheet of paper. "If you can't remember these names carry this, but it would be better to memorize them and throw it away."

Batista looked at the paper. On it were the names of high ranking military men.

"These men will help you. See each of them yourself. How you do it is your business, I am simply the carrier of information to draw many different factions together behind one man. Do you know where the Bay of Isabel is?"

Batista nodded his head.

"Good, in six nights be there, with a truck and several trusted men. A ship will sail into the bay. He will have three red lights, but when he enters the bay he will turn them off. He will make two sweeps of the bay. You are to blink a light four times. When he sees this, he will come to you. There are grenades and many machine guns, compliments of the United States. I'm sure they will come in handy. But remember, you must not move until the other government is in. Let them do the first fighting."

Batista looked at the passing people. "Your employer is very organized."

Vandall laughed. "Don't worry about the names on the list, each of these men will do as you say. Let's just say certain people have their nuts in the old vise, and for a few small favors after you are in power, a plantation here, something there, they will follow you to the gates of hell. The students are no problem, my men inform me you are quite the underground leader."

Batista did not answer nor pay attention for the remainder of the drive. Vandall let him out on a corner in the market section. Vandall looked at the standing sergeant. "To your health, El President?"

Batista did not know if Vandall was being sarcastic or sincere. He didn't really care. There was much to do, much to do. He must contact his men in connection with the students. He must not forget the boat in six days, and the meetings with the generals.

Batista walked quickly. He did not feel power within himself, he did not see the people standing and cheering as he spoke. He saw only a street filled with people who would storm over the palace. People who would carry him to the palace. The streets were red with blood, and the people were without faces. A faceless mob of people, willing to die for Batista. He hailed a cab. Success, success was inevitable.

———————

Molly stood in the middle of Elizabeth's room. There were the first pair of shoes she wore, numerous stuffed animals. Ribbons from riding, photographs of her and her horses. She did not feel sadness nor the passing of time, she just felt alone. The trunks lay packed at the end of the bed. Soon they would drive to Havana and Elizabeth would board the ship for Boston.

To Molly it seemed that she had never really known her daughter. She could not point to one moment in time when she could say she knew her daughter. Molly had seen the changes in Elizabeth only the past months. It frightened her, but she knew there was no controlling her daughter. What Molly saw she did not like. She had noticed the advances Elizabeth made toward Smiley and also seen the troubled look on Smiley's face. She held no animosity toward Smiley. She knew Elizabeth was young and ripe, and would be trouble for any man, but she wondered why and how Elizabeth had become this way. Her life was so easy and trouble-free, she had been such a lively, wonderful young girl. Loved by her father, spoiled, maybe that was it, but Molly did not think so. It was within her, in her person, there was nothing in her environment, nothing that molded the girl. It was simply her, her cells and blood, her mind that made her the way she was.

Molly looked around the room and sighed. She prayed Elizabeth did not find misfortune in the world, but she hoped deeply she would not do anything to destroy the bubble her father had placed around her. Molly wanted to talk to Cam about Elizabeth, but each time she gathered her nerve and had the conversation planned in her mind, she would look into Cam's eyes and could not bear to speak to him regarding her feelings about Elizabeth.

Elizabeth was quiet, riding in the car to Havana. For years she dreamed of this moment. To get out of Cuba, Cuba, with its flies and heat and Cubans. She wanted desperately to be away from Cuba and away from her father and mother, and not watched like a cow. She wanted the city, with its lights and restaurants, fine men and dancing. Her mind swam with the dreams of her journey. For all her desires, she never once let on to her father. Cam was made to believe Elizabeth loved the ranch, and the freedom. He never saw the selfishness of Elizabeth's desires.

Standing on the dock, Cam watchced the ship slowly glide out into the harbor. He held Molly close to him. When the ship was a mere dot on the horizon, he looked down at Molly. Molly smiled into his eyes. They did not speak, but stood looking at one another. The ride back to the ranch was quiet. The night stars glistened and the moon hung tranquil on the horizon. Lying in bed in the early morning, Cam kissed Molly on the forehead. "I guess we're getting old, Molly."

It was only then Molly sobbed and a tear ran down her face.

Elizabeth breathed deep the ocean air. One more day and she would be in Boston. Boston, with its large green parks with oak trees. The books she had read about Boston had imprinted in her mind the sights and sounds. It was as though she had already been there, and only needed to land to be able to travel that city. Standing on the deck in the evening, she thought of the school and the men. She knew her school was private, but there were other colleges in Boston. Colleges with bright young men, men with stately names and east coast accents. Men who would show her the town. Men she would sleep with, strong, assured young men, not afraid of her, but men she could lavish her fire upon.

Roberto Alvarez listened nervously to Batista. The time was drawing near. He looked at the man and saw the fire within him grow as he talked. He talked of American help and American guns. He told of the backing of the military and how the students would pour down the streets following the army. The room buzzed with excitement. All except Roberto, who did not like the talk, the sound of guns, and seeing the man Batista. It was as though he saw him truthfully for the first time. Here was a man like all the others, preaching blood and guns and army. Roberto did not trust the man, the man with the army uniform and the dark, darting eyes. He wanted to speak out, but he would be labeled an enemy and placed on a list, a list like Mendosa's. Power bred enemies and hatred. He watched the other students beam and praise the presence of Batista. His glory spread through their veins. His dreams were their desires. It was madness.

He looked over at Fernando and saw Fernando caught up in the fever. Standing and watching Batista talk and the students listen, he looked around the room and wondered how many here would die. How many would be nothing but the lifeless building blocks for another dictator.

During the frenzy of the meeting, Roberto slipped from the room. Outside, he felt the night air touch his skin. It was wrong. Why, he did not really know. But revolution, death, destruction were not the tools of a benevolent leader. They were but an extension of all the leaders of Cuba before him, power-hungry, greedy men.

Entering the apartment, he smiled at Carmella. Carmella looked at his long face, "You must be failing."

"No, it's nothing, I think I'm just tired."

Carmella yawned. "I'm tired myself. One more dance, one more American asking me how much, and I think I'll die."

Roberto smiled. At first her dancing with the Americans made him angry, very angry. But now it did not bother him. He looked at Carmella. "You are my poison."

Carmella looked at him with mischief in her eyes. "Come to bed and we'll see what kind of poison I am."

(39)

On July 23rd, early in the morning as General Mendosa slept, the army stormed the presidential palace. Mendosa woke to the clinking of machine gun bolts and the stern look of General Juan Ramon Trujillo. Over the radio in the afternoon the population of Cuba was informed that they were now ruled by a five-man council that would decide the fate of their lives. General Juan Ramon Trujillo was the new governor of Cuba. The people in the fish market listened for a brief moment and went back to fish. The workers cutting cane and stacking tobacco would not hear the news for days. The white community was thrown into an immediate uproar, speculating as to the attitude toward the Americans of the new government. They wondered if the army would be necessary. The troops at Guantanamo were placed on alert. Within three weeks the United States officially told the world that they did not back the new government of Cuba. American troops were trucked to private American holdings. An uneasy calm hung over Cuba.

Cam immediately armed his bosses and filled the house corners with rifles. He cleaned and oiled his pistol and personally rode vigilance over the ranch. There were marines garrisoned several miles from the ranch, headquartered at the refinery, so Cam did not feel any great danger in the immediate area.

During the confusion, Smiley and three workers, for one hundred dollars apiece, spent several evenings unloading boxcars of sugar. Smiley guessed there were over twenty thousand pounds of sugar hidden in the barn.

Molly was visibly shaken by the takeover. Tired of the turmoil, she seemed to age several years in two weeks. Cam could do nothing to comfort her. She did not sleep, but would sit or stand, holding her hands in front of her. Her face lost its pink roundness, and became drawn and tight. She was not impolite, but she was distant to everyone. Cam, anxious over her mental stability, became curt to the workers and seemed to be in a hurry to do everything. He became silent and grouchy, and soon Smiley did not bother to see him.

Three weeks after the takeover, Roberto Alvarez and Carmella stepped out of the cab by the corrals. Cam for a moment forgot his troubles and smiled, but as Roberto walked up to him, he once again withdrew into his cold shell. Roberto was taken back by Cam's look. Cam said before any formal greetings were passed. "You may have your job. There is an empty house you and your wife may move into."

Cam looked at the pretty Cuban girl. "I am sorry, Senora, but it is not a good day."

Carmella looked at Cam with sad eyes. "I understand, Senor, the country once again is in turmoil."

Roberto walked toward the empty house. It was good to be here, now that he was a graduate of the university. Cam Stearns paid well. It was calm, restful. So many months in the city, and more and more Roberto thought of the ranch. His vigor and politics seemed dulled or useless to him now. Here, on the land, there was a respite, a sanctuary almost. There was not the sound of the cars, the constant buzzing of the city. There was the sound of the chickens and dogs, the horses, a freshness in the air. Here was a good place to put to use his education, a place to hide and think about his life. Roberto needed time. Here he would work and draw money, and rest and sort out his thoughts.

Soon he would be a father. In eight months, Carmella had told him, and here they were back on the ranch. Roberto was happy about Cam giving him his job back. It was good. The child would be born and well fed and not have to deal with the city, at least not yet. But in the child's day, he too would go to the university and maybe there would be a different Cuba by then. Carmella held open her arms for Roberto to hug her. "This is a fine place for a baby."

"No clubs to dance at out here, my lady," Roberto said.

That evening Roberto sat on the porch alone. He was away from Havana. Luckily they did not want to kill him. Soon Batista would make his move. His friends would storm down the streets behind the army sergeant and the country would rock once more. He stood and looked into the house. Carmella was hanging curtains, already planning the furniture, the color of the bedspread. It was peaceful. Here there would only be numbers and ledgers.

Two months later, Sergeant Batista, with the support of the students and many military men who had helped Trujillo, took over the government. A different five-man council was established and Geraldo San Martin was elected Governor of Cuba. Batista was shaken by the verdict of the committee, but he did not show undue concern nor remorse.

Already San Martin was making speeches against the Americans. He called for the expulsion of American business. Batista knew it was impossible for the Cuba people to develop without the help of the United States. Vandall, meeting Batista in the fish market, shrugged his shoulders. "Sorry," he said simply, "but I suppose everyone can't be right all the time."

Batista looked at Vandall with a smirk on his face. Vandall looked bored. God, he would hate to have children and let them see personally the drive behind the men who ruled the world.

Vandall looked at Batista and changed his tone. "San Martin's stand against the United States will prove to be disastrous. The ruling people of Cuba with money already grumble. Let the rich eat and all is fine. Once they start to grumble they will follow anybody. In a few months it will be time. Until then, play your cards right, Mr. Batista. Listen and you will soon hear the dissatisfaction of the generals and the wealthy, and at that time you will become Presidente of Cuba. There are several men who stand in the way, but time has a way of changing all things."

Batista lay with his head between the large bosoms of Lillian. She stroked his brow as he looked sullenly at the ceiling. "It will be different," she said soothingly. "There is time my love, time. You will see."

Batista rolled over and pushed Lillian back onto the bed. He began to kiss each of her ribs. I am no fool, he thought, kissing her belly button. It is my destiny. Lillian's hands gripped the back of his head and he heard her sigh.

With the second government shakeup in a few months, Molly became more nervous and aloof. Everyone noticed the decline in her health and the palor of her skin. Even Cam Jr. became alarmed. He tried his best to comfort his mother. Laughing and talking in practical terms. "There is no way, mother, that Cuba can live without us. It is all talk, you will see. There will be no more killing of Americans in this country."

Molly looked at her son. "But I worry so, Cam. Your father, there are many things that have happened during your life, your father can be such a violent man. I worry that he will be hurt. I don't know if he could live without this plantation. It is his life."

Cam Jr. looked at his mother. "Mother, if Dad and you would have to leave Cuba, he would not die in desperation. Knowing father, he would plunge into some other endeavor."

"That is easy for the young to say, but not so for others."

There was no one who could reach Molly. Each day she seemed to be more and more lost in her own thoughts, more and more withdrawn.

Finally, no one talked about the situation, but a dark cloud hung over the house and it was as though everyone walked in the gloom. Cam began to not be at home for dinner, preferring to come in late and be alone. Molly went to bed early and woke late. Her garden was maintained by one of the worker's wives Cam had hired. Bertha cooked for everybody. Cam Jr. and his father did not mention Molly except in passing. It was as though she was a ghost, a part of the house, but unseen, unheard, a walking, living shadow whose black weight bore down on everyone. Smiley avoided the house, only meeting with Cam over the ranch and the daily situation as reported by the papers. There were no killings, no riots, no armed rebels assaulting plantations. Everyone waited, guns ready and nerves taut.

Batista was tired. The past weeks there had been the same dream. There was a lion, a great black lion that would begin as a tiny dot at the end of a tunnel, slowly growing until its large dark face blended into Batista's mind, smothering him with its great roar. He would awake sweating, but once again asleep, the dot would return.

Rafael looked at Batista sitting behind the desk in his army uniform. Rafael knew Batista seethed inside. The work, the years, and then the revolution, and he was still a sergeant. Granted, a very powerful man beyond the sergeant's stripes, but still a sergeant. "You look tired, Sergeant," Rafael said. Batista rubbed his head. "It is nothing, but yes, I am tired."

Rafael lit a cigarette. "Well, the Americans are ready for another shipment of sugar. Jo Jo is in town to meet the ship."

Batista smiled for the first time in days. "Good, good, is everything ready?"

"Yes, the sugar and the rum are all ready, but I think maybe the Americans also have sugar of their own."

Batista shrugged his shoulders. "That is all right. I told them all they must do is pay a tax and it was fine."

"And if they don't pay the tax, and try to underhand our agreement?"

Batista looked bored. "Then their man here in Cuba will meet with an unfortunate accident."

Rafael smiled, exhaling the tobacco smoke. He rose. "I will meet with Jo Jo this afternoon and arrange for the shipment of the sugar. When everything is ready, I will have the money delivered to you."

Batista nodded. As Rafael reached the door he turned. "Oh yes, did you read about the sugar that was stolen from the depot?"

Batista shook his head no.

"Don't you think it's strange? Who would steal sugar in Cuba unless they were shipping it out of the country?"

Batista stopped rubbing his head and looked at his confidant. "That is a good

247

point, one worth looking into. I will put the word out, you also. Any information will be rewarded, the docks, the workers, it will take time, but someone will hear about it."

Rafael walked out into the street. Americans and their stupid laws, there would be a fortune here, a large fortune.

Jo Jo did not like the Cuban, but he was polite. Michele had been explicit in his orders. "Be polite, whatever you do. Remember, everything they do is right, they hold the key to our success."

Jo Jo understood, but he still did not like the greasy Cubans, with their white smiles and their black eyes. As far as he was concerned, it would be easier to kill each one as the sugar was loaded and then come back for more.

Rafael looked at Jo Jo. He knew the American did not like him, but the feeling was mutual. It would be easy to cut his throat and take the money. But it was not time. A few shipments, enough money, and then maybe cut his throat and feed him to the sharks. "There is no problem," Rafael said, "our ship will carry the goods to your waiting ship. You will give me the money as soon as our captain returns with word that you have the sugar."

Jo Jo nodded his head. "That is good, very good."

Jo Jo sat in the bar and looked past the whores. Of all the girls back in the states, he never messed with any of them. If Smiley had received the letter, he should be at the bar any minute now. Looking at his watch he felt anxious, he was a stickler for being on time.

Smiley adjusted his eyes to the dim light of the bar. Approaching Jo Jo's table, he extended his hand. The two men shook hands and Smiley sat. Jo Jo smiled faintly, wiping his brow. "Hot as hell in this bug-infested country."

Smiley laughed. "You'll get used to it."

"Are you ready?" Jo Jo asked. Smiley nodded. "Twenty thousand pounds ready."

Smiley reached into his pocket and spread a map out on the table. "Here," he pointed with his finger. "Here is a small fishing village. In three days, have your boat there. I will meet you."

"Good, good," Jo Jo rose from the table. "There is no need for anything further, I will see you in three days. I will be on the boat. After the boat is loaded, I will come with you and you will have your money."

"Fine, that's fine."

Smiley drove slowly back to the ranch. It was going to be easy, almost too easy. He would take one of the trucks from the ranch and fill it. Covered with cane, there would be no difficulty. Already his mind moved to the next shipment and where he would get the sugar. There were several ideas in his mind, but none of them were concrete.

Rafael listened to the woman. She was in her thirties, and showed the years of her trade. Dark skinned, and infinitely tired, she told her story slowly. Yes, the American had met another American. Rafael held out a picture of Smiley. The whore nodded her head. "That's the one, senor, that's the one."

Rafael pulled the twenty dollar bill from his shirt pocket and handed it to the woman. "If you see them again, tell me."

The information was passed along to Batista. It was evident there was more sugar, sugar from this other American. It only took an afternoon to locate the American, and several hours to dispatch men to sit along the road. They would watch, and the sugar would not make it to the intended rendezvous.

Smiley drove the truck slowly. The dawn was beginning and he felt light and at ease. Drawing close to an overturned wagon drawn by two oxen, he felt no alarm. A shotgun blast shattered the window, and Smiley fell into darkness.

Jo Jo waited on the dock for three hours over the appointed time, and then the ship sailed once more out to the open sea. The captain entered the port of Havana and proceeded to the Isle of Pines. He would meet Rafael and continue with the rest of the deal.

For a day Jo Jo sat with Rafael. The captain returned, and Jo Jo handed over the briefcase filled with money. Rafael smiled and rose from the sofa of the hotel room. "It has been a pleasure, my friend," he said. Then, nearing the door, he looked at Jo Jo. "It is unfortunate that your other shipment did not make it to your ship."

Jo Jo looked alarmed. Rafael continued. "But I understand the truck was met with a shotgun, and the driver is no longer with us."

Jo Jo's eyes narrowed. "I don't know what you are talking about."

"Of course not," Rafael taunted, "it must have been another shipment for another person."

The door closed. Jo Jo pounded his fist into the table. "One day, you greaseball," he spat, "I will personally cut your balls off and shove them down your throat."

Batista counted the money carefully. American cash, good American cash. With this he would become Presidente. Only a few shipments and he would have enough money to insure his success. It would be soon, sooner than even Vandall expected.

That night he did not dream of the lion but slept soundly, the thought of the government in his control comfortably in the back of his mind.

Smiley could not comprehend the dark. He knew it was dark, he remembered the blast and the feeling as the windshield glass shattered into his face. But he was not dead. Although the darkness was too deep, and there was no sound, no feeling, he knew he was not dead. His mind reached out, but there was nothing. Nothing to bring him back, nothing but the dark and a deep ache that blanketed his body.

Cam had heard the engine of the truck start during the night, but thought nothing of it. Smiley had been restless the past weeks, working late into the night, tinkering with the trucks and other small odds and ends around the ranch, so when he heard the truck pull away from the barn, he had not risen from bed. To Cam it was just another moment in the last months that weighed him down. His mind was constantly on Molly. Molly with the drawn and drained looked, her listlessness and seeming withdrawal from life.

He found himself more and more going through the days lost in thoughts of earlier times. Times with Elizabeth and Cam Jr. Times with Molly when her face beamed and the entire ranch seemed to glow with her smile. He had grown restless the last weeks, drinking and daydreaming, not paying any atttention to the ranch. The reports of the cash flow became a dull drone as Roberto read them off.

Even Roberto became disturbed at the change in Cam and Molly. It seemed there was no life within them, each day was a dark trek into an unknown world in which only they lived. But there was nothing he could do. His pregnant wife could not understand, she would never really know the role Cam had played in Roberto's life.

It was not until late afternoon that Cam became worried when Smiley did not return. He started the Ford and began driving toward Havana. Maybe somebody along the way had seen him. Maybe he was in Havana with a whore. Whatever it was, it was strange, and Cam did not feel good about the matter. He drove slowly, not seeing the landscape around him. He thought nothing, until out of the corner of his detached gaze, he caught the glistening of shattered glass beside the road. Cam did not know why, but he stopped the car and walked back and looked at the shattered glass. Scanning the gravel of the road, he looked into the deep grass and saw the blood. Moving quickly, he saw the mashed grass and the booted feet of Smiley. He looked and saw the bloody mess that had been his face. "Smiley, Smiley," Cam cried, picking up the body. "My God, my God, is there no end?"

Smiley felt his body being lifted. He tried to speak, but there was no sound. Cam carried the limp body to the car and sped toward Havana. People on the streets stepped back in horror as the car passed with the bloody, faceless man propped in the back seat. Cam drove to the hospital and carried Smiley through the emergency entrance. He sat down heavily as the limp body was wheeled away.

For two days Smiley lay between life and death. Gone were his eyes and half of his face. The evening of the second day, Cam was allowed to enter the room. Smiley lay, his face bandaged all except a small slit for his mouth. Cam stood and looked down at the limp form. The bandage moved slowly. "Jo Jo, Jo Jo," the slit in the bandage said, "sugar." And there was no more. Cam stood and looked at the form on the bed. So many years, so many shared experiences. He did not cry, but in his heart once again he felt the cold steel grip of hatred. "Jo Jo, whoever you are, I will find you."

Molly watched Cam's mouth as he formed the words. Then she began to scream. A long, shrill scream that even the children in the school could hear, and Mr. Baca stopped his teaching, caught in the moment of anguish and grief. She screamed and screamed, until she could scream no more, and she crumbled to the floor, convulsed with sobs. Cam stood over her and could say nothing. Cam Jr., hearing the screams, ran to his parents' room. He rushed through the door and saw his mother on the floor and his father kneeling beside her. Father and son helped her to the bed and said nothing.

Lying in bed, Molly's face was not hers. Bertha came into the room and pushed the two men out. "Leave her, leave her with me."

Cam stood by the bar and drank the rum straight. Cam Jr. saw the hard lines in his father's face and the distant look in his eyes. "She'll be fine, father."

Cam looked at his son. "I don't think so," he said distantly, "this time I don't think so."

Cam Jr. looked at his father and began to cry. "Father, father, why?"

250

Cam reached out and pulled his son close to him. "There are no answers my son, only time and life."

Smiley was buried on a warm, rainy day. Cam and Cam Jr. watched as the dirt was thrown over the grave. Molly had not moved from her bed since hearing the news, and for the past days spent her time singing children's songs and talking to herself. Bertha bathed and fed her like a small child, and talked to her like she was her daughter. Cam could not bear to enter the room, and had Bertha move his things into another room.

Cam left Roberto in charge of everything now, and Roberto, being a capable man, directed the ranch. Being Cuban, the workers responded well to him.

Mr. Baca tried to cheer up Cam whenever they would meet, but there were no words that brought him back to the plantation. He wore the pistol that Smiley had given him again, and during his time sitting on the veranda, be began his plan to search and find this man Jo Jo and his friends. In a few days he would travel to Havana and talk with Mr. Vandall. It would be a start. Already he had phoned several people who had shown interest in his horses. He would sell them. With the horses gone, there would be only the cane and the tobacco and Roberto could handle all phases of the ranch. He told Roberto one evening that he would draw thirty thousand dollars a year as overseer of the ranch.

Cam made plans to send Molly back to the states. There were hospitals there that might be able to nurse her back to life. At least, there was a vague hope. The doctors who had driven from Havana all shook their heads and looked at Cam sadly. "She is unable to face the world, senor," they would say. "Perhaps a change, a different place."

Cam wrote Elizabeth and told her the news, but so far he had not received a letter in return. Elizabeth, whom he had loved so much as a child, seemed like a long lost memory to him now. A mirage that swam in front of his face, untouchable, unreachable.

After the funeral, Cam Jr. told his father he would go to America and attend a college in Colorado, to learn what he had always dreamed to be, a national park ranger. Cam saw his world disappearing around him. It was as though he were a boy and his sister had just died. He was alone once again with the cliff.

One evening, sitting in his room when the house was quiet, he could see the small, twisting stream and the hawks that rode the up currents from the valley below, and he remembered the smell of the juniper and the pinon trees, the feel of the dry New Mexico wind as it touched his face. He remembered the last night he spent there, the lost, alone feeling that engulfed him, and the last look down and over the ranch as he turned his horse and headed for Las Vegas. "The dreams, the dreams," he muttered, remembering Molly and her eyes the first night they met. The smell of the steak as she sat down at the table with him. He remembered the warmth of her skin when they made love in the mountains and the excitement they shared at the world that waited for them in Cuba. And for the first time he felt as though it had all been a mistake. The dream, the hope, the travel to a strange land. They could have lived and had children in New Mexico. And then there would have been no Smiley, no death, no revolution, no riches. They would all still be together, the children, he and Molly. For the first time in many years, Cam felt empty. He felt like he had that day many years ago when he stood over the twitching body of the man he killed. Empty, without remorse, and the name Jo Jo burned into his mind and into his soul. It would not end until he met this man. Cam's life took on a new purpose.

For three weeks Cam stayed on the ranch and sold the horses. Arrangements were made, and one bright sunny day he drove Molly to Havana. Two nurses took her aboard ship and traveled with her to Miami, where she was placed in a sanitarium. During the drive she did not speak, but sat and looked blankly out upon the land that they had shared for so many years. Cam spoke to her softly, but she did not respond. It was not until she was on board the ship that Cam, alone on the dock, began to cry. Small tears that ran down his face and dotted his coat.

A week later, Cam Jr. left Cuba. Cam shook hands with his son on the dock, and looked at him closely. "Be good with your life," he told him as the boarding whistle blew, "be good with your life."

As the ship disappeared into the ocean, Cam was truly alone. That evening he sat in his hotel room, looking out on the streets of Havana. He sat long into the night, silent, his mind a blank, and the morning rain found him still in the chair, his eyes bloodshot and his mind tired.

For two days Cam sat in his room. He did not lose himself in alcohol, nor did he fly into fits of depression. He sat quietly, watching the street. On the afternoon of the second, day, he walked from his room to the docks and looked at the building where he had often met with Bill Hood. He walked down the avenue where he had driven away from the approaching riot. It was as though his mind was a movie, playing back all the bitter memories of the past years. He did not think of the lavish parties at the plantation, or the school he had started, or of all the years and ironies of life that had given him the ranch.

Back in his room he sat as though in a trance, and before him loomed the face of Teddy Roosevelt. His voice was a distant whisper. *"There are those of us destined for blood,"* he heard, *"people of the same mold, no matter how different the backgound, you and I, Cam Stearns, are men of this nature."*

Cam felt the stiffness of the pistol in his belt. For one brief moment, he thought of Molly and reached for the pistol, but his hand relaxed and he set his gaze once more out the window and to the now rain drenched street.

In the morning Cam rose, shaved carefully and left the room. He paid his bill and drove rapidly to Joe Vandall's office. Vandall stood and watched Cam enter the office. He had read about the foreman and heard about Cam's wife. He looked closely at the man approaching him, but could detect no different character than the man he had talked with earlier in time. He was firm in his stride, and his face was cut hard and straight. His eyes, though, seemed to bore deeper into one, and a coldness could be detected in his mannerisms. Cam sat down in the chair in front of Joe's desk. They did not shake hands. "I heard about your foreman, Mr. Stearns." Joe said, "I am sorry."

He did not mention his wife. There was no need, and Joe did not possess the tact to formulate the word in a way as not to be offensive. Some things in life were best left unsaid. Joe looked at Cam. "What brings you here, Mr. Stearns.?"

Stearns looked at Vandall. "Work, something to busy my mind."

"What of the plantation, Mr. Stearns?" Joe was cautiously watching the man.

"The ranch is in capable hands and I really have no interest at the present time in its development."

"I see," Vandall said, thinking to himself, is it time? He knew it was lonely men who made up this organization, men apart, so to speak, men without families or love, finding in the words country and honor a resting place for their internal loneliness. But was it time? It was a touchy and tricky position to be in, finding and screening men to the last detail, men who would have to kill or spend their lives hiding and running. He looked at Cam carefully and did not speak. But here, he felt in his bones was a man, here was a man tested in battle, tested in life, a man who has already killed other men. Joe looked at Cam and smiled. "My position is a very delicate one. You must forgive my hesitation, but there are so many situations that one must be in, it is difficult at time to make the final step."

He quickly jotted down on a scrap sheet of paper his home address. "Come to my house this evening around six or seven. I am a bachelor, so no need for promptness. I will be there, we will discuss further this question."

Cam folded the note slowly without looking at it. "I will be there," he said, rising, "good day, Mr. Vandall."

Vandall rubbed his face with both hands after Cam left. Jesus what a world, he thought. This Batista bullshit was wearing him down. The coup, all the work and then the fucking Cubans put in another man who hates Americans. His orders were to bring about a peaceful revolution. What that had meant exactly, he did not know, but he figured the United States could in no way be implicated except in an advisory fashion to any details leading up to the revolution. But now with the events of the past months, the continued slander of America in the papers and this new president yelling and screaming about Americans, there had come new orders. Any steps necessary by American agents to speed the installment of Batista in office should begin at once.

Joe looked over the stack of papers on his desk. Five names ran through the briefs. With these men out of the picture, there would be no stopping Batista, and when he would step into office he would have the government and the people completely behind him. There would be no counter revolution, at least not for many years.

General Alfredo Mercado, a powerful military general, Trujillo's right-hand man, the lesser generals behind him Batista's men, but held in check by Mercado's power.

General Jose Griego, a man of seemingly overfed stupidity, but, in actuality, a cold, caculating man, able to perform any job. Presently he was in charge of ridding the country of opposition to Trujillo's power. Not like the powers before him, with public executions, but with death squads, that went out and left no trace of the men they murdered.

Professor Armando Gutierrez, who, from his position of professor of history at the university, constantly spread anti-American sentiment to the students. What a first had been mere talk had lately become more and more open violence toward American owned interests.

Secretary of the Treasury Eugene Lucero, a brilliant man in his own way, but unfortunately pulled by the existing government.

And finally, the Department of Agriculture head, Ernesto Malendez. Already bringing forth motions for the high tariffs on American goods and high taxes on the Americans themselves that would eventually drive them out.

With these men gone, there would be no proverbial horse's head to guide the horse, and the Presidente would fall rapidly with no support. Batista's men could take their places and America could once again feel secure with her investment. It was a sticky assignment, one that must be done without any slip-ups. A Cuban could not be trusted to do the job. It must be an American, an American who could do the work without being caught.

Until today Vandall had been perplexed. There were several good men in his small realm, but non that he would feel really comfortable with. But Stearns, Stearns might be the man. Vandall sat back in his chair and stared into the cheap oil painting of a slow moving southern river, surrounded by dogwoods. It was possible, but it must be led up to gradually. One could not just tell a man to kill five people. But Stearns knew the rules. Now that he was alone, with all his misfortune built up within him, he was the man who possibly could be given this assignment. No more contact, nothing, just simply do this. Then once more back to life.

Cam left Vandall's office and drove to the downtown section of the city. Downtown Havana was not like the outlying tin shacks blending in with the cramped, tiny houses. It was new, hiding itself in the insides of the city. Here were the large banks, the real estate offices, shops and lavish restaurants. Cam stood for several moments in front of the sign that read Bradford and Son, before stepping inside and listing his plantation for sale.

(40)

When Elizabeth sailed into Boston Harbor she became a new person. Here were the pictures her mind carried in all their reality. For three days she walked around Boston, the cool breezes causing her to buy a sweater. She had never seen anything so beautiful. The houses, the neatness of it all. Here were smiling faces and so many different clothes and stores.

On the third day, she took a taxi to her school. Set on a rolling, pine-covered knoll, it was beautiful, standing there looking like the embedment of tradition. She was both taken back by the beauty of the school and afraid of what lay inside the large oak doors. She envisioned ladies in stiff wool grey skirts and white starched blouses, their hair bunned and pinned. Dresses must be to the floor, they would say, hair bunned, silence in the halls.

But what Elizabeth actually found were women professors in their early thirties and forties, very modern. Elizabeth, having never seen America, was not informed about women's rights. Her life on the plantation was not muddled by the issue. Elizabeth soon learned that here, here were the fighters. They would never be servant women.

Elizabeth was entranced by the school. The girls were from wealthy families from all around the country. They secretly smoked. Smoking was not one of the things even liberated women did. They drank bootleg rum. Men were a different matter. There would be no pregnant girls at Wordsley. The girls, when allowed off the campus, were very well chaperoned. The various men's colleges around town held dances, and the girls were bussed over to them. They were allowed to dance with the boys from the college and then they were bussed back. There were a few girls who managed to sneak in some light petting, but mostly all went in order and place, arranged by the great Mrs. Bailey, headmistress of the school. Well dressed, very proper, she expounded her thesis on life, and people obeyed. Women must stand up for their rights, women were proper, dignified, the equal of any man. They did not drink or smoke like filthy men, nor did they cavort with men until the proper time. The proper time became a topic among the girls. When was the proper time? After several months, Elizabeth and several girlfriends, through enough dances, would arrange clandestine meetings with brave men. They were faceless men, men met in dances and then met in the dark for lovemaking. Alisa and Sally were both semi-wild, free creatures like Elizabeth. The cruel, sarcastic side of Elizabeth disappeared. The brief period of time she spent with Smiley made her shudder. Here at the school she was a girl, a young girl, free for the first time. Life was enjoyable, the dances, the classes, the sneaking around. The first months were joyous times she would always treasure.

Right after fall classes, the news of her mother and Smiley dampened Elizabeth's spirits. Her father wrote her and told her he thought it would be best if she could arrange lodgings with somebody during the summer. If not, he was sure he could, through many businessmen in Cuba, but if she could on her own it would be more enjoyable for her. Elizabeth spent days in a dark, quiet stupor. Not the fall colors nor the singing of the birds nor encouragement by her friends brought her to herself. But, after a period of remorse, she accepted the facts. She did not mourn Smiley, but she felt empty knowning he was gone. For her mother, she felt more a sadness than grief. All her life she was so devoted, but the ranch was like a prison, with the fighting and the shooting, it was not like here. It was so different in Boston without the ever constant fear of revolt.

Elizabeth wrote her father telling him of her intention to take the train and see her mother. But Cam wrote back saying the doctors at the present time thought it best for Molly to be left alone in her world. Maybe in time, she would relax and she would return to the real world. She wrote her mother religiously every week, but there had been no reply. Letters to her father as of the past several months were unanswered.

Now truly for the first time, Elizabeth felt her own life approaching.

Never until this moment with all the grief did, she understand that life was a singular affair. No matter the love or the hates, the commitments, life was walking on one's own two feet. She stopped being the young, flirty, giggly girl, and became, almost overnight, very serious in her actions. The meetings with the young men by the wall stopped, sneaking and drinking with the girls stopped. She began to look around her and see the world as a passing enjoyment in life. Not a mere day to day passing for her personal fancy. The more she looked at the world, the more she was amazed at the intricacies and wonders around her.

One night, sitting in her room, her childhood dream of becoming a nurse returned to her. She was surprised at how she had forgotten that dream she had while at the ranch. And looking back, she thought of the two years playing the tart, and her coldness toward everyone around her. It was the knowledge that she was only a minute member of humanity, spinning through space, that she would carry through her entire life. She would finish her semester at her college, and then she would enroll in a nursing school. Here was an outlet for her great desire that filled her to help her fellow man. Women's rights and sufferage was a noble cause, but now she would devote herself to her career. Suddenly there were no color barriers, no classes of people, no right or wrongs, only the need to help and become fulfilled in this helping.

When her father received the letter telling him of her plans, he sat in his rented hotel room with the cigar smoke and thought to himself, the bird has learned to fly. And he thought of the little girl he used to toss in the air, and the afternoon when, although she did not know it, he watched her ride. He returned her letter with, "helping mankind is a noble course for one's life."

He thought it ironic how a man such as he could have instilled in his daughter such a deep regard for humanity. Sitting and looking out his window, knowing that the course he had chosen would lead only to trouble and bloodshed, he felt perplexed and confused, but also trapped in the world to which he was committed.

Cam Jr. left Cuba with the weight of seeing his mother deteriorate and the death of Smiley. But upon arriving in Colorado and his first sight of the Rocky Mountains, he immediately fell in love with the cool air and sparkling rivers. His studies enchanted him, and there was not a weekend that he did not fish or hunt, or go hiking with his friends. In his quiet, thinking way, he knew he had found his life. There was no strife, no inner concern over his livelihood, he would live, here in the mountains with the deer and trout. Carrying on Roosevelt's dream of national parks, he would spend his time crusading for more public lands, and battling the mining and lumbering interests in every way. He remained as he always was, slow to anger, carefully analyzing all that was around him. Like Elizabeth, he was not concerned with the world of politics, only the life in the woods and the drive to protect for all mankind the loveliness of the outdoors. He was not overly concerned with humanity. He saw the earth as a place of trees and animals, beings far superior to man in their adaptability with the earth and their sublime crusade to co-exist peacefully with one another, each in some way, relying on the other.

During his third month of school, he became completely enchanted by a Miss Jo Ann Smith. A petite blond girl from Colorado Springs, her father was a cattle rancher. Possessed of the same love for the outdoors as Cam, they began to date, and soon were madly in love. Both though, were intelligent enough to do nothing rash, and began a quiet relationship. Cam Jr., having attended the school on the plantation, was painfully shy, but with Jo Ann, he slowly began to articulate his ideas about life and the natural state of the world. Together they were warm and loving, and found peace and solitude in their weekend jaunts to the mountains.

Joe Vandall and Cam sat in the Imperial Hotel bar, Even after Stearns had met Vandall at his home, Joe did not approach Stearns with the difficult assignment. It was Christmas Eve, and Joe decided he would say nothing until the New Year. He felt confident that Stearns would not blink an eye at the task, but human nature had a way of changing, and this was one assignment which he did not want to go wrong.

Both men were in a pleasant mood. The bar was noisy and crowded, and even a Santa Claus stood outside ringing his bell. "Never seems like Christmas over here," Joe said. "When I was a boy, we always had a tree and popcorn, and presents hidden around the house. I remember the excitement for weeks, wondering what we would receive."

"Christmas is for children," Cam said. "We had good Christmases ourselves on the ranch."

Joe noticed there was no sadness or bitterness in Cam's voice. No emotion. Just a statement of fact.

"Cam Jr. and Elizabeth will see their first white Christmas this year in the states."

Joe smiled. "Your children are well, I presume."

Cam sipped his drink. "They are in love with their country. I suppose never having been there, they are more appreciative than most. In their letters they go on and on about the country, both from different sides. Elizabeth talks of the automobiles and the modern attitudes in Boston. She is alarmed by the stock market and many simple things, but she loves it. Did you read about the police in Chicago arresting the women for bathing in suits that showed their legs?"

Vandall laughed. "As if the cops had nothing better to do."

"I hear from Elizabeth that there is a nationwide uprising of the young, they are smoking cigarettes and wearing shorter dresses."

Vandall looked at Cam. "Kids, let them enjoy it. Hell, in time they'll have to face the world like everybody else."

Cam laughed the first genuine laugh. Joe had never heard him laugh. "True, it doesn't bother me. I like the new fashions myself, nothing wrong with a little naked flesh. From all account of the newspapers, America is just having growing pains now. What with the headlines about booze and gangsters, the stock market falling, it seems to be a very volatile time."

Joe waved his hand for the waitress. "Another one?"

Cam shrugged, "Why not?"

"Have you seen the new cars, Cam?"

Cam nodded his head. "Beautiful, aren't they? I have thought about trading mine, but it runs so well I hate to. I like those new two-door roadsters."

Vandall snickered. "On the money the government pays me, I'm lucky if I can afford to walk."

Cam agreed. "If it was up to the government, you would work for free. Thank God for democracy, so even the government has to tow the line."

Cam looked over the milling crowd of people who were in the adjoining

257

ballroom of the hotel. "Seems the country is growing, huh Joe? There must be a lot of money floating around, more and more people every year. I hear there's a lot of money coming into Cuba. Bootleg money."

Cam had never found out anything about Smiley, but he knew that in some way Smiley had gotten himself involved with some rum runners, and that was the reason he had been shot. To the government of Cuba there was nothing but money to be made, laws in the United States did not have any bearing in Cuba. People willing to run liquor were welcome, just bring the cash. Everyday American men could be seen walking on the docks. Ship after ship left Cuba, her holds filled with rum and sugar. The vengeance that Cam had felt at first over Smiley had subsided, and now he only thought of Vandall and his work for the government. One day, if it was in the cards, he would stumble onto someone or something that would put him on the track of Smiley's killers, but for now his sole drive was to work for Vandall and wait for him to give him his directions.

Cam was fully aware that there was more to Vandall and the United States interest in Cuba than what he knew. He knew it was a dirty business, and he also knew the United States was not in flavor of the new government. What the plans were, what his role would be, he did not know. He was not a fanatic, but he felt obligated to whatever the cause was.

To Cam, the United States had become his new family. She housed his children and had made everything possible for him. Now that the ranch was no longer his life, he needed the feeling of being needed and so do whatever his benefactor wanted. He must only wait for Vandall to begin to settle in his own mind that Cam could be trusted in any capacity. But for now it was enough that it was Christmas and life continued. Cam Jr. and Elizabeth were both with friends, they received money every month from a trust from his bank in Florida. Molly was unchanged, but at least her poor soul was at rest.

(41)

Christmas in Colorado for Cam Jr. was the most beautiful sight he had ever seen. The tall mountains that circled Denver didn't seem real, they were so spectacular, and the ranch of Jo Ann's father was beyond his imagination. During the day they had driven into town and listened to the carolers, and then that Christmas Eve night there had been turkey dinner with her folks and grandparents, followed by hot spiced tea and the opening of presents. Cam Jr. was so enraptured by the day that it was not until he was in his room that he thought of his mother and father and sister.

The past months he and Elizabeth had written often, becoming through the mail much closer than they had ever been at home. Both showed concern over their father, and both wondered what he was really doing, as they suspected he was not living on the ranch.

258

Lying in bed, Cam Jr. looked out the window at the falling snow, and although he was happy and in love, he could not help but be saddened by his mother and father. He wished his father would leave Cuba, he knew he would be happier in the west. Although he did not know the history of his father, he knew he was raised in New Mexico. Occasionally he would read the newspaper, and the accounts of the happenings in Cuba would be briefly covered. The Cuban government was not pro-American, he gathered that. And the people of America were at an emotional high. What with bootlegging and gangsters and radio and movies, it seemed that nothing could dampen their spirits. In bed, with the snow outside the window, Cam Jr. said to the ceiling. "Father, please, please change your world."

Elizabeth spent Christmas with a girlfriend in upstate New York. She was the daughter of a wealthy man who owned several large car lots. The house was two stories, wood, and surrounded by trees. During the holidays cars came and went constantly with presents and goodwill. The ladies wore the new, daring dresses and many had fur coats. The men were wealthy and dashing and drove the latest cars. Everybody seemed to have a flask of alcohol. The house was decorated beautifully with a tree that stood in the den a full twelve feet tall, with gold tinsel trailing to the floor.

Elizabeth received letters from her brother and father, but nothing from her mother. Molly did not know the difference from day to day. If the children had gone to see her, sitting in her room filled with dolls and children's puzzles, they would have grieved even more. But as they were miles away, they could remember their mother as she was when they last saw her. A busy, happy woman.

Elizabeth thought of her father the most. The strange, quiet man who seemed to watch over her every moment of her life. In Cuba, without family, alone on this day.

On Christmas day, as the children stood outside in the snow and sang their carols, Elizabeth felt the saddest. The last of 1920, and the family was scattered around the world. It did not seem right that it should be so.

On Juanuary 7, 1921, Cam Stearns sat in his hotel room and methodically thumbed through the pile of newspapers and magazines he had bought. After several hours, Cam began to look more closely at the magazines. Here was a world in print that he had somehow missed during the last years. All the years on the ranch he had read books and newspapers, but it seemed that his mind had always been preoccupied. But here today he seemed to look at a world he had not imagined for the past nineteen years. Here were pictures of ladies and men, new automobiles, and Cam began to miss his country.

For the first time, he felt an apprehension about Vandall. He did not feel hatred or vengeance or a drive to be anything anymore. He sat and thought of all the years, the dreams, the hard work, and it did not seem like much now only a blink, a brief moment in time.

He began to think of New Mexico, and the dry, sunny heat of the summer. The snow-capped mountains that could loom in front of one for hours on end. The last time he had seen New Mexico was when he was in his twenties. There were no automobiles, nor any roads, and gas stations. He thought of Poncho cooking meals for the people in their automobiles. Maybe he even had a gas pump in front of the restaurant. Funny, he had not thought of Poncho in years. He had never written him. Just another memory he erased from his mind once they were on the ship to Cuba. He thought of the dusty streets and the hot summers, but he also thought of the spring, when the aspen began to bloom and the robins returned to the valleys.

And in that moment Cam Stearns changed his life. He wanted to return to New Mexico. He would buy a ranch there. He stood and looked out the window. The plantation had not sold but he would go back to where he came from, for another new beginning. Let Cuba be Cuba. Let the United States handle her own problems. There would be a day, a day when there would be no Americans in Cuba. Cam knew this, this little island would forever be in strife. One day, the United States would no longer wish to content with this strife and leave Cuba forever. When the time came, it would all have been for nothing. At least if he left now, Cam knew he would leave a winner.

Cam packed the few belongings he had in the room and drove toward the plantation. Driving through the setting evening sun, he felt relaxed, and for the first time in months he felt alive and breathing, and not merely a walking transparency.

In the house at night he smelled the familiar smells. He looked at the painstakingly laid out china and vases. With Cam Jr. gone, the house was not kept up now. Bertha stayed at home and Roberto and Carmella moved into Smiley's old house. Standing in the house Cam felt the years. He set his bag down and walked slowly from room to room, and although he felt at home, he knew there was nothing here for him now. Only memories and dreams, and he was not ready to have his life become that just yet.

In the morning Roberto saw Cam sitting on the veranda. Cam stood, and Roberto saw, for the first time, a genuine smile on Cam's face. "How are you, Roberto?"

Roberto shrugged his shoulders. "As well as one can be with a pregnant wife."

Cam laughed. "Well, let's go into my office and have a chat."

By the end of the evening, Roberto was dazed and flabbergasted. Within a few days he would become the major owner of the plantation. Mr. Baca would receive ten percent of the net cash each year. Roberto would send Cam a percentage of the profit until the plantation was paid off. Cam had called the firm, and the dates were arranged for the signing. As he hung up the phone, Cam had told Roberto, "Within two days." Roberto had looked at the man sitting behind the desk. "Why?" he stammered. Cam looked at the boy he had helped through school. "I don't know, Roberto," Cam answered truthfully. Roberto rose and walked to his home. That evening he sat dumbfounded and told his wife of their fortune. In the early morning he was still on the sofa, awake and slightly worried.

Cam did not walk around the ranch, but he sat on the veranda and thought of the days after Kettle Hill, the days lying in the hospital. The days lost and dark, and then he would see the house and the barn and the drying sheds and he would feel afraid. Afraid of the time, the ever encroaching time.

Two days later, he signed the ranch over to Roberto. After the signing, he shook Roberto's hand and said nothing. Leaving the house with several suitcases, he turned his back on the Stearns plantation. The contract handed over everything on the ranch, including the car. For years Cam would receive a handsome payment, and with the money in American banks, Cam was a very wealthy man. A man with no credit, but with over eight hundred thousand dollars in cash. Starting the autombile, he looked at Roberto. "I'll leave it at the docks," and then he smiled, looking with eyes that did not hide the sadness that would always be there. "Go well with your life, Roberto, and may you have many sons for your plantation."

Roberto Alvarez would become a wealthy and influential tobacco and cane man in Cuba. He would slowly invest money with the beginning of Batista, and fall into Batista's group during the oncoming years. He would own trucking lines, several restaurants and two large hotels in Havana. He would become a quick, sure-acting man who had four sons and two daughters. During the Second World War, his plantation would flourish, and completely would miss the economic depression of the United States.

With each passing year, he would become further and further entranched with Batista. He lived a life of luxury and well being, without being ostentatious or vulgar. He was good to his help and discreet with his other women. Not until Fidel Castro would his world crumble.

(42)

Cam booked passage on the Florida Lady for Miami. He would see his bankers, travel to see Cam Jr. and Elizabeth and then head for the west. He had only one more thing to do in Cuba, and that was to see Mr. Vandall.

Seeing Cam enter his office, Vandall did not show his surprise. He had been so sure that Stearns was the man. Stearns walked up to the desk but did not sit down. He looked Joe straight in the eye and said. "Your secrets are mine, Mr. Vandall," he said, "I am going home."

Joe looked at the fortyish man standing in front of him and smiled. "I missed my chance a long time ago."

Both men shook hands and Cam Stearns took a cab to the docks.

It was a warm, balmy day in Havana when Cam sailed out into the ocean. The further he got from Cuba the more his mind seemed to come alive. Like New Mexico before Cuba, it too would become a memory.

Cam was not prepared for the growth and rapid industrialization of Miami. True, he had lived only miles away, but coming from Cuba with its poor progress, he could now see how small it was, and how limited it was to the very rich. In the states it seemed that everyone owned a car. He was to discover the extent of the car revolution sweeping the country. He knew about the radio, but until now he had not thought of it much. Here there were radios of every description. The college students were not mere characters in Life Magazine, but young, daring people to his eyes. The beaches were covered with girls unafraid of the authorities or laws passed to ban certain lewd swimwear. Women wore knee-length dresses at night with their hose rolled below the knee. Credit was beginning to sweep the country, and everywhere he looked Cam saw signs offering credit. Sewing machines, refrigerators, radios, watches, everything could be bought on credit.

Since Roosevelt's death and Harding's election, Stearns had not followed politics, but back in the states he was overwhelmed by the political arena. The general concensus was that soon Coolidge would be in office.

The United States seemed to be basking in an utopian world. Dancing, new music called jazz, kissing and smoking swept the campuses, along with fads ranging from outlandish men's clothing, to sitting on flagpoles.

After a few days of walking through the streets of Miami, Cam did not feel that he had missed anything at all. Here there was a rush to life, no stable feeling one gets from the land, but a mad dash to buy everthing and make more and more. Cam bought himself several suits and casual clothes.

Seeing the bankers didn't take much time. A Mr. Richards, president of First Florida Bank, was all handshakes and teeth and went on and on about the huge profits to be made on the stock exchange. Cam, although rich and comfortable, did not understand the first thing about stocks and declined investing his money. He knew cattle and land, and would stick to these, he assured the banker.

Cam's wealth already overwhelmed him, and the thought of people like the Rockefellers and others made him shiver. He could not comprehend such people. They were not people, they were institutions, living in a world all their own.

Besides being overwhelmed by the apparent wealth and ease of life in America, Cam was also struck by the poor that lived side by side in the city. Florida was filled with Cubans and Blacks, both vying for low man on the pole. He thought it ironic in the states, while in Cuba he thought it only a natural order of life. But here, living away from the country for so long, he believed in the dream of Americans more than the realty. For all those with cars, there were still the people sweating and digging for each meal.

Also Cam was impressed by the apparent openness of the breaking of the prohibition laws. Not confronted with them in Cuba, he also found himself drawn to the speakeasies that dotted the town. He found it a rather amusing experience, going through the locked door, and he was amazed at the splendor and extravagance of the establishment. Sitting in the bar, he was astounded by the number of white women, and he found it hard to believe that he was truly in the United States. A few drinks and several songs by a sexy blond in a very tight sequined dress, and Cam began to scan the floor for single women. A small, slender girl in her twenties caught his attention. To Cam she looked like his daughter, a girl with a look of innocence, without being innocent. She saw him looking at her and walked to his table. She sat down without being invited and smiled at Cam, showing her small, even, white teeth. "Beats selling shoes," she said casually. "I suppose." he answered. Cam had not thought of women for several months ever since Molly had gone to her sanitarium. But this girl seemed to swim in his mind and he followed the outline of her breasts with his eyes. The rest of the evening they danced and made small talk. At four in the morning, they took a cab to Cam's room. Once in the room, the girl removed her clothes and lay back on the bed. Cam looked at the young, naked form at the smooth tautness of the skin. He toyed with her body for hours before entering her. She was young and alive, and in the early morning, gone.

Waking alone, Cam quickly saw the emptied billfold and flopped back down on the bed. He ran his fingers through his hair and got up. He was not angry, nor did he comtemplate his stupidity in leaving his billfold so accessible. It had been good. She needed the money more than he did. He dressed slowly and took a cab to the sanitarium.

Walking up the large white sidewalk, he was impressed by the neatness of the grounds. Large palm trees shot to the sky and scattered flower gardens seemed to give the place a sense of serenity. Inside, Cam was met by a courteous nurse, her manner was polite, but curt and businesslike. It was not until he saw Molly that he lost his composure.

She was standing in a small corner of a fenced area used for recreation. There were stone benches and grass, small shrub-lined paths one could walk through. Molly was looking out past the wire that separated her from the real world. She wore a long, blue gown, with slippers that matched. Her once beautiful hair was dull, and bunned on her head. Cam stood and watched his wife for several moments. Then, with slow, steady steps, he walked up behind her. "Molly," he said softly.

The lady that turned was no longer Molly. Her face was drawn, but not sickly. Her blue eyes, once sparkling and alive, were vividly blue, but were passive, afraid and fleeting. She looked at the man standing before her, but there was no look of recognition or of love. Cam stood cemented in space for a brief moment, then he slumped and reached out and touched Molly's hand. She was warm and alive. He raised her hand lightly and kissed it. Molly looked at Cam and smiled, saying, "You are nice."

Then she turned and looked once more out beyond the fence. Cam walked beside her, and holding her lightly, they walked to a stone bench. "The children are fine, Molly," Cam said as if they were sitting on the veranda in Cuba. "Elizabeth is in school to become a nurse, and Cam is in Colorado. I understand a fine land, with large mountains and clear water. They would like to come and see you, but you never answer their letters."

Molly looked at Cam and moved her face slightly as he spoke, but she did not answer. Cam continued calmly, quietly, with the serenity and the quiet of the place. "I have sold the ranch. I'm going back to New Mexico. Do you understand New Mexico, Molly?"

Molly looked at him with her sad, blue eyes. She reached over and lightly touched Cam's hand and her face turned toward him. As one tear fell from her eye, she said, "home, a new home."

But once again she fell silent. Just then a whistle sounded and Molly stood. "Dinnertime, I must go."

Cam nodded his head and stood. "You look fine, Molly."

Molly turned and walked slowly toward the complex. For several moments Cam looked around the grounds, the carefree flowers and palm trees, the endless quiet. We should all be so lucky, he thought to himself as he walked through the gates.

The train ride to Boston from Florida gave Cam time to rest and think. The past months had been so rapid, an endless accumulation of misery. Between sleeping, Cam read the magazines and rags that swept the country. He was astounded by the local news, the gangster articles and the coverage of stills and smugglers that were caught. He liked the new fashions, the haughtiness of it all, but he saw it as only a passing fad. When he was young, there had been no parties nor automobiles for him. Enjoy them, he thought to himself.

Cam saw the beauty of the east coast for the first time in his life. The endless tree forest, the large, snow-covered pasturelands. He was in awe of the beauty of the country. Leaving a tropical climate for the first time in years, he was back into cold weather. Boston lay gripped in ice and snow, and Cam stood on the passenger rail waiting for a taxi. He breathed the cold, crisp air and for a moment he remembered he and his father on cold mornings, the snow shining from the early sun when they would hunt for deer, with this thought, his lungs felt young and alive, filled with newness.

His first stop was a clothing store, where he bought an overcoat and sweater, with gloves and a hat. He felt warm and comfortable. He did not write and tell Elizabeth of his coming, as there was no need. But sitting in his room, he thought of his daughter as he called her dorm. The dorm mother was very serious and amid the sounds of girls arguing in the background, he only waited three minutes for the word to spread that Elizabeth was wanted on the phone. Elizabeth answered and Cam could hear her independence in her tone. "Elizabeth," he said, "this is your father."

"Daddy, where are you?"

"I'm in town, to see you."

"Why didn't you write, Daddy?"

"I'm in room three fifteen at the Waldorf. When can you come."

"I'll come around seven."

"Good, then we will go to dinner."

"I love you, Daddy," the voice said as Cam hung up the phone.

Cam sat at dinner and looked at his daughter. He had never seen her so happy, so full of life. She was dressed like most of the college girls, with slight traces of rouge on her knees and cheeks. He remembered Molly years earlier. The long, stiff, restrictive dresses. Here indeed was the voice of the new woman.

Elizabeth talked on and on about the college. Her classes and the young doctors she met during her studies. Cam smiled and agreed with all she said. "Find yourself one of those young doctors, Elizabeth," he kidded. "You're sure of one thing, a doctor will never need a job."

"Who are you to talk," Elizabeth joked back, "look at what you've done with your life."

Cam looked at the sleeve of his missing arm. "Yes, but I was lucky, Elizabeth. Most men like me forever use a shovel or work for other men."

264

Elizabeth, seeing a change in the mood of the conversation, quickly changed the subject. "It's so beautiful here in the summer, Daddy, you can't believe the freshness of the air, the sight of the sailing ships as they dart in and out of the whitecaps."

"It looks very beautiful," Cam agreed, "but a little too busy for me."

"What are you going to do?" Elizabeth asked.

"Oh, I think I'll go back to New Mexico. Look around and maybe buy a small ranch somewhere. I know things have changed through the years, but I feel an urge to see my home. The proverbial elephant, going home to die."

Elizabeth looked cross. "You're not going home to die. I've even noticed you have finally given up those terrible cigars."

Cam looked at his daughter and felt warm and content inside. She was a wonderful, pretty girl, so intune with her life and times. She was very different from him. "Your mother is well, peaceful. I feel she will be there until she dies, Elizabeth. I went to see her and talked to her, but she is not with this world. I don't really even think she knew who I was."

Elizabeth looked down at her plate. "Poor Mama. This life is so strange at times. Some people just can't seem to take the darker sides."

The rest of the evening they talked, and the next day Elizabeth did not go to her classes. She and her father drove around the city. "Spring will come soon," Cam said, parked by a set of docks, "and it will be green and beautiful. I leave on the train this evening. I will write to you as soon as I get settled."

Elizabeth did not show any sadness but looked out upon the ocean. "We are all like the ocean. Restless, moving, always going or coming, will any of us ever find peace?"

Cam held his daughter close to him and stroked her blond hair. "Remember that I love you Elizabeth, throughout your life, always remember that I love you."

As the train pulled away from Boston Cam felt tired. He was alone, knowing no one in New Mexico except Poncho and his wife. Between Boston and Colorado he knew only his daughter and his son. He sat and watched the city pass slowly by, to be replaced by the granite outcroppings and tenaciously clinging trees. The train rolled through the farm belt of Iowa and Kansas. The farmers were just now feeling the significance of the machine age. The tractors stood lifeless, waiting for the last snow of the year. Going through the flat land of Kansas, he was struck by the expansiveness of it all. Used to an island where one could drive to either end in a few hours, he was in awe as he had been in awe when they took the train to Florida.

But now there were tractors and cars, trains with sleepers. Radios in the stations that kept one abreast of the weather and the news. There were radio shows and advertisements of every name and description. And there was even the airplane, and the news that soon Ford Motor Company would have in service an airplane that would take people from coast to coast in a little over thirty hours. Smiley had been right. One day the air would be filled with airplanes, going and coming from all places in the world.

Having never been in Denver before, Cam loved the outline of the city. Nestled between the peaks of mountains, it lay in its boomtown splendor. Cattle, gold and silver were the money that paved its streets. Large lumber operations gobbled up the huge fir and spruce trees. As modern as Boston, with its newly paved streets, it was the hub of the rich mountain west. Looking at Denver, Cam wondered how New Mexico would look after twenty-three years.

Cam Jr. was shocked when he opened the door. Cam looked at his son, so different from the Boston young men he had seen. He was standing in Levis and cowboy boots, an off-white yoked western shirt pulled out over his trousers. For a moment their eyes locked. Cam stepped into the room. It was a two-room apartment, only blocks from the university.

"Jo Ann," Cam Jr. called. Cam watched a young, pretty cowgirl come from the other room. He looked at her young face and the ease with which she moved. "This is my father, Jo Ann. Dad, this is your daughter-in-law."

Cam looked at the girl and then at his son. Setting his bag down, he stepped foward and huggged Jo Ann. He did not speak for a moment but held the girl. He felt her tense for a moment in his arm, but slowly relax. Stepping back, he looked at his son. "Good luck, Cam," he spoke softly. But then, he began to laugh. "Does your sister know about this?"

Cam Jr. nodded his head yes.

"Then the stinker knew all the time I was in Boston, and she said nothing."

They sat in the apartment all evening. Cam was warm and comfortable. Jo Ann had slowly won him over. He liked her young, bouncy spirit. He could see her on the ranch. A nice ranch, judging by her bearing. "Do your folks know?" he asked. "We were married at the ranch. My father would love to meet you. Cam Jr. has told him all about Cuba and the revolutions. By now, my Dad thinks you are a one-armed ten-foot-tall giant."

Cam looked at his son. It was a reassuring feeling, at least someone in the west knew him.

Jo Ann and Cam Jr. had a summer job at a forest lookout tower high in the mountains. They were both excited about that. Cam smiled to himself. He could see the newly married couple running all over the meadows. Two months with no company. He could expect to be a grandfather soon.

The next afternoon Cam and the newlyweds drove to the Smith ranch. Mr. Smith was all Cam had imagined. A tall man, over two hundred pounds, with sandy hair and a dark complexion. He wore loose fitting work clothes and heavy winter boots. He was sitting in front of a large rock fireplace in the den of his home, surrounded by deer heads, rifles and the smell of leather.

The room had a mad order all its own. It was a jumble of outdoor creations and gear. Fly poles and duck decoys.

He stood as the trio entered the room, and shook hands warmly with Cam when they were introduced. "Mr. Stearns, sit down, sit down."

"Nice fire," Cam said, "it's been years since I sat around a fire in the winter."

"Damn winter's about to let go," Mr. Smith said gruffly, "older I get the more I hate the winter. Whiskey, Scotch, any drink you want."

"Scotch," Cam answered. Cam felt happy and warm, staying with the Smiths for a day.

Off in the distance, beyond a grey veil of fog the sun set quickly. The animals pawed the still frozen ground as great circles of air came from their nostrils. It was a good place, this west. Not perfect, but Cam felt his mind stir and his body long for the mountains.

In late March 1921, Cam took the train from Denver to Albuquerque. Boarding the train, he bought the Denver Post. As the train climbed down out of the Rockies and entered the plains separating Colorado and New Mexico, Cam watched the sun set over the land he would see and know again in the morning. He was restless. He felt alone, alone as the day he rode to Las Vegas.

Scanning the newspaper, he chanced to see a small news brief, datelined Havana. It read, "An American working in Havana was found dead earlier today. Dead from multiple stab wounds. An official statement by the government of Cuba states that it has received information that he was killed by revolutionary forces. Presidente Batista, newly elected president of Cuba, stated he would do all in his power to find the killer of a Mr. Joseph Vandall . . . ."

Cam laid the paper down and closed his eyes. Cam would never know of the five men slated for execution and the turmoil Joe went through in thinking of a man for the job, and then finally doing all five himself. The last two, with the aid of Batista. He would never know it was Batista's men that repeatedly kicked and stabbed Vandall. Nothing would ever come of the murder. The United States would bury Joe's body in a small cemetery in Louisiana, and another agent would simply take his place.

(43)

Michele Diangello felt the power of the Packard as he pulled away from the curb. Business was good the past year. What with the shipments of sugar and rum, he was making ten thousand dollars a week. Making so much, he had rid himself of all his other ventures. There were no longer girls nor hijacking shipments of clothing. Selling his wares directly to the big boys, he avoided all the trouble that wracked the liquor trade. Already there had been over eighty murders in Philadelphia. Michele knew the names, Capone, Spiegel, Lansky. But he avoided all contact except with the Philadelphia people and sold directly to them. With this he knew whoever was in power would buy his merchandise. He had no ties nor obligations. He did not sell his wares on the street nor try to horn in on the action through the speakeasies. Very few people knew he smuggled. To most he was a proper and well-to-do man who owned several clothing stores in Philadelphia and Chicago.

Jo Jo handled all the logistics of the operation. From the loading and unloading to the various drop-off points for the merchandise. Michele dealt directly, picking up the money when the merchandise was inspected. Through the years there had been no rip-offs, no non-payments. He cheerfully took the money and slowly began buying properties in western cities. He bought lots in Denver and San Francisco. Cheap property in Arizona. He no longer dressed flashily, he dressed in

267

style, but subdued. He did have a new car, but that was only what an upper class man from the heights would do. His one child, a two-year-old daughter, was pampered and loved by him and her mother.

Life was good for him. There was money and fine restaurants. The clothing stores in their own right made money. Michele's house was filled with radios. A radio in every other room. He had the latest refrigerator. He felt comfortable, and looking back on his life he marveled at time how he had been so lucky. He would think of the real gangsters, and remember when he was a child dreaming of living a life like theirs. But now it was different. He would sit with his wife and child and dream of his properties in the west.

Jo Jo, on the other hand, had become hard and ruthless. The trade was so lucrative he began to sell off parts of the shipments without Michele's knowledge. Then he secretly placed the money in banks in Florida. To Jo Jo's knowledge, Michele had no idea as to his activities, and never would. Jo Jo knew Michele's liquor went directly to Capone-controlled outlets. He also knew that Moran was his chief competitor and was not willing to come over. Jo Jo sold his rifled hooch to Moran's people. To the best of his knowledge, only he and the man next to Moran knew of the arrangement. Jo Jo knew that one day Capone would rid himself of Moran and that it wouldn't make any difference. It was simply business. He did not like Michele less, nor did he feel mistreated, it was simply business, and he couldn't see not cashing in while it lasted.

It was impossible for the country to forever outlaw booze. Already it was a national mockery. Companies issued kits to make juice that told explicitly how not to make the illegal substance alcohol. Government issues by doctors for medicinal purposes were commonplace. It was the vogue by the wealthy to serve their guests sparkling champagne and the best of Canadian liquors.

Michele rested comfortably in his easy chair and listened to the radio. Already the political contest was beginning. Michele, like most other Americans, was tired of Wilson, the war years, and the never ending platform that America must spread its doctrine around the world. By and large most Americans were tired, and held little concern for the rest of the world.

Michele believed the country was symbolized by the youth. They seemed completely involved with anything that was fancy and worthless. They did not seem to understand that comfort came from work, whether it was legal or illegal. Michele only thanked God that his own child was young, and he hoped that the frivolous age would soon pass, and the world would get back to normal values. But at the same time, he remembered his childhood, the comfort of his home and the ambition that made him what he was now. Now, sitting in comfort with cash flowing in a steady stream, he only considered his early violence in business as a means to an end.

To Michele, educated and wealthy, the country was run by hypocrites. One day expounding on democracy and equal opportunity, and the next turning its eyes from the racial and social injustice that filled the streets. Every day the radio broadcast stories about the farmers and coal workers who worked hard and starved. On one side of the coin were men like Michele. Men who pursued the dollar and became rich, and others who worked long, dreary days and remained poor.

268

Although many men Michele knew played the stock market regularly, Michele kept to his land purchases and preferred to forget the market. He felt an apprehension in the country. No matter the high amount of material goods the American public owned, no matter how well-dressed were the men and women, there was an air of hopelessness about the people. An air that everything would end soon, so one must do as much as possible.

Michele's wife Nancy now considered her curiosity about Michele's vocation as a passing obsession, as there were no more strange men around the house, and the stores were doing well. She never asked him questions, although she knew he tampered with alcohol. She also knew that he was not a typical gangster of the newspaper variety.

Nancy loved her daughter. The child's room was filled with toys of all kinds imaginable.

But Nancy had changed. She had been a shy girl, raised in a typical strict Italian home where the women knew her place and did not venture forth from the home. But recently she had become active in women's rights. She wore the short dresses and powdered her face and knees. Being attractive, she liked the way men looked at her, but would never think of going beyond the lines of propriety. They joined the Philadelphia country club and they both took up golf. On the weekends they would drive through the country with friends and picnic. She even went so far as to drink small amounts of Scotch, and she voiced her opinion that the government must have been the driving force behind outlawing booze, and that they secretly backed many large distributors for the under-the-table money that was used for clandestine operations in foreign countries. At first Michele scoffed at such an idea, but what with the demand for alcohol as it was, and the ease with which it was brought into the country, he sometimes also thought that it may be some great masterminded conspiracy.

Jo Jo stepped from the ship. These trips to Cuba were becoming common occurances for him now. He was picking up Spanish, and he knew several lovely Cuban ladies who kept his free time far from boring. Although at first Jo Jo did not play with other women, with his new-found fortune, and with his new business associates, he began to enjoy the various women who filled his life.

Batista, who Jo Jo did not meet with, was always represented by several men who made sure Jo Jo had whatever he wanted. They were his constant companions, always on the lookout for theives. With prohibition in full swing, many men came to Cuba for sugar and rum. Also many American dollars, made illegally in the states, began to appear in nightclubs and hotels around Havana.

The country seemed to be staying on an even keel. For the past years there had been no riots or small bandit groups in the jungles. New schools, and new improvements to the city could be seen everywhere. Cuba had her own radio station, and electricity was being installed all over the country. The people were satisfied with Batista, who gave firey speeches and extolled the role of the United States in Cuba.

Jo Jo sat confidently at the bar of the Imperial Hotel. To his left sat a buxom Cuban lady in her mid-twenties. Copying the look of the American flapper, she wore a light knee-length blue dress and a small hat with her short cropped hair neatly underneath. With every opportunity she rubbed her ample bosom into Jo Jo's arm. He had never been with this one before, but one of Batista's men had brought her over to his room early in the morning. She had come into the room when Jo Jo was half asleep, undressed in a very professional manner and lain down beside him in bed. It had been a most delightful way to wake up.

After breakfast, they went to the bar where Jo Jo was supposed to meet Rafael. Rafael entered, a little late as usual, with the normal disdainful look for the American on his face. Even after many shipments, the two secretly hated each other. Jo Jo, because Rafael was a Cuban, and Rafael because Jo Jo was nothing more than an American gangster. Living too high, screwing good Cuban women, and acting like he owned the world. Jo Jo still swore to himself that he would kill Rafael before it was over.

Jo Jo looked at Rafael and told the girl to meet him back in the room, slipping her a twenty dollar bill. She walked away happily. Rafael sat down but did not smile. He watched the girl walk away. "Nice, no?" Jo Jo taunted. "Very nice," Rafael agreed. Rafael hollered across the bar and ordered a drink in Spanish. Sitting and waiting for the drink, he smirked. "We have a slight problem now, senor. You know there are many men who come here for sugar. Each day seems to bring more. We even have college boys now, out to make a fast dollar. Have you heard of all the hijacking lately?"

Jo Jo waved his hand in the air. "We have nothing to worry about. Our ships do not get touched."

"Maybe so, senor," Rafael continued, "but here it takes more and more to get people to look the other way."

"Why? There's nothing illegal here," Jo Jo said.

"That is right, but there still is to be a higher tax placed on the sugar."

Jo Jo looked astonished, and almost lost his temper. "Why? There is no reason."

"I only follow orders, senor, it is not my doing. Only ten cents on every pound, just a little."

What Jo Jo did not know was that during the past few months, several representatives from large bosses back in the states, their bankrolls swelled by prohibition, were sending men to Cuba, to establish ties with important officials. Through bribery and large kickbacks, they saw in the future a gold mine for their interests. The government, little more than swindlers themselves, flocked to the new people. There was talk of hotels with large floor shows and open gambling. Gambling that would pull more tourists in from the states and bring fast money into Cuba. Batista met personally with many of these men. Smiling and wining and dining them, their bills were paid and the women were free. Millions of dollars would flow into the Cuban economy, making it a very profitable place to be for many.

For the peasant, life did not change. The rich people coming to the country came with recommendations from judges and various political sources. Millions of illegal dollars could be cleaned in the hotels and casinos of Cuba and brought back legally into the United States. But with these people also came the wish that lesser people be cut off from the source of sugar and rum. Already ships manned by crews working for large families roamed the sea, stopping and searching all ships they crossed. Ships carrying sugar and rum were taken, the luckless crews were thrown overboard, their story never to be told.

Jo Jo sipped on his drink and after a few moments of silence said. "Well, I suppose there is nothing much we can do."

Rafael stood from the table. "Enjoy your woman, senor, the ship will be loaded as usual."

Jo Jo finished his drink and paid the bill. Entering his room, he looked at the girl lying naked on the bed. "Well, my Cuban rose, there is nothing idle about your thoughts."

He began to undress, and it was not until his trousers were half-way down, that he saw the thin smile on the girl's face and the small black pistol she was holding.

Standing naked over the twitching form, the girl calmly placed one more round into Jo Jo's head. Then she dressed and took the moneybelt from the lifeless body. Rafael will be happy. Batista would never miss the American. There were many others to take his place.

Sitting in Rafael's house, the girl stroked the man's hair as he counted the money. "This is very good, my sweet," he said. "Soon there will be another one, and we will both become rich."

The girl took the three thousand dollars he gave her and placed it in her purse. "You know where to find me," she said, "Anytime. You know how I feel about the Americans."

For three weeks Michele waited for Jo Jo. There had been no delivery, and although there had been other shipments that were late, Michele was worried about this one. During the fourth week he received a call from Atlanta. "Word is your man is dead, Michele," the voice said. "Better find yourself a new boy."

Michele placed the receiver down, his face ashen. For several weeks he went through each day in confusion. Then finally, he placed all his stores and his home up for sale.

Taking his family, he moved to Phoenix, Arizona, where he opened a clothing store and a furniture store, and forgot about his life in crime.

(44)

Cam found in New Mexico a new land. Albuquerque was no longer a dusty, small town, but spread out on either side of the Rio Grande. Bernalillo was still small, but filled with gas stations and restaurants. The cities were laid out completely by class, the whites on one side and the Mexicans on the other. But what most impressed Cam was the miles one could still see. He had forgotten about the vistas of New Mexico, and he would spend hours driving around the state and looking at the scenery.

He drove slowly toward Las Vegas. Here was still the dusty, dirty, adobe-filled town. The Montezuma hotel was boarded up, but still grand, even in decay. He was apprehensive as he drove toward the old restaurant, but a smile crossed his face when he saw the two gas pumps outside. He walked into the restaurant and it was as though he had never left. There were the same tables and chairs, the same style grease cloth coverings. Plastic flowers filled vases and a faded "Molly's" was still painted in red on the window.

He sat down and looked slowly around the restaurant. From the back he could hear whistling, and the sound of a small baby crying. Soon a short, fat, white-haired Mexican man came from the back. "Senor, senor, I am so sorry, but I deed not hear you come in."

As Poncho drew closer, his eyes narrowed and he looked at the man sitting by the window. It was not until he saw the missing arm that he knew for sure. "Meester Stearns, Meester Stearns, the years, they have been so fast."

Cam stood, and the two men shook hands without speaking. It was then Cam had to fight to hold back the tears. Both men sat and smiled at each other. "Where eez your wife? Where eez Missus Molly?"

Cam looked at Poncho. "She is dead, Poncho. Died in Cuba."

"Blessed Mother," Poncho crossed himself and whispered a short prayer.

"God, he takes the kind first," he said softly adding a few moments later, "how was Cuba.?"

Cam looked out the window. "It was many things, Poncho, many things."

Strangely there was nothing else to say. How could he tell his story and make this good man understand? "How is it here, Poncho?"

"Like when you left, only now there are the cars and the gas, but all in all eet eez the same. We have grandchildren now. There eez nothing new here."

Poncho looked at the man and he could see the traces of loneliness that Cam tried to mask so well. "Life, she eez not always what we dream, no senor?"

"No Poncho, it is not. How is your wife, Poncho?"

Poncho laughed. "She eez beeg and fat now, Meester Stearns. But happy. All the grandchildren, she loves. If she eez not making something to eat, she eez making something for the babies to wear. Soon eet will be spring, and she will begin making the winter clothings. Much snow was on the mountains this year, there will be much water and many flowers."

Cam looked out the window again. Here it was, almost May. The past week had seemed like nothing. Dotted with visions of his wife and chidren, he knew for the first time how really lonely he had been. Poncho broke his thoughts. "What brings you back to New Mexico?"

"Going to buy a ranch, Poncho, going to buy a ranch and settle these bones down."

"That, she eez good. There are many nice ranchos north of here. This, she eez good country. Not all busy and growing like Albuquerque and Santa Fe. She eez still free country here."

But then Poncho looked annoyed. "There are many problems now. The whites and the Mexicans, they are fighting over the land. My people, they say the Spanish, they give it to them, your people, they say eet eez theirs because they buy eet from Spain. Not a week goes by that some kind of shooting don't happen here in town. But most of the people, they only wish for peace and not trouble. Stay out of the bars, senor, they are trouble."

Cam looked at his old friend. "The bars have never been a problem to me, Poncho."

Cam was amazed at how the town had changed. To be sure, it was not a thriving city, but it did have new gravel roads and many automobiles. It was still a blend of Mexicans and cowboys and Indians, but as far as one could see everybody lived in their own section of town. The cowboys made life lively on the weekends, and judging by the looks Cam received from the Mexicans, feelings were running high.

Much of the land had been homesteaded by white settlers. Whites who came in and who were backed by the judges took over land that had been granted to Mexican families by the Spanish. The Mexicans, unable to compete with the large ranches, were slowly pushed into smaller and smaller hamlets. Constantly resentful about losing their land, they stole from the whites as often as they could. Fences were cut and cows ran out. It was a standing rule that any Mexican found on private property was immediately shot. The sheriff was not called, and the body was dumped by the road.

Cam quickly rid himself of his suits, and decked himself out in jeans and western boots and shirts. Although the automobile was around, the only way to really travel the country was still by horse. The ranches lay few and far between and outside of town the only power was electric generators and hand pumped pumps or windmills.

The land around Las Vegas is a treeless expanse of gamma grass and rock. It slowly climbs to reach the foot of the mountains and the tall pine and spruce trees and the trout-laden beaver ponds. It is land made only for cattle and an occasional herd of sheep. Bone dry land in the summer, and cold windy land in the winter.

North of Las Vegas was all white land, and the poorer, hilly, rock and pinon land south of Las Vegas, belonged to Mexicans. Mexicans filled many ranch jobs, but after work there was little or no blending of the two cultures. A few Mexicans owned large prosperous ranches and dealt with the gringos. These people were disliked by their own kind, but generally did not care.

With prohibition in full swing, many smugglers traveled through the country with trucks and cars filled with booze heading for points east. Although most of the country was fully into the jazz and flapper rage, here life was like it had been for hundres of years, men still wore guns and played hard.

Riding around the country, Cam looked at the large herds of whiteface cows and slowly the old feeling of the earth began to fill his mind. He did not think of Molly nor the children, but for several weeks he rode and camped around the country. Riding into ranch headquarters, he would dismount and talk to the owners, memorizing the names of the ranches. There was the Flying Diamond, The Forked Lighting, the Dead Horse Ranch, and the Pecos River Ranch. All were vast, sprawling ranches with many full-time cowhands. The cowboys were a flashy bunch. They wore pointed Mexican boots with their pant legs tucked in, and on their heads, large, droopy cowboy hats. Many wore brightly colored bandanas and braided horsehair bracelets. All were armed with whatever weapon they could find. Old 30/40 Kregs, the new Winchester repeaters, but by far the 44/40 pistol was the favorite. People still talked about Billy the Kid, and the large range wars that used to plague the state. It was still a place where men did not ask questions and could care less where you came from or what you did. It was how you treated them that mattered. And most of the men and bosses liked the silent stranger with one arm, and had no objections to his riding their ranches and camping on their land.

To Cam it was needed time alone. Alone with the sun during the day the stars at night. He slowly felt his body returning to life. He would fix fence if he saw it down, but mostly he rode slowly, talking to the bay mare. Around him was nothing, nothing but grass and cows. Each night camping with the stars, he would sit and look in the fire, and if one would have come across him they would have thought he was some primeval beast, the way his eyes shone in the fire.

After two weeks of riding, Cam returned to Las Vegas and went to the realtors around town. Brown and Macbride, and Las Vegas Realty both assured him they had what he was looking for. He made appointments with each for different days so they could drive out and look at the ranches.

Spring was in full blossom, and the runoff from the mountains filled the numerous small gullies and ditches. On the sides of the mountains the aspen could be seen greening and the brown open areas filled with blooms of many colors. It was not beautiful land like Colorado or the east coast, but it was large, free land with room and space and Cam felt at home.

Sitting in the restaurant in the evening, he looked out at the sun setting on the small adobe town, and although he did not smile, he felt happy.

Within two months, Lou Grange had found Cam the ranch he wanted. A small place, by the standards of western ranches, it encompassed only five thousand acres. It was a brown pinon-covered tract of land nestled on the side of the mountains. Two miles of the Pecos River ran through the northeast corner of the ranch. At one time being Mexican land grant land, it had been homestead by a bandit from Kansas. The man, wanted in Kansas, came to New Mexico Territory and moved onto the ranch. A solitary man, he built a small adobe home. He ran a few cows, kept a few goats and shot wild game. He seldom went into town or saw other ranchers around him. Not until a neighbor's dog dragged in the arm bone of the man was he remembered. He was found dead by the river, bitten by a rattlesnake. He was buried where he lay, with a board plank that read, "Here lies Mr. Reed."

Cam loved the ranch at first sight. The clear water of the river, contrasted with the brown earth around the pinon trees. Rising in the morning, he could see the tall, snow-capped peaks to the east and the mountains looming hundreds of miles to the north. It was a dry region, but the grass greened when it rained.

By fall he had four hundred head of cattle purchased in Mexico waiting for the train to bring them into New Mexico. Two brothers from Las Vegas, Ross and Virgil Cutler, were hired and were in the process of building themselves a cabin for the winter. They were uneducated, rough young men. Dirty and scornful, they were nonetheless hard workers and knew cattle.

Ross, a small, bow-legged man with dark hair and a habit of letting his chewing tobacco drip down his chin, would go for days without a word. Riding the fence

274

or looking for cattle, he loved the solitary life. He did not dream of women nor think of the town. It was as though in his own simple mind there was only the one life of the ranch. When he did talk, he talked in short bursts, condemning automobiles, fancy clothes, and the government.

His brother was the opposite. A tall, brown-haired man with hazel eyes, he smiled and always seemed to be happy. Whenever there was a day off he would ride the twelve miles into the small town of Pecos and spend his money on drinks and whores. He did not gamble, saying one day to Cam, "I'd rather fuck, at least then I know where I'm throwin' it away to."

Both men were good marksmen and hated Mexicans. To them Mexicans were worse than Indians, and if Cam had not given the order that Mexicans were not to be shot if caught on the ranch, they would have gladly shot every Mexican they saw.

For weeks Cam thought of the ranch and tried to decide on a name for it. Then one early morning as the sun rose, he looked out at the red filtering through the low, dense pinon trees, and thought to himself, Sunrise Ranch.

That afternoon the men began carving out the name on a large plank to hang over the gate. His brand would be a circle with four lines, representing rays, one for Molly, each of the children and himself.

Cam worked hard, seven days a week. Working from dawn to dusk, the days ran together. Falling into bed at night exhausted, he did not have time to think of his wife nor feel lonely. He knew one day he should ride around and say hello to the ranchers around him, but each day he had the time, he found an excuse not to go. But lately he found himself thinking of women, and how nice it would be to have someone around the house and someone to talk to beside the Cutler brothers.

One day riding by the river, he heard the laughter of small children. Riding up to a large bend in the river that cut through a tall gorge, he saw two small girls splashing in the water. Looking around, he noticed three horses tethered to a tree. Cam rode up to the children and stopped his horse by the edge of the river. "You two shouldn't be here without someone watching you."

The two girls, no more than seven or eight years old, looked at the man. "We can swim."

Then Cam saw the woman step from behind the horses. She was not a beautiful woman, nor was she ugly. She was tall and large-boned, but she carried her head straight and her eyes looked directly into Cam's. Cam noticed the tightness of her shirt against her breasts and momentarily looked away. "If you are the owner sir, I am sorry, but my girls and I were riding on the other side of the river, saw this lovely place, and the children did so want to swim."

Cam got down off the horse. "No trouble," he said, "it's good to hear a little laughter around here."

The lady looked at the man. She was curious about the one arm, but she did not ask. "Well then, will you join us for some lunch? We have chicken, some cole slaw and a few oranges."

Cam looked at the little girls, now paying no attention to the adults, and then back to the woman. "I would like that, thank you."

"Good, my name is Mary Douglass."

"Cam Stearns. And this is the Sunrise Ranch."

The lady looked around. "It is beautiful, Mr. Stearns, you are a lucky man."

"I hope your husband won't mind," Cam said, sitting down by the river. Mary looked at the little girls. "My husband is dead sir," she said, without a trace of sadness in her voice. Cam did not speak, but felt a warmth spread through his body.

Every chance he got, he looked at the woman. He noticed the high, pronounced cheekbones and the hands that showed the signs of hard work. Her features were hard, but her eyes were soft and blue like Molly's. The little girls minded her well when she spoke to them, and were polite to Cam. "Nice girls," Cam said.

"Thank you, Mr. Stearns. Do you have children?"

"Two," Cam answered, "both grown and away now."

"And your wife?"

"She died. She died over four years ago."

Mary looked out across the river and said nothing.

After the chicken was gone, Mary rose from the ground. "Well girls, we had better be going. By the time we get back to the ranch it will be late."

"Visiting the Dead Horse?" Cam asked. Mary looked at him. "Yes, my uncle owns it. We came from Arizona to take a vacation."

As Mary got on her horse, Cam said quickly. "Would you like to go to dinner in town tomorrow? I hear there is a silent movie playing also."

Mary looked at the man, surprised at the suddenness of his offer.

"I'll pick you up in my car," Cam added. "My, my," Mary laughed, "a car in the midst of the wilderness. I thought all you cowboys loved were horses and fast women."

Cam looked at the lady, at least ten years his junior. "Who says we don't?"

"Mr. Stearns, I would be happy to. It's been a long time since I did something just for fun."

Cam stepped into the saddle and watched the three ride away. He could not help but look at the rear end of the lady as she bounced in the saddle.

That night sitting in the house, the kerosene light sending its faded light off the white walls, Cam could not help but feel happy. He thought about the lady, and the more he thought the more he could picture her sitting on the horse and the way her mouth moved when she spoke.

Lying in bed, he thought of Molly and a dark sadness came over him, but he felt she would understand. If in her mind she ever found out, she would understand. Cam pulled the blankets up around his shoulder. No matter what, no matter how tough or brave or how many wars he fought, he was lonely.

The Cutler brothers watched as Cam stepped into the car. Ross spat a large gob of tobacco and looked at his brother. "I'll be back late, Virgil," Cam said as he cranked over the engine. Virgil nodded his head. They watched the car bounce away over the rutted road. "Wonder where he's goin'," Ross said. Virgil looked at his brother and laughed. "Looking for women, you dumb fuck, one thing you ain't never gonna do."

Ross looked at the now fading dust cloud. "Nope, guess yer right, might be dumb, but I ain't that dumb."

Mary wore a light brown summer dress. Cam looked at her and thought of all the women through the east he had seen with their flapper dresses and rolled hose, and he smiled thinking, of the down-home women here. Mary was bright and happy, getting into the car. She seemed to enjoy the feel of the wind as it touched her face as they drove.

They entered town, and Cam pulled in front of Poncho's restaurant. Mary looked at him. "That was fun. These automobiles are relaxing."

Poncho saw Cam walk in with the lady. He felt happy for the man, no man should be alone, especially not one he knew. Sitting at the table, Poncho did not let on he knew the man, but waited on the table with an air of prompt and courteous attention. Cam knew that he was doing this for him, and felt warmly toward his friend.

Mary looked at Cam. He seemed like such a sad man, so quiet. The one arm intrigued her, and she would know in time. He did not talk about the past in any way. The conversation riding into town and now sitting in the restaurant was about the ranch or the weather. He asked about her and Arizona, but never about anything personal. It was as though he did not want to invade anyone's privacy, and he also did not want his invaded. He was a polite man and one used to being comfortable, she could tell. He did not talk like the normal cowboy nor did he carry himself like the average man. He was confident, haughty at times, but also not afraid of anything. His eyes attracted her the most. The off-green that seemed to penetrate all that he looked at. She immediately took a liking to him and as the dinner progressed, she found herself leaning over and touching his hand as they talked.

Cam also liked the woman. She was fresh, a talker, unlike him, and able to keep a conversation going. He knew that she loved the outdoors and loved to fish. She was worried about her daughters, as with the growth in the cities, the younger generation was getting out of hand. There was bathtub gin and wild parties. She could not see how the world could continue like this.

With the passing of time and touch of her hand on his, Cam felt himself happier than he had been in years. After dinner they sat and watched the sun go down, and then rose and walked to the theater. Charlie Chaplin was playing. "This is my first movie," Cam said as he bought the tickets. Mary looked at him. "Well then, you should really like this."

Cam sat and watched the movie and was amazed by the magic of it all. He laughed at the antics of the small, athletic man, and it was not until the movie was over, that he noticed that he was holding hands with Mary. Rising, they talked about the movie on the way to the car. Cam had been truly enthralled by it.

Riding back in the night with the bright stars overhead, Mary leaned her head back and looked up into the heavens. "This is a wonderful place. Here we are, two people and all these stars."

Cam let Mary out in front of the Dead Horse Ranch main house, and walked her to the door. Standing there he told her, "I really enjoyed this evening, Mary."

Mary looked at the tall man. "I did too, Cam. Maybe another time."

As he drove back to his home, Cam felt happy. There would be another time. He knew there would be.

Walking to her room, Mary saw the two girls peeking out from their room. "Will he be our new daddy?" Anne asked. Mary went to the girls' room and put them back in bed. "You never know," she said, kissing each child. "you just never know."

Cissy looked at her mother. "He is a nice man. I would like him for a daddy."

Mary lay in her bed and breathed the fresh air from the open window. She thought of the man and the fire within her burned deeper. There was something about him, something she could not put her finger on, but he was exciting. He was not like most men, only wanting to bed you and then leave you. She had had enough of those men, hopefully they would stay in Arizona and not bother her. But Cam, he was a gentleman, a serious man who might have a dark past. Nevertheless he was a good man, and lonely.

For Cam life on the Sunrise Ranch became quiet and peaceful. After the first date, he and Mary saw each other at least twice a week. If they were not driving to town, they would go for rides around the ranch. The two little girls, not at all shy, grew closer and closer to Cam, and while Cam had always been responsive to the needs of his own chidren, he had never been very affectionate with them. But with Mary's daughters he found himself picking them up and holding them often. They were two bright happy girls, who loved the ranch.

Although Cam and Mary both felt in their hearts they were becoming closer than mere friends, they were careful to keep their feelings in check. Several times by the river Cam had burned with desire for the woman, but he maintained his composure. Sometimes at night Mary would lie in bed and dream of Cam's caress, but she tried her best not to let on about her emotions. When they would go to town to eat, Poncho could see the look that the couple had for each other, but he had never had a chance to be with Cam alone, to tell him that he knew the lady loved him.

Cam found himself working and thinking of Mary all the time. Rising in the morning and cooking his own breakfast, eating a warmed-over lunch and whatever he could throw together in the evening was more than tiresome. But Mary always seemed to have a pie for him or homemade bread that picked up his home cooked meals.

Ross and Virgil were careful not to mention the woman, but behind Cam's back they began to make jokes and laugh about their love-struck boss. One day, feeling brave, Ross looked at Cam as they slurped on a can of beans. "Sure would be nice to be able to eat some decent food on this ranch."

Cam looked at him sourly and did not speak for a moment, but then said, "well then, learn to cook," and there was no more of that.

By the time the cattle arrived from Mexico the fences were all finished and the holding pens and shoots erected. The old house that Cam moved into was fixed and tight and the Air Light generator was on the way by rail. There were gas tanks, a half-completed tack room, and a large shed for feed. The hay barn would be finished in several weeks. Although the ranch was not the place of splendor as the one in Cuba, it was a well put together and tight western ranch.

Everywhere was the scent of cattle and the ever-present flies swarmed around the mounting piles of horse and cow manure. Cam's home, a five-room affair of adobe, was cool in the hot summer days. Set against a deep brown gully surrounded by pinon trees, it was gracious and blended in with the country.

During the few evening when he had time to sit on the front porch, he would look out and feel awed by the rapid changes in his life. The sound of the cattle, the dry whistle of the wind through the trees. The ranch reminded him of Smiley, and at times he would think how nice it would have been to do this with Smiley. He was a friend. Although he liked the Cutler brothers, they could never be like Smiley.

On Sunday morning as Cam rode in from checking a fence, he noticed his stove pipe burning. Entering the house he was met by the smell of coffee and the aroma of pie. Mary was in the kitchen and she smiled as he entered. "I was sitting over at the Dead Horse and the girls were going to town with their uncle, so I thought I would come over."

Cam looked at the woman and he felt a great sadness fill his heart. "You shouldn't have done this Mary, it's so much work."

Mary looked at Cam. "Work, what's a little work."

The rest of the day they sat around the house and talked. For the first time they talked of their earlier lives.

As the sun was setting, Cam told her of Cuba and the land, the greenness of it all, and the plantation he had sold to return home. Mary sat and listened, and for the first time she realized the depth and complexity of this man. This man who had taught himself to read and run off half way around the world to start a new life. She found out about his children, but she did find out anything about his first wife. Simply that she died. He told her about Smiley and the Rough Riders. He even told her of the fighting on the plantation and the killings that occurred.

Cam wanted her to know all about him, to take from her mind and feeling that he was something beyond a human man. He wanted her to know he was like everyone else. After Cam had talked, they sat on the porch in silence. Mary took his hand and pressed it against her cheek. "Well, if you aren't going to say anything else I will."

She looked into Cam's eyes. "I love you, Cam Stearns. For what it is worth, I want you to know, I love you."

Cam looked at the warmth in her eyes and touched her face with his hand. "I love you too, Mary, but it is very hard."

Mary nestled her head on his shoulder. "I know, Cam, I know, it is so strange, so very very strange."

Both people had shared their pain, both had known love and felt its highs and lows and both were confused by their mutual love, here in New Mexico. One returning after so many years, one running from a life she wanted to leave behind. Here, meeting by a river and falling in love. After a few monents Mary raised her head. "Make love to me, Cam."

Cam leaned over and kissed her on the forehead. They both rose without speaking and entered the house.

Ross and Virgil sat on the porch of their cabin braiding a rope. They watched the two move inside. Ross laughed. "Well, maybe soon we'll be eatin' good food."

Virgil looked at his brother. "Maybe, maybe not, but you don't be sayin' nothin' about this to anyone."

Mary lay sleeping, curled against Cam's side. Cam lay looking out the window at the morning sun. A small wren chirped somewhere deep in the pinon trees. Although he felt happy and warm, he was perplexed. He had not wanted to fall in love. But he knew he loved this woman with her two daughters. However, he was married, married to a woman who did not even know he was alive. Moving through her days of dolls and make-believe. Shut up tight in a green manicured prison. But Cam also knew he could never divorce her, it would be impossible. He would have to tell Mary. He felt Mary move and watched as she opened her eyes. Looking at the woman, he felt sad.

(45)

Molly drew the blue blanket tighter around her face. There was a man, a man who came in her sleep. A tall, light-haired man with one arm who smiled at her and held out his hand. "Molly, Molly," he would speak, and Molly would stand and reach for the man but he would always be beyond her reach. She would run, run as fast as her legs would move, but the figure would stay ahead of her.

At first the dream had been like this, night after night. But now there were two people. The man and a woman. The woman stood beside the man, but with her back to Molly. Molly would run in circles around the couple, trying to see the face of the woman, trying until her lungs burst with pain and her legs shook from exertion.

Then she was awake, awake and tired and sweating and rising from her bed to find her small doll. "Elizabeth," she would say to the doll. "You know, I know you know. I wish you would tell me."

And then the door to her room would open and the nurse would be there. There to help her put on her clothes and tell her about the day. And Molly would stand not talking but moving her head trying to grasp what the nurse said. But there was nobody who understood, nobody except her doll Elizabeth, who would listen and look at her with those great blue eyes and say nothing.

It was in August when Molly began to dream of the fire. Waking at night screaming, she would tear at the burns on her face and hands. *All around her the blaze swept. She would be walking through a small clearing in the pine trees. To her right a large bluejay would circle and then a rabbit would dart by. Then she would smell the smoke and see the large grey-white cloud of smoke blot out the sun. Then she would run from the wall of fire. Run blinded by the smoke and singed by the dancing flames but always behind her would be the screams, the screams of two people trapped by the fire. She did not see them but the screams for help ripped through Molly's mind.*

280

Then she would awake, clawing at her face, breathing the acrid smell of the fire. And there would be no scream, no sound, only her cries with the day. The nurse would hurry into the room and hold her and talk quietly to her, but no one understood.

(46)

Cam rode and looked at the ranch. It had been a terribly dry year. The grass, normally as tall as a man's knee was short and cropped close to the ground. The river was down at least five feet and small stagnant pools of water stood where current used to run. The cows, sturdy Mexican beef stock, did not die as others would have, but remained skinny and gained no weight. Although they did bellow with hunger, there was no chance they would die. Only if it was a severe winter, and the snow was so deep the cows could not dig through the snow and find food, would they die. With the dry weather the people of the area were also seething. Word spread of the growning hostilities between the whites and the Mexicans. Already several people from both races had been found dead. With each body, men became more and more on edge. Guns were placed around the houses and all men began wearing their weapons.

Las Vegas simmered in the heat, the town severly divided. The country's political arena was constantly being racked by scandal after scandal. Politics under Harding was little more than a hop scotch affair. The Secretary of the Interior, Albert Hall, had been indicted for swindling the country out of millions of dollars of oil money.

But the country seemed not to be bothered by anything at all. There was a growing trend by the people to try and forget that there was a world outside the United States. Living was still high, booze ran free and politics was a different world.

In the west there was little if any change. Fighting the weather with cattle and crops, there was little time nor inclination to waste one's time worrying about what the big cities on either coast were up to. To Cam and his two workers there was only the drought and the ever increasing risk that the cattle might not make it through the winter. Cam would have to ship large quantities of hay from Colorado to feed during the winter, and if the calf crop in the summer was not good, he would loose many thousands of dollars.

(47)

Cam Jr. scanned the uninhabited wilderness around him from the Park Service fire tower. For miles around there were the towering firs and spruce and deer and rabbits. Beneath the lookout point, he could hear Jo Ann putting the dishes away from breakfast. It was beautiful here. Situated on Mt. Baldy, the fire station has a view of all the surrounding area.

Linked by radio with a station in Crested Butte, Colorado, they would report any sign of fire within their ever-scanning point of view. There had been several small fires earlier in the season, but now with the weather so dry, the fire season was at its peak.

For the past five nights, every evening had brought an accumulation of dark clouds that would rumble and roar, but send no moisture to the ground. With the night, the clouds would let loose their torrent of lightning. So far, there had been no fire, but Cam Jr. knew this was only luck and each night he and Jo Ann stood and watched the lightning carefully.

For the two newlyweds it had been a beautiful two months. Outfitting at Crested Butte, they had ridden into the lookout with five horses, loaded with enough supplies for the summer in the mountains. There were beaver ponds around them filled with hundreds of small trout. They had discovered many patches of berries, and between rounds of looking for forest fires, they ran naked through the woods and made love in every conceivable place they could find.

Cam Jr. could not believe his life could be so good. Here, away from the world, there were no newspapers, no daily reports of graft and murder. There was a simple rhythm to life, punctuated by the cool evenings and the sound of fish frying on the small shepherd's stove. They had seen many deer and a few brown bears. But mostly they saw each other. Making their daily report to the ranger in Crested Butte, they would report, then listen for his reply and sound off.

There was nobody in their world to draw them apart, no mortgages or payments to make them slaves to the system. Only the trees and the wind and the lonely part of the mountains where they lived and loved.

After a month, Jo Ann knew she was pregnant but said nothing to Cam Jr. In the evenings, lying on the floor covered by their sleeping bags, she would see the small, living boy beside her. She would call him Joseph, and he would be raised loving the outdoors and the nature around him. He would not ever be raised in a town nor trapped by life as so many of the people she saw now.

Although there were many people living rich and expensive lives, most of Colorado was poor. Miners and lumber people, they slaved, trapped by the large companies who paid little if anything and kept the men chained to the company store and the warehouses. Working for no retirement nor sick pay, they were poor, hard men. But her son would be a free person, a lover of the wild and the free. Here in this great land with the mountains and the clear air he would grow and live his life.

At night, feeling the touch of Cam Jr., she would lie warm and content, letting her body respond to the caresses of him. She loved the feel of his hand and the warmth of his kisses. He was a gentle, caring man. But she would not tell him of the baby until the winter, when they were down from the mountain and warm and snug in their home.

As Cam Jr. scanned the northern horizon he noticed the clouds build up earlier than usual. Large, white clouds billowed over the mountains. Maybe these will bring rain, he thought. He scanned the mountains for a few more minutes then climbed slowly down the lookout tower.

Jo Ann walked from the small cabin and sat down beside the spring that trickled through the meadow. He sat down beside her and handed her a small, yellow wildflower. "For the flower of my life," he said. Jo Ann smiled. "It's so lovely here, too bad we only have a few more weeks."

Cam Jr. wrinkled his nose. "I know, then it's back to Denver and another year of school."

Cam Jr. hated the idea of school, but he knew each year brought him close to his degree.

The winters were pure drudgery. Each winter he would look out at the snow-covered landscape and dream of the summer. The occasional outing he did as part-time work to check the wildlife was fun, but still not the days of sunshine and cool air. It was as though like the wildlife, he slept during the winter, dreaming of the summer and the fishing.

He looked at Jo Ann and his fly rod leaning up against the cabin. "Let's go catch a few fish for lunch."

Jo Ann stood, "sounds like fun to me."

Getting his pole, they walked hand in hand down the well-worn trail they had made to the beginning of the beaver ponds. They had counted over fifty beavers in the stretch of ponds that began at one end of a small gorge and continued all the way to a box canyon that even during the summer was usually in the shadows. Here were grouse and chucker and many elk and deer.

When the wind kicked up, he looked at the sky and then at Jo Ann and said, "we'd better get back to the cabin. It seems as though the weather is worsening."

Jo Ann looked at the sky. "Looks like a bad one."

They reached the cabin as the wind hit the mountains. It was a terrible wind, whipping and bending the trees. Deeper in the forest they could hear the crash of trees that could not withstand the onslaught, and Cam Jr. looked nervously at Jo Ann. "I'd better climb up and take a look."

Climbing the tower, Cam Jr. was buffeted by the fierce wind. Once on the platform, he found out they were completely surround by the dark clouds that as of yet hand not released a drop of moisture. Between large claps of thunder, Cam Jr. could see the lightning split through the sky. Looking at his watch, he saw it was four o'clock, but it looked as though it were dusk. He cranked the radio and listened for the reply of the officer in Crested Butte. "Hello, Cam Jr.," the voice came across the line. "There's one big one up here," John said. "Wind, and lightning, I can't see a thing past the edge of the clearing." Cam Jr. replied.

"Well, you'd better get in the cabin. From all reports we're due for a big one tonight."

Cam Jr. looked once more around him. Climbing down the ladder, he did not notice the lightning rod that hung from the tower nor did he hear the remainder of the wire break free and fall to the ground. He found it hard to open the door into the wind. Once inside, he sat down and looked at Jo Ann. Neither were afraid, it was just another storm, a large storm to be sure, but it would pass.

"Guess we sit and wait it out." Jo Ann smiled, walking toward him and slowly unbuttoning his shirt. Cam Jr. reached out and slid his hands effortlessly around her small bosoms. "Nothing finer to wait out a storm," he smiled into her eyes. "Nothing finer."

Cam Jr. woke with the crash of the lightning. He jumped quickly from the bed and struggled into his clothes. Not looking back he ran outside. To his front, great waves of flame shot around the cabin. The wind blew first one way and then another. Looking around, he could not see a break from the fire. Running back into the cabin he grabbed Jo Ann's hand, dragging her behind they ran outside. But then Cam Jr. stopped and held his wife. There was nothing but a circling, boiling wall of flame. He looked deep into the eyes of the terrified girl and held her next to him. The heat scorched their hair and blistered their skin. They gasped the hot air into their lungs and ran back into the cabin. "Rain, please God, rain," Cam Jr. screamed.

The cabin was like a hot house, within minutes they could not breathe, and pouring water into a bucket and onto a blanket, they lay on the floor and covered their heads.

The skeletons would be found like this. The charred remains of two people, sprawled next to each other. There would be a small article in the Denver Post, with a report of the fire and the loss of the lives.

The next summer the new trees would spring from the blackened soil and the underbrush would grow around the beaver ponds. The beaver, untouched by the fire, would splash and rebuild their homes. The deer would return to lick the charcoal.

By the 1950's, only small traces of the fire would remain among the large, healthy trees. Bluejays would once again soar through the branches and rock chuckers would whistle through the day.

Molly woke screaming. The two bodies exploded in flame before her sleep-filled eyes. One, a tall young man, screamed. "Molly, Molly, mother, mother, I love you."

For the next three weeks Molly would sit in the corner holding her doll and whispering to the lifeless form, "you know and I know, you know and I know."

As Cam rode to the house late in the afternoon, he saw a strange automobile parked by the house. Approaching slowly, he was surprised to see Poncho sitting on the porch. Dismounting, he saw the look of dread of Poncho's face. As he neared the porch, a fear filled his heart as Poncho stood and placed his arms around Cam. "Your son and his wife, they were killed in a fire in Colorado, Cam, ' he said between sobs. "The sheriff sent me out to tell you."

Cam fell into the chair on the porch and covered his eyes with his hand. Slowly he began to weep and let the darkness come over him. Poncho stayed for several hours. He helped Cam inside the house and talked to Virgil and Ross. The men said nothing, but walked slowly back to their cabin.

It seemed as if all life had left the ranch. For three days Cam did not leave the house. Sitting, staring at the walls, he thought of nothing. He did not shave nor change clothes. The men did not try to see him or talk to him. They were men of the west, hard men who knew in their simple fashion that there were many things

284

a man must come to grips with himself.

On the fourth day, Cam came from the house dressed and clean. "I will be back in a few weeks," he told the men, "you know what to do."

Cam began the long, lonely drive to Denver. He would bury them there. There in the mountains that they loved.

Mary rode to the ranch on the sixth day. She had begun to wonder where Cam was. He had not been by nor had there been word. Riding into the house area, she was surprised to see his car gone and two hands working on the corral. "Where's Cam?" she asked Ross. Ross looked at the lady. "He went to bury his son and his wife, Mary," he said softly. "They were killed in a forest fire."

Mary held her clenched fist to her mouth. "Oh my God," she gasped, and began to cry. The two men stood and watched the woman. They could do nothing. Soon she turned the horse and began to ride back toward the Dead Horse Ranch.

The funeral was a somber affair. Elizabeth took the train from Boston. Jo Ann's parents and relatives stood around in a daze, and Cam did not speak. After the funeral, it was as though he was in a dream. He took Elizabeth to the train station and stared, as though in a trance, as the train pulled from the station.

Starting the drive back to the ranch, he felt as though there was no life left in his body. All he could think of was so far, for so many years, for so little. The second night he bought a bottle of whiskey and outside Raton, New Mexico, he stopped the car and drank the bottle. In the morning it was a barren, lifeless world. The trees were but mirages in front of his eyes and the miles and miles of land were but dead voids on the face of the earth.

On the train ride back to Boston, Elizabeth did not grieve for the loss of her brother as much as she did for her father. For Elizabeth life had a meaning, in a few years she would be a nurse. Her studies, her never lacking for dates, kept her life even and enjoyable. To her Cam Jr. would never be dead. He would live forever as he always was. But riding back, she thought of the years they had been together, raised in the same house. It was as though they had never really met. For her father she could only see the look of utter loss that engulfed him the day of the funeral and the day she left on the train. They had talked little during the week they were together. Only in passing did they speak of Molly, and it was as though they touched on a matter Cam had rinsed from his mind. Elizabeth wished there were something she could say or do to change her father, but there was nothing. Only time.

Riding back to the ranch and entering the house, Cam looked around him and, for the first time, he began to cry. He stood and listened to the wind as it rustled in the dry trees, and he sobbed. Sitting in his chair with the darkness, he rose and walked wearily to the bed. "Oh God," he muttered as he lay down, "Dear, dear God."

The next morning Cam was up early and Ross and Virgil met him by the tack room. He looked sad and weary. Both men smiled and shook his hand and Cam understood. "It's a real strange life, Mr. Stearns," Ross said, looking away from Cam. "We just live and work and one day we're nothin' but a memory to the world. Leavin' all this space and time and work to be done."

285

Cam lifted the saddle onto the horse's back. "We've got cattle to check. A lot of hot, dry days."

The next weeks were but blurs to the men, riding all day, counting the cattle. Cam rode long past the other two men. He worked and grunted, and after the weeks slowly he began to speak. One night, sitting by the stove in the kitchen, Cam looked at Virgil and smiled. "It's a good life out here, Virgil, a real good life."

Virgil felt the gloom lift from Cam and smiled back at his boss. "It's a good life, for sure," he agreed. "A man couldn't ask for no more."

After the men had gone to their own house, Cam sat and for the first time in weeks, he thought of Mary. He left the house quickly and drove to the Dead Horse Ranch. Mary was sitting on the porch when Cam drove up. She stood, seeing him get out of the car, and ran to his arms. Holding him tightly she cried into his shoulder. She did not speak, nor did Cam, but they stood holding each other. "I need you, Mary," Cam said, "I need you."

Sitting on the porch, Cam held Mary and looked at the New Mexico night. "I have to tell you something, Mary," he said softly. "Something you must know."

Cam told Mary slowly and carefully about Molly and the sanitarium in Florida. Mary sat in the darkness and looked at the man. Cam looked at the lady by his side. "So you see, Mary, we cannot marry. Do you understand?"

Mary did not speak, but sat and covered her face with her hands. As Cam stood up, he looked at the motionless form and walked to the car. "It is best, best that you know."

In the morning Cam heard a car pull up in front of the house. Standing on the porch, he saw Mary and the two girls getting out of the car. They carried suitcases and the car was filled with their belongings. Cam felt his heart jump, and with bold strides Mary walked up to him and set her suitcase down. "You are a strong, silent, brave man, Cam. I love you and I have come to live with you."

Cam looked at the woman and two little girls and he kissed Mary lightly on the forehead.

Virgil and Ross spent the afternoon helping rearrange the house. In the evening, sitting at the table, the men ate chicken and biscuits and salad. They were not uncomfortable nor judgmental. For the first time the house was truly a home, and both men felt warm as they walked back to their cabin. Lying in their separate bunks that night, Ross said into the dark, "man needs a woman. I suppose life just deals some strange hands sometimes."

Virgil rolled over in his bunk. "She's a good woman," he muttered.

For several months the gossip would spread through the countryside about Cam and Mary, but with time and people seeing the two together, the gossip stopped and the town and the ranchers forgot about the two people living together without marrying. Cam became active in the Cattlemen's Association, and Mary would drive any distance and for any reason to help out a neighbor.

The dry season passed and the winter was mild, enabling the cattle to maintain a small amount of weight. In the spring there were over two hundred calves, and spring rains swelled the Pecos River and snapped the drought.

Besides the Cattlemen's meetings, life on the ranch was a continuation of the day before. Although there were scattered outbreaks of violence around the country between Mexicans and whites, there was no trouble on the Sunshine Ranch. The calf crop was good enough that Cam bought a new car and a truck and enlarged the home. Ross and Virgil were given a raise.

With Mary, Cam was content. Each evening there were good meals. She was a strong woman, never one to complain. She was brave and self-sufficient and did not need to be constantly praised or pampered. A strong, sturdy woman, she slowly loved the bitterness out of Cam, and with her steady rhythm of life, their home was happy and filled with a quiet, peaceful tranquility.

For the remainder of the decade, Cam and Mary would live a comfortable western life. Watching from the fringes the direction the United States was taking, Cam was no longer obsessed with any matter of life except the ranch. While in Cuba, he had read extensively and followed the course of the nation, but in New Mexico he cared little for the government or political policy whether it be local or federal.

Because New Mexico was wild and wooly, he carried his rifle and pistol in the car and marveled at the police when he went to town. He thought he saw a breaking down of the country, a flighty outlook on life, but it did not bother him. Pampered by good cooking and Mary, life was a simple matter of cattle, and the worries about rain and snow and grasshoppers. Prohibition was a thing for the large cities, although many ranchers in the area ran stills to pay for needed items. In New Mexico it was not a matter of life or death. On the Sunshine Ranch there was no loss of stock, and besides the occasional hobo that wandered through, or a wetback, there was nothing to distinguish one day from the other, except the weather.

Cam was healthy and tanned. His skin was lined around his eyes and chin, and his hair had whitened. The sun bleached his eyebrows. Upon seeing Cam, one would think he was a cowboy, slightly over the hill, but tough, tough enough not to bother, and he lost his arm in a tractor accident or stomped by cattle.

As in Cuba, Cam became a trusted man of the area and also known for his hard work and the success of his ranch. To Cam there was only one success, work, work made the breaks and pulled out the extra cash. He took up deer hunting again, and loved the feel of the autumn wind as it touched his face.

Cam became, if nothing else, a part of the land he owned. He knew every tree and gully, each cactus. He knew the dove that would fly over in their grey masses, and the deer that came down from the distant high peaks to winter in the pinon-covered lowlands.

The two girls grew to love this man, with his stories of wars and far away places. Cam would sit in the evenings and tell them stories and the girls would sit and listen, enchanted. He was not strict with the children, as he did not have to be. There was an aura about him that they felt and knew. Although he was kind and pleasant, he was a silent man. A man that Mary gave his own space and his own time. In his mind, Cam was a far different man from his appearance. Life seemed useless and terrifying at times. He loved the ranch, he knew this, he loved Mary and the kids. But with each day there always seemed to be a yearning. Not a yearning that would ulcer a stomach, but an ache. An ache that was there, no matter how happy or comfortable he was. He did not tell Mary of this feeling, nor did he let the world see it, but it was there, hidden in the droop of his eyelids and held by the slightly cold gaze.

In 1927, Ross married a girl from Lincoln County, New Mexico, and they lived in a home twenty minutes ride from the main ranch home.

Virgil, still single, lived in the cabin. It was a hard life, but life was good for Virgil. His dreams did not carry him past being a cowboy.

From the day she entered Cam's life, Mary loved the ranch. She loved the quiet and the sunsets, and she especially loved to ride. When Cam was off she would go to the corral and saddle a medium-sized quarterhorse mare. Riding alone, she felt the happiest. With the thought of the home and Cam, and the children well, her body would relax and her mind settled into the sound of the saddle and the horse. It was a dream to Mary. A dream come true. Raised in Arizona, she was from a middle-income family. Schooled fair, she was sweet and innocent and lured by the talk and moves of a man from Denver. Pregnant and married, and pregnant and married again, her life had become a torture. The man traveled and whored and did whatever trick came his way. After several years, a few beatings and many crying nights, she returned to Arizona where she found no answer to life. Working two jobs to support the children, it had been through luck that she had come to New Mexico. Pure luck. And pure luck to have found Cam.

At times she would look at Cam and truly feel that he was only a stranger. But at other times she would look at the man and her heart would be filled with him. In either case, she loved the home, the ranch and the life her children led. She loved the feel of Cam's hand and the look on his face when he ate her food. When they fought, which was not often, they would yell and scream and forget the whole matter. She did not think of not being married to Cam. Maybe in town she would, or back home. But here there was nothing but oneself and one's thoughts.

Sometimes she thought of the woman in Florida, walking around her room. What she looked like, how they met and their lives together in Cuba. But soon she found this painful, and she blocked it from her mind.

If she had one fear, it was the fear of becoming pregnant. There was nothing she dreaded more in life. She did not wish to have a bastard child. Although they had never discussed children, she knew Cam did not wish for them either.

The girls, closing out the 1920's, were two young cowgirls. Both tomboys. They were strong, horse-riding girls. Both filled with life, and at night they talked in their room about boys at school and the development of their breasts.

Cam knew soon that they would be trouble. Mary tried to ignore the widening hips and budding breasts of the girls. When the stockmarket crashed on October 24, 1929, Cam was looking at his six-month-old calves. When news of the crash came, he shrugged. He owned nothing but a ranch, and a ranch paid for, with enough cattle to feed an army for months. He had a river and trees and doves in the fall and deer in the winter, and if he wanted to, he could saddle his horse and ride to the top of the mountain and get grouse and elk.

There was no stockmarket for him. Just cows, cows that bred and ate and made steak. If he lost everything, he would have his ranch. A ranch was not a piece of paper. It was land, solid and real.

At dinner that night, Mary asked, "what does it mean, Cam?"

Cam looked at Mary. "To us, nothing," he answered, "but to the country and the world, it means a changing point. I think it's time to pay the fiddler."

Mary looked at her hands and then at the girls. She could think of nothing to say except, "there's pudding for dessert."

(48)

From the time Elizabeth stepped from the train in Boston, after her brother's furneral, her pursuit of life became an obsession. Elizabeth hated to not feel that she had accomplished something with each day, be it cleaning the apartment or reading a book. She became a busy lady, very opinionated, and over the middle years of the 1920's, very serious. She looked back on episodes of her life as mere building blocks to the person she was now.

A nurse by 1925, and working in the largest private hospital in Boston, she was known by the doctors as a very competent woman. As with all people who constantly work around the sick and dying, she fully came to realize the small thread of existence the human race clings to, and although she had never been religious nor thought of religion before, she became a devout Catholic. Baptised and confirmed, she spent many hours of each week with volunteer work at the Catholic hospital and with home-ridden people. Elizabeth was one of the few people in life who could truly mask her feelings and play a part for the person with whom she talked. She was a smiling, bubbly person, rustling in her stiff uniform, brisk of manner and confident.

She once again became interested in women's rights and attended many meetings. She would continuously pursue this until her death.

Slowly she dated less and less. She decided, in a matter of fact way, that she would have to marry someone like her, or there would be no chance for happiness. Although she went out with several doctors and various businessmen around town, there never seemed to be a spark or any sign that she would want to spend her life with any of them.

She was a very perceptive woman, and around her she saw a frivolous society. Having been raised in Cuba, she discovered the many faults in the unjust system of American life. She would debate any subject with anybody at any time, and loved mostly small gathering of people drinking wine and talking of the world.

In the late 1920's, she began working with handicapped children. A nurse friend became ill, and Elizabeth volunteered to take her place for several days at a city hospital for handicapped children. The children touched her like nothing else in her life, and each evening after working with them, she cried. It was their eyes. The small creatures with their tired, pleading eyes.

In 1928 she resigned her job at the hospital, and took a lesser paying job at the children's hospital. Although it was a taxing job that left her exhausted, it was also very fulfilling when a child was helped. She circulated printed material asking for funds for the hospital, and become relentless in her pleading with the hospital and the board of regents for changes.

When she first began working at the hospital, it was a cold, white, lifeless building. The children were fed and worked with in a clinical manner. Being handicapped, their basic belief was that they were beyond hope, with no purpose, except to be forever held prisoner in a small hospital.

Elizabeth immediately began pestering the hospital for flowers and color, for some game rooms, for radios for music. At first many opposed her, but her drive and will and the success of her work with the children and money from her city drives prevailed.

Several articles were published in medical journals about the work, and the new approach began to be used by the Boston Hospital for Handicapped Children. Walls were painted bright colors, paintings were placed in the rooms. With each day of therapy, the children also had time for games. Living each day surrounded by people who would not speak correctly, or walk, children with stubs of arms and no legs, she began to see more clearly most of the people who called themselves normal. Every day she marveled at the walking, talking, frivoulous people, and more and more she decided that most people had very small minds.

When the stockmarket crashed, she was rubbing the nob on the end of a nine-year-old boy's leg, preparing the child for the rigors of using a wooden leg. She looked at the radio as the news was announced, and looked back at the boy. She could see the fear and concentration of the child's face, thinking about walking. "It will be fine, Charles," she said tenderly, "a few weeks and a few falls and you will be walking."

The boy touched Elizabeth's hand. "I hope so, Miss Stearns. I really hope so."

That night at home she read the paper slowly and laid it down "Piss poor world," she muttered to herself, and then she thought of the small boy thumping down the hall of the hospital.

(49)

For several months Molly dreamed about the fire. Each night there were the same faces and the same cries, "mother, mother, I love you."

But then the dream stopped, and Molly no longer dreamed. Her sleep became a dark void, suspended in time between sleeping and walking. So deep it was not rest but oblivion. During the day she no longer took notice of the dolls that had comforted her, but she either sat in the day room looking out into the garden, or she sat in the garden.

In several spots in the garden there was a presence that came to her at times. Not something one could touch or hold, but a feeling that came to her and reached into the corner of her closed but safe mind. She would sit unspeaking for days, and then by 1926 she no longer talked at all. In all other ways, she looked normal. She was clean, she kept her room neat, she dressed and brushed her hair. She wore no makeup, her skin was a clear white.

To Molly there was no world. She had never been young, never danced or made love. There was only the day. The morning sun and then the day, ending with the darkness when she lay in bed. To the world she was a slow-moving ameba, unfeeling, not sad in appearance, not violent. Molly was a neutral entity.

In 1929 Elizabeth drove from Boston to Florida to see her mother. Through the years Elizabeth had felt the compulsion to go, but there was always the fear. Cam no longer visited Molly, the pain was too great.

It was a warm June day, and Elizabeth had been surprised at how airy and cheerful the home was, as she followed the nurse to the garden. Dressed comfortably in a light summer dress with large red flowers, Elizabeth suddenly felt free and alive this day. Maybe it was shedding the heavy clothes of Boston, she did not know, but the touch of the warm air through the light dress excited her and made her feel happy and gay.

The nurse pointed at the woman sitting on a stone bench in the garden. To her left was several orange trees bright with summer life. Elizabeth stood and looked at her mother. She did not rush up to her, nor did she feel a surge of anguish. She just stood and looked at the woman who seemed peaceful and rested. To Elizabeth, she seemed like one of the children at the hospital. The time, Elizabeth thought, the time. She walked up to Molly, who looked at her, but seemed not to really see the figure before her eyes. Elizabeth sighed, taking a deep breath. "There have been so many years, so many changes."

The lady moved over a tiny bit on the bench, and Elizabeth sat down. "My life has been good, mother. I have a wonderful job working with handicapped children. Boston is a beautiful place. So green and crisp, it does get tiresome at times, but it is nice."

Molly turned her head and looked at Elizabeth. Her eyes took on a puzzled look and she said, barely above a whisper, "Elizabeth."

There was no tone of recognition in her voice, as if only the name stirred her memory. Elizabeth knew this and smiled, taking her mother's hand. "That's right," she said. "I have never been married," she continued. "Although there were some pretty wild times in my life, you would never guess it now. Most men think me the very competent, dedicated nurse with the sex appeal of a wet dish rag," she laughed. "They should have known me sooner. This generation has not lived up to the standards you desired, but which one does? Cam Jr. and his wife are dead. It was such a tragedy for Dad. I think he will never come to grips with the fact."

Molly watched the young women talk. She noticed the smoothness of her skin and the way her eyes seemed to decipher her surroundings. She did not formulate an opinion on the woman, but she felt comfortable with her. Elizabeth continued. "He lives with a woman and her two daughters now. Twice a year or so we write, but his letters are very vague. More about the weather than anything going on in his life. One day I will travel to see him. I would like to meet the woman. He will not marry her. I feel sad for the woman for she must truly love him."

Elizabeth scanned the garden. This was such a tranquil place. "The world is having quite the to do now. Money isn't worth anything, banks are closing. People are starving right here in this country. Crime is soaring. It seems there is nothing but turmoil. I don't really know what will happen, but we live I suppose, good or bad, we live."

And then Elizabeth said no more. She stood and looked at the woman, the woman with the flowers and the grand parties, and she remembered, when as a child she would sit by her bedroom door and peek out and watch the people. She would listen to the horses tethered outside and smell the cigars and hear the laughter and chatter of all the gaily dressed men and women. She remembered the kitchen with Bertha and her mother, and how one could stand by the kitchen window and see out to where her father kept the stallions. It was then, that she began to cry. Not grief-spurred sobs but tears that ran down her face. She knelt down before the sitting lady. "Mother, mother. I wish you well."

Elizabeth stood and walked away from the form that could just as well have been the bench or the orange tree or a small bird that flew overhead. Elizabeth went directly to her hotel room where she slept for several hours. She then put on the new swimsuit, went to the beach and allowed herself to be picked up by a man. She made love all night long, and in the morning boarded the train for Boston. The tanned man, three years younger than she, looked dazed as she packed. "Why so soon?"

Elizabeth looked at the man, still in bed as she left the room, and winked as she closed the door. The train ride back was comfortable. Seeing her mother had broken the wall of disbelief Elizabeth had held for all the years. Her mother was well, there was no need to worry. The man had been delicious in a way, but in many other ways he had been nothing.

Back in Boston, Elizabeth returned to work, relaxed and once again dedicated and very Catholic.

(50)

After the crash in 1929, life did not change for Cam and Mary. Although the rain was little and the cattle thin and sickly, the bills were met. Relying on the money he had left in the bank, Cam met each day resolute and strong. It was a great help that he owned his land and outright and did not owe the bank. Many ranchers in the area dogged it out stubbornly, but soon loans came due and many people were forced from their property to become faceless numbers in the throngs of people that sought out other places to live and feed their familes.

It was not until 1933, when the banking system of the United States folded, that Cam was truly thrown into the depression. In one day the hard worked for security blanket was gone, and Cam was broke. He held his property, but there was nothing else. He became a spearhead for angry ranchers, and twice organized groups of men to travel to Santa Fe and speak to the governor. Each time they were turned back by state police and national guard, with lifeless words and no action. The ranch, blessed by a running river, became a holdout. Mary and the two girls worked the summer in a large garden, while Cam and the men struggled with the cattle. Many ranchers in the area killed large portions of their cattle in an attempt to drive the price of meat up, while others, pushed from their ranches, slaughtered their own cattle and left them to rot.

If Mary was grieved by the change in the country, she did not let on to Cam or the children. Up before anyone else in the family, she fixed meals and worked in the garden. Although there was no money for new clothes or trips to town, the family stayed together, and Ross and Virgil more and more came to respect the woman. At times even Cam would become depressed, but Mary would talk to him about the future and the promise of Franklin Roosevelt, and soon Cam would once again fall back into the task of survival.

When Roosevelt was elected in 1934, Cam said to Mary, "well, maybe this son of a bitch has some balls. At least he carries a grand name."

Shut off from the world except by radio, they never really understood the plight of the many Americans during the depression. They ate and were warm. There was beef and venison, and although they had no new clothes, the clothes they wore were mended and clean.

With Roosevelt in office and prohibition over, life seemed to take a sudden upswing. Federal monies pumped into the failing banks, work programs gave the destitute work, and the country began the slow climb back to prosperity.

By 1938, although they were not rich, Cam was comfortable. They had money in the bank and the drought had snapped. The girls, now fully matured, had minds of their own.

In 1938 both Anne and Cissy married young cowboys and moved to ranches in the area. Mary cried at the weddings, but once back at the ranch she seemed to become younger and life became dearer. For the first time in their time together, Cam and Mary were truly alone with each other, and Cam began to see more and more of the woman with whom he lived. Mary was always there, listening to his ideas about the ranch, helping in any way she could. It was as though they had just met.

Once a month they would drive and see the girls. Cam would sit with the young men and talk cattle or horses.

Cam liked Cissy's husband, Raymond Pierce, immensely. He was a large, robust man in his late twenties. With short, blond hair and blue eyes, he seemed to have the look of a naughty child. A happy man, one very seldom saw him without a smile.

Anne's husband seemed to Cam a worthless sort, but he put up with Michael Campbell's attitudes like any good father-in-law. Each time leaving Raymond's ranch, he would be laughing and smiling, but leaving Michael's, he would be serious and quiet. Mary would look at him and touch his arm. "It's her life now, Cam, nothing concerning you and me."

"I know," Cam would scowl, "but what a worthless man."

Cam knew Mary only saw the man as husband to her daughter. But to Cam there was something evil and sinister in the mind of the small, wiry man with the piercing eyes and short laugh. It worried him, worried him enough that on several occasions he felt like dragging the girl from the house and taking her back to the ranch. But with the soothing words of Mary he would settle down and dismiss the idea from his mind. Still, he would look at Mary and say, "one learns a lot about people living a life like I have."

When the German tanks rolled into Poland in 1939, Cam laid aside the book he was reading and looked out the window at the sprawling pinon trees. A chill came over him. He looked at Mary and said, "it's unavoidable Mary, the country will go to war. It's unavoidable."

Mary sat quietly and put down the trousers she was mending. She thought of the two men married to her daughters. They will go, she thought, they will have to go. Cam saw the fear in her eyes. But there was nothing he could say or do. Mary looked at him. "We've come so far, radio, movies, medicine, climbing out of the depression. And now this, why, Cam?"

Cam thought of Cuba and he remembered the feeling of the battle. The cries of the smell of gunpowder, the surge that spread through one's body as the enemy rounds sang overhead. He thought of Smiley, and the planes, and the rebels in Cuba. "Only God knows, Mary," he said, "only God knows."

Elizabeth passed the depression years with the children. Although the hospital was severely cut back and it seemed there never was enough of anything, her strength carried her through the days, and when times were better, people who worked with her told others how they relied heavily on her never-ending spirit.

For six years she shared apartments with at times up to five other nurses, various men in love with various nurses, and two cats. Boston struggled on with its poor and destitute, but somehow they managed. Everyone was beginning to feel relieved when the news of Germany entering Poland came, and the war machine in the United States began to gear up. Elizabeth began making plans to enter the service as a nurse. They would need women, strong, able women, women to work and help the soldiers. She and several friends decided to see what would happen, if the United States did enter the war, they would join the nurse corps immediately.

On December 9, 1939, Molly stepped from her room and looked down the hall of the hosptial. "Where am I?" she asked a nurse walking by. The nurse looked startled. "You are in Florida," the nurse answered, composing herself. Molly looked around her. "Where is my husband?"

The nurse held out her hand. "Come with me," she said calmly. "Let's go talk to the doctor."

The head doctor at the hospital looked at the woman. He had seen so many sick people through the years. "You have not spoken in years, Mrs. Stearns, do you know that?"

Molly looked at the doctor. "What year is it?" she asked slowly, feeling for her words. "It is 1939," he answered. "My God," Molly said, "my dear God, where have I been?"

That night, lying in bed, Molly thought of her children and her husband. It had been over nineteen years, nineteen years she had been locked inside her mind.

But now she was alive, alive and well. But lying in bed and thinking, she was afraid. So much time, so many years, who knows what her family was doing or where they were. "My God, my dear God," she prayed into the dark, "thank you for the light."

_____

Cam slowly put the letter down and closed his eyes. A cold shiver ran through his body. He picked up the letter and began to read again.

"Dear Mr. Stearns: Through the years I have seen many cases in my life, but none like your wife. Several weeks ago, she suddenly began to speak, and has completely regained her memory. She has asked many questions concerning her family, but knowing of the passage of time, I have avoided her questions as best I can. I am writing you to inform you that your wife is well and could be released at any time. Not knowing your present situation, I thought it best to inform you. I know this is a very delicate family situation, and I will proceed along the lines you wish."

Cam rubbed his forehead and listened to Mary inside the house washing the lunch dishes. Through wars and revolutions, now at fifty-four years of age, Cam did not know what to do. He must not tell Mary yet, he knew this. He would call Elizabeth and tell her, and maybe she would know what to do. Molly was but a memory now, after the years, all this time, just a memory. But she was still his wife. Looking around, he thought, I should have filed for divorce, but who, who would ever think this would happen.

That evening as Mary bathed, Cam rang the operator. He only hoped the party line would not listen. "Daddy," Elizabeth answered, "it's a good connection."

Cam held the phone and listened to Elizabeth. He could think of no small talk to lead into the conversation, so he blurted it out. "Elizabeth, your mother is well and wondering about us."

Elizabeth froze with the phone in her hand. A friend sitting in the room saw her palor and thought she might faint. Elizabeth stammered, "Oh Daddy, what can we do?"

Cam heard the fright in his daughter's voice. "I think you should go to Florida and take her to Boston with you. It's been so long, Elizabeth, so very, very long."

"Daddy, what about Mary, does she know?"

"Not yet," Cam answered, "not yet. Write me when you get back to Boston."

Molly walked from the hospital with a small bag and her hand clutching Elizabeth's. Neither woman spoke, but tears streamed down their faces. Sitting in the cab on the way to the train station, Elizabeth could see the bewilderment on Molly's face. Everything was so different. The cars, the people. For hours on the train they would sit in uneasy silience, both trying to avoid the unavoidable, but both knowing the question must arise. Elizabeth did not mention Cam Jr.'s death, but when they talked she talked about the depression, the war in Europe, the advancement of the radio, all the many and wonderful inventions that had occured while Molly had been away.

Molly, although strained, looked well. She still had the sparkling eyes and her chin, though now loose, was straight. Her hair, sparkling with white, blended with the

295

the light palor of her skin. "Life is marvelous, Elizabeth," she said as the train moved through Georgia. The new trains amazed her, and it was here that she mentioned Cam for the first time. "When your father and I went to Florida to take the ship to Cuba, we rode on the train. It was a large, black affair with the coal dust covering everybody. Nothing like these new trains."

What amazed Molly the most were the young people. The world seemed to be happy and content. Although she read the paper about the war in Europe, the general attitude of the government was that it was a war across the ocean. The Japanese were not interested in us, only in China, and Hitler would remain in Europe. America was too far away and too mighty to be bothered by the Nazi menace. This attitude would change abruptly in several months, but for now the war was only in the newspapers.

Molly was flabbergasted at first by the new, daring fashions the women wore. In Florida the swimsuits had shocked her, but seeing that nobody seemed to pay any attention, she kept her feelings to herself.

The night of the second day she looked at Elizabeth. "Where is Cam Jr.?" she asked calmly, "is he well?"

Elizabeth looked at her mother and held her hands. "Mother, he is dead. He was killed in a fire in Colorado."

Molly looked at Elizabeth and Elizabeth could see the grief spread across her face, but there were no tears. She slowly turned her gaze out the train window, and for the rest of the night and the next day she did not speak, but looked at the countryside as it slowly passed by. The greens and brown of the earth. During this time, she thought of her dream, the fire, the calls for her.

The next morning as they walked to the pullman car for breakfast, Molly looked at several young men with their young wives. She said to Elizabeth, "he was a good boy, a very good boy. I am happy he died with his wife and in love. That is very important, love."

After breakfast the women stood on the back of the car and let the summer air blow around them. Molly took a deep breath and looked at her daughter. "Is Cam's wife a good woman?" she asked, her gaze unflinching from Elizabeth's eyes. Elizabeth looked at her mother, and both women fell into each other's arms. "Oh, mother," she cried, "my dear, dear mother."

Sitting back in their seats, Elizabeth told Molly about Mary and the ranch. Molly sat and listened but did not speak, and when Elizabeth had finished, she took a deep breath and smoothed an imaginary wrinkle from her dress. "Your father was always a strange man, so hard at times. You know, I knew very little about him. I met him as he was about to go into the army. We fell in love through the mail, did you know that? I never thought I would fall in love again, after my first husband died and everything seemed so black and dark."

"I never knew," Elizabeth said, but Molly broke in. "There are many things you don't know about your father and me, Elizabeth. My first husband was a kind, gentle man, a hard worker. Your father was driven, driven to be somebody. A hard, resolute man from New Mexico, he clawed and struggled for what he got in Cuba. It was the shootings and the fear that finally got to me, I suppose. So many people dead and hurt. But your father went on in grim determination. I suppose it was me that made him leave Cuba. He loved it there. The challenge, the excitement, the power, all of those things. I know he has changed now. I shall not interfere with his life. Heaven knows he has suffered enough, but one day I will see him. Not now, not in Boston, but one day I shall see him. Life has taken us apart, and that is how it must remain.''

Elizabeth looked at her mother and did not speak. Molly looked at Elizabeth and smiled weakly. ''Now, my dear child, tell me about your life and your nursing and why in God's name you have never married.''

Waiting for Elizabeth's letter to arrive was misery for Cam. He did not enjoy keeping the news from Mary, but he could think of no other way. He received the letter from Elizabeth late in the afternoon, and as he sat down to open it, his heart raced.

Dear Father,

Mother is well and knows all that has happened. She seems strong, considering all she has been through, and the sudden influx of information after having been away for so long. We have discussed you and Mary and she does not want to be of any bother. She tells me to send you her deepest regards and hopes that one day you will meet again. She feels it best that things remain the way they are. She knows you have suffered much, and that life at all times is not what we dream or desire. With the money that you sent she has rented a small apartment and is working for the Red Cross now. She feels we will be at war soon, and tells me about her dreams. There is something about her dreams that mean much in her life, and they have an uncanny way of becoming true. She is well, father, and I see her often. She seems to enjoy her work with the Red Cross. It fills a need in her and what with her life, she has a way with people, a deep understanding of grief and anguish that sick people go through. She thinks it best that she not write, and hopes you understand.

Things are much better in the city now. The streets are no longer lined with beggars, and although everyone says we will not be pulled into the war, I feel there is no way we will be able to avoid the conflict. It is strange, but in your life you will see three wars. It seems like such a waste of men and money, but we are all only players in this game.

Give my best to Mary. I suppose it is different with the two girls married and off. Stay well, my father.

I am your loving daughter, Elizabeth

Cam took a match from his pocket and lit the letter. He held it until the flame neared his hand and released it to fall on the floor. ''Bless her God,'' he said, ''let my wife live the remainder of her life in peace.''

When the bombs fell on Pearl Harbor Cam listened to the radio and walked outside to see Virgil and Ross. ''Fucking Japs,'' he said, as the men began heating the branding irons. ''Fucking Japs anyway.''

Within six weeks both Raymond and Michael were called into the army. Cissy and Anne came back to the ranch and Cam, feeling old, began to follow the war closely. Both of Mary's daughters joined the Red Cross and rolled bandages. Mary, in between her work, also helped in any way possible.

Cam and Virgil watched as Ross rode into town to join the army. ''There'll be many dead," Virgil said, looking at Cam, "many, many dead."

In Boston, Elizabeth put in for duty with the newly formed WAC's, volunteering for any assignment they wished to give her. Molly worked from dusk to dawn in the rest centers and at the railroad yards, passing out magazines to all the young men going off to war. There were so many bright young faces, with the smiles of boyhood. Each face made her sad, as she knew so many of them would never return.

The country geared for war as men marched off and many thousands fled to Canada. Cam sat feeling old and useless. Volunteering for the air guard, he studied the designs of enemy planes and spent hours sitting on the porch scanning the sky. Looking at the silhouettes of the planes passed out by the government, he thought of Smiley, and how Cam had said that the plane would never amount to anything. So fast, he thought to himself, everything is so very, very fast.

As the fighting spread across the Pacific, Cam and Virgil spent the evening listening to the radio and following the battles closely. When the tide turned in the Pacific with the battle of Midway, both men jumped into each other's arms with joy. The women, more than the men, were under a great strain. Husbands off to war was more depressing than brothers. When word came that Ross had been killed in action, a cloud covered the household for many days. Virgil, being the tough cowboy, did not show his anguish, but his wife and Mary and the daughters cried together. When the body was shipped back to Las Vegas, the funeral was attended by both Mexicans and whites. If nothing else, the war had brought to a halt the hostilities between those two races. After the funeral, Virgil and Cam went to the bar and did not return to the ranch until the next afternoon. After that it was many months before Virgil would speak of his brother.

Cissy's and Anne's husbands wrote as often as possible, but at times the letters were so censored it was impossible to tell what they were trying to say. It was not until the tide of war had turned that Anne received a letter from Michael. He had been wounded and would be home within the month. Although worried, Anne felt relieved that at least he was alive. The day the train arrived, Anne and Mary waited at the railroad station. Cam and Virgil were busy branding, while Cissy worked in the kitchen making a good meal of chicken and potatoes and pie. When Michael came off the train on crutches with only one leg, Anne fainted. Mary, looking at her prostrate daughter, hugged the young man with tears in her eyes. "It's all right, Michael," she said, "there is still a life."

Cam had not liked the young man before, but now they had a common bond, each having lost a limb, and they became close friends. Cam marveled at the strength of the young man as he once again adjusted to life, and was proud that he did not fall into fits of gloom and self pity. His only comment on his wound was one evening sitting on the porch when he looked at the sky and muttered, "many men worse than me."

After a month, Michael and Anne moved back to their own ranch, with the help of some good hands, Michael had his ranch productive within no time.

As the fighting in the islands progressed, Cissy became noticeably worn by her worry over Raymond. When word came that he had been wounded and would be home soon, she was beside herself, losing sleep and almost in a daze. But when the day came and train pulled in and Raymond was complete, her face lit up with happiness.

Now with both girls once more gone from the Ranch, Cam and Mary were alone again. To Cam the war seemed almost unreal. The newspapers carried the day to day coverage of the battles. It was as though there really was no war except for the crippled men walking the streets, and the stars in the windows of homes in town.

Life in the states was comfortable. The war brought jobs and money and a national unity. Although there was limited rationing, it was not a bother and life was much more enjoyable than the previous lean years. There were baseball games and movies and radio programs each evening. There were cars and nylon stockings and an unconcerned attitude of the young. Sometimes Cam would sit scanning the sky for enemy aircraft that he knew would never come, and think how utterly unbelievable it all was. Here on this tiny, spinning planet there were men fighting and dying as he sat peacefully. It was all a matter of distance, he concluded, distance, time and luck. It was the new weapons that horrified him, he remembered the charge up Kettle Hill and the smell of the powder, but now there were planes with bombs that destroyed blocks and whole towns. Men with rifles and machine guns protected by tanks and artillery. He thought of World War I and his war, as he began to call it. And it seemed that if nothing else man was beginning to make enough weapons that one day he would destroy himself.

After the allies had retaken Paris, Elizabeth was shipped to Paris and worked in a hospital. She wrote Cam often and told him of her life and experiences. Her letters were filled with compassion for the numerous wounded, and also of the beauty of the country and the reception by the French people. It was here Elizabeth met a young doctor, and two weeks later they were married. Honeymooning in a small hotel with a bottle of red wine, they both decided that when they returned to the states after the war, they would move to the country and he would open a country practice.

Doctor William R. Bradley was a small man with immense, dark eyes. Not a handsome man, but very dedicated, and Elizabeth loved him greatly. He could work for hours, sleep lightly and return to work as if he could live forever at this pace.

Receiving news of the marriage, Cam was happy, and it seemed that his life was complete. One day they would have a child, and he would be a grandfather. The thought of being a grandfather somehow relaxed Cam and he became more amiable and loving to Mary.

During the years of the war Cam had been confused in his feelings for Mary. At times the thought of Molly would come upon him and he would look at Mary and picture Molly in her place. He could see Molly, working, cooking, listening to him. And it seemed strange that a woman who had been through so much with him, and was his true wife would be somewhere on the east coast while he was here. Mary never knew about Molly being well, and ignored his fits of moodiness, thinking to herself it was the cattle or the war.

Cam, being a man who dreamed little, would dream of Molly. But he would dream of her when they were first married, the cocky way she would stick out her hip. And he would lie in bed, his eyes open, and think of the first time they met and he could smell the steak and the coffee and hear the rustle of her skirts as she sat down beside him. He remembered the first time they made love and the way she bounced in the saddle as they rode into the mountains. With Mary he was content and peaceful, but with Molly there had been the passion and the desire, the drive to please. With Mary he was always comfortable. The fighting and driving to become wealthy was over, the learning to read and write was gone. His life was so different when they met, and although he decided he did not love her as he did Molly, he was comfortable with her and did not try to make of her any more than she was.

V-E Day, Cam and Mary and Virgil sat quietly around the kitchen table and drank a bottle of wine. There was no great commotion, but a feeling of relief. Toasting, Virgil said. ''Now if we can only finish off them Japs.''

A tone of bitterness flowed with his words. That night, lying in bed, Mary said, ''Cam, do you think it will be over soon?''

Cam patted her on the stomach. ''Yes, it will be over soon.''

On V-J Day, everyone went to town and watched the fireworks display. It was a joyous day, soon all the young men would be home and the town would once more filled with young men.

Although the times were prosperous during the war, there was always the death that hung over people like a cloud. But the men coming home would not all find happiness and relief from life. There were the thousands upon thousands who would forever carry the scars of war, mental and physical. For many it was returning to lost wives and broken homes, new starts to try and regrasp the life where bullets did not cry through the night and friends did not lie lifeless on the ground.

For Cam, life on the ranch was the same, same cattle, same problems, life was not different, the world was.

Elizabeth and William departed France four months after the Japanese surrendered. The last months in Europe there had been an endless barrage of men, healed enough to be shipped home. It was a joyous time in France. Each night the town came to life, men and women crowding the bars and dance halls, drinking and loving away many of the memories. The streets were filled with men rebuilding the torn and destroyed houses. All through Europe, families went back to farms and life began anew. Mile upon mile of crosses dotted the countryside, and children played around the broken wreckage of bunkers and tanks. Shell holes were plowed and animals turned out to graze on battlefields.

Holding hands, Elizabeth and William watched as the shoreline of Europe disappeared beneath them. The engines of the airplane hummed, and both people felt the stirring of their new life together. They had decided they would move to Iowa. There was nothing in the world that would not grow, there gardens burst with watermelons and cantelope, tomatoes the size of softballs. Elizabeth would listen to him and picture the green countryside with the mammoth cottonwood trees. It would be lovely. William's grandmother had given them a two-story house with a wrap-around rock porch.

Three hours away from New York, the plane, without warning, exploded in mid-air. There was a tremendous explosion, then a dreadful plunge into the ocean. Everyone on board was killed instantly.

Cam did not receive word of the tragedy until one day in the mail a letter came, with familiar handwriting on the envelope. He did not open the letter immediately, but sat on the porch and looked at the writing on the envelope. Opening the letter, he began to read:

Dear Cam,

Our lives take so many turns and life is not always kind. I really do not know what to say, or a manner in which to break the news to you. Our daughter and her husband were killed in an airplane crash returning from France. Several days ago she was buried, along with her husband, in his home town. There was no way to contact you discreetly because of our situation. A hole has been torn from my heart. Poor Cam Jr. and poor Elizabeth. The years are our enemy. Only yesterday they rode and played in Cuba. We were so young, you so brave. One day we shall meet again. I hold you in my heart. Molly.

There was no return address on the letter. Cam folded the letter and put it in his shirt pocket. He rose slowly, sighing and walked to the stables. He saddled a horse and rode deep into the ranch. It was a cool day. The white powder clouds drifted lazily across the deep blue sky. Scattered through the pinon trees he could hear the singing of the cicada. Looking around him, everything seemed so real, so alive, the colors were as he had never seen and the sound of the cicada like the song of a small child.

Cam rode for many hours. He rode until the sun set and he turned his horse back toward the house. Mary was sitting on the porch when he returned. "I was worried," she said as he walked up to the house. Cam sat down beside her. "Elizabeth is dead," he said slowly "My daughter and her husband are dead."

Mary covered her mouth and looked at Cam. He looked at her and slowly he began to cry.

In 1948 Cam was sixty-three years old. He ventured to town little, no longer interested in the Cattlemen's Association nor town. He lived a solitary life on the ranch. Mary would go to town to shop and for errands and he would stay at the ranch. There was no other world except the trees and the cattle and the horses. He never lost his temper, it was as though there was nothing serious enough to make him become excited. He once again read extensively and became acutely interested in the affairs of the world. His hair was grey, his features slightly rounded, though he was still slim. His eyes were still hard and piercing.

Mary was round and plump and content. Cooking and cleaning, she enjoyed her life. There was no change from Sunday to Friday, no break in the routine.

But in the common experiences of each day Cam found peace and comfort. There were no letters to outside people. No family. He thought of Molly sometimes. Wondering where she was, and what she was doing, while he was on the ranch. But it was just another ache in his heart that he covered with the tasks of his life. The world seemed strange to Cam. It was a mechanical, complicated world. A world belching gas and smoke and still filled with hate. There were rumblings of war in Asia. The Russians encroached in Europe. It seemed there had been so much fighting during his life, and yet nothing changed. Everything just became larger and more complicated. An endless parade of Roosevelts and young men with much ambition. The world was restless, angry, oppressive. All except for little valleys and mountains where people hid from life and lived and breathed, afraid to leave their small, secure worlds.

At sixty-three, Cam did not look forward in life, but found himself more and more reaching into the past. He remembered small aspects of his life as a youngster in New Mexico. Everything seemed so much simpler then, but he knew this was only because he was a child. For his parents' life had still been a struggle and hardship. So many people it seemed were cheated in life. Born by chance into a world in which they must live and produce.

One evening, sitting in the living room reading Life Magazine, it suddenly came to Cam that there was a God. Some super intelligence that focused and knew all the trials and tribulation that was life. With this small revelation, Cam became calm, and the days passed in his recollections and dreams of the past.

Molly, now fifty-eight years old, settled into a small brick home on the outskits of Boston. After the war and her duties as a Red Cross worker, she took a job in an orphanage. It was a rewarding job for her, and seeing the smiles of the young ones to which she administered helped soften the pain of her life. The death of Elizabeth had been a deadening blow to Molly, but unlike her earlier experience, she did not fall into a world of darkness, but of half life. Without the work and the extra hours she put in, Molly knew she could not handle the grief. She was at work at five in the morning and worked until well past nine every night. It was ironic that a woman such as she would choose to work in a place that, no matter the smiles or laughter, was still a sad place.

The children ranged in age from eight to fifteen. Many were adopted into good homes, but most stayed until they were fifteen, when they were transferred to homes for people from ages fifteen to eighteen, and then placed out into the world. Each child who left the orphanage Molly knew, she would never see again. They were on their way into the world, to be buffeted and knocked around as all people were. But they were used to the sadness and loneliness of life. It was the eyes that attracted Molly the most. The young, knowing eyes of the growing faces, so aged and hardened by their life.

Molly had never dated any men since her discharge from the hospital, nor had she been attracted to any. There were men during her Red Cross work that had asked her out, many younger, a few older, but she politely declined. Always busy with one activity or another to have an excuse. Her two children left dull, painful memories in her, but Cam walked in front of her eyes each day as if they were still together. She was not bitter about Cam and his woman. She had come to grips with the situation and found in it just another twist in life that cannot be explained nor rationalized. She did wonder at times whether Cam thought of her. Sitting in the house late at night, with all the business of the day gone, many times she would feel him close to her, a small essence in the air, and she did not feel alone. She prayed she would see him again and be able to reach out and touch his face. It had been so many years, so many lost years.

For Molly the days passed with the seasons. Looking in the mirror, she was round and grey, still very blue-eyed. So out of the times, she knew. Marveling at the younger people. The daring look of women's fashions and the seemingly uncaring attitude of the young men.

Cam and Smiley had been such hard working, driven men, men who believed in the country and their life. But now there were so many people that thought life was just a dream, a party that was plentiful and never-ending.

Molly had been horrified by the war, the mass destruction and the atrocities the Germans and Japanese inflicted on people. But she had been most horrified by the atomic bomb. A weapon so dreadful, to her it marked the beginning of the end. She could see no future for the world. Sometime, somewhere, it would begin, and once again the world would be at war, but this time there would be no winner, all losers.

But in Boston she kept her sanity. The large, sprawling beautiful parks, the ever-present ocean with its seagulls and smells. There were the sailboats and the power boats. The endless hum of a large city with its automobiles and buses. It seemed so strange, but she had seen the passing of the horse and the complete takeover by the mechanical beast, the automobile. She had seen the airplane and the train, so many things.

Molly saw the end of her life approaching, and with each passing day it was as though she embraced the thought. Although she had come to grips with her life, she maintained her sanity on a narrow thread of work and simple thoughts. Avoiding the complicated, she no longer questioned anything, there was no answer and no question. Just the day, whether it rained or snowed or was sunny. Whether it was spring, winter or fall, it was a day, another day in her life and one less she would have to cope with.

On January 3, 1949, Mary walked out onto the porch of the ranch house. It was a cold, terrible day, with the wind blowing the snow into her eyes. Cam and Virgil had left early in the morning to check the cattle. The storm had raged for three days, dropping several feet of snow, and plunging the thermometer to less than fifteen below.

As Mary stood on the porch, she felt very weak, and a slight pain swept through her left side. She placed her hand on the supporting log of the porch roof and slowly slid to the porch floor. Sitting on the floor, the icy wind kicking the snow in her face, she knew she was dying. She did not cry out nor feel afraid. She only looked out upon the ranch, and quietly and peacefully, she died.

Four hours later, Virgil rode into the corrals. Cam was checking another fence. Walking to the house, Virgil found Mary, partially covered by the blowing snow. He looked down at the half-frozen form and began to cry. He picked her up gently and carried her to the bedroom and placed her body lovingly on the bed. When Cam returned, Virgil met him in the corral. He walked up to Cam and held his shoulder, the tears streaming down his face. "Mary's dead, Cam," he said brokenly. Cam looked at Virgil and fell into the man's arms and wept.

The funeral was private and simple. They buried Mary by the small stream under a cottonwood. The daughters and their husbands and Virgil and his wife were there. Afterwards there was a small, quiet dinner, and then everyone slowly went home.

Cam stayed for hours, looking at the grave. In his mind there were no thoughts and he had no more tears. He returned to the house and sat in his chair until he slept. In the morning he saddled his horse and rode the ranch. In the late afternoon, he looked out toward the area where the grave was. "You should have died in the summer when it was pretty, Mary. You deserved that."

An icy wind blew from the north, and once back in the house Cam built a large fire and sat down, feeling very old and very tired.

For the next months Cam threw himself into the ranch. Each day he drove himself. Virgil, seeing the old man working too hard, tried to tell him to slow down, but to no avail.

But soon the work and the winter passed, and one evening, sitting on the porch, Cam thought of Molly, and for the first time in months, he truly felt alive. He did not know where she lived, but he knew it was in Boston. There were private detectives, and this would be easy for them. Nothing to do but locate the woman, and he would go, go and see her. He felt excited. A thread held him to life.

In June he received a letter from Bailey's Detective Service. They had located Molly. They enclosed the address where she lived and the place she worked. Cam immediately began packing. He put on his best pants, and in town he bought new boots. As he drove to Albuquerque where he was to take the flight to Boston, he marveled at the largeness of it all now. He had lived on the ranch so long, isolating himself from life, the world had began to pass him by. Day by day, until years passed. Stuck inside his books and his work, there was no other world. But seeing the newness of the cities, he felt vibrant for the first time in months. His eyes scanned the pretty girls and the lines of the new dresses. Here were people on the go, moving people.

Sitting on the plane as the attractive young stewardess gave him a drink, he looked at the people. But once in Boston is when he really began to feel different. Standing in the airport, wearing his boots and hat, a tiny child ran across the room calling, "Mommy, Mommy, look at the cowboy, look at the cowboy."

Cam smiled. Cowboy, he hadn't thought of that in years, but he suppose that was what he was.

It had been years since he had been in Boston. The town had expanded on all sides for miles, but he marveled at the greenness of it all. The freshness of it. It was not brown and dry like New Mexico. Here were flowers by the thousands, and the cries of the seagulls and the smell of the ocean. And for the first time in a long time he thought of Cuba, and he remembered the lushness of the country and the varied and beautiful flowers. The smell of the blue-green ocean and the taste of fish. And he felt a yearning feeling come over him, like when he was young with his dream of cattle and Cuba.

He wanted to go to Cuba and see the old plantation. After Roberto had paid off the plantation, there had been no more communication. He wondered how he was, how many children he had. How the cane grew and the tobacco. There was nothing to stop him, nothing in the world. He had property and enough income that he could spend his last days traveling around the world if he wished. If he died, Molly would get the ranch, that was the way his new will read. And Virgil would receive the cattle, with instructions to Molly to let him remain, running the place until the time she wished to sell.

Virgil had never been like Smiley to Cam, although they had spent many years together, shared many griefs, from losing wives and brothers. But now in Boston,

Cam thought of the old, tough, weathered cowboy and he smiled to himself. Virgil was a good man, a tough, good man, but like Cam, he too was a dying breed. There were cattle still, but like the end of the horse and buggy, it was tractors and trucks. No chow wagons and dust, but air-conditioned houses and refrigerators. This was all well and good, but soon there would be no more of the men who roughed it and stuck it out. There would only be pampered, soft men, spending days in trucks. The world was on the move, and it waited for no man.

Cam had the cab let him off a block from Molly's house. It was a peaceful, tranquil neighborhood, older, and classy. The homes were brick with large, rock porches and the yards were green and well cared for. As it was June, everything was new and fresh from rain.

It was Sunday morning, and only Cam and the paper boy were on the street. For several days Cam had been sightseeing around Boston, trying to think of what to say, what to bring to her. He wondered how much she had changed in the years.

Finally he admitted to himself that there was nothing to say and nothing he could bring to her.

Standing by the door nervously, the doorbell unanswered, he thought he heard some noise in the back yard. He walked to the back, and looking over a three-foot wooden fence, he saw Molly, sitting under a sun umbrella reading. Cam looked at her and saw the years, the roundness of the body and the drooping bosoms. Her blond hair was now grey, but she still bore herself regally. The strong chin and prominent cheekbones were still there. He entered the gate and walked toward the woman. As he neared, Molly heard the soft footsteps and looked up. She saw the pinned up sleeve. She did not move nor speak, for a few seconds it did not sink in. Then Cam stood over her and she saw the green eyes and heard his voice. "Molly," and a pause, "I wished to see you."

Molly slowly stood, and they fell into each other's arms. They did not speak, but stood together and listened to the birds in the large oaks, and the rise and fall of their breathing.

(51)

Roberto Alvarez and the plantation were doing well. After receiving the plantation from Cam, Roberto and his wife had moved into the large house. He also moved his parents from the work shack to the home.

For the first years, he almost doubled production. The United States, recovering from the war, had bought everything. Batista, firmly entrenched in the government, let the planters do as they wished, while he sat back and enjoyed the illegal money pouring into Cuba. Rural Cuba would remain rural Cuba, but Havana and other major ports would become mecas for gambling, women and joy. Large resorts began to dot the country. While the United States was wracked by the depression, Cuba still enjoyed a large influx of Americans who came for the beaches and the gambling.

Roberto did nothing different with the plantation except that it moved more smoothly with the new machinery that made the work easier and faster. But even with the new automation, he still employed many men and always had the workers houses filled with families.

Mr. Baca continued on at the plantation with a nice salary, and spent the rest of his life teaching in the school. He died one evening, sitting in his house watching Bertha cook. She turned from the sink and he was slumped in the chair. Bertha knew immediately he was dead, and she went to him and cradled the tiny man in her arms and wept. He was buried on the plantation, and another school teacher came from Havana.

For Roberto, the passing of Mr. Baca marked a turning point in his existence. He felt for the first time the brevity of his life and in everything he did he was meticulous and sincere. He was a strict overseer of the men and did not tolerate any nonsense, and he was respected. At least he was Cuban, the workers agreed, and not one of the Americans who owned and operated many of the other plantations.

In 1921 Roberto and Carmella had their second child, a baby daughter. She was a round bubbling, happy baby, showered with attention by her mother and grandmother. Roberto would look at the child and think of her world and how completely different it would be from his. He would see and smell the small fishing village, and remember the tired, worn look of his father as he set the tiny sail.

Now his father was old and crippled, and he would sit in the garden looking in the direction of the sea. Sometimes Roberto would drive his father to the ocean, and the old man would sit and look at the fishing boats. He would look at his son and say nothing, but upon returning home he would smile.

Roberto's mother, so used to the toil of life, loved the large house with the noise of the people and the child. She supervised all aspects of the kitchen, and was one of the first to rise in the morning.

Through the years, there had been a few small uprisings in Cuba, but nothing of consequence. The rebels were quickly and quietly rounded up and shot, life was good for the rich, but the proverty level remained high. Roberto no longer thought of his days in college, but he often remembered the time he saw Batista and remembered the feeling he felt when he saw the man.

There were no simple answers for Cuba. During World War II, Roberto followed the war closely, but besides an occasional navy man seen driving around the country, or the reports of a buildup in Guantanamo, or German subs being sighted, there was no war in Cuba. Sugar and tobacco were still in demand and although they were lean years, they were not lean like they had been in the fishing village.

Roberto would look at the plantation and think of his problems, and know that they were nothing compared to most. It took Roberto nine years to pay off the plantation, and although he thought of Stearns often, he no longer kept in touch with him. He kept Stearns, big desk in the office, and often he would think of the man, sitting behind the desk with the sleeve pinned up, smoking a large black cigar, and he would wonder where he was and how he was, and about his wife and children.

Roberto loved his wife very much, and although he would visit girls in town when he made occasional trips, they were nothing to him. When his two sisters had moved to the United States, there had never been word from them, and besides a few old photographs, they no longer existed in the minds of the family. Life on the plantation was comfortable and simple, and the war came and passed.

By 1949 Roberto looked around him and saw a change in the state of affairs, a young man, Fidel Castro, attending the University in Havana, began to make his presence known around the country. Hearing of him in a bar in Havana, Roberto made a point of going to a small rally and listening to the fiery young man speak. Roberto was transfixed by the man as he had been transfixed by Batista years earlier. He saw in the dark, intense eyes the same desire for power, the same inner energy that would drive the young man to either an early death or the fullfillment of his dreams. But he also saw a young man who did not like the United States nor any current goverment policy.

For Roberto it was a disturbing night. He saw the fire in the eyes of the students gathered around the speaker. He knew, that there would come a reckoning. One day the man Castro would make his move. Surprisingly, the young people had no opposition from Batista. There were no signs of military nor police, although Roberto felt certain that several of the students at the rally were loyal to Batista. Or maybe after all the years, Batista was now too comfortable and cocky and could not be bothered by the young student who talked revolution and the down-fall of the Batista regime.

Victoria, Roberto's first daughter had, much to his relief, little or no interest in Castro or in politics in general. For her, life was gentle, and she had never been far enough away from the plantation to know of anything else. There had always been plenty, and as far as she could see there always would be. She was a bright, attractive girl, simple in many aspects of life, carefree and happy. Roberto knew she drove the young men wild, and he knew also she could be flirtatious at times, but he loved his daughter and did not keep an overly watchful eye on her as many Cuban fathers did of their daughters. He did wish at times that there had been a brother to watch over her.

After the evening of watching Castro, Roberto once again returned to the plantation, and over the months he forgot the young orator. Caught up again in the rhythm of the seasons and the crops, there was little that disturbed his life. But soon word began to spread through the people. First a small sentence here, and then the talk of the men about the rebels, and the rumors spreading through the workers about rebels looking for men. Soon small groups of soldiers would be seen walking through the countryside, and then began the reports of the shootings and bombings throughout the country.

Once again, the country armed itself. Driving through Havana, one could see and read all the posters that appeared overnight. The anti-capitalist and anti-American propaganda began to reappear, along with anti-Batista posters. Roberto did not pay much attention to it, although he did go about armed, and always left his home protected by armed men.

His daughter, after two years of college, fell in love with a young doctor, and in the summer of 1951 she married and moved to the far side of the island. After the marriage, Roberto and Carmella felt for the first time the touches of age, and for many weeks the plantation seemed to be bathed in a quiet sea of contemplation. But as suddenly as it came it passed, and the two began to hold parties for neighboring people and began to travel to Havana and other cities together.

More and more of the plantation work was handled by other men, as Roberto began to enjoy his life of leisure and the company of the round, plump lady that was his wife.

(52)

Fidel Castro sat in the hot, smelly bar and looked at the man in front of him. The man, a young, skinny blond, smiled a toothy smile and between puffs on the cigarette, spoke in excellent Spanish. For Castro, it was a dream come true. An accumulation of all the fragments that had driven him relentlessly on, every waking moment of his life. This little man with the cigarette-stained fingers had the tools, the almighty guns that were needed. "They have watched you for years," the man continued, "watched your every move, and now is the time, they believe. We all share a common goal, the eradication of the United States, with all its half-truths and lies."

"Your country is very careful," Castro said, weighing his words. Here was a man who could be anything, as far as Castro knew. Maybe a man working for Batista, and not a representative of the Soivet Union as he said. But there was something that told Castro that this man was actually a representative of Russia, a lethal man, capable of any deed for the good of his country. He would talk to him and stall him and then, through his contacts, he would have the man checked out. But it would be right, he knew it would be right and he would have his new weapons and all the ammunition he needed, and then he could take his rightful place in government and bring his country out of the grips of capitalist society.

Rising from the table the skinny, twitchy man looked at Castro. "Call for me here," and he handed Castro a card. "Ask for Bill, is that not easy?"

Castro smiled and stood to shake hands with the man, but the man turned and was gone. As he sat back down, several men walked from the bar and sat down around their leader. Castro snorted and lit his cigar and began to laugh. The others laughed with him, and they spent the rest of the evening drinking and planning.

Frank Waters sat at the bar and drank his beer slowly until the Cuban group filtered out the door. Fuck this shit, he thought to himself, lighting another cigarette. Months and months of following this Cuban greaseball around, and finally a touch. The boys back at the office would love this, finally a touch between the young rebel and the Russians. All their suspicions could be substantiated now, and they could really go into high gear with fear. Why they just didn't send somebody in and blow the young buck's head off was beyond Frank. The hell with all this spy versus spy crap, just get rid of the guy and wait for the next one and then get rid of him. From what he had seen of the office over the past years, he wondered how in the hell the U.S. kept its hands in the pockets of any country with the bumbling antics of its secret societies.

Frank Waters walked down the damp street and lit another cigarette. Well, now they would get their guns, and not have to steal them from the army. It was becoming very clear.

In the morning, Castro stepped between the legs of Rosetta, the youngest whore. Looking at her naked body, for a moment he felt a pang of regret, but then he turned away and walked from the apartment. They would never come here again. It was stupid he knew to bring these women here. Still, there would have to be another apartment now, one that only he and the handful of friends he trusted would know about.

He felt the freshness of the day as he walked the streets. Stopping at a pay phone, he made several short but direct calls. Within a few days he would know if this man was planted by Batista, and if he was, then he must disappear, quickly and efficiently he must disappear.

Castro hailed a cab and rode to his own apartment. He cleaned up and dressed, and headed for the university. It would not be long, a few more weeks and he would have his law degree. The government was not fighting a young, stupid farmer from the mountains with pig shit and dirt on his hands. This time there would be a problem, an educated problem.

Frank Waters looked at the men around him. They were disturbed by the news they had waited for for so long, and now none of them wanted to break it to the upper offices. Waters lit another cigarette and walked from the room. Lord, he thought, I'm glad I'm just a lowly runt. Decisions, decisions, whatever happened to good old quick and clean killing.

Frank headed down the street towards his home. He had a few days and he knew a petite young Cuban girl.

It took several days for the memo to pass through channels and reach the right desk in the United States. It took several more days, and passing through various hand to reach the desk that sent back the reply. "Watch the two persons carefully."

Frank Waters was once again called in and given the assignment. "Find out as much as possible, and when anything important is found, return to the office."

Frank stratched his neck and walked out into the city. It would be boring he knew, but it beat working for a living. Getting into his car, he opened the report and began to read it, carefully and slowly.

Code name "Bill" was everything the United States did not want him to be. A man raised in the United States, at one time or another he had worked for every anti-American organization he could find. Finally, after many years, he must have been approached by the Russians and took the final step. Now here he was in Cuba, acting as the go-between between the young rebel leader and the Russians. Good for you, old Bill, Frank thought to himself, made the big time. Frank closed the folder and began to drive the car. It would not be easy. As far as anyone knew, this Bill had no vices, no lady friends in Cuba, no drugs, no liquor, he was a loner, a very solitary and dedicated loner.

Waters moved into a muggy, cramped room down the hall from the Russian spy. With no phone to tap, Water set up sensitive listening devices to monitor all sound in the room, but after several weeks of listening to the toilet flush and the sound of a man brushing his teeth, he knew this would not get him far. Tails had led to nothing. Walks to dingy restaurants and ever dingier bars led to nothing. Sometimes, tailing the man, Waters would wonder what the higher ups were doing while he wore the rubber off his shoes and sweated through the light shirts. It was almost impossible for him to imagine that the fate of this tiny island rested in his hands. So far nothing led to anything, incoming mail was useless, there was none. It seemed impossible that this man Bill could be anything except a solitary writer, or a hermit. The man as far as Frank could see had never suspected he was being tailed, he did nothing evasive in any way, just repeating day after day his meanderings around town.

Then finally one Sunday morning in front of the bus depot, Bill bumped into a man. To most the collision was an accident, but the trained eye of Frank, he saw the tiny slip of paper pass between the two men. He did not get a good look at the man, just that he wore a dark suit, which was unusual in Cuba, and that he was in his forties. He was soon lost in the crowd. Bill continued walking, and soon returned to his apartment.

For the next several days Bill did not leave his apartment except to make occasional phone calls from a pay phone down the block. A tap on the phone revealed nothing until the following week, when it uncovered that a meeting had been set up between Bill and Castro. It would be in a small cafe, popular with students. Risky, Frank though, but everybody makes mistakes. For two days men worked quickly, planting bugs all over the restaurant, until the evening when Castro came in with two burly men who sat at another table. Frank sat outside with two other men from the department and listened intently to the conversation.

Castro looked at the small, spindly man and smiled. He had checked out the man, and true to his word, he was as he said. "The weapons will be delivered as promised," Bill said, "but I will not tell you about it here, we must take no chances. Outside, after we leave, I will tell you."

Frank marveled at the surprise twist to the plot, and could not help but admire his foe. After several hours of small talk, the men walked out into the street. Looking directly at Castro, Bill leaned close to him and spoke for several minutes. Castro smiled and shook the man's hand and they parted. Frank yawned and looked at his partners. "We should have killed him. Him and the rebel."

The other two men said nothing, but just sat and looked bored.

Three days later, besides tails and bugs, twenty men in dark clothes met the Russian submarine thirty miles out of the Bay of San Louise. The weapons were exchanged quickly and the rubber boats started for shore. Within two days the weapons were safe and protected, deep in the mountains of Santiago, while Castro took the final exams for his degree.

Intelligence men in Cuba relayed the messages once again down the chain of command. From all they could determine, the weapons were in Cuba. Now there was nothing to do but wait until something happened.

Military aides were sent to Batista with the information. Batista, though concerned, could not help but feel safe and powerful in his country. There had been nothing to rock the ship in years. The army, to the best of his knowledge, was behind him, the government was stymied by his political influence and the backing of the United States. How could a college student with only a handful of men shake his power? What Batista had forgotten was that he too had once been a nothing, a lowly army sergeant with a dream, a dream of power and glory.

On the morning of May 2, 1952, Fidel Castro, with a hundred or so of his followers, stormed down the hills and attacked the army base at Moncada. At first, the soldiers fell back from the sudden onslaught by the students, but with the deadly calm of trained soldiers, they regained their composure and killed and captured the entire force. Taking Castro to a back room, they joked and pointed as the captain used a cattle prod on his testicles, and they laughed when the young revolutionary passed out in his own vomit.

Batista, smug in his victory, took a personal hand in the trials of the men. Some were hanged, several were shot, but to show his benevolence, he sentenced Castro to hard labor for fifteen years.

Castro, though jailed, became an underground folk hero, and his picture was posted on many streets of Cuba. Slowly his following grew.

Although the country prospered and the tobacco and sugar flowed, most Cubans remained peons, unable to climb out of their existence, listening to the whisper of revolution that spread through the country.

The United States, comfortable after the intended coup's failure, did nothing to follow up on the insurgence. Russians entered the country unchecked, and many men like Frank Waters were transferred to other countries in South America.

It was not until after Castro's eventual release from prison and his fleeing to Mexico where he trained his fighting force for the return to Cuba, that others would echo Frank Waters' sentiments. "We should have killed the mother fucker, all this spy shit is for the birds."

The attempted revolution had little effect on Roberto and his family, although he was relieved when it was over. He knew what would happen to him and people like him if Batista were shaken from power. There would be endless killings, takeover by the new government, large holdings by the wealthy would be redistributed and the work of a lifetime would be gone in an instant.

His wife lived her life insulated by the ranch, while his daughter grew plump and complacent in the home of her doctor husband.

Only Roberto worried, sitting alone on the veranda remembering the days of his youth when he dreamed of social change. Before the good food and wine, the servants and fine clothes. He remembered the days with Stearns, and the ache he felt, working for the man. And now he was as Stearns had been, a power, a comfortable power. Revolution would mean an end, an end to him and everything he loved. It must never happen, he knew, it must never happen. There must never be a communist country around him, or he would have to flee, flee to the United States and begin a new life when he was already approaching old age. But for now Castro was in jail, and the workers were once again cutting the cane and stacking the tobacco.

His horses pranced around their paddock and his wife sat in the house, cool and comfortable and relaxed.

(53)

After their reunion, Molly and Cam were inseparable. Cam moved into the house with Molly, but each had their own room. It was as though they were young again, and each would think of the days of their past lives, but not speak of them.

Boston was fresh and lovely. The green of the trees and the vastness of the ocean held Cam and Molly. They dined out each evening and took tours and rides each day. There were the gulls to feed and the days to touch. Neither of them felt any sexual desire, but more the closeness of dear and true friends. Neither spoke of the children or Cuba or Smiley or New Mexico. It was as though there was no before, no after, there was only each day that they woke and washed and met in the kitchen over the smell of toast and coffee. There were no maids nor parties, no desire to be anywhere but where they were, no plans for the day.

At first they walked together and talked of the world and the sights and smells around them, and then they began to walk and hold hands and laugh as if they were children. To the neighbors it was a shocking thing, the old man that moved in with the lady who always kept to herself. But Molly and Cam did not care, the neighbors did not know about their life, that they were married.

It was a joyous time, a time when nothing the world offered hurt them or brought them down from their days together. Cam forgot about the ranch, and the cattle. There was only Boston, with all the young people, and the Kennedys, and the drives by the ocean. There were the beautiful young girls with their bare legs and midriffs and the young men, enjoying the easy life.

There was Korea, but there would always be something. World War I, World War II, Korea, what the hell, the country had made the step. His step, his young step in Cuba was the beginning, the beginning of the conquest, he knew that now. He saw it, spurred by Roosevelt and the others who followed, pushing their dreams, convincing the people, but it was nothing, it was only power and money and greed. It was a mistake, he concluded, a bloody and awful mistake that now must only take its course and end where it will. In his later years he enjoyed the smell of the house and the sound of Molly moving in the kitchen and the birds that sang in the trees. It was simple, simple and enjoyable, there was no great amount of money, but there was enough. There was no desire to travel the world or take a cruise to Europe, everything was here with them, and he knew it was only because of one thing, love. Love for Molly.

For the first time in her life, Molly found a deep, restful peace that seemed to cover her each day. Cam, now old and slow, was not a fearful person, going to be killed by rebels or by his desire to prosper and grow. Now he was a man who saw the end of his days approaching, and enjoyed so very much the touch of her hand or the smile she gave him in the morning. There was no sex nor pressure to perform, it was only life. There were no teas to give or parties to go to. There were only the two of them, sitting in the evening, sipping wine over a delightful dinner by the ocean.

She loved this strange old man, this man of wars and hunger, this man who had been through and survived an exciting life. He was still different from most. He was different from other old men who sat in the park and played checker or swapped war stories. He was alone, alone but not tired, not defeated, not pushed into the much of the world. They had lived to see the death of their family, the split of their lives, only to be once again together, and maybe, Molly would think, closer then if there had been no turmoil, no heart-wrenching aspects to their life. She would never understand, but in all truth was nothing to understand. There was simply Cam, Cam and his green eyes and his smile and his stumbling with buttons on his shirts. She was safe and warm and loved. She knew beyond everything she was loved by this old warrior, loved beyond words.

If there was a part of Cam's life that began to stir him, it was Cuba. For the first time in years he followed the developments in Cuba. It began with the attack by the young rebels on the military base. It was a chance, remembering, a small clipping in the newspaper while he sat on the porch. Nothing large nor obtrusive, just a report of the action and the capture of the rebels. But to Cam it was a remembering, a remembering of the guns and the rebels, the turmoil that was his younger life, and he began to read the paper and search out the small, obscure articles that covered the happenings in Cuba.

With the imprisonment of Castro, the curiosity that filled him subsided, but the thoughts of Cuba still remained. He would sit and think of Molly when she was young, moving around the plantation, the sound of the children outside, blending with the hum of the bugs and the creaking of the wagons as they pulled the large loads of cane and sugar. And it was with this that Cam knew he would return, one day he would return. He would not tell Molly, she would not understand, and it might make her worry. He would tell her he was going to the ranch to get the paper-work straight, as he was already planning to sell the ranch. He would put the money in C.D.'s and leave them to Molly in his will.

Boston was nice, it was removed from the things his life had been. There were no people who knew his history, and he like it that way. But each day his mind toyed with the idea of Cuba, to see Roberto and the plantation, to see the change or lack of it in the land over the years. And he secretly began to make his plans.

(54)

For Castro, jail was the ultimate test of his endurance. The days were days of hard work and abuse, the guards were pigs, with their sweaty, greasy smiles and their big clubs that sent men sprawling to the ground. But with each day he vowed that he would escape, he would be free once again, and this time he would not be foolish enough to think a mere handful of men could perform his task. There would be bargains and deals made with powerful people, there would be not merely students but trained and dangerous men, men capable of murder, men who would kill and attack for money, not for the people. And then and only then would he be able to fulfill his destiny.

He would change Cuba. He would drive from the face of Cuba all the whites and the capitalists, and all the Cubans sympathetic to the whites and the Americans. He would take the land and give it to the people who deserved it, all the people who for centuries had cut the cane and staked the tobacco. They would have new shoes and food and places for their old people, there would be collective farms and schools.

If he did nothing else in jail he read, he read everything. While other men thought about raping other men, and the jail filled with the dregs of Cuba, he alone stayed different, he alone had a fire in his eyes that made men listen to him, and when he found people that proved trustworthy, they would sit and talk of the new day and the new order, and the day they would flee from these walls together.

And while he sat in the jail and picked the lice from his body, still his name filled the mouths and minds of many, from peons and students to lawyers and professors. Men such as he, caught up in a dream of equality and freedom for the masses. And they filled the streets with propaganda and told their children of the brave man in jail.

Sometimes visitors would come to him and tell him of the country, the streets with his name painted on brick walls, and Castro would sit and smile and look out past the wire and the high brick wall. "It is my destiny," he would tell them, "my destiny that will fulfill itself. These walls, this time is nothing but the training fit for me, my cross to bear for the moment. But there will come a day, a time, a place when all will see and know."

Castro did know one thing. If and when he was released from prison, he must leave Cuba. He must go to another country and from there train his men and gather his support. All must be in readiness. In Cuba he would be watched, they would hound him and see him out, and this time they would kill him. But far away, he would be nothing, nothing but a fester to Cuba, a defeated rebel who would be laughed at by Batista. Batista would sit and tell his generals, "let him come, this time we will shoot him, like we should have last time," and they would light their expensive cigars and look at their finely dressed and manicured women, and discuss their mistresses.

And Castro began to hate, to hate deeply and intensely, with the cold, calculating mind of an attorney, reduced to figures and laws that held no feeling or detail to real life. And he swore, he swore to the God that he did not believe in, that when he was free and in control, there would only be Cubans in Cuba and only criminals in jail. While he was alive Cuba would be known around the world as Cuba, Cuba the independent nation, alive and well and on her own, not a puppet of any other nation.

Roberto did not like the changes he saw in Cuba. Once again the country was tense and ill at ease, but now Cuba was not a small island, remote and quiet beside the United States. Because of this Cuba was important, important to other nations as large and greedy as the United States. Countries willing to back anybody or anything that would give them a foothold off the shores of North America.

And with each day, Roberto saw the changes in the people. There was a hope, a hope for the people. Real or not, it was a hope, and more and more people began to long for the ousting of Batista and the new order to come. It was because of this, Roberto guessed, that in 1955, in order to quell the rising tide against him and prove he was truly a benevolent dictator, Batista ordered the release of Castro from prison. It was a joyous day, and Castro paraded in the streets of Havana, but gave no fiery speeches nor promised any reform.

He quietly slipped out of the country one evening, accompanied by several trusted friends. Their tiny ship sailed for Mexico, with their dreams and the dreams of the Cuban people. From this day on, workers would hear reports and read leaflets circulated by undergound presses of the growing army Castro was building. They were told that the day would come when they must pick up their tools and march for the rights of the people, and drive the Americans from their shores. And more and more of the people held Castro as their answer, an answer to a life that was not life but a drudgery, and a sin on the face of the earth. They did not know that Castro's force consisted of a few measly men, nor that there was a shortage or money, but it would have made no difference. They did not know of the deals with Soviet agents nor the desire with which their folk hero dreamed of his triumphant return.

By 1955 Cam had sold the ranch. The past years had rolled gently by, and both he and Molly moved slowly and awoke each morning with the aches and pains of old age. Cam would look into the mirror at times and wonder how he was alive, or if he was alive. He could not go on forever, but it seemed that he would.

The money from the ranch he deposited in C.D. notes, and left everything to Molly. Molly knew nothing of this. It was February of 1955 and as they were eating breakfast, Cam looked at Molly and said slowly. "I'm going to go to New Mexico and see the ranch for a few weeks, Molly. I haven't been there in years, and I would like to see how it is holding up."

Molly looked at Cam and for a reason she did not know, she searched his face. She felt strange, and dropped her gaze. "It should be enjoyable Cam, are you going to fly?"

"Yes," he answered, "it's quicker."

For the next several weeks there was no mention of Cam's trip until one morning Molly heard him packing his bag. As she stood on the porch and watched the old man walk to the cab she waved. Back inside the house, she sat for several hours and looked at the iced streets of Boston. "Be careful, Cam," she said, "be careful."

That night she lay in bed and fought for sleep. Early in the morning she awoke and sat up in bed. She had not dreamed in years, but she had dreamed something, something she could not quite remember. She could remember that there was a car and men, many men, strange men in green clothes and with guns. Men that sat and looked down the road for the car, while they smoked and looked nervously at each other.

She rose from bed and walked to the kitchen, where she made a cup of tea and sat listening to the clock in the living room echo through the house. In the mid-morning she called the airlines, checking to see when a Mr. Cam Stearns would be

315

returning from Albuquerque, New Mexico, but there was no Stearns registered on any of the flights from Boston or returning. She put the phone down and returned to her chair, where she sat the rest of the day, alone, tired and very afraid.

Sitting in his room, Cam slowly let time encompass him. Havana was far different from his memories, and he felt the heavy weight of time on his shoulders. There was very little that resembled the Havana of his youth. There were still the street vendors and the ever-present smell of fish and the ocean. But there were miles of hotels and gambling casinoes. One never escaped the steady rumble of the traffic.

For two days, he had traveled around the city in a cab. The docks were completely changed, the old offices of Bill Hood were torn down and replaced.

He sat in his room and sipped on the gin and tonic and looked out over the city. "We fought to make you like us," he said to the lights, "in that we have succeeded."

Outwardly Havana had changed, but Cam felt the seething violence of the city and saw that the scrawled graffiti on the walls was still the same. Only now, it was Castro's picture that sprang at one from dirty street corners, but still it was the American pig, the hate America posters.

It took several days for Cam to muster the courage to rent a car and drive out to the old plantation. The fear of change, he supposed. But early Sunday morning he left the traffic and noise of Havana and headed for the old home. Once out in the country, there were not the severe signs of change. The fields of cane and sugar lay as before, but now there were the large trucks and gas stations. But the land, the land itself had not changed. There were still the hunched-over figures of bodies in the fields and the gang bosses riding to the left and right. There were still armed men at most stoppings, and soldiers that walked along looking tired and mean. But it was still the land, still the cane that was supreme.

As Cam turned off the main road, he noticed the plantation was as before, here where he had planted cane was cane, and there, tobacco. He could see tobacco sheds in the same place, newly built ones, next to the rotting shells of those he had built, and as he drew nearer the house, he saw the workers' houses still clean and freshly painted. In the field where he had raised his horses were horses, and across the field were still cattle where he and Smiley had brought in their few head of cattle. For a moment he could almost see Smiley, laughing and joking as they roped and branded the cattle. Driving into the main complex of the plantation, Cam saw the remains of Molly's garden, now much smaller, but still neat and tidy, and the house. The house was the same. The white adobe sat as princely as the day they had left. There were the paddocks where Elizabeth had ridden, and the building that had been his office.

He saw an older looking man sitting on the veranda of the house, and with the noise of the car, a woman, round and plump and middle-aged appeared at the door. Seeing the car, she immediately stepped out of sight. Cam got out of the car, and watched the man, straight and strong, walking toward him. At first the man showed no sign of recognition, but then the man's pace quickened and he smiled and held out his hand. "Mr. Stearns," Roberto said, "time has once again brought us together."

Cam looked at the handsome Cuban man with the dark eyes and the fleeting smile and said. "It looks well for you, Roberto, I am happy."

The two men sat on the veranda and talked for many hours. They talked of the plantation and of time, children, deaths, and late in the evening they sat and said nothing. Silent with the hum of the mosquitoes and the hot, humid air. Finally Roberto said. "We have a room ready for you, Mr. Stearns."

Cam walked through the old house slowly. There were so many memories here, good memories, and sad, so many years. Here locked in the paint and walls of this house were many ghosts, unspeaking, dormant, waiting for more life, more memories.

Sitting in the room filled with different furniture, he remembered Molly and the children, the young, happy faces. He did not sleep that night, but lay in the bed and looked into the darkness. After all, it was just a house, a house no longer his. Another man's home now, and a man he no longer knew. A man like himself, filled with love and hate and terror for the future.

In the morning he visited Mr. Baca's grave, and later before lunch, he walked across the yard and knocked on Bertha's door. "Bertha," he said as she came to the door, "you are old, like me."

The Cuban lady, seeing Cam, began to cry and both hugged each other warmly. For several hours they talked, and unlike his conversation with Roberto, Cam told Bertha of the death of his children and the recovery of Molly. As he walked from the door there was silence as both old people knew they would never see each other again.

After lunch, Cam shook hands with Roberto and started back toward Havana. He drove slowly and looked at the land, the rolling hills. It was beautiful, still one of the most beautiful places in the world. Every green imaginable to the eye could be found in Cuba.

The four men waited patiently. They were rough looking men, dressed in rags. Their hands were torn and rough from the cane. In their eyes could be seen generations of hate, hate bred in the fields and the shacks of the workers. As the car approached, one said. "He is white, he is white."

The car slowed to make the curve and as it did, the machine gun bullets tore through the door. Cam heard the report of the machine gun, but no more. There was no pain, no thought. The men looked at each other and melted back into the jungle. "White pigs," one spat as he ran, "soon there will be no more Americans in our country."

It took the authorities several weeks to notify Molly in Boston of the death of her husband. She did not cry at the funeral. Standing alone in the cold rain, there was no more to cry about, no one left to cry for.

That night in her home, she slowly walked around the house and removed the photographs of Cam from the walls and placed them in an old chest, then she sat by the window. Only then did she cry Soft, silent tears. "It was your destiny, Cam," she said to the window, "it was your destiny."

www.ingramcontent.com/pod-product-compliance
Lightning Source LLC
Chambersburg PA
CBHW011341010726
47493CB00009B/2905